A Well-Trained Lady

A *Well-Trained* Lady

JESS HEILEMAN

VAGABOND PUBLISHING

Cover Design: Ashytn Newbold and Jess Heileman
Image of Girl: Jess Heileman
Cover Background: Valentyn_Volkov©DepositPhotos.com
Rose Vectors at Beginning of Book and Chapter Headings: Jane_Hulinska©DepositPhotos.com

Library of Congress Control Number: 2020913596

ISBN Paperback: 978-1-7329851-2-4
ISBN Ebook: 978-1-7329851-3-1
Published By: Vagabond Publishing, LLC.

To all those who have helped me along the way.

CHAPTER ONE

"Cursed driver," Mother hissed, following the abrupt shift of the carriage. "Surely London streets are maintained well enough to avoid such unnecessary jostling." When neither Papa nor I responded, she gave a disgruntled huff. "I hope the traveling coach is not so poorly sprung for our trip."

Papa's regard remained set on the veiled darkness of Mayfair passing by. "I have already spoken to Mr. West about seeing to its maintenance. He assured me it shall be ready by Friday's departure."

My gaze shot to Papa's shadowed features. "Friday? But Parliament will not be adjourned for another month yet. I thought we were to remain in London with you until our removal to Branbury Court for the Thortons' house party."

"That had been the plan, but—"

"Considering Lord Thorton is no longer in London," Mother interrupted, "I do not see a purpose in lingering. I have accepted your aunt's invitation to Sandson Hall."

A lump formed in my throat at the memory of my last

visit to Sandson and the continuous censure I'd been forced to endure at Aunt Priscilla's hand. I'd readily deemed Mother pleasant in comparison to her venomous sister, and Mother was a more toxic serpent than most. "Is Papa not to join us then?"

"Of course not." Mother sent a pointed glare to Papa. "Though it would be easy to make a list of Lords that don't allow their seat in the House to dictate half their year's plans."

"As though you'd wish me along?" When Mother didn't counter his statement, Papa gave a wry chuckle. "And your list would only serve to condemn the men that shun their responsibility. Selfish, ignorant—"

"Your father will remain behind." The firmness of Mother's voice ended Papa's rant. "But I require a respite from the stench of London."

I withheld a groan. "And how long shall our stay at Sandson be?"

Mother did not speak for a moment, allowing me to stew in my worry. "Not quite a fortnight. Unfortunately, Priscilla has other plans that prevent us staying longer, so we must return to London for another week before our departure to Branbury Court."

Despite the promise of our eventual return to London, any amount of time spent with Mother and Aunt Priscilla for company seemed entirely too insufferable. Surely, I was old enough to remain behind with Papa. "Must I join you?" The question slipped from me, and I instantly wished it back.

Even in the darkness, I could sense the full strength of Mother's glower, and I shrunk under its intensity. "Of course you must, foolish child. You have procured no invitations elsewhere, and I will not allow you to remain behind without a *suitable* chaperone." She paused.

"Besides, we cannot risk you encouraging any more suitors before Lord Thorton offers for you. The last thing we need is to have him return from France to encounter more tales of your meandering heart."

Indignation coursed through me, but I masked it with arrogance, an emotion Mother did not consider weak. "It is not my fault that gentlemen so eagerly arrive at the incorrect opinion of where a lady's affections lay."

"And yet how many other ladies have as sizable a collection of rejected suitors as you have managed in the past three Seasons?"

Unwilling to speak on it further, I lowered my gaze to my lap.

"Come now." Papa interrupted the heavy silence that had engulfed the small cab. "Only a handful of those lads you forced at her were even tolerable enough to be considered. And Lord Thorton seems superior to them all. Should we not then rejoice that Arabella has proved herself indifferent to men's feelings?" I winced inwardly as he continued, regardless of his noble intentions. "To think, if she had accepted the first suitor who came along, we would be attending the Brimhall's ball tonight in the agonizing company of Lord Penthrop."

Mother lifted her chin at Papa's assertion. "Considering that Arabella is likely one rejection away from forever sealing her pretentious reputation, and marring ours along with it, I would say Lord Penthrop is certainly preferable to no husband at all."

"You cannot be in earnest?" Disbelief saturated Papa's tone. "Even a title cannot overcome the fact that the man is a spineless cross-bencher."

"Always politics with you. And yet being your wife, it has become obvious that one's political abilities have little to do with the true value of a man."

My lips parted at Mother's slight, but Papa simply turned his attention from her, his posture slumped from weariness. Poor Papa.

"Close your mouth, Arabella," Mother said. I was hardly surprised she could see my mistakes, even in the dark. "You will never procure an earl's affections by such untoward displays."

The carriage jostled again, and I righted myself and my *untoward* expression as Mother hissed another remark regarding inept drivers and Papa's lack of oversight on such matters. I released a muted exhale, gladly turning my attention out the window to the shadowed streets until we arrived at Lord and Lady Brimhall's Town house.

Papa assisted us both from the carriage, then offered Mother his arm. The two of them started up the stairs as though all was perfectly well between them. The very image of marital contentment. And it was all a lie. But over the years I had discovered that all marriages adhered to the same pretense. Even the supposed love matches within the *ton,* the ones that were so often touted as an ideal, were nothing but a farce in the end. I would admit those individuals who claimed love as their marital badge of honor were better performers than most, but upon closer examination the truth was there—love always faded.

And though I had once been as naïve as other young ladies, thinking I would one day marry for love, it was no longer the case with me. I wanted a marriage of convenience. A marriage where I would not need to fret about my love for someone fading, nor feel the agony as I witnessed the unavoidable disenchantment take hold of my husband through the years. I was not strong enough to bear the loss of love. Not again.

I followed my parents through the doorway and into sight of our awaiting host and hostess.

"Lord and Lady Godwin," Lady Brimhall said, nodding her welcome, "I am so glad you could make it." She looked to me. "And you, Miss Godwin."

I dipped into an elegant curtsy and rose, receiving approving nods from both Lord and Lady Brimhall. "Thank you."

"It is such a lovely night for a ball." Mother looked to Papa, who offered a nod of agreement. "It is not nearly as warm as it has been the past few evenings."

Lady Brimhall now looked to her husband. "We are quite fortunate. Are we not, dear?"

I was hardly surprised to find Lord Brimhall's eyes were still upon me, only removing them when a jab of his wife's elbow reminded him of his insolence. "Yes. That is … I do believe …" He paused, tilting his head to the side as though he wasn't certain what he was supposed to be agreeing to.

Lady Brimhall gave a taut smile at her husband's idiocy, while the three of us pretended not to have noticed his error.

"Oh, see there. It is Sir Tillard and his daughter." Lady Brimhall seemed a touch too eager in her declaration, and Mother and Papa offered a brief nod before continuing on.

Moving through the crush, countless gazes followed us, and the crowd parted as we neared. There were many gentlemen I recognized, but I skimmed over their eager expressions so as not to be pressed upon for a dance or to engage in unwanted flirtations. After three Seasons, it had become a hardship feigning interest in those with whom I had little desire to interact.

"Miss Godwin!" I turned toward the distinct voice of

Lady Beatrice. She gestured with her fan for me to join her. Her incessant gesture meant she would have gossip to share.

"Go on." Mother peered over her shoulder at me before directing an overdone smile to Lady Beatrice. As the eldest daughter of a higher peer, Lady Beatrice had easily obtained Mother's approval, a circumstance for which I was most grateful.

Lady Beatrice looked pretty in her ivory silk, though not even a stunning dress and fine jewels could compensate for the angular nose she had inherited from her father.

"Where is Miss Browning?" I glanced around for her ever-present companion.

"Marianne is just finishing the set." Lady Beatrice leaned closer, and her voice grew to a whisper. "And I daresay she was quite pleased when a *certain gentleman* asked her to partner with him for the quadrille."

"Indeed?" I pretended interest, counting the requisite number of seconds Mother had taught me to allow until I could change the subject to something more pressing. "And have you decided if you will accept Lady Thorton's invitation for the house party at Branbury Court?"

Lady Beatrice whipped her fan open to conceal her features from me. "I have not yet made a decision."

I forced a smile, confounded by Lady Beatrice's unwillingness to speak of any invitation without giving airs to her importance. And yet, in part, I envied her. As the daughter of a duke, Lady Beatrice's delight came not in the invitation itself, for those were expected, but in the amusement of choosing which of them to accept. "Do you have another engagement you are considering?"

Her eyes skirted about the room, as though making certain I was still the most promising person to be speaking with. "The Meads have invited me, and therefore Marianne, to Hampshire at the start of next week. I have already accepted and do not yet know how long our obligation there will be."

"The Meads?" I concealed my surprise. "How unexpected."

"Most unexpected. But when you have an unmarried son set to inherit such a fortune, an advantageous match must be sought out."

I gave a nod of agreement, concealing my irritation. "Certainly. I only wonder what Miss Gilbert will think of the invitation. I do believe she was hoping to be the one receiving it."

"Receiving what?" Miss Browning stepped directly between Lady Beatrice and me in a most irksome manner.

I removed myself to a more suitable distance with practiced ease. "We were speaking of poor Miss Gilbert, likely beside herself having not received the Meads' invitation to Hampshire."

Miss Browning tipped her head to the side. "It is the fate of those of us with little more to offer than our exquisite looks and our incomparable charms." She gave a small giggle, and I knew she meant to lighten the reality of her situation. It was dreadfully unfortunate that, despite Miss Browning being fairer and a touch more amiable, her father had no title to lure gentlemen to his daughters as Lady Beatrice's father had.

"Do not fret. I shall find a grand match soon enough." Miss Browning reached out and rested her hand upon mine as though I required consoling. "And consider yourself blessed that your own father is a wealthy viscount, for there are few gentlemen who would not desire such an agreeable suit."

I acknowledged her improper comment with a tight nod.

Lady Beatrice flicked her fan with her wrist, pushing a bout of warm air toward me. "And when is Lord Thorton set to return from France, Miss Godwin?"

"I believe just before his house party at Branbury begins."

She shook her head. "I still think it odd that he should depart midway through the Season, and for a trip to the Continent, no less. If I didn't know better, I would think he was trying to escape something."

I veiled my irritation. "And yet the truth is quite the opposite. His mother has assured me it was a last hurrah before *settling down.*"

Miss Browning giggled. "Oh, what a match you shall be. He is the most handsome of men. And to be the wife of an earl." She released a dreamy sigh. "You are so fortunate."

"We are not engaged yet, Miss Browning." Yet even I knew it was only a matter of time before he would offer for me, and pride filled me. Lord Thorton was an ideal choice. His offer, unlike the others I had received, was one I actually wished to obtain. Not only was he a sought-after earl, but he was handsome and confident. He seemed wise enough to have not lost his fortune in gambling nor poor investments as others had done, and his estate was said to be one of the finest in England. But most importantly, when he looked at me, his eyes were not clouded with emotion and desire. He looked at me as few men did —a woman who met his list of qualities needed in a wife and nothing more. Yes, I was fortunate indeed.

"Bella?"

My eyes fell on the young lady who approached me, a wide, excited grin spreading across her plain features. I scanned her unembellished, muslin gown and unadorned, brown hair. The curls heaped on each side of her head accentuated her heart-shaped face to an unflattering fault.

"I am Arabella," I said curtly. Lady Beatrice and Miss Browning ducked behind their fans, muted whispers adding to my impatience. "But to those with whom I'm not well acquainted, I am addressed as Miss Godwin."

The girl's face turned scarlet, and her smile faded. "Forgive me. I assumed you would recognize me."

I tried to place her unremarkable face. She hardly appeared old enough to be attending a ball, yet something about her did seem oddly familiar. "I'm sorry, but I have no recollection of you." I glanced toward Miss Browning who had peeked over her fan. She looked as though she were about to start another fit of giggles when she lifted the fan again. How I wished this homely child would seek companionship elsewhere. How had she even managed to obtain an invitation?

"It's me." The young woman's large, brown eyes implored me to remember her. "Ruth."

My legs threatened to give out beneath me. "Ruth Seton?"

She nodded, and her exuberant smile once again brightened her face.

"Forgive me for not knowing you directly, but it has been ages since I've seen you." I reached out, clasping her hands in mine, searching for a likeness of the girl I once knew. "How much you have grown."

"And you look precisely as I pictured you, though your hair is a touch more golden than I would have thought." She leaned in closer. "But your eyes are the same dark blue." She sighed, taking in the rest of me. "You must be the most beautiful lady in all of London!"

My amused laugh did not drown out the huffs from behind me. "You were always one for exaggeration." I released her hands and glanced behind me at the affronted expressions of our onlookers. "Lady Beatrice, Miss Browning, may I introduce you to Miss Seton?"

They lowered their fans further and nodded in unison, Ruth waving her hand in a gauche manner.

"She was our neighbor at Fellerton when I was young," I said, feeling a sudden need to clarify our connection.

"Well then," Lady Beatrice said, taking hold of Miss Browning's arm, "we have no desire to prevent the two of you from becoming reacquainted."

Uncertain if I felt relief or aggravation at their prompt departure, I inclined my head in farewell, all too aware of the giggles trailing behind them as they left us.

"Is it not wonderful that we have crossed paths after all these years?" Ruth's smile widened. "I only wish Augustus were here." I stiffened at hearing his name, but she did not seem to take notice of it. And why would she? She did not know the agony he'd caused me. "I'm certain he shall scarcely believe me when I tell him I happened upon you this evening."

"Your cousin is not here, then?"

"No. He abhors balls and would not be persuaded otherwise."

The tension in my body eased at knowing I would not be forced to pretend polite ignorance at seeing him again. "That does not surprise me in the least. Too constricting for him, I daresay."

Ruth laughed. "How well you know him."

Knew him. "But I do hope he is well?" I asked, out of obligation.

"Oh, very well. He has taken over the role of patriarch most admirably since my uncle's death."

I reached out and touched her hand. "Oh, Ruth. I'm so sorry to hear of your loss."

Her smile lessened. "It was most unexpected, but we are managing."

I tipped my head to the side. "That must have been hard on all of you. I know how fond of him you were, as were your cousins."

She nodded, her eyes glistening in the candlelight.

I glanced around, having no desire to bring her to tears at the Brimhall's ball. "And has Augustus *settled down*, then?" I asked it with a tone of indifference, as though the answer would not affect me, for it most certainly should not.

Ruth nodded. "He certainly has."

My heart dropped at her confirmation, despite how I reprimanded it. Of course he should be married by now. It had been years since I had last seen him.

"In truth," Ruth said, "you would hardly believe him to be once so full of mischief. Though, he does still tease us from time to time, and we are always glad to see it."

I tipped my chin downward, uncertain whether she was still answering my question or if she had misunderstood me entirely. "Does his wife appreciate his teasing?"

Ruth quirked her head to one side. "Augustus is not married." Her hand lifted to her mouth. "Oh, is that what you meant by settled down? How silly of me. Of course I should have known that. No, he is still most eligible despite him being the kindest, most handsome man in all of Dorset. All of England, really." She paused. "Though I admit I likely hold a biased opinion on the matter."

I could not prevent a smile, though whether from the ridiculousness of her declaration or the clarification of Augustus's bachelor status, I could not be certain. "Your cousin was always most handsome," I said, unwilling to admit more. "And how do you enjoy Dorset? I heard the landscape there is quite breathtaking."

"Oh, it is. When I first went to live with my aunt and uncle, I was certain I could never grow to love it as I loved Bath, but I have. And you would love it there also."

I had once wished to visit Dorset more than any other place in the world, but that was years ago. Now I had not the slightest desire to set foot within the county, let alone be anywhere near Augustus's treasured estate, Fairhaven. "Perhaps I would."

"Arabella, dear." Papa stepped to my side. "Your mother sent me to check on you."

I glanced over at him with a grin, eager for him to realize who I was speaking with. But he was already staring at Ruth, his face blanched and his mouth agape.

"Ruth?" His whispered voice was hoarse, nearly indistinguishable.

I scanned his awestruck features, utterly confused how he had known her when I had not.

Ruth beamed up at him. "I am surprised you recognized me, Lord Godwin."

Papa pressed his eyes shut and opened them again, as though he thought Ruth might be a figment of his imagination. When he had confirmed she was still there, his gaze returned to me.

"It is her, Papa," I said with a laugh, taking hold of his arm.

He gave a slow nod. "It is obvious. She looks very much like her mother did at her age."

Ruth's expression filled with delight. "Do you truly think so? My aunt has claimed the same thing—that I remind her of Mama, when Mama was younger—and I have often wondered if she speaks the truth of it or if she simply means to please me. I do have her hair and brown eyes, of that I am certain, but I recall Mama being the most beautiful woman I have ever known. Yet, when I look in a mirror, I feel I am quite plain." Ruth's words gushed from her, and I again felt a smile coming to my lips without the slightest encouragement. There was the chattering girl I'd loved so well.

Ruth tipped her head to the side. "I don't necessarily count it as a bad thing—to be plain that is—for I have been told many a time there is more to a person than their appearance." She glanced sideways and drew in closer to us, lowering the volume of her voice. "But, in all honesty, I wouldn't complain if I were to be thought beautiful." She straightened. "So, you saying I resemble Mama, Lord Godwin, is the greatest of compliments, and I thank you with my whole heart."

"Then you're most welcome." Papa's lips lifted into a rare, full smile, but when he caught sight of me it lessened. "And who is it you are here with, Ru—pardon me—Miss Seton?"

"Our neighbors, the Whitmores. That is who we are staying with while Augustus and I are in London. You see, Mrs. Whitmore is Lady Brimhall's first cousin, and the Brimhalls were generous enough to allow me along this evening when they were told of my visit to Town. It is my first ball, you know." She glanced around. "It is all quite overwhelming, so many people in their finery, and I don't believe I've seen so many candles in my whole life, let alone in one room."

Papa and I gave slow nods.

"Oh yes, the Whitmores. I should be happy to introduce you, if I could only place them." Ruth's face scrunched, and she rose onto her toes, scanning the crowded room. "Oh, they are here somewhere." Papa seemed equally conscious of her tactless manners before she lowered herself. "I'm certain I shall find them in time."

Papa glanced over his shoulder, his eyes returning to Ruth with a gleam of urgency. "Well, it's likely best if you go find them straightway. You do not wish them to worry after you."

I took in Papa's inscrutable profile, unsure why he would say such a thing when we had just found one another. It wasn't as though the Brimhalls held such large functions that one could truly get lost for long among the crowd.

Ruth's smile faltered at Papa's admonition, and she glanced toward me. "I would hate for the Whitmores to worry on my account, especially after their kindness toward me. Perhaps I should go in search of them."

I reached out and took hold of her hand. "Then go. But let us depart with an agreement to correspond now that we're older and more capable of such things?"

Her brow creased momentarily, before her face brightened again. "Oh, yes. *Now that we're older and more capable.* I should enjoy that, and it makes our goodbye feel not so permanent."

A sense of relief overcame me. "Precisely."

Papa cleared his throat, and Ruth instantly dropped my hand, taking a few steps backward. "Farewell, Bella. Farewell, Lord Godwin."

Papa and I dipped our heads in near unison, and I offered a parting smile. "Farewell."

We watched as she disappeared through the crowded room.

I released a sigh. "Poor dear. Though I love her regardless, I cannot help but think how altered she would be if her mother had not died. It is apparent her aunt's tender disposition is far too lenient for her spirited nature, for I have hardly met a lady so neglected in her training."

Papa looked at me, his expression pained.

"Who was that pathetic creature?" Mother's voice startled me, but Papa turned toward her, his face now masked of emotion.

"I'm not certain. It seems the young woman had Arabella confused with someone else."

My head flinched backward in confusion, and Mother's suspicion moved to me. "You did not know her, Arabella?"

Uncertain why, I followed Papa's lead and shook my head. "No."

Her gaze drifted back to the place in the crowded room where Ruth had just departed. "Why the Brimhalls would invite such riff-raff to one of their balls is beyond me. I should likely not have come had I realized who we would be forced to keep company with this evening. Mr. Hall and his young new bride are also in attendance."

Papa nodded. "Well, my dear, it is fortunate, then, that we must not remain in such offensive company a moment longer." Mother's attention settled back on Papa as he gave a brief tip of his head in my direction. "Arabella mentioned she had a headache coming on, and I assured her we would not be at all bothered to return home without delay."

Mother scanned my features with skepticism. "Arabella appears perfectly well to me."

I lifted a hand to my temple, instinct pushing me to go along with Papa's deception. "The headache is just beginning. But the spots in my vision are growing larger, and I fear I will soon grow faint." I glanced around at the many faces surrounding us. "I would hate to swoon in front of all these people."

There was nothing Mother disliked more than making a scene, and, after a brief moment, she gave a small huff. "Very well. But, because you are so *ill*, Arabella, you shall be staying abed for the entirety of tomorrow. And that includes missing the theater."

Mother always knew precisely what consequence to hold over me. But when I looked to Papa, it was evident there was a reason for his ruse despite me not knowing it. "Then let us be on our way."

CHAPTER TWO

*T*he clock on the mantel ticked in a most tedious rhythm through the empty sitting room. Each click marked another irretrievable second of my life passing by, and one less moment I had until our looming departure to Sandson Hall. I dropped my sampler to my lap and glared at the small clock mocking me, as though it would do some good. It did none.

"There you are, Arabella." The shrill tone of Mother's voice commanded my attention. She had scarcely spoken a word to me since the ball, yet I suddenly favored the silence of the past few days to the wrathful glint in her focused regard.

I took a steadying breath, attempting to give nothing away. "I did not realize you were searching for me."

Her jaw steeled as she moved to the window, placing her back to me. "I know you are aware of the reason for my vexation, so you need not act an innocent."

My gaze dropped to the cream-colored rose I had been embroidering, dread pulsing through me. She must have discovered the truth about Papa's and my encounter with Ruth. No wonder she was furious. I opened my mouth to offer an apology.

"Priscilla will be most displeased." Mother gave a disbelieving shake of her head. "Not to mention the timing of it all is most inconsiderate."

I closed my lips, unable to find a correlation between the timing of our chance meeting with Ruth and its effect on Aunt Priscilla. Could she be referring to something else entirely? I needed to tread with more caution.

Mother whipped her head toward me. "What have you to say?"

"In truth, I'm not certain what you are speaking of."

"The Leavitts?"

I tried not to cower at the intensity of her stare as she started toward me.

"What of them?" To my great relief, I truly had no idea what Papa's cousins had to do with anything.

Mother leaned over me, taking hold of my arm, her fingers cold and sharp on my skin. Her eyes bore into me, searching my features for any hint of deception. After what felt an eternity, her grip slackened. "You truly do not know?"

"Know what, exactly?"

Mother dropped her hand from my arm and straightened. "Your father has decided to send you to the Leavitts' for the next several weeks, instead of allowing you to join us at Sandson Hall."

"Papa's cousins?" My heart leapt when Mother gave a brisk nod. "But we are set to leave any minute for Sandson."

"I know." Disgust coated her words, as though she'd mistaken my amazement for displeasure equal to her own. "I am in full disagreement to this arrangement, though your father will not hear a word of it."

I swallowed, cautious to not appear too eager over the joyous news. In truth, had the revelation come at any other time, I would have thought it far from ideal, but knowing the Leavitts' company could be more easily borne than the company I would find at Sandson Hall, I was obliged to consider myself most fortunate. This certainly had to be Papa's reward for my silence regarding Ruth and his unwillingness to speak to me of it—accepting an eleventh-hour invitation to free me from the clutches of Mother and Aunt Priscilla.

Mother was watching me as I pulled myself from my thoughts. In an attempt to look more displeased by the news, I dropped my shoulders and released a small puff of air. "But what shall I do at the Leavitts for so long?"

Mother sat herself on the opposite end of the settee. "You shall be acting as companion to Mrs. Leavitt. Apparently, Mr. Leavitt believes your *cheery spirit* shall be just the thing to improve his wife's ailing health."

I set my focus on the embroidery sample on my lap, refusing to take Mother's doubtful tone to heart. "And shall I go to Branbury straight from the Leavitts' then?"

The exhale Mother released sounded more like a hiss. "Yes. It appears that is what your father intends."

I gave a slow nod, realizing this providential development could be taken from me as quickly as it had been given. "But do you not oppose my going?"

"Of course I oppose." The shrill tone altered Mother's voice. "But as I have already stated, Charles will not hear me on the matter, despite my reasons. As if he has ever dictated your social arrangements to me before. It is most unlike him and utterly infuriating."

"Mrs. Leavitt must be melancholy indeed, for Papa to be so determined."

Mother huffed. "Yes. I suppose she must be. Though

her timing is most inconvenient as is Mr. Leavitt's lack of foresight to not send for some other young relation to cheer her. One less inclined to receiving invitations than you."

I thought to mention Sandson Hall hardly counted as a noteworthy invitation, but I held my tongue, allowing the silence to settle. I would not risk her temper, nor my freedom.

"At least Charles was correct in one regard—your continued absence from London will ensure that you will not haphazardly encourage any more suitors while Lord Thorton is away."

My throat constricted as I thought of Papa saying such a thing. Surely he only mentioned it in an attempt to appease Mother. Hadn't he?

Watching me, Mother's lips curved at the edges, and I cursed myself for not better concealing my quandary. "I am at least relieved to discover you were not aware of the arrangement, as Charles had assured me." Mother's eyes shifted between mine. "To think that either of you would willingly deceive me would be unpardonable."

Ever so slowly, I released the air I hadn't realized I'd been holding in. "I knew nothing of the Leavitts' invitation."

A light knock sounded on the door, stealing both our attention.

Mother stood. "Yes, Harriston?"

The butler gave a slight bow of his head. "The coach is ready for you, my lady."

"And have my daughter's trunks already been hauled back inside?"

Harriston tipped his chin downward. "They are being moved now."

"You presume to collect me when your work is not yet complete?"

He gave a small bow. "Forgive me, my lady."

Mother just shook her head. "These Town servants are utterly remiss."

I quieted my tongue, unwilling to risk provoking Mother further.

Mother's regard returned to me. "Well, be certain to arrive at Branbury in time to dress for dinner on the first day of July." She started toward the door but paused, looking back at me. "You must realize that Lord Thorton is likely your last chance at a match of that caliber. Do not forget it."

Placing my sampler on the side table, I stood and faced her. "I know what is expected of me."

Mother scrutinized me one last time. "I would certainly hope so by now." Without another word, she walked from the room.

I took a moment to gather myself. When Papa walked past the door, indicating for me to join them in the entry hall, I followed obediently.

Mother tugged on her gloves. "I am of a mind to delay my departure so that I might at least see Arabella off."

Papa hardly looked affected by her threat. "You shall do no such thing. I am more than capable of seeing to the task."

"I believe we often hold different opinions, though mine don't seem to matter as of late." Mother shook her head, grasping her reticule. "I shall not pretend we are parting on good terms."

"And yet, I implore you to enjoy yourself." Papa sounded less than sincere. "Considering the guestlist, I'm certain Arabella's absence will allow you to more fully enjoy your time at Sandson Hall."

Mother pursed her lips and lifted her chin, moving toward the open door. "Farewell, Arabella. Charles."

"Goodbye, Mother." I stepped through the doorway after her, still in shock that she was climbing into the waiting coach without me.

"Farewell, dear," Papa muttered, stepping behind me. We watched in silence as the coach rolled forward and down the street.

"Papa, I want to—" I glanced over my shoulder, only to find he was no longer there. Hurrying back into the entry hall, I caught sight of his retreating figure. "Papa?"

He paused and ever so slowly turned back toward me.

Despite his visible reluctance, I would not allow this opportunity to pass, not after all my futile attempts at obtaining a private audience with him the past few days. "I want to thank you for allowing me to visit the Leavitts. I know Mother was not pleased with your interference, but I am grateful for it."

He gave a slight nod of acknowledgement and again turned to leave.

"Also," I called, halting him a second time. "I was hoping you could offer an explanation as to why we were not to mention Ruth to Mother."

Papa lowered his chin and rubbed at the bridge of his nose, as though the mere question exhausted him. "It is complicated, Arabella."

"Yet, is it not reasonable that I should be made aware of the situation before I begin a correspondence with her?"

His eyes returned to mine. "I can say no more. I have sworn I would not speak of the Setons, and I'm nothing if not a man of my word." He paused, indecision evident in his features. "That is why I must allow for this."

"Our correspondence?"

"No. Not that. Though if you do write to Ruth, take caution to ensure your Mother does not intercept your letters."

I nodded absently, my thoughts still on his previous statement. "If it's not that, Papa, then what is it you are—"

His stern glare silenced me. "Do not make me regret my interference in keeping you from Sandson Hall."

I swallowed. I had grown accustomed to Papa's aloofness, but I was not used to his anger being directed toward me. "Forgive me."

He considered me briefly then shook his head. "Now," he said, his voice once again gentle, "go find some way to entertain yourself. I have work to attend to."

Even after Papa disappeared into his study and closed the door behind him, I could not convince myself to move. Why had Papa been so harsh with me? And why had he sworn to not speak of the Setons? I had always supposed my parents had been friends with the couple, just as I had been friends with their daughter. But my memories were so vague, I hardly felt sure of anything anymore. With one last glance at Papa's closed study door, I made my way back to the drawing room.

I WAS SO INCREDIBLY BORED. Papa had spent the remainder of the day after Mother's departure at Westminster, and I hadn't said a word to another person besides our housekeeper and Leah, my lady's maid, in nearly twenty-four hours.

My restless mind seemed incapable of needlework, so I placed my embroidery next to me on the settee and scrutinized the painting above the fireplace. I was never particularly fond of the piece. It was of the seashore—

though that was not the part I disliked—with a boat painted in the background sailing away. It always left me with a disquieting feeling, as though I was being left behind at a place I'd never even been.

A knock interrupted my pondering. The door opened and Leah stepped inside.

"Yes?"

"Your father wishes to speak with you in the drawing room. He said the coach should arrive any moment."

"Thank heavens," I muttered, standing. "Do be sure to grab my sampler and the two books on my writing desk."

"Yes, miss." Leah was already in motion as I walked from the room.

The drawing room door was open, and I strode in to find Papa reading the newspaper in his wing-backed chair. I scanned his relaxed posture, and it eased me. "Good morning, Papa."

He glanced up from his paper. "I thought you might enjoy a cup of tea before your travels."

My eyes fell on the tea tray. "How thoughtful of you. May I pour you a cup also?"

He nodded and handed me the key that Mother typically retained, folding his paper and setting it on his lap.

I moved to the tea chest and unlocked the top drawer, retrieving a few of the leaves and locking it once again. "Would you prefer lemon or milk?"

"Lemon."

Papa's regard remained fixed on me while I readied his cup. "And how was your day at Westminster?" I asked, a touch self-conscious under his continued scrutiny.

"The Leavitts have written," Papa said abruptly, disregarding my question.

I lifted my brow. "Oh?" I carefully handed him his tea.

"It seems Mrs. Leavitt is not well enough to travel to Dorset at this time."

My chest tightened, and I took a seat with my own cup in hand. "But Leah said the coach will be here any moment to retrieve me."

"Yes … well … I have secured you another invitation for the time being."

"Another invitation?" I attempted to conceal my bewilderment. "Where to?"

Papa pulled his pocket watch out and studied it.

"Papa?"

When his eyes lifted, there was a peculiar flicker that left me unsettled. I raised my cup of tea to my lips, hoping it would calm the sudden churning in my stomach.

A knock splintered through the silence and Harriston stepped inside. "A Mr. Brundage and Miss Seton have arrived, my lord."

My gaze shot to Papa so quickly that the warm liquid I was attempting to swallow was instead inhaled. I sought to pull in a breath, but the attempt was in vain, and a fit of coughs seized me.

"Are you well, Arabella?" Papa asked. I had just enough sense to nod.

"Is she choking?" Ruth's voice only heightened my state of dread, realizing she and Augustus had been shown into the room.

Papa stood, and started toward me. "I believe she has just swallowed wrong."

I held up a hand toward him, gesturing for him to stop. "A mo—ment," I choked out in a throaty voice, rising to stagger toward the window. My coughing continued and my chest burned, making it impossible to right the rhythm of my breath.

"Lift your arms." Augustus's voice was humiliatingly

close, and I refused to glance in his direction. After eight years without so much as a word from him, to have him find me in such a state was too much to suffer.

"I'm ... well," I said through more coughs.

"Still just as stubborn, I see." There was amusement in his voice.

I contemplated piercing him with a scowl for teasing me in my distress, but it would not serve my purpose with a reddened face and tears streaming down my cheeks. Finally, out of sheer desperation, I lifted my arms to shoulder height. Augustus stepped behind me and took hold of my wrists, lifting them until they were straight overhead. Though his proximity did little to ease me, within moments my coughing ceased and bit by bit my breathing regulated.

Without a word, he released my wrists.

I lowered my hands to wipe at my eyes, unwilling to lift my gaze to his. "Thank you."

Papa gave a loud clap of his hands. "Well done. I shall need to remember that trick."

Augustus dispelled the heat engulfing my back by moving to a more suitable distance. "My father always claimed lifting your arms above your head like that opens up the chest cavity to allow for more air. Though I'm not sure of the truth in it, it has always seemed to work."

"Well I'm glad you thought of it." Ruth moved to my side. "That was awfully frightening to witness. And to think, if you'd not been here, who knows what could have happened."

I straightened in exasperation. "A moment or two longer and I could have righted myself." I compensated for the heat that now pooled in my cheeks by offering a tight laugh.

Ruth nodded, though it was obvious she was not convinced.

Without thinking, I glanced at Augustus. My breath nearly caught a second time at the striking man that stood before me. How tall he now was—though I was certain Lord Thorton was taller yet—and his hair had grown darker, a soft golden brown that nearly matched the undertones of his tanned skin. But his honey-brown eyes were the same, as was his delightfully irritating grin. "After eight years, how does it feel to suddenly reappear and be deemed my hero, Mr. Brundage?"

He only laughed, but the familiar sound, though now deeper, somehow set me at ease. No. It could not. Not after his neglect. I fortified the wall around my heart, assuring it would be impenetrable to his disingenuous charms.

"Can you believe, after all this time, we are together again?" Ruth's question pulled me from my thoughts. "We shall have such a grand time these next few weeks."

My stomach knotted, and I glanced toward Papa.

Guilt glinted in his eyes. "The invitation I was telling you of is to Fairhaven."

"Fairhaven? You have begged an invitation for me to go to Fairhaven?" A slew of emotions coursed through me, but I had not the time nor the capability to sort through them.

"It seemed a feasible alternative after you and Miss Seton discussed your mutual desire to be reconnected at Lord and Lady Brimhall's ball."

My mouth hung open, and I could not convince it to shut. What would ever prompt Papa to do something so utterly insolent? What must Augustus think? Had he assumed I had been the instigator of the invitation? Augustus stood with a look of utter confusion on his face that confirmed my quandary. This would not do. I had to say something. "Mr. Brundage, I believe we owe you an apology. It is not Papa who typically sees to my social affairs, and I believe it is quite obvious he is unaware of the protocols." I sent a corrective glance to Papa, who appeared to care little for my public correction. "It is one thing to beg an invitation from family or dear friends, but it is quite another to beg one from an old acquaintance."

Augustus did not bat an eye at my affront. "Do not apologize. Though I admit I was ... surprised to receive Lord Godwin's missive, I assured him we would be willing to accommodate you."

My heart dropped at Augustus's lackluster assurance, and I rebuked it for betraying me so quickly. It was precisely the reminder I required. "I hate to disappoint anyone, but I'm not certain Fairhaven is the best situation for me at present."

Ruth took my hand in hers. "Please don't refuse us now. I am entirely set on it. Besides, we have already sent word of your coming to Aunt Marina and hired a larger post-chaise for our travels." Her pleas tugged at the piece of my heart she still held.

"Ruth, I do want to be with you. I simply ..." My voice faltered, and I was unable to finish under Augustus's unwavering consideration.

Papa cleared his throat. "Well, Arabella, I fear you must make a choice." He now used his politician's voice. "I have business to attend to and shall soon be retiring my duty as chaperone. If you prefer to join your mother and Aunt Priscilla, I can have a coach hired within the hour."

I glanced back at Augustus, and one side of his mouth lifted in an uncertain half-smile. Surely, Augustus's company was preferable to the company I'd find at

Sandson Hall. Or was it? After all the heartache I'd endured, I hardly felt certain.

"To Sandson, then?" Papa said, taking an impatient step forward.

Even the name grated at my soul. "No," I said softly, holding his gaze. "If Mr. Brundage is certain he can tolerate me for a time, I will accept his *invitation*."

Ruth's squeal of delight forced my notice from Papa's contented expression just in time to brace myself against the force of her arms wrapping around me. "You shall not regret it," she said in a hardly distinguishable pitch. "It shall be exactly as it used to be."

It could not be, but now was not the time to say such things. Allowing the unseemly gesture only as long as was necessary, I placed my hands upon her arms and pulled back as though I was admiring her. "I'm certain we shall have a grand time."

"Now that it is decided, you'd best be on your way." Papa stepped forward with a hand extended to Augustus. "It was good to see you again, Mr. Brundage. Please give our regards to your mother as well as our condolences to your entire family for their loss."

Augustus gave Papa's hand a firm shake. "I will. Thank you, my lord."

I studied Papa's profile. How did he know of the late Mr. Brundage's passing? He was not there when Ruth had spoken of it at the ball. Could it be that Augustus had mentioned it in his reply to Papa's missive?

Ruth's waving hand pulled me back to the present. "Goodbye, Lord Godwin. I do believe I shall be forever indebted to you for allowing Bella to visit." She glanced at me, a giddy grin upon her lips. "I still cannot believe it is true. Though we are standing here, in this very moment, I am waiting to wake and realize it was all a dream."

Papa returned her smile, but it was tainted by sadness. "Well, I am pleased to oblige you this time." With one last lingering glance, he moved to me. "Enjoy yourself, my darling," he said before leaning in to place a kiss upon my cheek. He lingered by my ear, and I thought he wished to say something, but then he pulled away.

My eyes searched his, but whatever it was, he had already hidden it away. "Take care of yourself, Papa."

"You also." He gave one more hurried nod before walking from the room.

Drawing in a deep inhale, I looked to the others.

"Do not look so worried," Ruth said, unable to conceal her excitement. "You shall love Fairhaven."

I forced a shaky smile and stepped forward. "Shall we depart, then?"

"Oh yes, let's do." Ruth bounced toward the doorway at a quickened pace. She glanced over her shoulder in the threshold to make certain I was following her, and I took a few hurried steps to catch up.

When Ruth disappeared, Augustus cleared his throat behind me. "Bella."

I stilled at my name on his lips. "You must not call me that, Mr. Brundage." Hesitantly I turned toward him. "We are no longer children, and seeing as we have not retained our friendship the past several years, it would be most appropriate if we were to use formal address."

The hurt that pulled at his expression pricked my conscience, but what else could he expect? It was the truth of it, and by no fault of mine.

"Forgive me, Miss Godwin," he said, amending his error. "I simply want you to know that I was under the assumption you were aware of our invitation. I would not have presumed to come, otherwise."

"I have no doubt of that," I said, cynicism seeping into

my voice, despite my best efforts.

Augustus released a heavy breath. "Well, it is not yet too late to change your mind. I know that you don't wish to disappoint Ruth, but she will come to understand."

"If I did not want to come, I would not have agreed to it." I paused, not certain I wished to ask the question looming in my mind. "Unless it is your preference I remain behind?"

He hesitated. "No. I don't believe it is."

I lifted my brows. "Very reassuring." His chuckle followed me as I started forward again. "Mr. Brundage?" As I faced him, my heart attempted to lodge in my throat due to its ridiculous thumping. I swallowed down the lump, but it only lodged in more firmly. "Your family is not aware of what transpired between us just before you left Bath, are they?"

The corners of his mouth twitched. "What exactly did transpire between us, *Miss Godwin?*"

My whole body grew hot and my face pinked from his apparent amusement. "You very well know what—"

"Are the two of you coming?" Ruth stepped back into the doorway, and I startled, clasping a hand over my chest. "Is something amiss, Bella?"

I took to clearing my throat. "No. Not in the least."

Ruth's gaze flitted to Augustus and his shameless grin. "Forgive me if I interrupted you. I thought you two were right behind me, so I was talking endlessly to no one but your butler." She glanced behind her into the entry hall. "And one of your maids."

I stepped with her through the threshold. "What is it you were saying?"

"Oh, nothing really." She swatted at the air between us. "I was simply waffling on again. You know how I have a tendency for such things."

I glanced over at Ruth, suddenly overcome by the realization that Ruth was here with me. I took hold of her arm, not wishing to conceal my delight. "I adore your waffling," I said, pulling her close.

"I am relieved to hear it. Though you must promise to inform me if your opinion changes on the matter."

"What a thing to say. As though I could ever tire of you." I noticed Leah awaiting my directions on the lowest step. "Come along, Leah."

"Yes, miss." She moved to step and thudded onto her foot, apparently forgetting the stair between her and the ground level.

"Careful there." Augustus reached out to steady her by the arm as she teetered forward.

Her cheeks were ablaze as she took in Augustus's handsome face. "Forgive me, sir."

Augustus gestured for her to go on ahead. "We all misstep from time to time."

The lovely pink of her cheeks instantly made me regret Mother's recent hire. There was no need to have such a young, pretty thing for a lady's maid. "Make haste, Leah," I said, unable to curb the harshness in my voice. "And do be more careful. You shall be of no use to me if you break an arm." I nearly winced at how much I had sounded like Mother.

Leah's shoulders caved and her eyes dropped to the floor before she hurried out the door ahead of me.

I offered my curious onlookers a tight smile knowing it would do me no good to appear distressed by my overreaction. "Shall we?"

With only a touch of hesitancy, Ruth stepped through the door, but Augustus looked behind him in the direction where Papa had disappeared. "I suppose we must."

CHAPTER THREE

I glanced around for Augustus's horse, desperate to discover it was saddled and waiting nearby. There was no horse. "Do you not intend to ride, Mr. Brundage?"

He stepped to my side but did not look at me. "I did not bring a horse with me to Town. I hope it is not disagreeable that I shall be riding in the coach also." His words were friendly enough, but his tone was distant as he offered his hand to assist me inside.

My stomach clenched at the thought of hours in his company, especially after my unkindness toward Leah. "It is not disagreeable in the least." I lightly placed my hand in his before ascending into the carriage. When he removed his support, I brushed my fingers against my traveling dress to diffuse the sensation of his touch and took the seat across from Leah. I thought to smile at her, but she did not look up.

"Is it not a most pleasant day for travelling?" Ruth asked, ducking her head as she entered the carriage. "I admit I have a small inclination to worry, and I thought of all the ways our travels might be ruined, yet I'm beginning to believe I fretted in vain."

Had she not yet realized her cousin's intentions to ride with us as I had?

Ruth gathered her skirts from behind her and positioned herself on the rear-facing seat next to Leah. "Hopefully tomorrow will prove equally amiable for the remainder of our journey."

I patted the seat next to me. "Will you not sit here?"

"I would," she said, looking a touch sheepish, "but I fear my stomach prefers it if I face backward. I know it's odd, but I suppose it is what I grew used to over the years, and now I cannot convince my body otherwise."

I had nothing to offer besides an unenthusiastic nod before I focused out the window nearest me. I shuddered to think what Mother would say if she were to witness an unrelated gentleman taking the seat next to me—and without a proper chaperone present. But then again, I would not be here at all if Mother had known of Papa's forced invitation for me to visit Fairhaven.

The carriage shifted under Augustus's weight, and I sensed him move in beside me. The decently-sized cab now seemed infuriatingly small as he shut the door and gave two distinct taps on the roof. With the initial jerk of the carriage reminding me what I had just agreed to, I attempted to draw in a calming breath. The air was stagnant and heavy.

"And you," Ruth began, and I glanced at her before realizing she was speaking to Leah. "You must be Bella's maid? Leah, was it?"

Leah sent me a hesitant look, and I gave her a slight nod of permission.

"Yes, miss."

"Are you from London?"

"No, Somerset." Leah did not offer more.

"Somerset? Of course, you would be from near Bath. I spent my childhood there. Oh, how I miss it. Though I must say, you will probably love Dorset just as much if you allow yourself. It is beautiful beyond description. And there are some great footpaths near Fairhaven you must take, for there is no better way to see the surrounding area than exploring. Do you not agree?"

Leah gave a slow nod and looked to me, her expression clearly entreating me to intervene. It was one thing to be made to ride inside a carriage with your mistress and her friends, but it was quite another to be treated as though you were one of them. Poor thing.

"How tired you look, Leah," I said, eager to make amends for snipping at her on the way out. I tilted my head to the side and examined her. "You must be exhausted from all your labors to have me readied so early. Do you care to rest a while?"

It took only a moment for Leah to realize the liberation I'd granted her. "Thank you, miss. I believe I may just sleep all day." Leaning against the side of the carriage, she closed her eyes.

Augustus's gaze flicked to me, but I pretended to not notice.

"The houses in this part of Mayfair are quite large." Ruth looked out the window again, her hands resting on the shallow sill, taking in the passing scene.

"Is your Town house nearby?" I tried not to feel self-conscious with Augustus listening.

Ruth shifted in her seat to more fully face me. "Oh, but we do not have a Town house. We've been staying with the Whitmores just a few streets over. Mrs. Whitmore has a daughter—Candace—who is about to turn one and twenty. Only a year older than me." She brightened. "And

35

only a few months younger than you. Do you recall me mentioning them at the ball?"

"I recall you mentioning the name Whitmore." I paused, attempting to keep the jealousy from altering my voice. "Though I did not realize they had a daughter about our age."

"Oh yes. And she is the loveliest person in all the world. Is she not, Augustus?" I refused to look at him, but Ruth's eyes danced as they returned to me, evidence that Augustus had not refuted her claim. "You shall love her as readily as I do. I am certain of it."

"Then I shall look forward to our introduction."

"I am surprised you do not yet know one another, being that this was her second Season."

I clasped my hands in my lap, uncertain how to explain, particularly under Augustus's watchful eye, that I would have known Miss Whitmore had we moved in the same social circles. We did not. True, we both attended Lord and Lady Brimhall's ball, but that was likely an anomaly, considering the Whitmores had not been invited based upon their own merits but as relations. Yet I could not say as much without giving airs to my higher status, and I had no desire to make Ruth, or even Augustus, feel lesser. "Likely the sheer number of young ladies during the Season prevented our meeting."

"Are there so very many?"

"Oh, yes. Hundreds just among the *ton*."

Ruth quirked her brow. "I imagined far less, but I suppose I would not know as I've not had a Season."

I tilted my head. "Is that not why you were in Town?"

"No. Well, obviously we were for a small part of it, but that was not our purpose for coming to London. Augustus had business to attend to, so he brought me along knowing how I longed to visit Candace. And we saw much of Owen in the evenings. You remember Augustus's brother?"

"Of course," I said, though most of what I recalled about him came from stories Augustus had told me. "Does he reside in London now?"

"Currently." Augustus offered a tight-lipped grin in lieu of more information, so I returned my attention to Ruth.

"So how long was your stay?"

"In the end it was just over a fortnight." She looked at Augustus. "And aren't you glad we stayed those extra few days, cousin? For had we not, I never would have encountered Bella at the ball."

Unable to refuse my curiosity, I glanced at Augustus. His expression was steeled, but the uncertainty in his eyes was still distinguishable. "To be sure," he said, his dull tone contradicting his affirmation.

After a brief pause, I covered my hurt with a forced laugh. "Your cousin does seem most overjoyed by our reacquaintance, does he not?" I sent him a wry smile, knowing full well how to pull him from his melancholy, though I wasn't certain I wished to. "I hardly believed Ruth when she made mention of it, but you *have* become somber."

Ruth's expression filled with contrition. "I … well, I did mention it, Augi, but—"

I gave a dismissive wave of my hand. "Oh, Ruth, do not fret. It was imperative that your cousin should grow up at some point, and I fear such a thing requires a less *mischievous* temperament."

Augustus appraised my features before his mouth curved upward on one side. "Mischievous? I believe your memory escapes you."

My heart lifted as it always had when we used to tease

one another, and I looked to Ruth. "Did he not taunt me mercilessly with his boyish tactics during his visits to Blacksley?"

Ruth tightened her lips together, her eyes now alight with glee, and she nodded.

Augustus shifted in his seat to face me more fully, resting his arm on the back of the bench. "What boyish tactics are you referring to exactly?"

I lifted a brow at him, ignoring the accelerated pounding of my heart and the warmth of his hand so near my bare neck. "You rubbed mud in my hair, put frogs down my frock, and hung my favorite doll from a tree."

"That was before our truce."

"And what of the time you took me fishing?"

He gave a half-hearted shrug. "What of it?"

My mouth opened in disbelief at his blatant oversight. "The way you bashed that fish with a rock is still seared into my memory."

He began to shake with laughter, and I resisted the strangely familiar urge to join him. "The blame there should not fall entirely on me. You had to have realized that fish must first die if they are to be eaten?"

I pierced him with my most unamused stare, waiting for him to appear sufficiently contrite.

After a moment he filled his cheeks with air and released it slowly through his mouth, resuming a more appropriate demeanor. "Forgive me. I never meant to distress you."

"Not even the time you nearly shot me with an arrow?"

He removed his arm from the back of the bench and pointed a lighthearted finger at me. "That was an accident, and I apologized."

"Or the time you carried on as though William Morris,

the pig man's son, was fond of me—writing me those horrendous love letters?"

His lips squeezed shut, and he placed his clenched hand atop them to conceal his growing amusement. "Not an accident, I admit, but they were not horrendous. I heard you telling Ruth how well-written you thought them."

My mouth parted. "You spied on us?"

He paused, then dipped his chin in mock contrition. "I now see that admitting it does not help my plight."

I took in Ruth's contented expression, unable to conceal my pleasure. "After everything I suffered at your cousin's hands, I'm beginning to wonder at my decision to come along." My intention was to tease, but the smile melted from Augustus's lips. Time seemed to stop at seeing him so altered in countenance. Yet why should I be bothered that his conscience was pricked by my words? The guilt was not mine but his own. "Luckily for him," I said, unable to prevent myself from righting the situation, "I have always been willing to overlook his troublesome ways."

The corners of his lips curved upward again, though the smile lacked its previous radiance.

Unsure how to proceed in the ensuing silence, I focused on Ruth. "Tell me of Fairhaven. I long to know everything about it."

She beamed back at me, needing no further insistence to fill the quiet. "Fairhaven must be one of the finest houses in all of England." Ruth paused. "Well, to be completely honest, I don't believe that would be a fair assessment, as I have not visited many houses outside of Dorset." Her brows pulled low. "In truth, I haven't visited many houses *within* Dorset either. Yet I have seen a great many from the outside, and Fairhaven, though not as large as some, is equally beautiful. Not to mention that the countryside gets more mesmerizing the closer you get to the coast. Do you not agree, Augi?"

Augustus nodded in my periphery.

Ruth leaned forward. "Do you think we could take Bella to the seaside?"

"If she desires it."

Ruth reached out and touched my knee. "Would you like that?"

"Very much. I have never been to the sea."

Ruth sighed. "There is nothing like it in this world. The waves crashing against the beach. Oh, and the smell. Cousin, tell Bella of the way the air smells. It is almost as though you can taste the salt in the air. And the way the water covers your feet ... it feels as though you are being pulled out to sea, like the ocean is yearning to keep you if you'd only let it."

I attempted to hide my dismay at such a notion. "I am certain I shall not be brave enough to venture in."

Ruth blinked rapidly. "But to go all the way to the ocean—and for the first time—to not go in?"

I sensed Augustus watching me again, and I tilted my head, allowing a kind smile to touch my lips. "Observing your enjoyment will be quite enough to satisfy me." I glanced at Augustus. "And do you enjoy the ocean as much as your cousin, Mr. Brundage?" I asked, hoping to make him aware of his unpleasant habit of staring.

He did not look away but offered a thoughtful grin. "I'm not certain anyone can enjoy the ocean as much as Ruth, but I certainly try."

I gave a nod and looked back to his cousin.

Taking it as permission to continue, we listened as Ruth described the shells, the sea birds, the quality of sand and on and on with whatever came into her mind. By the time we reached our first stop, I felt desperate for some quiet.

Augustus saw to acquiring the next team of horses while we took our midday meal inside the posting-house. Ruth was thrilled with the food and spoke of her love of all types of pies, from minced meat to fresh blackberry. At the second stop she recounted the first time she had tasted ice cream and by the next we had discussed her favorite teas to alarming detail.

By the time we reached the coaching inn that night, I felt strangely exhausted. I hardly received as much interaction in a day with my parents as I did in five minutes with Ruth. Now, after ten hours of her endless chatter, I realized that the constant pace had worn me down more than I cared to admit.

Eager to sleep, I went directly to my room. But the lumpy bed and the rancid smell of the place made sleep hard to come by. I tossed and turned with dreams of Papa and Mother quarrelling with the Setons. Then came my repeated nightmare, one I thought I had finally quelled.

In the dream, I stood at a window staring out at countless people passing by, none of whom I recognized. Each movement, each sound, disquieted me, but I waited. And waited.

Augustus never came.

CHAPTER FOUR

I squinted into the morning light, the throbbing in my head too insufferable to take in much else besides Augustus awaiting us near the carriage. "I trust you ladies slept well?"

I wasn't certain any person could sleep well in such a place, let alone with the torrent of nightmares I'd endured, but I forced a smile. "Perfectly. And might I inquire about the length of today's journey?"

Augustus held out a hand to assist Leah into the cab then offered the support to me. "Not half a day's travel from here. If we encounter no complications, we shall arrive with ample time to rest before dressing for dinner."

My head throbbed, and the thought of another moment bouncing about in a carriage was unbearable. "Superb." I accepted his offered hand and ascended the steps, my aching body protesting each movement. I settled myself across from Leah into the same seat as yesterday. Ruth soon followed, resuming her rear-facing position before Augustus again moved onto the bench next to me.

When the carriage lurched forward, I looked to Ruth. "I still desire to know more of Fairhaven before our arrival. You had begun yesterday, but we changed topics before you were able to relay much of it."

Ruth clasped her hands at her chest. "I could talk of such things for hours."

"By all means, please do," I said, relieved I would not need to offer much in the way of conversation once Ruth began.

Augustus's gaze was once again on me, but I did not meet it as Ruth began her explanation of Fairhaven's scarcely noteworthy history. With a few nods and well-placed smiles, Ruth continued on with little need of encouragement.

By the first stop to change horses, she had finished detailing the rose garden—apparently Fairhaven's most *mentionable feature*—and moved on to describe the orchard. As Ruth launched into the different varieties of fruit grown, my eyelids grew insufferably heavy.

I stifled a yawn and glanced at Leah enviously, her head resting against the window, and her eyes closed. How fortunate she had no one to make a good impression on. Refocusing on Ruth, I forced myself to remain attentive. The rhythmic movement of the carriage lulled me deeper into exhaustion, but I would not succumb. It would be completely improper for me to fall asleep while Ruth spoke, especially sitting next to Augustus.

"Miss Godwin."

A light tapping on my arm followed the voice.

"Miss Godwin," the deep voice was familiar and exceptionally close.

Despite the heaviness of my eyelids, I forced them open. The vibrant colors of a summer afternoon were framed by a tilted window contrasting the interior of the swaying, more dimly lit—coach? I lifted my head and a strong hand helped me upright.

"Don't let her miss it, Augi!"

Augi? My faculties returned in near unison with the mortification that consumed me. I glanced sideways with dread as Augustus returned my look of embarrassment with one of utter amusement.

"I ..." I didn't know what to say as I ensured my hair had not dislodged from the pins. My training had entailed memorizing appropriate excuses for any foreseeable misstep; unfortunately, falling asleep on a gentleman had not been among the list. "I must have fallen asleep." My deficient excuse sent the rising warmth to my cheeks.

Augustus's smile grew. "I did not mind in the least."

Ruth watched the exchange with nearly as much enjoyment on her face as her cousin.

"I'm sorry if I drifted off while you spoke, Ruth. I was very much enjoying your explanation of Fairhaven and"— I searched my mind—"the orchard."

She smiled. "It was not the first time someone has fallen asleep while I prattled on and it certainly shan't be the last."

I gave a timid nod, hoping my acknowledgment would not be taken offensively.

Ruth's unaffected expression moved to her cousin. "Tell Bella where we are."

"Branbury Court is about to come into view." Augustus's intent stare only deepened the awful shade of red I could feel settling into my cheeks and neck. "I hated to wake you, but we figured you'd be disappointed if you missed it."

I swallowed. "Who told you of Branbury?"

Augustus did not look away. "Your father wrote of it in the missive he sent—both the upcoming house party as well as the anticipated engagement between yourself and Lord Thorton."

My fickle heart lurched, quickly followed by a wave of guilt surging through me. But why should I feel guilty about such a thing being withheld? It wasn't as though I'd hidden the truth, we simply hadn't ventured on the taboo topic yet. And there certainly had never been an opportune time to mention my forthcoming offer. Not with Augustus here. Eager to be free of their expectant gazes, I looked out the window nearest me. "I had not realized we passed by Lord Thorton's estate on our journey, though I admit I am eager to catch a glimpse of the place."

"It will be on my side." He pointed out his window ahead of us. "At the edge of this clearing of hedges—just there."

I moved slightly toward him, but could only see the darkened wall of endless foliage from where I sat. Augustus pressed himself against the bench, allowing me more room for viewing. I leaned a little farther, ensuring I did not touch him, only to find my attempts were in vain.

"I shall wait." Gesturing for him to return to his place, I corrected my posture.

"But you shall miss it." Ruth's voice was frantic. "You can only see it for a few moments before the hedges will again block it from view."

I glanced back at Leah who was awake but seemed to have little interest in the happenings inside the carriage. Reassured by her unwavering view out the opposite window, I inhaled and leaned even farther over, craning my neck. It was hopeless. I still could see nothing.

A warm hand settled on my waist, and the touch of

Augustus's other arm wrapping around my back forced the air from my lungs. Slowly he pulled me toward him until my face nearly touched his window. His strong grasp held my weight effortlessly. "Is that better?" I felt his voice vibrating in his chest which did little more to ease my racing heart than his warm breath on my neck.

"Yes," I whispered just as a large estate came into view. My ears rang and my neck tingled, but I attempted to focus on what I saw and not the sense of yearning that Augustus's touch evoked. Branbury was tucked significantly back from the road, a long private drive leading toward the house. The gray stones reflected the sun and, though I could not see it exceptionally well due to the distance, I could tell it was enormous in size and sufficiently grand. "Branbury Court," I said to myself. "How ideal."

I watched my future home until it was once again hidden from view. Before I considered how my proximity to Augustus was no longer necessary, he slipped his hand from my waist.

The heavy folds of my traveling dress repositioned under my forceful hands. "Thank you, Mr. Brundage."

"It was my pleasure," he said with that familiar, mischievous tone.

I refused to let it rattle me. "Well, if all goes according to plan, I do believe I will be quite pleased to call Branbury Court home in a few months' time."

"Why did you not tell us you would soon be engaged?" Ruth gave a small pout. "I was quite amazed when Augustus mentioned it before waking you just now."

"Forgive me." I clasped my fingers tightly to keep myself from fidgeting. "But as the arrangement is only anticipated, I do not yet speak of it openly." The excuse was hollow, but what else could be said? Surely not that I was just as uncertain as to the reasons for my blatant omission.

Ruth nodded, her expression cheering a touch. "Well, now that I've been made aware, it is you who must do the talking. You must tell me everything."

"There is not much to tell."

Ruth scoffed. "I can hardly expect that is the truth of it."

"Lord Thorton is an earl." I gave a small lift of my shoulders, hoping she would accept the only answer most people required.

She bobbed her head. "And?"

I fixed my eyes on her, refusing to let them drift to Augustus. "Well ... he is wealthy, connected, and ... a most superior gentleman. Not to mention, I believe us to have similar expectations of marriage."

Ruth gave a small frown. "But why do you love him?"

I stiffened.

"Ruth," Augustus said, drawing her consideration. "Perhaps this is a conversation Miss Godwin would prefer to have in private."

Ruth glanced around the small cab, as though she were uncertain of what he alluded to.

"With *only* you."

Ruth lifted a hand to cover her gaping mouth. "Oh! Of course. Forgive me, Bella. I assumed ..." She looked at Augustus then back at me. "Never mind. We shall venture there later when we are *alone*."

Too confounded to offer Augustus my gratitude, I simply nodded.

"To think your future home is not three hours from Fairhaven." Ruth appeared unaware that Augustus had likely intended for her to leave the matter entirely. "We shall have to visit one another regularly once you are settled. Perhaps we shall even attend your wedding."

"We have one last stop before arriving at Fairhaven." Augustus's hasty interruption reverberated through the small space. A disruption I was grateful for.

Ruth released a squeal, the sound piercing through me. "I can hardly believe we shall soon be home. It feels an eternity since we left."

Augustus chuckled. "It does always amaze me how a fortnight in London can feel so dastardly long."

"Surely you jest, Mr. Brundage." I eyed him. "I much prefer London to any other place I have been. There are so many diversions to keep one occupied."

"Well you haven't been to Fairhaven yet." Augustus tapped his knee into mine in a way that forced me to overlook my body's foolish response. "Perhaps your opinion is about to change."

It felt ungrateful to conclude otherwise, so I offered a tight smile. "Perhaps."

CHAPTER FIVE

$\mathcal{T}$he coach turned off the main road, causing us to sway in our seats.

"I see it!" Ruth pressed herself against the window, her neck craned. "Oh Fairhaven, how I have missed you!"

Her excitement was a touch excessive, but even I couldn't conceal my eagerness to catch a glimpse of the house I had heard spoken of over and over throughout our seemingly endless journey.

Leaning toward Augustus's window, I became distracted by his nearness yet again. The warmth of his breath caressed my neck when he drew closer still, and a shiver moved through me.

"I do hope Ruth did not set your expectations of Fairhaven too high," he whispered.

I shook my head, pretending I was unaffected by both his proximity and the intimate volume of his voice. "I am certain it shall prove to be equal to her praises."

Just then, the house came into view. A red brick structure accented with canted windows and white, Greek-inspired columns. It was three stories high, but the trees surrounding it somehow managed to enclose it as though it were nothing more than a mere cottage.

It was precisely how I envisioned it. "How charming."

Ruth wore a satisfied smile. "Isn't it the loveliest place in all of England?" She scanned the scene again as if taking it in for the first time.

A small divot in the drive caused my shoulder to bump into Augustus's chest, but before he could right me a third time this trip, I retracted back into the safety of my seat. "I can see why you consider it so, Ruth."

When the coach rolled to a stop, Augustus tossed open the door and stepped out to the obvious delight of two women hurrying out of the house to greet us.

"Mother. Sarah," he called, moving to them. Through the open door, I watched him place a kiss on each of their cheeks.

Ruth clambered out unassisted and hurried to the beckoning arms of her aunt. The squeals pierced the silence as the three women embraced. Had they not just seen one another a fortnight ago?

Augustus admired the group a moment then returned to the carriage to offer me his assistance. I took hold of his hand, his attentive regard warming me in combination with the women's shift of interest in my direction.

"They do not know," he whispered.

I paused mid-descent, furrowing my brow.

"The question you asked me earlier—if my family knew what had transpired between us. They are not aware of it. Not even Ruth."

Relief flooded over me, and I completed my descent. "Since you had the consideration to confess before introductions, I may come to forgive your excessive delay in answering—eventually."

He laughed, relinquishing his aid only to set his hand

on my back to guide me forward. "Mother, you recall Miss Godwin?"

"Of course I do." Mrs. Brundage's sparkling blue eyes danced happily in the daylight. "And how lovely you've grown, Miss Godwin. Though it should be no great surprise, as it was always apparent you'd be most handsome."

"You are too kind." I looked to the younger woman standing near. She was no more than sixteen or seventeen, with a feminine loveliness that offset the strong likeness to her brother. I wondered at how a plain woman like Mrs. Brundage should have such attractive offspring. Perhaps she had been a beauty in her younger years as her sister had been. Though it was just as likely that their looks could be credited to the late Mr. Brundage, despite my inability to conjure an image of him.

Augustus sent his sister an affectionate wink. "Miss Godwin, may I introduce you to my sister, Sarah?"

"But I've already met your sister." The memories of her were nearly too faint to evoke, as she had chosen to remain behind with her mother the only time I recalled them visiting the Setons, but it was important to make a person feel remembered. I gave her my sweetest smile. "Though I would not blame you if you do not recall, Miss Brundage."

Sarah's cheeks pinkened in a most endearing manner. "I remember."

I faced Augustus. "See, there? I'm not entirely forgettable." I turned back to Mrs. Brundage before he could respond. "Thank you for allowing me to visit. I very much look forward to becoming reacquainted with Ruth after all these years."

"And Augustus," Ruth added, causing my smile to falter.

I compelled the corners of my mouth to lift again. "Yes, of course."

Mrs. Brundage reached out and briefly took hold of my hand. "We are honored to have you here, my dear. But you must be anxious to rest after two days in a carriage. Come, I will show you to your room."

The mere thought of being alone was so entirely welcome, it was unnecessary to feign gratitude. "That would be wonderful, Mrs. Brundage."

I walked beside Mrs. Brundage up the front steps toward the entrance.

"She is so lovely." Sarah's voice was hardly discernible when I overheard it from behind.

"I'm certain we are not the only ones who think so." Ruth giggled. "You should have seen how your brother kept watching her, and when she fell asleep on him—"

"Ruth!" I spun toward her, my face flushed from the idea of Augustus's sister hearing such nonsense. "Did you say the stables were directly behind the house? I seem to have already forgotten your explanation."

Ruth sprang up the last of the steps to join me. "Not directly behind, but set to the northwest. Would you care for a tour later? I shall even introduce you to Guinevere."

"Guinevere?"

"My mare." Her eyes grew in size. "Did I not mention her yet? That is a most tragic oversight on my part. She is the most stunning horse you shall ever see. Her coat is all white, but her nose and feet look as though they have been dipped into a pool of golden-brown paint."

"She sounds exquisite." I linked my arm with Ruth's, ensuring she did not return to her cousin's side to gossip about my folly. "I shall very much look forward to meeting your Guinevere."

"She was a surprise from Uncle Henry. He knew how

much I missed Daisy. You remember my pony Daisy, do you not?"

An image of the lovely chestnut-colored mare surfaced in my mind. "Of course I do."

Ruth squeezed my arm in apparent appreciation. "Well, Uncle Henry felt awful that I had been forced to leave her at Blacksley. And when he had no success in retrieving her, he bought me Guinevere to offer in her place." Ruth sighed. "Every time I look at her, I'm reminded of how fortunate I am to be so loved."

I caught sight of Mrs. Brundage wiping a tear from her cheek. I doubted she had been as fond of her late husband in life as she apparently was in death, despite how sincere she appeared. Mother would certainly not shed a tear for Papa unless she thought it expected.

"Here we are." Mrs. Brundage stopped in front of a door and opened it.

The room that had been prepared for me wasn't as sizeable as the rooms I was accustomed to, but it had an air of comfort I was not familiar with. Everything, including the set of drawers, somehow looked friendly, as though nothing need be handled with care. True, it wasn't decorated according to latest fashions, but I was quite pleased with it.

"This shall do very well." I turned toward Mrs. Brundage who watched me anxiously.

Her face lit up. "I'm very glad you find it acceptable, Miss Godwin. I know it probably isn't as grand as you are used to, but I have always preferred comfort over extravagance." Her hand flew to her mouth. "Not that being extravagant is bad nor necessarily uncomfortable. I just prefer simplicity." The color in her face deepened to scarlet.

I offered a courteous smile. "I can see why you prefer

this style. It has a friendliness about it that perfectly suits what I have heard of Fairhaven."

Mrs. Brundage and Ruth beamed at my compliment, though Sarah didn't look up from her twirling fingers.

"And I'm just the next room over if you should need me." Ruth looked giddy with the idea of being so near.

"Dinner is at six." Mrs. Brundage paused. "Unless, that is, you prefer to have it postponed to a later hour during your stay?"

Unwilling to remind her that she was the hostess and therefore was the one to decide such things, I shook my head. "Six is most agreeable."

"Very good."

We stood a moment in silence before I clasped my hands before me. "I shall see you at six, then?"

Mrs. Brundage's eyes widened. "Oh, of course. Yes. We must be on our way." She nearly pushed the two young ladies from the room, and Ruth lifted onto her toes and waved at me from the corridor. "Do not hesitate to ask if you need anything."

I offered one last smile. "I will not. Thank you." As I closed the door, I let out a heavy sigh and leaned my head against it. After a few moments of silent reprieve, I made my way to the looking glass. Thankfully, I didn't appear nearly as fatigued as I felt.

A slight knock sounded, and Leah stepped into the room.

I met her gaze in the mirror's reflection. "Are you as exhausted as I am, Leah?"

Leah's lips curled upward ever so slightly at the corners. "Your friend has quite a talent for conversation."

"She certainly does. Though I hope it will only be a matter of time before I grow accustomed to it again."

Leah retrieved my discarded bonnet and the gloves I'd

tossed on the bed, and placed them in the wardrobe. "Mr. Brundage seems reason enough to endure any amount of prattle."

I spun toward her in my chair and rose to my feet. "I will not stand idly by while you speak of your superiors in such a manner." Recalling the touch of pink in Leah's cheeks when Augustus had spoken to her in London made my blood boil. "Mr. Brundage's position, as well as Ruth's, demands both respect and distance from someone of your station."

Leah dropped her head. "Forgive me, miss."

My headache intensified, and I rubbed at my temples. How I hated getting upset, but I could not tolerate such behavior from a servant. Leah's last employer may have allowed for the improper familiarity, but Mother had warned me of the hazards of permitting such casual conduct from a servant. A firm hand was needed, and yet my determination wavered when I appraised her downcast countenance. "Go see about my trunks."

She moved toward the door and stopped, turning toward me again, her head still lowered.

"What is it?" Though my patience was on unsteady ground, I managed to keep my voice unaffected.

"I have a missive from your father." She extended a letter toward me. "He told me to deliver it once we had arrived at Fairhaven."

I stepped forward to retrieve the letter, uncertain why Papa had not just given it to me on our parting. Was there a reason I was not to read it until now? "Thank you. You may go."

Leah hurried from the room, and I lifted the missive to examine it. This must be Papa's ill-timed explanation of why he had sent me here. I shook my head at the memory of how it had all come to pass, and broke the seal.

My Dearest Girl,

Though I am certain you shall later demand a more thorough apology, I hope you are not too disappointed in me nor in the situation in which you find yourself. After much consideration, including the regrettable reality that your mother must be kept ignorant of your whereabouts, I have concluded that the greater offense would be to keep you from one of your dearest friends now that Providence has reunited you. Particularly when it is evident how desperately she needs your guidance. Do assist her.

All my love,
    Papa

I flipped the page over in hopes of discovering a post-script that contained a more thorough explanation or the actual apology Papa had alluded to. Yet, it was hardly a surprise to find both omitted.

I released an agitated sigh and reread his scribbled hand a second time, my consideration drawn to the last three words of his text: *do assist her.* Was this to do with my comment after first parting ways with Ruth? When I had mentioned that I'd hardly met a lady so poorly trained? And why, if it was the reason, would Papa place the task on me? Surely he had no responsibility for Ruth.

But perhaps it was an act of charity for an old neighbor in obvious need of help. Papa did always see it as part of his role as a politician to give some opportunity to the lesser among us. And who better to offer Ruth that support? I surely had her best interest at heart, and, as one of the *ton's Incomparables,* I was well aware what aspects of training would be most beneficial to a lady of her situation.

A surprising surge of excitement rushed through me at the thought of amending Ruth's unfortunate upbringing, at least in part. Now I simply needed to conceive a way for her to request my intervention, for I would hate to be regarded as patronizing.

CHAPTER SIX

*a*n incessant knocking roused me from sleep. I opened my eyes to find that Leah had quit the room and my trunks no longer filled the space on the floor. I could not imagine how she had managed it all without waking me. I must have been in a deeper sleep than I had thought.

The knock sounded a second time, and I heaved a sigh, moving my aching body clumsily from the comfort of the bed. "Who is there?"

"It is Ruth." As I opened the door, her smile intensified. "I hope I did not disturb you?"

"Your interruption was most welcome. I had intended to rest only for a moment, but I am afraid my exhaustion got the better of me."

"And are you feeling much improved?"

"I am, thank you."

Ruth was now bouncing on her heels. "I came to see if you would care to take a tour of the grounds before dressing for dinner. I know you mentioned your interest earlier."

I glanced at the clock. It was nearly four already. "Will we be gone long?"

"The grounds are not so very big that we cannot make quick work of them."

I should have supposed as much, given the size of Fairhaven itself. "Very well. Let me retrieve my bonnet."

"Oh, but you shan't need it for such a brief walk. Besides, much of the way is shaded."

Despite her assurances, I started to the wardrobe. "It is imperative a lady wear a bonnet out of doors. Freckles are hardly an admirable trait."

Ruth's expression became thoughtful. "I shall retrieve mine also, then," she said, disappearing into the corridor.

Perhaps a quick jaunt wasn't such an ill-conceived notion. I would finally be alone with Ruth and could help her realize how much she required my assistance. Snatching one of my more basic straw bonnets, I hurried on my way, waiting to tie it into place until I was confident my fingers had regained their dexterity and could manage a decent bow.

Stepping out onto the circular drive with Ruth at my side, I stopped to admire the grounds on this side of Fairhaven. The sun was no longer above us in the sky, but the warmth of it served as a reminder to secure my bonnet in place.

"Are you two out for a walk?" Augustus was striding toward us from the side of the house, leather gloves in hand.

Ruth walked to meet him. "We are. And you are most welcome to join us."

Augustus's gaze flitted to me. "Thank you, but I do not wish to impose my company upon you."

Ruth laughed. "As though such a thing could ever happen. Bella, do tell him he is most welcome."

Augustus's eyes met mine, and I convinced the corners of my lips upward. "You should certainly join us. If you wish it."

"See, there? It is settled." Ruth took hold of her cousin's arm. "Shall we start our tour with the garden or the stables?"

When I realized her question was directed toward me, I glanced around. "I'm certain I will find pleasure in wherever you decide to lead us."

"I have been quite anxious to see Guinevere. I have missed her so very much while we've been away."

"Then let us not delay my introduction a moment longer."

Ruth's shoulders lifted in excitement. "This way, then."

Ruth rambled on as we followed the drive to the rear side of the house and a stable came into view. The woods around it seemed to nestle the brick building so completely that it appeared to be straight out of a children's story.

"Augi, do you not remember Mr. Ansely's reaction when Guinevere bested his racing stallion?" Ruth's question pulled me back to the conversation, if it could be called a conversation at all. "He was most vexed. Was he not?"

My regard moved to Augustus whose analyzing regard was, not surprisingly, on me.

"I remember," he said, giving me a brief smile before directing his attention forward. "Did he not offer to buy Guinevere?"

"Oh yes, and for a far greater sum than Uncle paid. Of course, Uncle refused, and I am eternally grateful for it. I couldn't imagine life without her. Sometimes I believe Guinevere is the only one who truly understands me." Ruth shot me a nervous glance. "I do realize she is a horse, but often I wonder about an animal's ability to discern human emotion."

I gave a tight nod, not wishing to disagree with the odd notion. "And was that the only time Guinevere raced your neighbor's horse?"

"Yes. And I'm certain it was also the last. Mr. Ansely seems most reluctant to have another of his stallions bested." Ruth sighed as we reached the stable doors. "In truth, if it was not so utterly thrilling to see the shock on his face following all his boasting, I should feel bad for him."

I pressed back a smile at her candidness.

"Well, come on," she said, walking in before me.

The smell of hay and horse manure overwhelmed my senses, and I paused, lifting my gloved hand to my nose.

Augustus stepped near. "Is all well with you, Miss Godwin?"

I lifted my chin, unsettled by his ceaseless consideration. Was he trying to glimpse a fault of some sort? A weakness? I was determined not to reveal whatever it was he sought. "Perfectly well," I said, walking through the threshold.

In the second stall a mare sifted a pile of hay with her muzzle. Ruth approached and pulled off her gloves, reaching out a hand. The horse lifted her head and sauntered toward us. "Isn't she exceptional?"

"Indeed." Though I had no great eye for such things, she was a lovely creature and truly looked exactly as Ruth had described—as though her white nose had been dipped in a pail of golden color. The mare gave Ruth's hand an affectionate nudge. "Do you ride often?" I asked, impressed by the familiarity they seemed to share.

Ruth beamed back at me. "Every morning with Augi and Sarah ... and Owen when he is home, except the Sabbath, of course."

"Of course."

"You should join us, Bella. Aunt Marina has a horse she no longer rides."

I had no desire to ride. I wasn't exceptionally fond of being atop an animal that had its own mind. Besides, I had refused to have a riding habit made, and thus had no proper attire for the exercise. "I would not want to impose upon your aunt's kindness any further."

"I assure you, it would not be an imposition at all. She would likely be grateful for it. Would she not, Augi?"

Augustus lifted his hand and placed it on the horse, causing the creature to give a small whinny. "You would be welcome to ride her."

I faced Ruth. "In all honesty, I no longer prefer riding. I haven't cared for it in years. Not since my fall."

Augustus shifted, and my conscience pricked me for mentioning it.

"That was a most unfortunate event." Ruth's tone was so casual that I wondered if she had already forgotten who was to blame for the incident.

Augustus dropped his hand from the horse and glanced at me. "It certainly was."

"Would you like to feed Guinevere?" Ruth bent down and pulled a carrot from a burlap sack set on the ground. "Carrots are her favorite. Well, besides apples. And I suppose she does love an occasional sugar cube, though the groom tells me they aren't good for her."

"That is quite all right." I gestured for her to proceed, having no intention of dirtying my gloves with such a task.

Ruth held the carrot out to the horse, and the mare quickly accepted her offering, giving Ruth another nudge with her head.

"Shall we take a look at the others?" Ruth asked,

though it was obvious she was reluctant to leave her precious pet.

"Perhaps Miss Godwin would allow me to show her the remaining horses?"

The unexpected offer left me searching for an acceptable excuse. When nothing surfaced in time, I stepped to his side. "Very well."

"Don't appear too eager," Augustus whispered, as I followed him farther into the stable. "I'd hate to give Ruth the impression that you actually desire my company."

"If it would suit you better, I could simply inform her of my thoughts so she need not speculate."

He laughed. "And what thoughts are those?"

I glanced over at him. "Am I so very difficult to read, Mr. Brundage?"

"You are an absolute conundrum." He grinned, but there was little humor in his eyes. "In truth, I have been trying to make sense of you since arriving at your Town house yesterday."

I swallowed. "Is that so?"

He nodded. "I suppose I thought I'd find you so very changed, and in many ways I have." He paused, and I warmed under his thoughtful consideration, against my better reasoning. "But in other ways, you have not changed at all."

I moved away from him, disappointed he should not have found me entirely changed from the ingenuous girl I had once been. And yet, though I was loath to admit it, I was also not oblivious to the conflict raging within me— the desire to revert back to that very person Augustus and Ruth had once known. But it would not do. I was no longer that person. I set my gaze on the stall where we had just stopped, eager to move on from his appraisal. "Now tell me of this next horse."

Augustus's regard lingered on me for another uncomfortable moment before he gestured to the horse. "This is Sarah's mare, Blossom. She is the tamest of all the horses, which is most fitting." We walked on further. "The empty stall here is where Owen keeps his horse while he's visiting."

"And how is your brother?"

"He is well." Augustus moved to the stall across from the empty one, and I couldn't help but wonder a second time why he didn't care to speak of Owen. "And this little lady is Mother's. We call her Buttercup."

I stifled my amusement at how uncreative some people were. With the same golden color from mane to foot, I should have thought to name her Hesperides, after the nymphs of golden light. Though I had to admit the horse was left wanting at being compared to a divine spirit of the Greeks. Perhaps Buttercup did suit her better.

Augustus lifted his arm when we reached the last stall, and a large, dark stallion walked toward his outstretched hand.

Despite my lack of experience, I was certain this horse was one of the most magnificent I'd seen. "Now that is a stunning horse, Mr. Brundage."

He ran his hands along its jaw and down its thick, muscular neck. "You should see him run." His voice was quiet, as though in reverence for the beast.

"I'm certain it is quite the sight." My words conjured an image of Augustus atop the large stallion, and my cheeks began to warm at my inability to push it from my mind.

"Then join us for a ride."

I met his imploring stare. "I was truthful when I said I no longer ride. I haven't since my fall. Papa hired a riding instructor to help me conquer my fear, but I refused his tutelage and haven't ridden since." I looked back at the stallion, slightly embarrassed I had felt a need to say so much.

Augustus took a step closer. "I'm terribly sorry for it."

"I did not tell you to earn your sympathies, Mr. Brundage, but simply to assure you of my reason for not accepting your invitation."

"But it was my fault."

"Yes, it was." I hesitated. "But had you not been the cause, sooner or later I would have come to the same conclusion—some things are simply not worth the risk." I felt Augustus studying my profile, and I shifted away from him.

"Yet some things are."

The air was stagnant as I drew it in, and I glanced back at Ruth. "Shall we return?"

The warmth of his hand on my arm penetrated my defenses, nearly toppling the wall I had been building between us. *One touch.* I was absolutely pathetic.

"Come, Bella." His voice was soft. "Can we not make things right between us?"

I spun toward him, yanking my arm free. "I asked you not to call me Bella." The uncertainty touching his features did nothing to prevent the anger rising inside me, my blood boiling from years of pent up, unresolved frustration. But I managed to maintain my composure. "You can hardly claim to know me anymore, let alone take such privileges."

His outstretched hand retracted, dropping to his side. "I wanted to stay in touch. Surely you must know that."

My hands clenched into fists at my sides, and an odd sensation prickled my spine. I longed to simply walk away, precisely as he had done to me, but I could not convince my feet of the wisdom. "How would I have known? You never told me." Tears blurred my vision as I glared at Augustus, but I refused to let them free. I had no intention of providing more evidence of my foolish care.

His shoulders dropped. "Please understand—"

"—that I was nothing more to you than a friend of convenience? A willing distraction from your boredom when you would visit Blacksley?" The accusation tumbled from my lips before I could stop it.

Grief etched deep into Augustus's features. "That is not true."

My chest rose and fell in quick succession, and I attempted to convince myself to say no more, to not let him affect me. I was resolute on adhering to the training I'd undergone. But the words had been held in too long, and I was powerless to contain them. "All those years and not a letter. Three Seasons. Three! And not a word from you. When you and Ruth left, I had no one." I looked away from his sorrow-filled eyes. "And you didn't even care." A blasted tear escaped down my cheek, and I swiped it away.

He took a cautious step forward. "But I did."

I ignored both the perceptible trembling of my body and the sincerity in Augustus's countenance. "Do not try to pacify me. Not now. Not when I've finally convinced myself to let it alone."

"And yet I entreat you to believe me." His voice was gentle and far too near when his hand found mine. At his touch, a peculiar ache surged through me—a longing to be what we once were. I glanced down, suddenly conflicted if I should pull away or welcome it. "If it had been my choice—"

"Are you claiming that you are not to blame for your disregard?" I lifted my gaze to his, curiosity nearly diffusing my anger. *Nearly.*

"That is precisely what I am claiming. And though I wish I could say more, I cannot."

I set my jaw. "Of course you cannot. Why should I expect any different from you?"

Augustus glanced back in the direction we'd come, dropped my hand, and took a step from me. I followed his line of sight to discover Ruth nearly upon us.

I forced a smile to my lips and stepped to meet her. "I was just about to retrieve you." Linking my arm with hers, I started us toward the stable entrance. "And where are we off to next?" I focused my gaze forward, my bonnet shielding my reddened eyes.

"Considering we don't have much time before we must dress for dinner, I figured you'd like to see the rose garden. With the roses in bloom, the smell is intoxicating." Ruth glanced behind her. "Are you coming, Augi?"

I did not look back for the echo of heavy footsteps told me what I needed to know.

"And have you concluded that your Guinevere has missed you as much as you have missed her?" I asked, desperate to draw my thoughts away from Augustus and the confusion he had just elicited within me.

"Oh, yes. I'm certain she has. I only regret that I cannot take her out until tomorrow."

"And where do you typically ride?"

"Oh heavens. So many places." The mind-numbing chatter on the different routes that were typically ridden was enough to settle me. As Ruth continued, my thoughts wandered back to my conversation with Augustus and what he could have meant by *if it had been his choice*. He had seemed reluctant to speak of it, which only strengthened my resolve in discovering his meaning. Yet why should he confide in me after I had made it quite clear we were no longer friends?

I glanced over my shoulder to find Augustus several strides behind us, his gaze cast downward. The pensive expression on his face reminded me of another time I had seen him appear so downtrodden—the days following the deaths of his aunt and uncle—and the memory stirred an all-too-familiar desire within me to forgive him.

The very thought of resuming the friendship we had once known made my pulse race. No. We would never be what we once were, as I was no longer an impressionable and naïve young lady. Besides, I needed to tread carefully considering my intentions to secure Lord Thorton. I could not risk everything I had worked toward, and I had no intention to hurt Augustus by allowing him to believe otherwise. It was not only best for all involved, but absolutely necessary that I keep my distance from Augustus. Or was it? A small sigh escaped me.

"Am I boring you?" Concern touched Ruth's expression.

"No. Not at all." I offered a reassuring smile. "Please go on."

With only a brief pause she picked up wherever she had left off. I kept my focus on her this time, refusing myself another thought of Augustus or a glimpse in his direction. Neither would strengthen my resolve in the least.

"Look at all the variations." Ruth dropped my arm to point out the exquisite shades of color. "Is the sight of it not spectacular?"

I scanned the rows of bushes with brightly colored blooms. "It is." There was no need to pretend delight. I drew in the sweet fragrance. "As is the smell."

"I told you it was intoxicating!" Ruth wandered onto the next row and stopped. "How extraordinary," she called. "These roses here have yellow at the base and red on the tips. I don't believe I've ever seen the likes of it anywhere but Fairhaven." She leaned in closer to examine the petals, leaving only the top of her bonnet still visible to me. "I wonder if they grow that way naturally, or if the gardener has used some strategy to make it happen. Regardless, I think I must declare this variation to be my favorite." She straightened, becoming once again visible, and glanced at a nearby bush. "Though those purple ones are also very lovely." Her focus changed again. "And I must admit that most days I tend to favor roses of the pink variety." A woeful sigh met my ear. "Perhaps it is unwise to make such declarations when I am not yet completely settled on my opinion."

"I do believe that is very wise of you. How tragic it would be to proclaim something so adamantly only to refute your selection later."

Ruth nodded, a sober expression on her face. "You are entirely correct. I shall continue to deliberate on the matter," she said, her voice in earnest as she meandered farther down the other aisle, stopping to study the flowers on each bush as she went.

"And what color most suits you, Miss Godwin?" Augustus rounded the corner of the walkway where I stood, causing me to tense. But his expression was softer now. "Or perhaps you are not yet certain of your choice either?"

"I am always certain of my choice, Mr. Brundage." At once I felt a hypocrite with the way my whole soul pushed me to change my resolve and forgive him. The nearer he came, the more I longed to forget all I'd come to know these past years and digress into the girl I'd once been— the girl who could never refuse Augustus anything, not even her heart.

No. I was not her any longer. I was stronger and wiser.

Reason must be my guide, as Mother had taught, not whimsical sentiments. "I prefer the white ones." I touched the soft, velvet petal of a newly budding rose. "It is refined yet still breathtaking."

Augustus stopped next to the bush I was admiring. He reached out and carefully pulled the bud from the branch before extending it to me.

I looked down at his offer. "I cannot accept that."

"It is only a rose, Miss Godwin."

I met his gaze. "Is it?"

He pressed his lips together, and lowered the rose. "Forgive me. I will not press upon you further." Sadness once again settled over his countenance. "But might I say, one last time, how truly sorry I am for everything? Had it been my choice, things would have been very different." He held my gaze a torturous moment, then he turned from me.

Panic surged through my whole body as he walked away from me. "Mr. Brundage," I called, unable to stop myself.

He glanced over his shoulder.

My heart was pounding, and my will turned traitorous. "Are you giving up that easily?"

He considered me a moment. "I was under the impression that is what you desired of me."

"Do you know nothing of women, Mr. Brundage?" My chest was abuzz from nerves.

He hesitated, but then started back toward me. "I'm beginning to think I do not understand them at all."

"Not every declaration a woman gives, especially ones pronounced in anger, should be considered irrevocable. As readily as a lady is to set her mind upon something, with a little persuasion, she yet may change it."

Augustus now stood before me, and ever-so-slowly he lifted the rose again.

I swallowed, wondering what I had just gotten myself into. But certainly there was not so much wrong with allowing some semblance of a rapport with Augustus. After all, he had saved me from a visit to Sandson, and he did seem sincere in his desire to make things right between us. In truth, it seemed heartless not to allow for it as long as I made my intentions clear. I quirked a brow at him. "A token of friendship?"

A curious smile touched Augustus's features. "If you will receive it as that."

Careful not to prick my finger on the thorns, I took hold of the rose. "I would like nothing better."

He did not relinquish it immediately, his hand situated just below mine on the stem. "Truly?"

"Truly." With my acknowledgment he released his hold, and I lifted the rose to smell it, glancing up at him as I did so.

Augustus's smile was radiant.

"What has the two of you looking so excited?" Ruth asked, walking toward us.

I lowered my hand, the rose dangling at my side. "We were discussing our friendship."

"Oh." Ruth glanced between us with a perplexed expression. "And what has been decided?"

Augustus's eyes flickered to me. "That we are to once again be friends."

Ruth scrunched up her nose, causing a deep line to form across the bridge of it. "And at what point were the two of you not friends?"

"We have always been friends." I glanced at Augustus for confirmation, and he cautiously nodded his agreement. "We were only in need of talking through a few things."

Ruth looked a touch hesitant. "I suppose those *things* are to stay between the two of you?"

Before I could decide upon an appropriate response, Augustus stepped forward and placed a hand around Ruth's shoulder. "Yes. At least for now."

"It's just as well. Why burden myself when you have begun to work it all out? So long as you do, of course. For I can't imagine anything that could cause a rift between the two of you."

Eight years without so much as one word from him seemed an adequate refutation, but I suppressed my comment. "Well, we are on our way to bridging it."

CHAPTER SEVEN

"The grounds were quite simple, but there was a pleasing quality about them." I watched Leah in the reflection, twisting a strand of hair and pinning it into place. "And though I long to be convincing Lord Thorton of our compatibility"—my eyes settled on the rose—"Fairhaven is certainly preferable to Sandson Hall."

Leah did not respond, but adjusted a few last golden curls before making quick work of weaving a ribbon through it. "Finished."

I leaned in close to the looking glass, inspecting my coiffure from each angle. "Well done, as usual."

"Thank you, miss."

I stood, taking several steps back from the vanity in hopes of catching a more thorough view of myself. It wasn't ideal, as my own full-length mirror would have been, but it was sufficient enough to see how the stunning silk gown I had chosen draped upon my curves perfectly. "A lady should be able to don her finest without a particular purpose," I said, with an air of indifference. There was no one here to impress, so why did my heart patter about in such an irritating manner?

Appraising my reflection one last time, I gave my cheeks a little pinch and walked from the room to make my way downstairs.

"Good evening," I said, gliding into the drawing room to find only Augustus and his mother present. Augustus turned toward me, a most satisfying smile alighting his features, and I could sense his struggle at keeping his eyes on my face. Forcing back my amusement, I gave him a nod of acknowledgment and looked to Mrs. Brundage.

"How lovely you are, Miss Godwin." Mrs. Brundage walked toward me with outstretched hands. "Though I am now regretting not having asked some of our neighbors to dine with us. You look too fine for our simple party."

I clasped her hands in mine. "You are kind. But I prefer an intimate dinner to one with too many faces I do not recognize."

"I quite agree." Mrs. Brundage hesitated. "I just wish Owen could be here. Or the Whitmores. They would certainly have added some liveliness to our small group."

"Will the younger Mr. Brundage be in London long?" My inquiry came partly from curiosity and partly from the desire to avoid speaking of the praiseworthy Miss Whitmore I'd already heard too much about.

Augustus and his mother shared an uneasy glance. "We are not yet certain," Augustus said, stepping to my side. "But we are hopeful he will return before your departure, at least for a visit."

"I should very much like that." I scanned the vacant room, hating to feel the outsider on whatever they were attempting to keep hidden. "And where is Ruth?"

Mrs. Brundage hesitated a second time. "She has gone

to convince Sarah to join us. I know Sarah is not yet out, her being only seventeen, but when we don't have guests, or our only guests are the Whitmores, we allow her to join us for the evening." Her eyes flickered to Augustus. "Ruth assured me you would not mind if we treated you with such familiarity."

"Of course I don't mind. It is fitting for you to treat me as such, considering Ruth is like my own family."

Mrs. Brundage's smile broadened, and she wrapped an arm around my shoulder. "In that case, we are happy to oblige you, my dear girl."

An odd warmth settled over me at her touch, and I crossed my arms to balance the wave of uncertainty that raced through me.

"Here we are!" Ruth called, pulling a blushing Sarah behind her. Her eyes stopped on me and moved over my gown. "Oh, Bella. Look at you."

The warmth that had filled my body with Mrs. Brundage's kindness suddenly moved upward, concentrating in my cheeks. "And look at you." Oddly wishing to pull the attention from myself and my unnerving blush, I gestured to Ruth then Sarah. "And Miss Brundage, you both look so lovely."

Sarah dropped her head. "You may call me Sarah if you like," she whispered.

I glanced at Augustus, who wore an approving grin. "I would like that very much. Thank you."

"May we go in now?" Ruth asked. "I'm absolutely famished."

"Oh, Ruth." Mrs. Brundage's tone displayed endearment rather than correction. "Go on then. Lead us in."

Augustus and I leisurely followed the others.

Leaning in toward him, I lowered my voice to ensure I would not be overheard. "Your sister is so quiet."

"At first. She takes a little longer to warm to people, but in time she'll prove herself to be just as silly as Ruth."

I considered Sarah, now several paces in front of us, whispering into Ruth's ear. The ladies exchanged a muted giggle before Ruth glanced over her shoulder in our direction.

"I hope she doesn't take too long to warm to me, for I hate to think my being here makes her feel ill at ease."

A side of Augustus's mouth quirked upward. "Of course it does. You make everyone feel ill at ease."

My gaze shot to his profile. "Whyever would you say such a thing?"

His irksome smile grew. "Because it is the truth." He stopped to allow me to step through the dining room ahead of him, but I hesitated, searching his features and longing to press him for an explanation.

"Is anything amiss?" Mrs. Brundage's question forced my consideration to our awaiting onlookers.

"Not in the least." I continued forward, unwilling to allow my emotions, nor my curiosity, to get the better of me.

As we settled around the drawing room fire, Ruth placed a hand over her stomach and leaned back into the settee. "Cook truly outdid herself tonight. I feel absolutely stuffed with roast chicken."

"It was delightful," I acknowledged, biting back my comment on appropriate portion sizes for a lady. With each folly Ruth exhibited, I grew more eager to begin our training.

Ruth glanced around. "So, how shall we occupy our time this evening?"

"We could simply converse," I suggested, too exhausted for much else.

Mrs. Brundage nodded her agreement. "Yes, that sounds just the thing."

"I know." Ruth sent me a pointed glance. "Considering how much Bella adores London, why don't we all share our favorite amusements in Town, then she will tell us if it makes her list also. I'll start." Her thoughtful hum disrupted the quiet. "The Royal Menagerie."

Sarah bobbed her head. "That would be mine also," she said, her voice almost inaudible.

Ruth gave her cousin a hasty smile and looked back to me. "And what do you think of it, Bella?"

"I regret that I have not had the opportunity to visit the menagerie."

Ruth flung herself forward in her seat to better see me. "But whyever not?"

Though I'd always wanted to, Mother had always insisted the menagerie was a place for people inclined to vulgar curiosity. It hardly mattered how many times I had reasoned that the exotic animals belonged to the Royal Family—gifts from dignitaries all around the world.

But I could not say as much to Ruth, especially not with the Brundages listening in. "I fear it was never a priority during our stay in Town."

"Well you must make it such during your next visit. It was extraordinary. There were bears, tigers, leopards ... even an elephant. I only wish they still had monkeys, though I know why they had to be rid of them—poor boy." Ruth's eyes widened at my questioning stare, as though she had a rousing secret to tell. "A keeper said a small boy had his leg nearly torn off by a monkey several years ago. Apparently, they were just out roaming free.

Can you imagine how frightful that would have been to witness?"

My hand involuntarily moved to cover my mouth. "That is horrible." Perhaps there was wisdom in Mother's refusal.

"Augi, tell her of the time you saw a rat run into the lioness's den. How the lion pounced so quickly that the rat hadn't even a moment to realize where it had sought refuge from the crowds."

Augustus pressed his lips together. "I do believe you summed the whole thing up quite perfectly."

Ruth gave a pout. "Oh. I suppose I did. Forgive me."

I gave an amused shake of my head, turning my regard to Mrs. Brundage. "And what is it you most enjoy in London?"

Mrs. Brundage, who sat next to me on the settee, waved her hand dismissively. "Oh, you needn't hear from me."

"We most certainly must."

Even in the dim light of the flickering fire, it was apparent her round face colored. "Well, I do always love going to Gunter's for ices."

A smile touched my lips. "That would definitely be on my list. In truth, it is one of the things I long for most when I'm away."

She leaned in, lessening the space between us. "What I wouldn't give for a lavender scoop at this very moment."

I put my hand atop hers. "We shall have to make a trip there if we are ever in London at the same time, for lavender is also my favorite flavor."

"Lavender?" Augustus repeated, drawing our attention. "Over bergamot? Or maple?"

I examined his disbelieving smirk and offered him a

scrutinizing look in return. "It seems not everyone is equal to our finer tastes, Mrs. Brundage."

Augustus gave a playful scoff, glancing past all of us to his sister at the far end of the settee. "Sarah, surely you'll agree with me?"

Sarah gave a timid head shake. "I prefer chocolate."

Augustus dropped his shoulders. "Ruth?"

Ruth bit at her lip, her expression apologetic. "Chocolate, also."

I looked back to him, attempting to conceal my amusement. "There you have it, Mr. Brundage. The votes have been tallied, and it looks as though you are the clear minority."

He bowed his shaking head in mock defeat.

"As your consolation, I promise not to scoff when you offer up your answer as to what aspect of Town has brought you the most joy."

He moved his gaze to the fire and leaned forward, resting his elbows on his knees. "I suppose if I must choose, my answer would be, without question, Lord and Lady Brimhall's ball."

Ruth's brow furrowed in near unison with my own. "But you did not attend the ball with us," she said.

Augustus gave a slow nod. "Regardless, it is the aspect of London that has brought me the most joy. For without the two of you meeting there"—his eyes slid to me, and I stiffened—"Miss Godwin would not be here with us now, discussing the menagerie and Gunter's."

Color filled my cheeks so immediately, I lifted my hand to see if I could feel the warmth through my glove.

Mrs. Brundage laughed. "Oh, Augustus. Look how you have made our guest blush." Her hand covered the one I had just returned to my lap, and she gave it a gentle squeeze. "Pay him no heed, Miss Godwin. I'm afraid he has always enjoyed rattling us a bit, and it seems you are no exception to his troublesome ways."

I sent him a pointed look. "I do recall that about him."

He leaned into the wing-backed chair and extended his feet. "Such harsh accusations you have both laid against me."

Mrs. Brundage wagged a playful finger at him. "Harsh, yet deserved."

Augustus's smile settled on me. "What are your thoughts on a mother scolding her son in front of a guest?"

My throat grew tight. "It is a mother's role, is it not? I know my own mother has scolded me more times than I can count."

His smile lessened, and his eyes flitted over my features, discerning too much.

"I am all astonishment that your mother could find anything to scold you for, Bella," Ruth said lightly. "I believe you are the most well-trained lady in all of England."

I turned toward Ruth, realizing I'd stumbled upon a viable means of introducing the notion of her training. "One must first find fault to remedy it. Surely you remember that I used to be quite the heathen, running about the woods as though I had not a care in the world."

"I remember," Augustus said.

The way he looked at me left me grasping for what I had wanted to say to Ruth. "Yes, well ..." It didn't come.

"Do you remember the first time you climbed that old, gnarled black poplar?" Augustus asked, stealing any opportunity I had to conjure my fading thoughts. "I had told you it would be impossible to climb wearing a dress, but you set out to prove me wrong."

"And I did."

He chuckled. "You certainly did." His expression turned reminiscent. "After that, we used to climb up the tree and wait for people to pass at its base." His eyes twinkled with mischief as they refocused on our watchful faces. "Bella had the idea to toss pebbles into nearby bushes to spook the poor souls passing by. Not that it worked, and we finally had to resort to making ghoulish noises, awful as they were."

Overlooking the slip of my Christian name, I shook my head. "That was not my idea."

"Was it not? I feel confident that it was."

I shot him a disbelieving glare. "As though distressing innocents was ever done at my suggestion."

"No, I suppose not." He paused. "Your talent has always been distressing chaps who had recklessly become smitten with you." Before I could voice my offense at such a brazen statement, Augustus laughed again. "Do you recall when I brought my friend, Robert, to Blacksley during a school holiday? He was so enamored with you, he could hardly speak any time you were near, poor fellow."

With the memory of Augustus's long-forgotten school mate, I pressed my lips together to ensure my laughter did not escape. "His visit was the first time I realized the intrinsic power that comes with being a female. It was quite eye-opening."

Augustus furrowed his brow. "You hadn't realized it before that?"

"Whatever do you mean?"

He glanced at his mother. "It is nothing. I don't intend to be corrected for making you blush a second time."

I surveyed him, knowing I should accept his excuse and permit a change in subject, but I found my resolve lacking. "Let me assure you, I have no intention of blushing at whatever you say."

He opened his mouth and closed it again, releasing a slow exhale.

I lifted my hand to my mouth, certain I could not keep my laugh in without physical reinforcement. "You are not implying that you were one of those boys who came under my *intrinsic female powers?*"

"A young lad's affections should not be mocked, Miss Godwin." He gave his head a correctional shake, though a grin now graced his lips.

Despite my assurances to the contrary, my face reddened in a most embarrassing display. I had realized his regard for me had begun to change, but that was not until right before he left Bath. Up until then, I had assumed his behavior was a result of the stupidity of boyhood. "All those times you teased me?"

He shrugged. "I'm far from proud that my initial response to this *mystical power* of yours was to act a jester. I would have much preferred Robert's speechlessness to such nonsense."

My mind sifted through memories of Augustus. Had his constant teasing truly been because of his affections for me all along? Regardless, it left me feeling somehow elated, even giddy. "Well, I'm glad I no longer have such an effect on you. I should hate to see what tomfooleries you would implement to gain my attentions now."

"Let us hope then that such drastic strategies might be avoided." Augustus stood and winked at me.

My mouth parted at his nerve before my lips betrayed me with a smile.

"Are you retiring already, dear?" Mrs. Brundage asked, a touch of concern in her tone.

His gaze lingered on me before shifting to his mother.

"A man can only undertake so much goading before his resolve weakens. Who knows what other admissions are at risk of liberation if I remain? But, by all means, feel free to gossip about the ones I have offered up once I leave you."

I stood to bid him goodnight at the very same moment he stepped in front of me to offer his farewell. Our bodies collided, but before I could be offset by the impact, Augustus steadied me. "Pardon me, Miss Godwin." He took a step back, my skin prickling from the absence of his warmth.

I stood there dumbly, unable to move.

"Goodnight," he said, reaching for my hand. I placed it in his, and he lifted it to his handsome lips before lowering it again and moving to his mother. "Do not stand on my account," he said, leaning down to kiss her cheek. He bid Sarah and Ruth goodnight in a similar manner and walked from the room.

Ruth tilted her head to the side and appraised me. "Are you going to bed also, Bella?"

Suddenly aware I was still standing, I took a seat again. "Not just yet."

Ruth and Sarah exchanged a meaningful glance, and I looked to the safety of the flames.

"For all his teasing ways," Mrs. Brundage said, interrupting the silence, "he is the best man I know. Well, he and Owen, of course."

Unwilling to discuss the qualities she believed her son possessed in my current state of malleability, I decided to change the topic of conversation. "He must take after his father then, for I have heard your late husband was a superior gentleman as well."

Mrs. Brundage's eyes grew wet. "Yes. He was that and more."

With only a little encouragement, Mrs. Brundage began to speak of Augustus's father. Her memories of him were filled with light and laughter, and I genuinely enjoyed myself as she spoke.

"My parents did not want me to marry Henry." Mrs. Brundage stared into the dancing flames. "They said he was beneath me, but I knew better. No matter how much they reasoned that I could find contentment in another marriage situation, I knew that there was not a better option." Her gaze settled on me. "There are people, Miss Godwin, that will make your life richer and more beautiful by being in it. Henry did that for me. Every morning, I woke grateful that I had chosen him."

"And what of your parents? Did they ever offer their blessing?"

"No, and for that I am sorry." She glanced at Ruth and Sarah. "Well, Miss Godwin, I believe you have heard quite enough for the evening. It is nearly eleven, and it seems I have already managed to put one person to sleep."

I looked to the opposite end of the settee where Sarah slumbered on the armrest. "Poor dear," I said, standing. "You and Ruth go on ahead. I shall see to Sarah."

"Goodnight, Aunt Marina," Ruth said, kissing Mrs. Brundage on the cheek.

"Goodnight, my dear girl." There was such affection in Mrs. Brundage's endearment that I could not help but wonder what it would be like to be so warmly regarded. "Sleep well, Miss Godwin."

"Thank you." I offered a brief curtsy before retrieving two candles off the side table. I handed one to Ruth and clasped my arm through hers, eager to finally have her alone.

As we ascended the stairs, I glanced over at her. "You were quiet tonight."

"I take great pleasure in listening to my aunt speak of Uncle Henry. It is almost like he is still with us when the warmth of her words flows through me."

"She does have an ability of making you feel as though you were somehow a part of it all."

"Yes. It was one of my uncle's favorite things about her. I can still recall the look of utter satisfaction on his face as he watched her tell stories."

The thought endeared me to the man. "They seem to have both made a fortunate match."

Ruth tightened her grip on me. "Indeed!"

"Speaking of matches, have you yet placed your affections on a gentleman?"

"Oh, no." Ruth shook her head as we reached the top of the stairs. "I'm not acquainted with many gentlemen."

"But you are out in Society, are you not?"

"Yes, but I've only been to a handful of gatherings and one ball—Lord and Lady Brimhall's ball—where I saw you, of course."

I nodded, debating how to best transition to the topic I'd been yearning to speak with her about.

"Besides," she said, as we made our way down the corridor, "I wouldn't even know how to conduct myself if I did fancy someone."

She had handed me the perfect lead. "I do," I said, a tad too eagerly.

Ruth giggled. "Well of course you do. Augustus told me you had gentlemen lining up to court you."

I went rigid. "Did he, now?"

"Oh, yes. He also mentioned that you had received more offers of marriage than any woman he has ever heard of."

My chest tightened at the thought of Augustus relaying such a thing to Ruth. Heaven knew what she must think of me, and him also. "Yes. Well, matrimony is not a decision to be taken lightly, as you well know." The moment the words slipped from my mouth I wished them back. "Forgive me, Ruth." I halted us. "I did not intend—"

"Of course you meant no harm." Ruth sounded as though she needed to reassure me and not the other way around. "It is hardly a secret that my parents did not maintain a happy marriage."

No. That secret was mine. "Regardless, I should not have mentioned it so casually."

"It is already forgotten."

We were nearing Ruth's door, and I could not let another opportunity pass. "I believe we got quite off course from what I was hoping to discuss."

Ruth quirked her head to the side.

It seemed I would never get it out without simply stating it. "I was going to offer to train you ... if you desired it."

"Train me?" Ruth asked, echoing my insensitive wording.

"Not so much train, as"—my mind raced to think of a more pleasant description—"instruct you on being a proper lady." I paused. "Not that you are not a proper lady already, as you clearly are, I simply thought it could be beneficial ..." This entire conversation had gone amiss, and I stopped myself before I made a bigger mess of it all.

"Training sounds wonderful." Ruth's eyes danced in the flickering light, filling me with relief. "But are you certain you wish to spend your time at such a task? I am quite aware of the effort it will take."

"And what else would I do for the next three weeks?"

Ruth's lips parted, as though she intended to say something, before she closed them again. "I suppose if you truly don't mind."

"We will begin first thing after your ride tomorrow."

Ruth squealed in delight, and I repressed my correction, knowing a fresh start would be beneficial to us both. "I shall see you in the morning, then."

I turned toward my room, but Ruth clasped my hand in hers. "I am so glad you came to Fairhaven." She moved close to place a kiss upon my cheek.

"As am I," I whispered, surprised that the declaration didn't feel false.

CHAPTER EIGHT

I picked at the toast from my breakfast tray as Leah finished pinning my hair into place.

"You rose early, miss."

I stifled a yawn. "I have promised to aid Ruth in becoming a proper lady, and we will begin this very morning. I shall require your help."

Leah gave a brief nod, sifting through the box of my jewelry. She selected a simple pearl necklace and placed it around my neck. "And how might I assist you?"

"Ruth will need her hair pinned in a more flattering style. Her forehead is far too wide for the arranged curls that are currently fashionable. A higher coiffure would be more pleasing, I believe, but I leave that to your discretion."

"That would suit her well."

A vigorous knock echoed through the room, and I waited for Leah to answer the door.

"Good morning." Ruth smiled at Leah and bounced into the room. "I was so excited to begin my training, I could hardly sleep. Augi teased me tirelessly about taking a longer ride this morning, but in the end, he made certain we were back early."

I spun toward her in my chair, cursing my oversight. "You told your cousin of our plans?"

She nodded, her expression turning hesitant when I did not mirror her excitement. "Was I not to do that?"

I took a calming breath. "It is no matter. I suppose I may require help along the way. But perhaps refrain from telling others."

Ruth bit her lip sheepishly. "Outside of my family?"

Evidently, she had already told the others. "Yes ... of course." Had I known Ruth would so carelessly mention our plans, I would have first spoken with Mrs. Brundage to ensure she did not think I offered such a thing because of her negligence. I'd simply have to make the point to do so soon.

"Agreed." Ruth offered a resolute nod. "Where shall we begin?"

I stood and ushered her into the chair where I had just been sitting. "With the simplest thing to change—your appearance. Leah will style your hair."

"But I have already had it styled." Ruth reached up to touch the ringlet curls piled around her face.

I pushed my lips together, choosing how to word my reasons kindly. "I believe a different arrangement will more fully compliment the beautiful shape of your face." I considered the ringlets set on each side of her forehead, affirming how it only served to widen her already heart-shaped face at the top. "We want to elongate your lovely features."

Though I was certain she didn't comprehend my explanation, Ruth nodded her agreement. Leah set to work, removing pins and loosening curls. When Ruth's thick hair hung undone, Leah separated it down the middle, twisting both sides and bringing them, and the remaining hair, to the back. With another twist upward and a few pins to hold it in place, Leah had managed a lovely coiffure. Freeing a few curls around her face, Leah took a step back.

I gave a nod of approval. "Much improved."

Ruth moved to look at her appearance, but I stopped her.

"Not yet. Wait until we have finished." I opened my container of powdered carmine, and a touch of red powder floated through the air.

Ruth eyed the powder dubiously. "What is that?"

"Rouge." I dabbed a small amount onto my fingers and added some hair powder to it. "The trick is applying just enough that it adds rose to your cheeks without appearing as though you are wearing anything at all." I dusted my fingers and touched the apple of Ruth's cheeks lightly. "And some on the lips for a touch of color."

I surveyed the subtle change and was pleased with the effect. "As for your dress …" I paused, and shook my head with a sigh. "I wish I could say I have one that would fit you, but I believe anything of mine would drown you, both in the chest as well as the hips. We shall simply need to commission a few fashionable dresses for you to wear."

"But I already own so many dresses. I'm certain they are sufficient."

I scanned the unembellished day dress she wore. "Sufficient is not what we are trying to achieve." I examined the neckline and sleeves, wondering what could be done to improve upon them. "Leah, grab my golden spencer, the one with the lace trimming. It has always been a little snug on me, and I daresay it will look splendid with Ruth's coloring." Leah moved to do my bidding, and I set my gaze back on Ruth. "As for your other gowns, Leah can attempt to update them as well. She is quite handy with a needle."

Ruth's eyes flew to Leah. "I would not wish to trouble her."

"I assure you, it is no trouble."

Leah returned to my side, and I took the spencer jacket from her, aiding Ruth in putting it on.

The final touch had been just the thing, and I spun Ruth toward the mirror, finally allowing her to see her improved reflection.

Ruth placed a hand over her chest, her lips parting in amazement. "How elegant I look." She glanced at me over her shoulder. "I can hardly believe it. May we go down and surprise the others with my transformation?"

I moved to Ruth's side. "We are not yet finished. It is one thing to appear a refined lady; it is quite another to become one."

"Of course," she said, gazing at her reflection again and smiling giddily. "What do I need to know?"

I pursed my lips, still unsure what lesson to teach first. "I don't want to overwhelm you, so we will commence slowly."

Ruth nodded, still observing herself in the looking glass.

"Let us begin by learning how to repress emotion."

Ruth shot me a quizzical look.

"A trained lady does not giggle, squeal, speak loudly or excitedly, touch others without purpose—"

Ruth's face filled with curious delight. "How does one touch someone with purpose?"

I gave a mischievous smirk. "That is a lesson for another time. For now, it is enough for you to know to keep a suitable distance from others. If an arm is offered to you, you may take it, but other than that, avoid all physical contact until I instruct you otherwise."

Ruth gave a quick lift of her shoulders. "That seems easy enough."

"That means no hugs."

Ruth nodded her understanding.

"No enthusiastic or longing grasps of the arm."

Ruth nodded again.

"And try to keep your excitement imperceptible."

She beamed, nearly bouncing in her seat. "Shall we go down then?"

"Ruth!"

"Sorry. Imperceptible." She drew her shoulders up and lowered them with a slow exhale. "Shall we walk down?" she asked again, this time imitating my tone.

"Well done." I looked to Leah. "Be sure to assess Ruth's gowns and see what can be done about them."

Leah's head lowered. "Of course, miss."

I waited for Leah to open the door for us then led Ruth out of the room, eager to show off my new pupil.

"Remember, Ruth"—I directed a stern look in her direction as we neared the drawing room entrance—"a lady does not allow others to know how she is feeling without a purpose."

Ruth bit back a smile and nodded.

I gave her one last appraisal. "You shall do wonderfully," I whispered, leading her through to the drawing room.

Augustus noticed us first and rose from his chair by the fireplace. Mrs. Brundage and Sarah turned their heads from where they sat on the settee before following his example.

"How lovely you look, Ruth," Augustus said when he had arrived at my side.

Ruth glanced at me, and I gave a nod of approval.

"Thank you, Augi. Bella had her maid style my hair, and she also let me borrow her spencer. Isn't it beautiful?" She pulled at the lapels of the jacket and swayed from side to side, no longer able to suppress her grin. "When I first saw my reflect—"

I reached out gently and touched her hand.

"Oh yes," she said, looking sufficiently contrite, before lifting her chin high into the air. "I thank you for your compliment."

Mrs. Brundage stepped next to her son with an amused expression. "I must say the style is very becoming on you, Ruth. How grown up you look."

Sarah released a small sigh. "I quite agree."

"It is one thing to look the part of a fine lady," Ruth said, appraising me before emulating my stance, "now Bella must teach me to act the part also."

"*Act* the part? That seems an interesting yet fitting description." Augustus smirked at me. "But I suppose if your desire is to learn to bat your eyelashes and become privy to the secret means of entrancing gentlemen, I can think of no finer tutor than Miss Godwin."

Ruth clasped onto my arm. "It is! How I long to be admired like Bella."

I pinned Augustus with a subtle glower. "Ruth, there is more to being a lady than simply being admired. But I suppose it is a difficult distinction to appreciate among the less cultivated of the sexes."

Augustus chuckled at my retort.

"I think it's a wonderful notion," Mrs. Brundage said cheerily. "And it's so very kind of you to offer your assistance."

Guilt pricked me. "I hope you do not think me pretentious in offering such a thing. I assure you, I do not find Ruth lacking in any way." It was a lie, but a necessary one.

"I had simply thought it would be something enjoyable to pass the time, while allowing me to continue in my own development as well."

Mrs. Brundage gave a kind smile. "I did not find your offer at all pretentious. It has been far too long since I've been a young lady in training, so your knowledge is much appreciated."

I caught sight of Sarah's rapt expression, but she quickly dropped her eyes to her hands when she noticed me watching her.

"You are welcome to join us also, Sarah." The offer came without my needing to consider it. "If that is acceptable to you, Mrs. Brundage?"

Sarah's hope-filled eyes lifted to her mother.

"I don't see why not. She is seventeen and will have her own coming out soon enough." Mrs. Brundage smiled at Sarah with encouragement. "Would you like to join Miss Godwin for lessons, Sarah?"

A beautiful flash of pink colored Sarah's cheeks. "Yes. If it's not too much trouble."

"Not in the least." I clasped my hands in front of my chest, confident Sarah's willingness meant she would soon grow to be at ease with me. "Shall we begin? Three weeks shall pass before we know it and there is much to cover before my departure."

"Yes. You best get started. And unless I'm needed"— Mrs. Brundage looked to me, and I shook my head—"I shall be catching up on my correspondence."

Pulling his eyes from his mother's retreating figure, Augustus met my gaze. "I suppose I better get to work myself. I'd hate to keep you from your ..." He waved his hand in small circles as though he was attempting to think of the correct word.

"Training," Ruth interjected.

He pointed at her. "Precisely."

"Well don't go far, Mr. Brundage. I may require your assistance at some point."

He appraised me a moment.

"There are several things of vital importance that will only be learned while interacting with a gentleman."

He leaned in closer. "Such as?"

I suppressed my amusement at his eagerness. "Dancing, for one."

The corners of his mouth twitched. "Will we waltz?"

"You and Ruth will waltz, seeing as she is the one in need of instruction."

I could tell he had no intention of relenting. "But she will likely need to see it demonstrated first."

I dipped my chin forward, refusing to look away. "Then I suppose we shall."

He gave a wink. "Capital."

This time I could not hide my smile, though I made certain to pair it with a disapproving shake of my head. "Perhaps our first lesson should be the handling of wicked flirts," I said, shooting Augustus a pointed look. "With one of England's finest specimens on display here before us, it seems a shame to pass on the opportunity."

Both ladies giggled, and I gave a triumphant half-smile.

"On second thought," he said, and I recognized the touch of mischief in his eyes as he continued, "I believe I can spare some time to see how you handle this most *unnerving topic.*" He leaned a shoulder against the wall, his brow raised as if daring me to continue.

"Very well, Mr. Brundage," I said, accepting his challenge. "Though I fear you will not find as much satisfaction in the lesson as you presume."

"I'll be sure to let you know my thoughts when you've concluded your discourse."

"Oh, but Mr. Brundage, my lessons are not lectures. Come," I said, beckoning him toward me. "Stand here."

He hesitated, clearly suspicious of my purpose.

I lifted my shoulders innocently. "I simply wish to demonstrate the protocol, as I believe visuals are easier to recall than explanations." I paused. "That is, unless you'd rather not?"

He straightened and took a few steps forward. "Here?"

I gave a tight smile to cover my exasperation. "That shall work. Now, say something flirtatious to me."

Augustus glanced at his sister and Ruth.

"Oh, come now. It is not like they haven't seen such coquetry on your part before."

Augustus squared his shoulders and moved his head side to side as though he was about to take part in fisticuffs instead. He gave a charming grin. "Miss Godwin, you are most handsome."

The ladies giggled wildly, and I rested the tip of my finger on my lips. "Surely you can do better than that." I took a step nearer him and bit at my lip. Augustus's eyes fell exactly where I had intended them to. "Tell me how the color of my eyes remind you of sapphires that sparkle in the sunlight, or how the way I move utterly intoxicates you, making all other things fall out of focus."

Augustus swallowed. "The way you move intoxicates me," he repeated, his voice stale.

It was nearly too much to see him so utterly discon-certed, and I cleared my throat to stifle a laugh. "Well," I said, glancing toward Ruth and Sarah, "you will have to simply imagine that he has been successful in his attempt. And once—"

Augustus stepped near and the warmth of him seeped

through my dress. "Miss Godwin," he said, his breath hot on my neck, "if you only knew the effect you had on me, you would not torture me so heartlessly."

My heart gave a decided thump, but I refused to let him come away victorious. "Much improved, Mr. Brundage. Now ladies, how you react to a gentleman depends entirely on what you wish to convey to him and to those who might be watching. Since in this example we are dealing with a *notorious* flirt"—I tilted my head to give Augustus another pointed glance—"my best option is to end our conversation with grace and minimize any harm he could inflict upon me."

"Harm?" Ruth asked, scrunching her nose in concern.

"On my reputation. Flirts and rakes alike rarely have the ability to aid a lady's reputation, but they can destroy it in one brief encounter if one is not careful."

The ladies shared a concerned glance, returning their eyes to me with new focus.

"You must make it obvious that you have no interest in their attempts, for both kinds of men are infamous in their inability to acknowledge dismissive cues. In my experience, increasing the distance between you and the offender is the first step, followed by a quickly contrived excuse of needing to be elsewhere."

"Mr. Brundage," I said in a pretend acknowledgment of farewell, taking a step away from the penetrating warmth of his body and lifting my hand to him. I glanced at Ruth and Sarah. "The withdrawal of my attention will not be viewed as a slight if I offer my hand to bow over." I nodded encouragingly to Augustus, and he obediently lifted my hand to place a kiss upon it. I overlooked the way my skin prickled with the tenderness of his display.

"The benefit of such a move, as you are able to see," I

said, gesturing to the distance between us, "is that we are now an appropriate distance apart."

Both ladies nodded in unison.

"Once that is accomplished, I must offer an excuse." I turned back to Augustus. "It was so kind of you to seek me out, but I promised—" I looked over my shoulder. "Add whomever would be a reasonable person here," I said, to clarify. "—*my mother* that I would join her directly, and she is not one to be kept waiting. Do forgive me." I offered a curtsy and turned as if to walk away. "Make certain you do not allow him an opportunity to persuade you otherwise, for he will certainly try appealing to your sensitive natures."

Augustus's hand gripped mine, spinning me back toward his infuriating smirk. "Please, Miss Godwin," he said in a most overly dramatic way, dropping down to one knee. "How unfair of you to dismiss me so cruelly. Can you not see how miserable a wretch I am?"

The sight of Mr. Brundage clasping my hand and looking up at me as though he was a love-stricken fool was too much, and the laugh I had been suppressing for days burst from me. "I most certainly can," I managed, amidst the chorus of laughter that followed mine.

I wiped at the tears that had managed to escape before wrapping my arms around my midsection. "I don't believe I've laughed that hard in years," I said. "Though it should be no surprise as you were the only one who could ever make me laugh like that, Aug—" I quickly corrected myself. "Mr. Brundage."

"That is quite the badge of honor you have placed upon me." Augustus stepped near. "I shall wear it with pride."

"As long as you do not bring it along for our next lesson." I sent him a disapproving glance. "Sarah and Ruth shan't learn a thing with such ridiculous and overly dramatic displays."

He looked toward his sister and Ruth. "I believe they learned a great deal. Did you not find the demonstration enlightening?"

Both ladies looked absolutely giddy. "Yes," they said in near unison.

My face warmed, too aware of what they were affirming, but Augustus only laughed.

"Well, I best leave you now before Miss Godwin bans me from her lesson on how to encourage a gentleman's pursuit. Considering how satisfying this one has been, I'm confident that one would be a dreadful shame to miss."

I shook my head. "You are incorrigible."

He smiled a most handsome smile, the smile that used to make me weak in the knees. I realized, to my great mortification, it still did. I placed a hand behind me, stabilizing myself on the back of the settee, watching him walk from the room.

"So much for no tomfoolery." Ruth sent me a knowing glance. "It is wonderful to see the two of you together again."

I cleared the lump from my throat, having no desire to give Ruth evidence of her foolish hopes nor acknowledge the nonsensical expressions they both wore. "Shall we start on our actual lessons?"

CHAPTER NINE

"*I* never knew walking could be so exhausting." Ruth slumped into a chair. "Or that one could do it wrong."

"Just be thankful we do not have access to the backboard Mother made me use." I examined Sarah's posture as she moved across the room. "Very nice, Sarah. Remember to lift your sternum as that will pull back your shoulders in a more natural way." Her figure went into a beautiful, natural alignment. "Chin up just a touch. Perfect." I looked over my shoulder at Ruth. "It is your turn again."

She tilted her head back and gave an exasperated groan. "Must I? We have been working tirelessly for the past few days now, and my whole body is aching, especially my poor feet."

I placed my hands on my hips and fixed her with a disbelieving look. "You make it sound as though I'm some sort of Napoleonic dictator."

She exhaled most dramatically. "I'm sorry, Bella. You are right. I believe I am simply in need of a short respite to rejuvenate. My head is still spinning with how many ways there are to communicate with a fan." She shook her head. "It is like a language in itself."

"That is the point, dear," I said, though I recognized I had required a lot of them since beginning our training. "What is it you'd like to do?"

Ruth sat up straight, brimming with excitement. "Augi offered to take us on a picnic. There is a lovely stream where we like to go. And would it not be divine to spend such a beautiful day out of doors?"

I pursed my lips. A short break was one thing, but a picnic was entirely another. Then again, I had been putting off speaking with Augustus about who had prevented him from writing to me. Nerves were certainly a part of the reason I had not accomplished my purposes, but the constant interruptions had not made the task any easier.

"We could continue our lessons there," Sarah offered timidly.

I glanced between both ladies' hopeful gazes. "Very well. If Mr. Brundage is available, I suppose some fresh air could be beneficial."

Ruth squealed in delight as she ran to Sarah's side.

"Ruth," I said, pinning her with a look of censure.

"Sorry." Ruth took a calming breath, just as I had shown her, and linked her arm with Sarah's. "Come," she said coolly, "let us fetch Augi."

"I shall wait for you both here." I moved to the settee. The quiet settled over me as I collected my needlework and took a seat. After removing my gloves, I glanced around the empty room. It was entirely too quiet.

"And where have your pupils got off to?" Augustus stood in the doorway, a few letters in his hand.

"Actually, they have just gone in search of you." I

slowly rose to my feet to face Augustus. "Something about a picnic they were promised?"

Tucking the letters into his waistcoat, he moved around the settee. "Is there time for such diversions as picnics in your schedule?"

I lifted my chin in response to the teasing in his voice. "No. But Ruth and Sarah have done well, and I believe they deserve a respite from their labors."

He shifted his weight from one foot to the other. "So, you are not to join us?"

"It was suggested we continue our lessons there. Unless you prefer—"

"No," Augustus interrupted. "I want you along."

My face flushed, but Augustus did not seem to notice as he settled onto the settee next to where I had been sitting. I glanced toward the door, uncertain if we should speak in such privacy, before tucking away my concern and resuming my seat. "If you have work to attend to, I am certain I could convince them to postpone the outing for another day."

"No. There is always work to be done, which is precisely why we should go. Besides, I've already met with two of our tenant farmers this morning, and I have no other appointments scheduled for the day."

"Ruth and Sarah will be glad to hear it."

"How are lessons coming along?"

"Both ladies are doing very well," I said, leaving out Ruth's complaints of the monotonous tasks I had them performing. "Sarah seems especially keen to learn."

"I'm glad to hear it. She appears to be warming to you."

"Yes—*despite the discomfort I inflict on others*—I suppose she is."

He quirked his head sideways. "You are not still vexed by my comment that you make others feel ill-at-ease."

I tipped my head to reflect his own. "Should I not be?"

"No. It was more of a compliment than anything."

"You fooled me, then."

He shifted his body to face me more fully, his knees resting against the skirt of my dress. "You, Miss Godwin, are a caliber of woman that commands attention. You are beautiful, capable, fashionable, articulate—"

"Please, Mr. Brundage," I interrupted. "A woman can only endure so much flattery before it becomes disingenuous, or, in your case, before it seems a desperate attempt to cover a previous folly."

He only grinned. "Bold, intelligent—"

I shot him an unimpressed expression. "What is your point?"

"I am getting there," he said, a laugh behind his words. "Humble?"

I straightened. "Was that one a question?"

He paused, and his tiresome smile grew. "Discerning."

I scoffed and nudged my shoulder into him.

"Did you just shove me, Miss Godwin?"

"It was obvious I had no other option. Who knows how long it would have taken you to touch on a mere portion of my *commanding qualities?*" I said the last two words in a deep, haughty voice. "We may be stuck here all afternoon." I tipped my head to one side and fluttered my lashes in a most ridiculous manner.

He chuckled and shook his head. "Humorous also, though I shall not be adding skilled impersonator to the list. You did quite an abominable job with that one. *Commanding qualities,*" he repeated in a mimicking tone. "It didn't sound a thing like me."

I smirked. "I beg to differ. Though you have still not offered me an explanation for the necessity of *your list.*"

He placed his arm on the back of the settee behind me.

"It is these qualities that make others feel inferior in your presence. Discomfort originates from comparison, and you are a difficult one to compete with."

"Insightful. Perhaps when I am finished educating Ruth and Sarah, I can offer you advice on giving compliments that are not so disparaging."

He laughed. "I'm declaring you a superior woman—"

"By informing me how miserable I make others."

His expression softened. "Forgive me. I meant no offense."

We sat in silence, and my thoughts involuntarily moved through the countless times I had been the one who had felt deficient. He was correct that nearly all had been caused by comparison of some sort—what I perceived I lacked or what I was informed I lacked by another. How I despised that feeling. That feeling had been one of my greatest motivations to work unceasingly at becoming the lady I was—a lady that rarely felt inferior or overlooked. A lady that deserved consideration and love. And I had accomplished it. I had achieved near perfection in Society's eyes, if not Mother's yet. And what greater scale was there in determining your own worth than others' reactions to you?

The knotting in my stomach contradicted my conclusion. I took a clarifying breath, sensing Augustus's regard on me. My heart raced, and I knew it was a warning cry, an attempt to stop my foolish desire of admitting what I had discovered during my moment of self-reflection. "I—" No. I would not let him affect me. I would not let him discover the truth about who I had become.

"What is it?"

I shook my head, casting my gaze to my hands. "Imagining for an instant that what you say is correct, what is to be done other than diminishing oneself for another's comfort?"

"Never diminish yourself."

I lifted my gaze, perplexed by his apparent contradiction.

"Think of the people you enjoy being around. What is it about them that makes their company desirable?"

I exhaled, allowing a hasty attempt to latch on to any of my peers who met his criteria. I thought to offer up Lord Thorton as an example, but decided against it after considering that what I liked best about him was how superior he made me feel. After ruminating for too long, I met his gaze and gave a timid shrug of my shoulders.

There was discernment in his expression. "How does Ruth make you feel?"

Of course. *Ruth.* Why had I not thought of her? "I suppose she makes me feel appreciated."

He nodded but said nothing.

I did not care to give more, but the image of Ruth's bright eyes lightened my heart. "She encourages me and accepts me." I paused. "She makes me feel valued without condition." Tears threatened my composure, but I forced the odd sensation away.

A smile touched Augustus's lips. "It is one of the things I adore most about Ruth—her willingness to treat people as they deserve—often better than they deserve. She somehow overlooks differences and simply finds some- thing to admire about everyone."

"But I am not Ruth." Nor could I be. Amid the circles I moved in, it would undeniably ruin my reputation if I were to follow her haphazard example, however well- intentioned she was.

"I'm not telling you to be Ruth. You can encourage others in your own way."

I feigned disinterest. "Learning to elevate another without a purpose is not a lesson often encountered in a young lady's training."

He paused. "But, thankfully for you, it needn't be taught. You have always been—"

"I'm not that girl anymore." I looked away, surprised at my own admission.

"I don't believe that." His voice was a near whisper. "Do you remember the time when one of your family's tenant farmers brought his daughter along to Fellerton? The little girl with the black hair and blue eyes?"

I warmed at the memory. "Yes. Elaina."

Augustus smiled. "Remember how she watched you tirelessly, though she refused to speak to any of us? Despite your encouragement and Ruth's persistent questions?"

"If only Elaina's father would have mentioned she was deaf sometime before they were leaving, then we might have better persuaded her to join our game."

"But when he did tell us, what did you do?"

"You know very well what I did. And it was hardly a sacrifice. I was growing too old for dolls anyway."

"You didn't simply give her a doll, you gave her Emily. Your favorite doll."

My lips parted, utterly amused by his admission. "You recall her name?"

Augustus chuckled. "That was not my point. It was supposed to be that you have one of the kindest hearts I have ever known. Perhaps you simply need to be reminded of it." As his hand moved atop mine, the warmth of his skin was both alarming and unnervingly desired. I drew in a breath, allowing the familiar sensation to settle over me. And for an instant, I allowed myself to believe that I was once again the carefree, kind-hearted girl he had known.

"There you are, Augi!" Ruth passed the far side of the settee with Sarah in her wake. "We looked everywhere for you and here you were all along—" She stopped mid-step, thrusting out her arm to halt Sarah as well. She looked at our hands, and I pulled mine free of Augustus's. "Were the two of you just holding hands?"

I glanced at Augustus. "No. Well, not really. You see we were just talking ... and ..."

Ruth quirked her head to one side. "I thought you said that a gentleman should not be alone with a lady unless they are set to be married."

"Yes. I did say that. But ..." I looked back to Augustus.

"That rule hardly applies to old friends," Augustus interjected.

Ruth's expression grew accusatory, and her hands moved to her hips. "A rule that one believes should hardly apply, still applies. Is that not what you said just yesterday, Bella?"

Sarah nodded in agreement, her cheeks lifting into a smile.

"Absolutely." I clasped my fingers together in my lap. "And I'm pleased that you not only remembered my exact words but ... that you also ... passed ... my assessment."

Ruth's eyes narrowed a touch. "Your assessment?"

"Yes," I said, trying to conjure up the remainder of my fabrication. "To ..."

"To demonstrate that your knowledge is not superficial," Augustus offered, coming to my rescue. "She thought it beneficial for both of you if, from time to time, she was to break one of her rules to make certain you are able to discern the error."

Ruth nodded slowly, obviously taking a moment to

grasp the concept. "So, we are to watch your interactions and point out when you err?"

I pressed my lips together. "Precisely."

"This shall be fun!" Ruth looked to Sarah whose smile confirmed her willingness to comply, but I was not surprised to see a glint of continued skepticism in her discerning eyes.

"Well, now that we have discussed that … idea, shall we be off?" I asked, eager to leave Fairhaven and this awkward conversation behind.

"I shall see about the basket directly." Augustus offered me a quick wink before he walked from the room.

I SET my plate on the blanket beside me to readjust my bonnet. "I'm so glad you joined us, Mrs. Brundage."

She scrunched her nose and lifted her face to the sun. "I always appreciate a summer picnic. Though I'm certain ours cannot compare to the ones you are accustomed to attending."

"It has been perfectly lovely." Perhaps she was right that it wasn't like the typical picnics I attended, but there was something about the simplicity of it all that was still pleasing. No servants hauling in tables and setting up gourmet dishes. It was just the five of us enjoying the summer afternoon and a small basket of food that Cook had prepared. It felt … perfect, really.

Mrs. Brundage's regard returned to me. "I do appreciate what you are doing for the girls. I hope you know that."

"Do not even mention it. I am thrilled to be able to return a small part of the kindness you have shown by allowing me to stay at Fairhaven."

She nodded, releasing a breath, and I was certain she wished to say something else, but her gaze went to the plate on her lap. Augustus continued watching his mother, waiting.

After a few more moments, she lifted her head. "I only hope you don't think me neglectful in my rearing of them. Especially considering their lack of instruction in some areas."

"Not at all," I said, glad for the years of practice I'd had in concealing my feelings. Besides, it wasn't as if I thought Ruth and Sarah truly neglected, only ignorant in certain aspects—aspects important for the future but not yet vital for the present.

"Well, you are kind to say so. But I fear I have been a touch too lenient with them both. I've tended to focus on morals, principles, and the like, and less so on Society's expectations of them." She paused, glancing toward the stream where Ruth and Sarah splashed, a hint of sadness in her countenance. "When Ruth first came to live with us, I felt such a heaviness about what she'd been through. The light had faded from her, and I worried we would not see it again. But slowly, as she healed and learned to trust us, it returned. I wanted nothing to ever dim it again. I wanted her days, as well as Sarah's, to be full of laughter and happiness."

"And you have given them exactly that." I reached my hand out, setting it atop hers. "And I assure you, they are some of the finest young ladies of my acquaintance."

Mrs. Brundage rotated her hand to grasp mine. "You are a dear girl, Miss Godwin."

I sensed Augustus's eyes upon us, and I turned to find a satisfied grin on his lips, his head nodding in agreement.

"Bella," Ruth called, waving her hand from the stream, "come join us."

Mrs. Brundage nodded her encouragement. "Go on, dear. We all deserve a little laughter and happiness from time to time."

"I shall come if I'm not expected to wade as you are," I called to Ruth.

Ruth's giggles floated on the breeze, beckoning me to her.

"Allow me." Augustus rose to his feet and offered his hand.

Accepting his gesture, I allowed him to assist me to my feet. "I trust you have no intention of pushing me in?"

He kept hold of my hand and tucked it into his arm. "Not today."

Ruth and Sarah had their dresses pulled up around their knees and were squealing in utter delight as the cool water flowed over their bare feet and ankles. I strangely envied their naivety, and the way Mrs. Brundage seemed to have no qualms with such untoward behavior.

"Are you sure you won't come in?" Ruth asked.

I watched the water flow effortlessly around them, and it was easy to recall the sensation from when I was younger—the chill and the rush. But I was no longer a child. "I'm afraid not."

As the ladies resumed their frolicking, Augustus led me from them along the bank. "Would you join them if I were not here?"

"Of course not. My mother has managed to add some sense to the girl you once knew."

"It's a shame." He flicked his chin toward the stream. "That water looks quite refreshing."

I looked up at him with accusation. "You are attempting to persuade me despite my refusal?"

Augustus grinned. "As though I would do such a thing."

"You would in a moment if you thought my resolve weak enough."

His hand moved to mine, readjusting it further onto his arm. "I should be insulted by your lack of faith in me."

I bit my lip, and his eyes moved to the spot. "So, you will not try to persuade me then?"

"You have my word."

I looked up at him from under my lashes. "Not even if I informed you that I long to get in the water?"

A smile pulled at one side of Augustus's mouth. "I know what you are attempting, and it won't work. I now have a point to make."

I gave a dismissive shrug. "How unfortunate. A little persuasion may have been just the encouragement I required."

He searched my profile. "I daresay you may come to regret having voiced that opinion."

"Perhaps." I sent him a teasing smirk. "Or perhaps not."

Augustus laughed, and I welcomed the sound. How strange it was that eight years had passed since our separation. Yet, now that I was with him, it felt but a moment.

We continued in comfortable silence until the ladies' delighted squeals grew distant.

"The view from the top of the hillock there is quite splendid." Augustus shifted his gaze from the hill on our right back to me. "Unless you are averse to the exercise?"

The provoking smile that lit his face was too much to suffer. Without a thought, I released his escort to lift the hem of my dress and started up the hill before him.

"You might have let me get a fair start," he called from behind.

"As though you were ever one to play fair," I said over my shoulder. He was hastening to catch up, and the look of determination on his face sent my heart racing and my feet moving faster. He caught hold of my wrist, but I managed to pull it free despite the laugh that threatened to hinder me. With one last glance at him, I lifted my skirts a tad higher and ran the rest of the way to the top.

Augustus finished the climb only a moment after me, and his eyes settled on my victorious smile. "I forgot how keen you are for a challenge," he said, his voice unaffected by the exertion.

I drew in a labored inhale. "No, you did not." I put my hands on my hips and fixed him with a most ineffective glower. "You are all too aware of my inability to refuse you." I stilled, realizing how that could be received. "Not you ... I mean your challenges ... as you said."

The amusement on Augustus's face was too much to tolerate, and I looked away, finally taking notice of the view. "It is lovely up here. Though the landscape is not so very different from Bath, is it?" I glanced around at the lush foliage that occasionally hid the stream from view. "Fewer hills, perhaps, but the same vibrant colors."

I watched him as he surveyed the landscape, a satisfied look on his face. "Perhaps that is why I was always so fond of Bath." He sent me a wink.

"Yet you prefer it here?" The question escaped me before I had a moment to think better of it.

His expression was soft, but his answer was evident.

I stared at the horizon in an attempt to conceal my irrational hurt. "It is your home."

Augustus stepped closer, and the sleeve of his coat brushed against my arm. "Do you know what aspect of Bath I have missed most?" His honey-brown eyes radiated the warmth of the sunlight so forcefully, I felt a need to look away, but I could not. "You, Bella. I missed you."

My whole body was abuzz at hearing the thing I'd longed to hear for so long, but I could not allow him to see the truth. It would do neither of us any good in the end. "I thought you intended to say it was taking the waters."

One side of his mouth lifted in a partial smile. "That was a close second."

The sounds of distant voices drifted on the breeze, filling the silence between us.

Augustus flicked his chin. "It looks as though Sarah and Ruth have caught sight of us."

I followed his line of sight to find Ruth waving and calling to us, though she was still too far for us to make out her words.

My gaze shot back to Augustus. How had I let the opportunity to speak with him pass? I was still desperate to know who had prevented him from contacting me or, more likely, confirm my suspicions. "Mr. Brundage," I said, in an attempt to gather my courage.

"Yes?" He closed the space between us and my legs nearly faltered beneath me.

"I was hoping ..." It was difficult to find the words with him standing so near, let alone the courage to speak them.

"What is it?"

I hesitated. The ladies were still some way off with a hill yet to climb. But even if I could find the resolve to ask my question, Ruth and Sarah would arrive before he could provide an adequate answer. "Mr. Brundage, do you recall the time Ruth was ill and we spent every free moment together, just the two of us, hidden away in the woods?"

His mouth pulled into a slow smile. "Of course I do."

The warm air surrounding us suddenly felt thick as I attempted to draw in a breath. "I only mention it because

I feel as though I have hardly had a moment to speak with you—alone."

Now it was his gaze that flicked back toward Ruth and Sarah. "We are alone now."

"For a moment. But it is never long enough."

He said nothing, but his brow pulled low, shading his eyes and making them appear colder.

Instantly I was overcome by my own indignity. I took a step back. "Forgive me. I should not have suggested such a thing." How foolish I was. We were no longer children. What must he think of me? Perhaps that I was exactly the type of lady he believed me to be—one who skittered about with gentlemen so I could have suitors lining up at my door. The thought nearly undid me, and I knew I could not allow him to entertain such a notion.

I could not meet his gaze. "Mr. Brundage, let me assure you, my suggestion just now was rooted in a nonsensical moment of nostalgia, nothing more." I paused, inhaling a shaky breath. "I am not the type of lady that—"

A soft chuckle caused me to glance at him. "Let me assure *you*, that thought did not enter my mind."

Relief flooded over me. "It is a shame Ruth and Sarah were not near enough to have heard my unseemly suggestion, or they rightly would have called me on it." I clasped my hands behind me. "Shall we start down and meet them?"

His gaze was thoughtful, when it came to rest upon me. "I shall make a deal with you. If you will stop the unnecessary and agitating formality of calling me Mr. Brundage, I shall agree to meet you wherever you deem fit."

I couldn't repress my smile, and his expression soon mirrored mine.

"Agreed?"

I gave an eager nod. "Tomorrow then. Two o'clock in the rose garden."

He drew in a slow breath, but nodded. "Two o'clock, then."

Guilt pricked at me as I took notice of his tightened jaw. "Are you certain you will have no regrets?"

He shook his head. "I'm certain I will."

I narrowed my eyes, unsure of his meaning.

"Regrets will come by either choice, but I have now sorted out which of those choices offers the regrets I can live with." He lifted his arm to me. "Shall we?"

With a touch of hesitation, I placed my arm on his, wondering what sort of regrets I had just accepted.

CHAPTER TEN

"We are finished for today?" Ruth glanced at the clock. "But it's not even two yet."

I gave a taut nod. "But you have both done so well—"

"Done well?" Ruth gave an exaggerated pout. "I was an absolute catastrophe! I shall never be an accomplished lady."

"Learning to pour tea *correctly,* especially for guests, is not an easy feat," I replied, desperate to hurry the conversation along. "A little more practice, and you shan't spill a drop."

"If it is so difficult, why did Sarah accomplish it with little trouble?" Sarah's face reddened at Ruth's inquiry. "I'm older, yet she manages it all so much better than I. I'm utterly hopeless."

I dropped my shoulders at the hurt in Ruth's voice. "That is not true."

"It is," she whispered with a quivering chin.

I moved in close to her side. "May I share something with you? Something I have not spoken of since its occurrence?"

Ruth nodded her head with a sniffle.

"My mother had retired upstairs after a particularly tiresome caller, when an acquaintance of hers was announced and shown into the drawing room." I drew in a quick breath to calm the constricting sensation that had settled in with the memory. "I sent word of her arrival to Mother and even had a tray brought in for tea, thinking Mother would be down soon. But when she didn't come straightaway, I decided to take advantage of her absence, and the unlocked tea cabinet, to display my talents as a hostess."

Both Ruth's and Sarah's gazes were now fixed upon me.

"I had done everything right. I remembered to ask her how strong she desired the tea. I put the leaves in first, added the milk after, and placed the spoon perfectly on the saucer. My mistake came in conveying the tea to my guest. I had very nearly made it, without a drop spilt, when my toe caught on the rug." I paused, my heart racing as I recalled the vivid scene. "It was as if time slowed for a moment, allowing me to see the consequence of my foolishness played out for an eternity before me."

"You spilled the tea on your guest?" Ruth whispered, lifting her hand to her mouth.

"The horror on her face as the hot liquid flew through the air toward the skirts of her expensive gown is forever seared into my memory."

A giggle escaped Ruth, pulling me from my mortification. Both hands covered her mouth and amusement shone from her eyes. "That must have been dreadfully embarrassing."

"It was," I said, surprised to find a smile coming to my own lips. "And the worst part of it all was that I had not only dampened my guest and stained her gown, but that my guest happened to be a very influential countess."

Both ladies glanced wide-eyed at each other before breaking into laughter.

The sound beckoned for me to join them and, when I did, years of hidden shame dissipated into the air around me. "So, you must not be so hard on yourself, my dearest. Until you have poured tea on a countess, I will not hear of your hopelessness."

Ruth's smile was so brilliant it radiated warmth through me. "Thank you, Bella."

I touched her hand. "Now go. I shall see you both at dinner."

Ruth took hold of Sarah. "Can we stop by to see Cook before heading upstairs? All that interaction with tea and no cakes has left me ravenous."

I grinned at her ridiculousness, but for once I had no desire to correct her for it. I watched the ladies walk from the room before retrieving the bonnet I'd placed out of view on the under shelf of a small table. I glanced at the clock one last time before hurrying to the garden.

"I do hope you have not waited long," I called as Augustus came into view.

He stepped to greet me. "Some things are said to be worth the wait."

My blush was immediate and entirely unreasonable. I had conquered nearly every visible reaction except this one, and each encounter with Augustus made my desire to triumph over the vexing response even stronger. "Do you suppose it will rain?" I asked, glancing at the sky for distraction.

Augustus looked to the blue, cloudless sky. "I think not. Though I suppose it is always a possibility—a very unlikely possibility."

I drew near and placed my hand in the crook of his elbow. "Then let us not delay." Augustus glanced back to the house, and my gaze followed his. "Do you fear someone at Fairhaven will witness our *scandalous* meeting and force us into matrimony?" I offered a small laugh to cover my nerves.

His eyes settled back on me. "No. Unfortunately not."

"Come then, *Augustus*," I said, to remind him of our agreement. "Will you not show me one of the footpaths I glimpsed at the edge of the grounds?"

He scanned my features. "If you are certain."

I stepped off the pebbled walkway, causing him to follow. "I am absolutely certain."

We did not speak as we sauntered down a narrow footpath, and more than once I thought to release Augustus's escort so we would not have to walk so close together, but I did not.

"It's not much further," Augustus said, pausing to assist me over a lifted root.

I glanced at his profile. "What is not much further?"

"Since the opportunity has arisen, there is something I've been wanting to show you."

As we rounded the next bend, our path met with another, wider one.

He guided us onto it. "This way."

"I know that look. What are you up to?"

"You will see in just a moment."

As we continued on, the earth on both sides of the lane rose upward until we were walking entirely below the surface level. An occasional root was visible above, protruding from the wall of dirt and ferns. I paused and released his arm to take in the enchanting scene. When I turned toward him, he was watching me. "This is a holloway, is it not?"

Augustus nodded, a pleased expression on his face.

"You used to speak of them. How they were formed by people travelling the same paths for so long the ground sank under the weight of it." I glanced around again, riveted by the delightful scene before me. The trees high above covered the path in a protective canopy, allowing only slivers of sunlight to reach us so far below. "It is magnificent."

"I thought you'd appreciate the experience after having endured my inadequate explanations for so long."

I smiled up at him. "Very much. Thank you."

He released a slow exhale. "Are you going to ask me your question now?"

Unprepared for his directness, I dipped my head to conceal my coloring cheeks beneath my bonnet. "How do you know I have something to ask you?"

"Though the old Bella wouldn't have hesitated at the opportunity to traipse about the woods with me unaccompanied, I'm nearly certain the new one would find such a thing entirely inconsistent with her training—only neglecting such propriety for a greater purpose."

I opened my mouth, but having no defense to offer, I closed it again.

Augustus took a step nearer, causing my breath to catch. "Come now. Friends must trust one another."

"Very well." I drew in a fortifying breath. "Who was it that prevented you from contacting me?"

He gave a slow nod, as though he had expected the question. "I will tell you, as I believe you deserve to know, but you must be aware that I was not only forbidden to speak of it years ago, but I was reminded of my agreement just before your visit. Breaking my word is not a choice I make lightly, especially considering your parents' willingness to allow you for a visit."

My chest tightened, and I could not be certain whether it was due to his revelation or the reminder that he knew nothing of Mother's ignorance regarding my stay at Fairhaven. "So, it was my parents who prevented you?"

"It was your mother who laid out the demand, though your father was present also."

With his confirmation, my mind filled with a slew of questions, and I wasn't certain which to ask first. "What threat could my mother possibly have imparted that would keep you from me?"

I was not prepared to encounter the sorrow that overcame Augustus's features. "I did it for Ruth."

"For Ruth?"

Augustus ran a hand through his hair. "Your mother threatened to ruin her reputation if I would not comply with her demands."

His accusation hit me with such force I took a step back to compensate for it. "Surely you misunderstood. Papa adored Ruth. He would never have stood idly by and allowed her to come to harm. And Mother ... she is harsh, but even she has limits." Didn't she?

His gaze bore into me. "Do you believe I would have given you up for any less of a consequence?"

My heart nearly burst at his declaration, and I moved my hand to cover the ache of it. "But why would they do such a thing?"

Augustus took a cautious step toward me, lifting a beckoning hand. "Bella, you are pale. Let us begin our walk back."

I gave a slow shake of my head. "I need to know."

"I would do anything to make amends for the hurt I have caused you. But I fear I cannot offer you more. I only have conjectures myself."

I swallowed. "They never gave you a reason?"

Augustus shook his head. "Your mother only said that if either Ruth or I were to attempt to contact you, she would make certain we would be made to regret it."

A rogue tear escaped down my cheek, but I didn't wipe it away. "Was Ruth there to hear such a thing?"

"No." He cautiously lifted his hand and wiped my tear with his thumb. His fingers lingered on my cheek. "Your father thankfully spared her that."

"But surely she knows of it now?"

Augustus shook his head. "I fear I could not bring myself to tell her the truth. Not then ... and not now."

"But what of my letters? Did she not wonder—"

He glanced away, silencing my inquiry.

"You never gave them to her?" My voice sounded quiet and distant in my own ears.

"It was for the best. Ruth was too young to fully understand the consequence. She would have risked anything for your friendship."

I gave an empty nod. With so many emotions circulating within me, I was uncertain which to give priority. I was livid that Augustus had allowed Ruth to believe she was forgotten, as I felt I had been. Yet I was relieved that Augustus had a reason for staying away, a reason I could not blame him for. Then there was the shame I felt at my parents' actions, and the betrayal for the years they had spent convincing me that Ruth and Augustus had moved on with their lives without me.

"Come, Bella." Augustus took hold of my arm, and this time I allowed him to lead me forward.

As we walked back in the direction we had come, my thoughts continued to whirl through my head. What would ever have caused Mother to be so severe, especially to someone as dear as Ruth? And how would she go about marring Ruth's reputation anyway? Even if Mother had not liked her parents, as Papa had mentioned, it was not reason enough to see her ruined. "What are your conjectures?" I whispered, uncertain I wished to know.

Augustus's gaze flitted to me. "Precisely that —conjectures."

"Please, Augustus."

He rubbed at his jawline with his free hand before looking down at me. "Are you aware of your father's connection to my aunt?"

I clasped the pearl necklace at my throat. "Only that they were neighbors all their lives."

"Perhaps I should not be the one to relay such—"

"If you refuse me, I shall likely never know." Any other time I would have been mortified to hear the desperation in my voice, but in this moment I hardly cared.

After a moment, Augustus gave a brief nod of acknowledgment, apparently seeing the reality of my statement. "They were once set to be married."

My eyes widened. "Mrs. Seton and my father were engaged?"

"Not engaged. Sort of *intended* for one another from a young age. Though I am not aware of all the particulars, I understand that it was your grandfather who sought to end the arrangement. Your mother's fortune, when presented as an option, was hard to refuse in the financial straits he'd managed to get himself into. Your father merely obeyed and married her instead."

I glanced up at him. "How do you know all of this?"

"My parents informed me of the complicated history when Ruth came to live with us."

The more he revealed, the more questions arose. "But

what does that have to do with my mother threatening to ruin Ruth?"

Augustus hesitated. "It seems that your father did not lose his fondness for my aunt after he married, nor did my aunt lose her fondness for him. They were always dear friends. Your mother, I believe, grew to despise both my aunt, and eventually Ruth, because of the attachment."

My gaze shot to Augustus, but I could not bring myself to inquire as to his meaning.

There was discernment in his eyes. "I don't know what their relationship was, but I like to think that they were both people of strong morals and maintained nothing more than a friendship."

It felt a strange thing to consider, Papa and Mrs. Seton as dearest friends, but the moment I allowed for it, a faded memory surfaced—Ruth and I playing as children, while Mrs. Seton and Papa laughed together at our make-believe game. The sound echoed in my heart, bringing a smile to my lips. "Papa and I used to meet Ruth and her mother at the stream between our properties. On occasion, we would picnic there." I furrowed my brow, attempting to recall when it had all ended. "But all the recent memories I have of Mrs. Seton were of a different person entirely. She grew reclusive and quiet."

Augustus's arm tensed beneath my hand, and his hand clenched into a fist. "Yes."

I did not speak, allowing him to fill the silence when he was ready.

"My uncle was much esteemed, but it turned out his kindness and generosity were nothing but a facade." Augustus shook his head. "And I was as foolish as anyone in thinking him honorable, of overlooking his concealed cruelty that slowly suffocated the life from my aunt." He paused. "I should have recognized his malice; then I might have prevented her death."

"But you were so young." I tightened my grip on Augustus's arm. "And surely you did not know they were to be murdered."

His eyes locked with mine, and he came to a stop, forcing me to do likewise. "My aunt's death was ruled a murder by the coroner's court, but my uncle's ..." He paused, indecision evident in his features. "Bella, my uncle's death was ruled *felo de se* ... self-murder. It appears he took his own life after taking my aunt's."

My throat constricted as I tried to form words. "I was told that they were poisoned. That the perpetrator had not been apprehended."

"I'm not certain we will ever know precisely what occurred. And though the evidence the coroner's court presented was condemning for my uncle, it also cannot go unnoticed that the Crown benefits from such rulings."

My legs swayed beneath me, and I blinked, attempting not to let the darkness at the edges of my vision engulf me. "I think I must sit."

Augustus's hand came to my waist in support, and I managed a few disoriented steps.

"Here," he said, aiding me onto the stump of a tree.

I closed my eyes and took several long, slow breaths, before opening them to find Augustus kneeling at my side. "How could Ruth bear it? To lose her mother at the hand of her own father, then to have him ... do such a thing. It must have destroyed her." I covered my face, the tears I had been withholding for far too long flowing onto my cheeks. "And I was not even there to give her comfort."

"That was not your fault."

The warmth of Augustus's hand moving across my back could not prevent the anger from boiling within me, and I shot to my feet. "No, it was not. My parents are to blame for that." Surrendering to the anger pulsing through my veins, I lifted my skirts and made for the path toward Fairhaven.

It only took a moment for Augustus to draw up alongside me. "Bella, what is it you intend to do?"

I wasn't certain of anything, except the need to confront my parents for the wrongs they had caused. "I will write to my parents and demand they tell me all."

Augustus grabbed my arm, spinning me toward him. "Bella, you must not." He held me tight and close.

"They lied to me, Augustus. They forced you both from my life, and I shall never forgive them. I had no one when you were gone." The words caught in my throat. "No one."

His expression softened, taking in every inch of my face. "But think of Ruth. If your parents were to discover what I have shared, it will be Ruth who pays the price." He paused, and his head tilted to the side. "They would remove you from Fairhaven."

A quivering breath fell from my lips, and I dropped my head in defeat. He was right. Unburying the awful truth now would only serve to ruin my present happiness and—if I handled it thoughtlessly—Ruth's future prospects as well.

I could sense Augustus watching me, and he stepped closer. "Do not allow their deceit to ruin this chance you've been offered. You deserve it and so does Ruth."

Though my body trembled, I lifted my gaze to his. "As do you."

He reached for my hand and lifted it to his lips. His

kiss upon my palm penetrated my glove and warmed my entire body. "As do I."

How strange it was, that only moments before, my entire world seemed to have shattered beneath me, yet as Augustus took my hand and placed it on his arm, I somehow felt restored. If only for a brief moment.

CHAPTER ELEVEN

*A*ugustus and I sauntered up the pathway from the rose garden in thoughtful silence.

As we approached the house, a part of our previous conversation lodged itself in my mind, unwilling to be overlooked. I glanced at Augustus. "What incentive would the Crown have to have a case ruled as a self-murder?"

"They receive everything, Bella."

I pulled on his arm, delaying us just before we reached the back door. "Everything?"

"The law states that if someone takes their own life, then all their property and holdings are forfeited to the Crown."

"But what if they were mistaken?"

"The few suspects in the case all had alibis, and once my uncle's true nature was brought to light—as well as his poor treatment of my aunt—it seemed the most reasonable cause."

"So, because of her father's actions, Ruth is left with nothing?"

"The Court of Chancery must still review the decision.

My father put in an appeal directly after my aunt's and uncle's deaths. His hope was to attain my aunt's dowry for Ruth, as that was not my uncle's property."

"But it has been eight years. They have not made a ruling yet?"

"It seems the Court has years' worth of backlogged cases they are just now ruling on. But in one way we are grateful for the delay—Owen, now being a barrister, is able to argue the case before the Chancery. He will attempt to recover the dowry, but he also hopes to make a case for lunacy or melancholy which would overturn the *felo de se* judgment and allow Ruth to regain her entire inheritance. It isn't likely they will rule in our favor, but he insists it won't do any harm to try."

"So that is why Owen is in London?"

Augustus nodded. "And helping to ready the case was my purpose for visiting." He paused.

That is why he didn't speak of his brother, nor his business in London. "And is Owen having any luck gathering evidence for such a thing?"

"Not enough. It seems my uncle's behavior was not much altered in the days leading up to his death."

"I'm certain he shall find something. For even a sane man who is intent on such a horrific crime would have altered his behavior."

Augustus's gaze grew distant. "Even a sane man," he repeated, though I could not be certain why.

"Is Ruth aware of it all?"

His focus returned to me. "She knows the case will soon come to trial, but that is all. I know I should not attempt to conceal everything from her, but she has already endured so much. I can't bear to make her relive even a moment if it is not necessary."

It was I who stepped closer this time, and I looked up

at him. "Despite your dubious beginning, Augustus Brundage, I am quite impressed with the man you have become."

The smile he returned ignited the internal battle within me with such intensity, I yearned to surrender. Desiring another moment before acknowledging how unsuitable our current proximity was, I reached up and removed my bonnet.

The door swung open, and I stepped away from Augustus.

"There you two are." Ruth looked between us, and an odd desire to embrace my dear friend consumed me. Yet I had no intention of cueing her to what Augustus had entrusted me with, so I offered a smile in its place. "I saw you walking up the path from the drawing room window and came to retrieve you. Where have the two of you been?"

Augustus and I shared an uncertain glance.

"This is one of your assessments, isn't it? The two of you walking alone together?" I nodded slowly, and Ruth's face lit up. "I knew it. I told Sarah that had likely been your intention, considering no one was told where you had gone, but she thought the two of you simply desired to be alone." She paused and her smile grew. "Or is she correct?"

Augustus laughed, and I shot him a corrective glance. "Not in the least."

Ruth stepped back to allow us inside. "Well, we shall have to remember to inform Sarah I was correct after our guests leave, for it does not happen often and I should like to bask in it."

"Did you say there are guests?" I asked, following her inside.

Ruth nodded, taking hold of my arm and leading me

forward. "The Whitmores have returned to Safford Park just this morning and have called on us to pay a visit. They have already waited nearly a half hour for the two of you to return from ... wherever you were."

My throat went dry, hoping Ruth or Mrs. Brundage had the foresight to offer a more permissible excuse to the visitors. "And what reason did you give the Whitmores regarding our absence?"

Ruth shrugged. "Only that we could not find the two of you, and that you had likely ventured off together as you used to do."

I nearly choked on the air I attempted to draw in, glancing over my shoulder at Augustus who appeared entirely unruffled.

Ruth continued forward, obviously unaware of my dismay. "We told them we weren't certain when you would return, but they would not be put off with how anxious they are to meet you, Bella." Ruth looked back at Augustus. "And, of course, Candace is most eager to speak with you."

I kept my gaze forward, unwilling to glimpse Augustus's reaction to Ruth's declaration regarding Miss Whitmore. "Well, as thrilled as I am to finally meet them, may I freshen up a bit first? I fear in my current state I may be somewhat of a disappointment."

Ruth appraised me. "But you look lovely, Bella." She tightened her grip, as though she had no intention of releasing me. "The Whitmores shall adore you exactly as you are."

I doubted that, but as the voices drifted toward us from the open drawing room doors, I realized there was no hope of excusing myself without being noticed. I swallowed down my apprehension and lifted my chin.

"Here we are," Ruth said, entering the room with me

on her arm. The chatter ceased and not two, but three visitors—a gentleman included—stood in unison with Mrs. Brundage and Sarah. I didn't allow my consideration to linger on the guests, but smiled at Mrs. Brundage who hurried toward us.

"Do forgive us for our tardiness," I said, reaching out a hand toward her. "Had we known there was to be company, we would have postponed taking a turn out of doors until later."

Mrs. Brundage took my hand in hers. "It is no matter, dear. We had plenty to discuss in your absence, but now that you have come, let us not postpone the introductions a moment longer." She did not release my hand, and neither did Ruth relinquish my arm, as she led me forward. The nearness of both women was both unnerving and yet somehow comforting.

"Miss Godwin," Mrs. Brundage stopped in front of an elegant woman with dark hair and matching dark eyes, "this is our neighbor and dearest friend, Mrs. Whitmore."

Mrs. Brundage released my hand, and I offered a small curtsy. "It is a pleasure to make your acquaintance."

The woman gave a tight grin and nod in return, her eyes indiscreetly moving up my figure as she lifted her gaze again. "Yes. We have heard so very much about you these past years, both from the Brundages as well as in London."

I straightened my posture at her insinuation, refusing to let her words affect me. It would take more than a subtly placed insult regarding mere rumors to cause me distress. In truth, I had become quite the expert at dealing with vindictive mothers, a necessary protocol I had developed with much success. Afterall, I did not lack practice. "How kind you are to say such a thing, Mrs. Whitmore," I said, in a saccharine voice. "And I have heard only the best about you also."

Her fingers stiffened then closed into fists at her sides, but she offered a tight-lipped smile.

"And this is Candace," Ruth said excitedly, neglecting my instructions on the proper handling of introductions. "I am certain you two shall be the dearest of friends."

I finally allowed myself a look at Miss Whitmore, not the least bit surprised to find a vexingly handsome lady with dark features that contrasted her almond-shaped, green eyes. Ruth had mentioned we were nearly the same age, but I couldn't help but think how innocent she looked. Had she truly made it through two Seasons without scathing such a countenance? *"Miss Whitmore,"* I said most intentionally, giving a nod. "I hope we shall be fast friends."

She smiled, though there was a touch of hesitancy in it. "Of course we shall."

Eager to move on, I looked to the gentleman, surprised to find a somewhat familiar face staring back at me. It wasn't that he was particularly handsome or entirely memorable, but the way his large ears reddened under my attention could not be forgotten. "Mr. Treynor?" I asked, confident I had recalled his name correctly.

He gave a swift bow. "I was not certain you would remember me."

"Of course I would. We met at a soiree held by my aunt not a month previous. Your mother"—I paused, trying to recall the connection correctly—"is married to my uncle's youngest brother, correct?"

"Impressive, Miss Godwin. And I, of course, remember you. Obviously ... as I already said that." He fidgeted, and I wondered what it was about a beautiful woman that made most men act so inept. "You look lovely

... as you did when we met. But you likely know that." His eyes widened. "Not that I think you vain, simply aware of your natural qualities."

I had watched him flounder about long enough. "And what brings you to Dorset?"

He swallowed, his ears turning nearly scarlet. "I have simply come for a visit, as you have, it would seem. Mrs. Whitmore is my aunt—my mother's sister."

"How splendid," I said, with not a hint of the wryness I felt. "And even more so that our visits should coincide."

The color that had congregated in his ears now spread into his face, and he tugged at his cravat. "It is most delightful, if you don't presume me too bold for agreeing." He gestured me to the chair near where he had been sitting. "Would you care to sit a while?"

Knowing I could not refuse him, I released Ruth's arm and took a seat. At least there had been no room on the settee next to him, though Sarah's position in the corner, with a book in hand, looked most ideal. "And what are the latest reports of Town, Mr. Treynor? I know I have been gone less than a week, but much can happen in that time."

He took a seat, as did Mrs. Brundage and Mrs. Whitmore, before nodding his understanding. "Where shall I begin?"

I gave a small lift of one shoulder. "Wherever you see fit."

He began with Almack's last ball of the Season, but even with the lure of an apparent scandal, my attention drifted to Miss Whitmore approaching Augustus on the far side of the room. He greeted her with the smile I had grown accustomed to receiving since my arrival. She leaned in close, spoke, and gazed up at him expectantly. He nodded and leaned back toward her, the low hum of his voice reaching me as she lifted her hand to rest on his arm, her attentive eyes not deviating from him. I steadied my breaths and shifted my regard to Mr. Treynor, struggling to keep my irritation imperceptible.

Why had Augustus not told me of his obvious attachment to Miss Whitmore? Though I was not so foolish as to be swayed by his constant flirtations, it was inexcusable to treat any lady with such untoward behavior when your affections were bound elsewhere.

"How mortifying for her," Ruth said, and I realized she still stood next to my chair. "It makes me glad I have never been to Almack's. Just hearing of the patronesses makes my skin prickle. I don't know what I'd do if I fell under their condemnation."

Mr. Treynor returned his regard to me expectantly.

Grateful Ruth had given me an appropriate direction for my response, I gave a nod. "That is most shocking. In all honesty, I'm relieved to have missed the entire incident." I paused, certain I could not focus on any more news of London. "And how long shall you be staying, Mr. Treynor?"

"I believe we are set to depart soon, but my aunt has accepted Mrs. Brundage's invitation to return to dine this evening."

"How wonderful," I said, disappointed at the news I had not requested. "Though I refer to your stay with the Whitmores. Will you be here long?"

"Oh." At realizing his error, his face reddened. "I shall only be at Safford a week, I'm afraid."

I tipped my head to the side, acting disappointed. "Well, we will have to make the most of your time here, shan't we?"

He straightened in his seat. "I look forward to it."

Mrs. Brundage rose from her place near the hearth. "Would anyone care for more tea?"

"I would not be opposed," Mr. Treynor called after her. "Nor would I refuse another cake or two."

"Let me help." Ruth stood to assist her aunt.

My gaze involuntarily slid back to Augustus and Miss Whitmore, both still oblivious to the happenings of the rest of us. How discourteous some people were.

"Do forgive their desire for privacy, Miss Godwin." The false sweetness in Mrs. Whitmore's voice drew my attention. "They were apart for months before Augustus came to visit us in Town."

My chest tightened, and I again looked to where they stood.

"You know how young love can be—a few days' separation is entirely insufferable."

I forced my focus back to Mrs. Whitmore, now fully aware why I had received such an unwelcoming introduction. She thought I meant to steal Augustus from her daughter. What a ridiculous notion. An indirect assurance that I would not interfere with her plans was all that was required for her to begin seeing me as an ally, not a threat. But I could not convince my tongue of my reasonings. "I am all too aware of the effects separation can have on *young* love." I blurted the words before I could think better of it, not only undermining my plan to make myself agreeable to Mrs. Whitmore but asserting myself as a formidable threat to her daughter.

Her posture went rigid, and her eyes became shadowed slits.

"Mr. Treynor," I said, focusing again on Mrs. Whitmore's seemingly unaware nephew, "remind me where your family's estate is."

I suffered nearly a quarter of an hour fretting about my brazen comment to Mrs. Whitmore while Mr. Treynor highlighted the appeals of Cornwall.

"Miss Godwin," Miss Whitmore said, ambling up with Augustus just behind her, "if you would not find it too much of an imposition, would you take a turn around the room with me? I do desire to know you better."

I did not look at Augustus but set my teacup and saucer on the side table. "Of course." I stood and looked to Mr. Treynor. "If you will excuse me."

He gave a nod as Miss Whitmore took hold of my arm in an all too familiar manner.

"Do you care to join us, Ruth?" I asked, hoping she'd be inclined to offer me her aid.

"No." Ruth moved into the chair I had just occupied. "I will allow you a moment to become better acquainted without my endless chattering."

Wondering if discernment could be taught, I allowed Miss Whitmore to lead me forward.

When we had moved a little way off, Miss Whitmore released a tight exhale. "And how are you enjoying your stay at Fairhaven, Miss Godwin?"

My gaze was fixed ahead of us. "It has been most pleasant up to this point." Though her eyes moved to my profile, I did not betray myself by showing more.

"Well, I am certain Ruth is exceptionally pleased to have you here. She has always spoken so highly of you."

I did not overlook Miss Whitmore's unwillingness to mention Augustus and how he felt regarding my visit. "We are both most grateful for the chance to be reac-quainted."

She nodded, but I could sense her hesitancy. I thought to be civil and offer conversation, but I knew that would only postpone the discussion she wished to have. After a few more moments of silence between us, she sighed. "In truth, Miss Godwin, I was astonished that you came to Fairhaven at all."

I glanced at her. "And why is that?"

She readjusted her arm on mine, lessening her hold. "Well, for one thing, there are rumors of an understanding between you and Lord Thorton."

"Rumors are not often to be trusted, Miss Whitmore."

She slowed our steps. "So, it is not true? There is no understanding?"

I set my gaze ahead again, uncertain of how much to divulge to this near stranger. If I said nothing, she would likely believe I had come to steal Augustus from her. But such a thing would do neither of us any good. "Not yet. Though I will not deny, to friendly ears only, that I do hope to receive an offer from Lord Thorton when he returns from France." There. It was said. And heaven knew I needed the accountability.

Another moment of silence passed between us as we neared the group again. "Well, I hope Lord Thorton is deserving of you. From what I've been told, you are one of a kind."

I glanced toward Miss Whitmore, surprised to see that she appeared genuine. "Thank you," I muttered, trying not to make it sound like a question. Was she using my own tactics against me?

She gave me a small smile before releasing my arm and moving toward her mother.

"What did the two of you find to speak of?" Augustus's curious expression reminded me of the offense he had given in refusing to warn me of his regard for Miss Whitmore.

"It is of no consequence to you," I said quietly, moving to step past him.

He took a step back, lifting an arm to block my retreat. "I certainly hadn't thought it to be of consequence until now."

I glanced around before fixing him with a scowl. "You should have warned me," I hissed.

His brow lowered. "Of what, exactly?" He leaned in close, just as he had done with Miss Whitmore.

The very thought unnerved me, and I took a step away. "You know precisely what I am referring to."

He followed my sight to Miss Whitmore. "Miss Whitmore?"

My stomach knotted at his acknowledgment. "Fortunately for you, I did not feel inclined to divulge your constant bombardment of flirtations."

His expression did not change, but there was a flicker in his eyes that left me feeling unsettled. "And how is what you accuse me of any different than what you are guilty of yourself?"

I stilled.

"Or did I miss you mentioning your upcoming engagement to Lord Thorton before *I* spoke of it when we passed Branbury Court?"

I lifted my chin, relieved to discover he was not referencing my flirtations toward him. "That is different. There is not yet an understanding between us."

"Just as there is not an understanding between Miss Whitmore and myself. We are friends."

My heart leapt, but I simply shrugged my shoulders. "Yet you seem quite familiar with one another and most eager to reunite."

A corner of his mouth lifted. "Is that jealousy I detect in you?"

My lips parted at the accusation, and I glanced around again to be sure no one had overheard him mention such a ridiculous notion. "Not in the slightest, I assure you."

"Being all too familiar with the sensation, I have become quite efficient at recognizing the same symptoms in others." The other side of his mouth now lifted until a full and most infuriating smile lit his features. "And *you* are most certainly jealous."

I pressed my lips together, so entirely vexed I could hardly draw a breath.

"Are you well, Miss Godwin?" Mrs. Brundage asked, stepping to my side.

I forced my eyes from Augustus. "Yes." I nodded my head a little too eagerly. "I was simply ... we were just ..." I could not find the words to continue.

Mrs. Brundage's brow wrinkled. "Well, the Whitmores and Mr. Treynor have just announced their intentions to depart. But they will return to dine with us"—she paused —"though our dinner will be a little later tonight, all things considered."

My face warmed at the realization that it was Augustus's and my tardiness she was likely referring to, then I noticed the others' collective attention already upon us. "It was such a pleasure to meet you, Mrs. Whitmore. Miss Whitmore." I hoped my false smile seemed genuine from across the room. "And an absolute delight to see you again, Mr. Treynor. I shall very much look forward to this evening."

Both Whitmore women nodded their acknowledgments, but Mr. Treynor moved to me and took hold of my hand. "As will I," he said, bowing over it.

The moment he lowered my hand, I freed it from his grip. "Until then."

With one final bow, he walked from the room, the others filing out behind him. Only Miss Whitmore paused, lifting her hand in farewell before also disappearing out the door.

"An absolute delight?" Augustus threw an inquisitive look at me. "If I didn't know better, I would assume you fancied Mr. Treynor."

I sent him a scowl, but he only laughed.

"Poor chap. If you aren't a bit more cautious in your encouragements, he is destined to be very much in love with you by the end of his stay."

I glanced around the now empty drawing room, relieved I no longer needed to whisper. "Language is more than words. Only a simpleton would so willingly misunderstand me, Mr. Brundage."

"Augustus," he corrected, with that smile of his. "And I'm not certain most men are as fluent in this language you refer to as you presume them to be."

I took a step nearer him. "Then they should be faulted for having neglected their studies."

He looked down at me. "And how would you recommend a man go about learning such a foreign subject?" He paused. "Not that I need it, per se."

"Of course, you would not." I sent him a mischievous grin. "But, if there was such a man who desired to gain insight as to the ways of women, he should consider joining my lesson tomorrow."

"I wouldn't miss it for anything."

Though the very thought of Augustus being present for our training sent my heart aflutter, I could not deny rendering aid to a friend in need. For of one thing I was sure. Augustus needed to be enlightened regarding poor Miss Whitmore's undeniable attachment to him.

CHAPTER TWELVE

"*I* am so glad you and Candace got on so well last night," Ruth said, as we worked on our samplers. "I know she was most anxious about meeting you, but I told her not to fret as you are the dearest person in the whole world." She paused. "Well, you and she both." She glanced at Sarah. "And Sarah, you, of course, would be included on such a list."

I hid a smile as I bent over my sampler.

Ruth dropped her needlework onto her lap, and her expression turned thoughtful. "I once overheard Owen and Augi speaking of Candace, where she was compared to a rare gem with so many lovely facets that she truly shined in comparison to others." She sighed dreamily. "I loved the imagery so very much that I have not forgotten it to this day. Is that not the most wonderful description of her, Bella?"

I pulled too swiftly on my embroidery string, knotting it. "Miss Whitmore was a delight," I admitted, though somewhat vexed at the concession. It was no easy feat to truly dislike someone of Miss Whitmore's nature, despite how much I had tried at first. Had she been more like her scheming mother, the task would have been simpler, but Miss Whitmore appeared to be both kind and genuine. With such an agreeable disposition, I might wonder how she had remained unattached throughout her first Season were it not for how her regard had lingered on Augustus throughout the evening before shifting to me. The memory of it did not sit well in the least.

I drew in a steadying breath, recalling Augustus's assurance that he and Miss Whitmore were no more than friends. I certainly noticed his high regard of her, but, for the most part, his declaration seemed to have been given in truth. Neither had sought another private conversation after the initial one, nor were their following interactions any more flirtatious than Augustus's were with me—less so, even.

"And what are your thoughts on Mr. Treynor?" I asked Ruth, longing to move on from further scrutinizing the situation. It did not matter where Augustus's—nor Miss Whitmore's—affections lay. I was resolved on attaching myself to Lord Thorton, for Lord Thorton was very much my equal.

"He seems a most affable gentleman."

I glanced up from my attempt to dislodge the knot. "And do you find him handsome?"

Ruth blushed, and her gaze darted to Sarah. "I suppose he is tolerable."

Sarah's eyes twinkled. "She finds him more than tolerable. I believe *quite fetching* were the words she used to describe him."

"Sarah!" Ruth's expression of betrayal lasted only moments before she broke out in a fit of giggles, inducing Sarah along.

I smiled at their silliness but shook my head for good

measure, refocusing on the blasted knot that would not come free.

"Have you begun today's instruction without me?" Augustus stood in the doorway, his consideration moving between Sarah and Ruth before settling on me.

My heart thudded in my chest, but I stood and put the knotted sampler on the side table as though unaffected by his appearance. "No. You are just in time."

Ruth glanced between us as I directed him to the back of the settee where there was more floor space. "In time for what, exactly?"

"Considering the visit of a *certain guest* here at Fairhaven, I thought it would be a beneficial time to discuss interacting with gentlemen. Particularly, how to ensure you are conveying your intended hopes during said interactions."

"You are going to teach us to flirt?" Ruth asked, elation saturating her voice.

I pressed my lips together, unable to keep my gaze from flickering to Augustus's smirk. "I suppose that is how some people view it."

Ruth tossed her sampler on the settee next to her and rose, moving to assist Sarah to her feet.

I joined Augustus behind the settee, ignoring the elated sensation in my chest. "I shall require your assistance again, if you are willing?"

His lips lifted at the corners. "Gladly."

"Yes ... well, there shan't be much required of you in this demonstration. You need only stand here for most of it."

Augustus's smile widened. "Am I to be relieved or offended by that?"

I gave a playful shrug. "I suppose it shan't matter either way, considering you have already committed yourself." I turned my attention to the ladies, who watched eagerly. "Now, before we begin—"

"You had not begun yet?" Ruth glanced between us. "I was certain you had. But I suppose the two of you are always flirting."

Augustus chuckled, but I curtailed it with a rebuking glance, already regretting my choice of inviting him along.

I placed my hands behind me in a display of calm, though I could feel the trembling inside. "I was telling Augustus yesterday that language is more than mere words." I drew in a breath. "To convey a message most effectively, you must not only say the right thing, but you must say it in the right way—intonation, pacing, and inflection are all vital."

Ruth and Sarah listened intently. Both of their brows drawn low in concentration as I faced Augustus. "I shall use the very line you teased me with yesterday as our first example. Though I will replace Mr. Treynor's name with yours."

Augustus nodded, his eyes brimming with amusement.

I overlooked his irksome reaction and moved to face him. "It was an absolute delight to see you again, Mr. Brundage." My voice was flat, evenly paced, and I did not linger on any word in particular. I gave Augustus a pointed look. "That is a woman being cordial."

The corners of his mouth twitched. "Yet what I *heard* was that I am an absolute delight to you."

I held up a finger, this time drawing a step nearer to Augustus. I looked up at him from beneath my lashes and lowered the volume of my voice just enough to obtain a sultry tone. "It was an absolute *delight* to see you again"— my words were slow and intentional, and I placed my hand gently on his arm, leaning toward him—"Mr.

Brundage." I drew out his name a touch slower, nearly whispering it at the end. When his eyes moved to my lips, I used the opportunity to wet them.

His gaze lingered, transfixed.

I lifted a brow. "Well?"

He gave a slow shake of his head. "It seems I stand corrected."

Both ladies giggled wildly, and I gave a victorious smile.

Ruth stepped forward and took hold of my hand. "You must teach us everything you know!"

"I will teach you what is necessary in order to accomplish your purposes. And I must caution you outright to use these tools prudently. The last thing you should desire is to haphazardly give any gentleman the wrong impression." I paused. "It is a lesson, I regret, I did not learn soon enough." I sensed Augustus's curiosity, but I did not meet his gaze. "Shall we continue?"

Following their agreement, I explained how to go about choosing what words to inflect, discussed pacing in their speech, and exemplified a few different intonations one could use.

"It is your turn," I said, beckoning to Ruth.

Her eyes widened. "I am to try? Here? In front of all of you?"

"How else should you learn?"

She shook her head and took a step backward. "I simply cannot."

"Come now, Ruth. Would you rather feel a fool with us, or with a gentleman you are attempting to impress?"

She frowned. "Perhaps I shall simply refrain from speaking to gentlemen altogether."

Augustus chuckled. "I could support that idea."

I shot him a hasty scowl before regarding Ruth again.

"You shall do wonderfully, and I will help you along."

She shook her head again.

"I will go."

I looked at Sarah, trying to hide my shock behind a smile. "Superb." I took a step away from Augustus and gestured her forward.

Sarah sent Augustus an apologetic glance before facing me. "May I try it on you instead? I know that might be odd, but it seems preferable to flirting with my brother."

I stifled a laugh. "Of course."

Sarah gave a nod and took a step closer to me, drawing in a slow inhale. Her eyes moved to mine with intention, but she paused. "What name should I call you, though? I don't know why it seems so complex, considering it is all for fun, but I'd prefer to address you as a gentleman. Unless you oppose?"

"Not at all. Perhaps Mr. Godwin is acceptable?"

She nodded, and then looked at me from beneath her lashes, her cheeks a lovely shade of pink from the embarrassment. "It was an absolute delight to see *you* again, Mr. Godwin." She had changed the inflection as well as the intonation—her voice full of sweetness and innocence— and it worked perfectly for her.

"Well done," I said, reaching out to squeeze her hand.

Augustus shook his head, a look of disbelief on his face. "Too well done, I daresay. And here I was thinking I only had Ruth to worry about for now."

"Sarah is seventeen," Ruth said with a beseeching look. "And it is not at all uncommon to see ladies younger than her out in Society."

He reeled back. "After that demonstration I will likely be postponing her come out for another several years."

At seeing both ladies' overdone pouts, I touched the hand hanging at his side ever-so-briefly. "Come now,

Augustus, do not tease them so. Despite your hindrance, they are resolved to become sensible ladies. Do you not think it best if they are made aware of all the techniques? Both for encouraging the gentlemen they hope to, as well as avoiding giving false hope to undeserving recipients?"

Augustus released an exaggerated exhale. "I suppose I cannot keep them little forever."

They beamed back at him, as I resumed my spot at his side. "Shall we continue, then?"

"Oh, yes," Ruth said, linking her arm with Sarah. "We have been looking forward to this lesson most of all."

Augustus lifted a hand toward them, pinning me with a look of validation. "See, that is precisely what worries me."

I shook my head at his ridiculous, yet charming, over-protection. "Before we discuss incorporating touch into your interactions with gentlemen"—Ruth and Sarah shared a giddy glance, and my own heart quickened in anticipation—"I want to mention a few tips for displaying your interest during a conversation. The first, and most significant, is that men desire to feel important and therefore must be flattered constantly."

Augustus laughed. "That is a most unfortunate generalization, I daresay."

"I assure you, it is not." His doubtful expression pressed me to continue. "As you well know, I have undergone a thorough study of gentlemen these past three years, and I feel quite comfortable offering my opinion on the matter. And I have yet to meet a gentleman immune to flattery."

Augustus's lips pushed together, and he crossed his arms. It was obvious he did not care to know how I had come to such conclusions.

I rested my hand on his arm. "I hope you do not feel I

am attacking your sex, for women are by no means immune to flattery. We are simply more aware of its use, and therefore it becomes a choice whether or not we will allow for it."

"And how does one go about flattering a gentleman?" Ruth asked, impatience evident in her tone.

"You must show great interest in what he has to say despite how dull it is." The ladies both laughed. "Do not speak of yourself, except to showcase your similarities. Compliment him whenever possible without sounding trite. And *never* disagree with him."

Augustus gave a disbelieving laugh. "Again, it is preposterous to believe that a man can be so easily swayed by any woman engaging him in such tactics."

"I did not say any woman. Flattery is an art, and like all art, there exists a range of skill. Only the most proficient have such great influence. That is why I feel it is important to teach."

Augustus glanced down at my hand still on his arm. "Because you are obviously one of the masters?" His smile did not reach his eyes, and I withdrew my hand.

The room was suddenly far too quiet.

"I believe we are in need of a demonstration," Augustus said, his false exuberance almost masking his concern. "Come, Bella. Show the girls what you mean."

"It will not work on you."

A side of Augustus's mouth lifted in a half-smile. "But I thought you were implying that even I am not immune to such things."

"Knowledge empowers a person. And seeing as I have shared a woman's secret tactics with you, you are now only as susceptible as you allow yourself to be."

"So I shall choose to allow for it."

"No. If Ruth and Sarah wish to see an example, it must

be authentic." I glanced sideways at them. "We must select an unknowing gentleman for the purpose."

Ruth threw up her hands. "If only Owen were here."

Augustus scoffed. "As though I would allow Bella to flirt with my brother."

His look of disbelief forced a laugh out of me. "Is that jealousy I'm glimpsing?"

"Mr. Treynor is the practical choice," Augustus said, completely disregarding my inquiry. "Besides, he is likely the only other man we are to encounter any time soon."

My gaze flickered to Ruth. "If we were to go to town, I'm certain we could find an unsuspecting candidate."

"You must not forego Mr. Treynor for my sake." Ruth gave a resolute nod. "It is not as though you are actually trying to obtain his affections." Augustus's brow furrowed, but Ruth didn't take notice. "Though I would hate to see him disappointed."

"I shall take a more friendly approach with him in order to prove my point. Flattery need not only be used for obtaining one's affection." Ruth gave a nod, but I took her hand in mine. "And, in the off-chance Mr. Treynor is inclined to think more of our conversation than I intend, I will simply mention Lord Thorton. That should keep him from anything more than a momentary disappointment."

Augustus released a heavy breath. "Yes. Tell him of Lord Thorton. You would not want to give the poor bloke any false hopes."

A knock sounded at the open drawing room door, and the butler stepped through.

"What is it, Branson?" Augustus asked the butler.

"A visitor has just arrived for Miss Godwin."

"For me?" I asked, more than a little uneasy. For who should know I was at Fairhaven besides Papa?

CHAPTER THIRTEEN

*A*ugustus's gaze met mine before moving back to the butler. "Did the visitor give their name?"

"Yes. A Mr. Leavitt, sir."

Disappointment pulsed through me, not at who the visitor was, but at the likely purpose for his visit. I sent Augustus an uncertain glance. "It was the Leavitts' postponed invitation that allowed me here."

Augustus gave a slow nod of understanding. "Do you believe he is ready to host you again?"

I shrugged, glancing at Ruth and Sarah, whose faces showed equal concern. "It is likely."

Augustus crossed his arms. "And do you wish for us to leave so that you may speak with him in private?"

Uncertain what Mr. Leavitt would relay about my current situation, I nodded. "If it is not too much trouble."

"Not at all." Augustus exhaled, turning to Ruth and Sarah. "Let us go see if Cook has made any cakes for us to sample."

Ruth stepped to my side. "I don't mind staying."

I touched her arm. "No. Go and enjoy a sweet."

With one last look at me, Ruth latched onto Sarah, and they made for the kitchen.

"You look ill at ease." Augustus hadn't moved, his eyes still on me. "Are you certain you wish to speak with him alone?"

I thought of Mr. Leavitt's loose tongue, and I knew I needed to assure Augustus all was well. He could not discover Mother's ignorance of my whereabouts. At least, not yet. "Mr. Leavitt is the dearest of men and is perfectly harmless."

"Very well." Augustus walked to the door where the butler still awaited direction. "Show Mr. Leavitt in."

Without a word, the man bowed and left the room.

Augustus paused at the threshold. "I shall be back to check on you shortly."

"Thank you," I whispered as he, too, disappeared out into the corridor.

The sound of men's voices greeting one another echoed through the doorway before Mr. Leavitt waddled in behind the butler, catching sight of me and gesturing with an extended thumb behind him. "Well, Mr. Brundage seems a most agreeable gentleman."

"He certainly is."

Mr. Leavitt scanned my rigid posture. "And have you enjoyed your stay here in Dorset?"

Realizing his concern for me, I brightened as much as I was able. "I certainly have."

"Good. Good." The jolly man's full cheeks pulled into a smile, obviously settled by my relaxed countenance. "Well, do come over here and give me a proper welcome." He reached a hand toward me, gesturing me forward. "I haven't come all this way to be treated as a mere acquaintance."

Obediently, I hurried to his side, placing a kiss upon

his cheek. Mother despised Mr. Leavitt's tactless behavior, but I had always had a fondness for the man. "Do you care to have a seat?"

"I've been sitting all morning, so unless you prefer otherwise, a moment to get my blood flowing would be most advantageous."

"Of course." I paused. "I see Mrs. Leavitt did not accompany you. Is she well?"

He heaved a long, drawn-out sigh, his big belly lowering at the effort. "I fear her health is not optimal, though whether it is a condition of the mind or the body is less certain." His brow furrowed. "She has been brought quite low since the marriage of our Amelia and has refused to travel these past few months because of it, though she would deny the causation."

I well knew I should comment on her grievous trial, but found myself unable to push aside my curiosity. "She is still in London then?"

Mr. Leavitt shook his head. "No. We were not in London this Season."

"But I ..." My words trailed off as I tried to make sense of Mr. Leavitt's declaration. I was certain Papa had mentioned they were in Town, for if they had already been home in Dorset, why would they have claimed Mrs. Leavitt's inability to travel as a reason for postponing their invitation?

"Do not fret, Arabella," Mr. Leavitt said, reclaiming my drifting thoughts. "She is not in dire straits. I intend to convince her to go with me to Brighton, and I daresay she shall be herself again in no time. Salt air does wonders for an ailing person's constitution."

I gave an absent nod, allowing the silence to over-whelm the room.

Mr. Leavitt cleared his throat. "I did not mean to

dampen your spirits with such news. Why don't we move along to the purpose for my visit?"

My heart dropped, and I was certain I did not wish to hear it. "May I offer you tea and cakes first?"

"No. I fear I must hurry back to Mrs. Leavitt." He rubbed his stomach, as though consoling it over the thought of missing out on cake. "She does not like to be long without me in her current state, and, unfortunately, the man I just saw about repairs for my stables had much to say regarding his thoughts on ... well, everything, really. I'm now running behind schedule, so I must be brief."

I stilled, preparing myself emotionally for the news of my immediate removal from Fairhaven.

Mr. Leavitt reached into his pocket and pulled out two letters. "I received a letter for you several days ago with your mother's seal." He appraised my expression. "I thought it a very strange occurrence, indeed, and wrote your father to see what it was about."

"Mother had already left for her sister's when"—I paused, uncertain how to word the Leavitts' failing to follow through with their invitation in a way to not give offense—"the Brundages offered to let me stay here. I suppose that is where the confusion came in."

Mr. Leavitt gave a tentative nod, though he appeared far from convinced. "I suppose that is similar to what your father has declared, though he mentioned giving your mother the wrong directions, or something or other, and here I am, hand delivering your missives like a regular post boy." He held out both letters and pointed at the top one with his other hand. "A second one arrived this very morning."

My gaze moved from the letters to him. "And is this the only reason you have come all this way?"

"Well, that and to see your pretty face."

My relief was instantaneous, and I happily accepted the letters. "I hope it was not too much trouble then."

Mr. Leavitt swatted his now empty hand at the air between us. "We are practically neighbors to Fairhaven. Our own estate is not even twelve miles from here, and the man I met with this morning is less than three, so it was hardly an inconvenience."

"Twelve miles? I knew you lived in Dorset but I had not the slightest notion you were that close to here."

"Yes. That is how I kept your father abreast on the news of the Brundage family. We have a few common acquaintances, though I've personally never had the opportunity to meet any of the lot until today."

My pulse quickened. "Papa had you keep him updated on the Brundages?"

A touch of concern etched into Mr. Leavitt's features. "Not the family in particular, but your friend, Miss Seton. Though I would report on significant happenings like the passing of the late Mr. Brundage. God rest his soul." He paused, his large head tipping to one side. "Did you not realize that is how your father knew so much?"

I gave a weak shake of my head, unable to tell him Papa had shared none of the news with me.

"Yes. Having realized our proximity to one another, your father wrote to me not long after Miss Seton was removed from Bath requesting any information I came upon. The Brundages seem to be a relatively quiet family, but on occasion I would hear something worth passing on."

My throat was tight, but I attempted to conceal my shock. "Well, I thank you for your willingness."

"It was my pleasure. Your father told me how

desperate you were to know Miss Seton was well in her new situation."

My smile was stiff. "Yes. In truth, I was beyond desperate."

Mr. Leavitt patted my arm jovially. "Then that is all the thanks I need."

"And yet it seems we are greatly indebted to you. First for you apprising us of Miss Seton, and second for your delivery of my letters."

"Think not a thing of it."

"But I must." Mr. Leavitt was much too forthcoming with information, and I could not allow Augustus to discover the web of lies I seemed to be stuck in. "If you receive any other letters, you must have them posted. I would not forgive myself for Mrs. Leavitt being left alone on my account."

He tilted his head to the side. "Always such a thoughtful girl."

Guilt pricked me as I rested a hand on Mr. Leavitt's arm. "Speaking of being thoughtful, you must not keep your wife waiting a moment longer than necessary. But promise me you will give her my regards."

"I'll be glad to." Mr. Leavitt patted my hand. "And I hope you are aware that you are welcome to come visit us anytime you desire. Not that your demanding agenda leaves much time for such trivial visits, but I am certain Mrs. Leavitt would prefer your company to mine any day. You need only show up at our door."

My mouth parted, but no words came out. The Leavitts had not extended an invitation to me at all. Papa had lied yet again.

Mr. Leavitt's expression sank in concern. "Is there something the matter, Arabella?"

I swallowed and forced out a smile, hoping to regain

my composure. "Yes. I am simply overwhelmed by your kindness. I shall not forget your offer. Here, now." I took hold of his arm to hurry him along before Augustus could return. "Let me see you out."

As we headed toward the front entryway, I glimpsed Augustus in my periphery walking down the corridor toward us. I kept my focus on Mr. Leavitt, leading him a touch more quickly toward the door.

"On your way out so soon, Mr. Leavitt?" Augustus called.

I barely managed to repress a groan when Mr. Leavitt halted, turning back toward Augustus. "I am afraid so, though I'm determined to convince Mrs. Leavitt to accompany me for a longer visit soon—once her health permits. I was just telling Arabella that we are practically neighbors."

Augustus took a few final steps toward us and extended a hand. "You would both be most welcome."

Mr. Leavitt took hold of Augustus's hand and gave it a shake. "Your kindness is most appreciated, Mr. Brundage." His eyes moved to me. "Do write your mother to let her know—"

"I surely will," I said, not allowing him to finish.

Mr. Leavitt's gaze flitted to Augustus for the briefest moment before he reached up and tapped his own cheek again. Desperate to see him on his way, I leaned over and placed a kiss upon the spot he indicated.

"I daresay, Mr. Brundage, that is the absolute best thing about growing old. I could hardly get a young woman to look at me in my day, let alone kiss my cheek, and now I have one of England's finest willing to dote upon me on command."

My cheeks now shook with fatigue as I forced another smile. "As though someone as beautiful as Mrs. Leavitt could ever be persuaded by any but a man of equal standing."

Mr. Leavitt laughed, his belly shaking in rhythm to the sound. "Such a dear girl you are, Arabella. And I will relay your amusing conjecture to Mrs. Leavitt as soon as I greet her. I am certain it will bring her much delight, though not as much as it has given me."

"And you will not forget to offer her my regards?" I took a few steps toward the door Branson held open, encouraging Mr. Leavitt on his way.

"Of course not," he said, following my example before stopping on the threshold. "Farewell, Arabella. Mr. Brundage."

Augustus stepped to my side. "Take care, sir."

I offered one last parting nod. "Thank you again, Mr. Leavitt."

With that, the portly man waddled down the steps and toward his awaiting carriage, and with his removal, I found it easier to draw a breath.

As I raised my hand in a final farewell, Augustus leaned against the doorframe, his discerning eyes on me.

"What did Mr. Leavitt want if not to remove you?"

I watched the carriage roll forward, determining what I should say. Augustus would rightly be furious to know Mother was unaware of my being at Fairhaven, especially after I had forgone the opportunity to admit such a thing on several occasions. Then there was the revelation of Papa's lie that would be too difficult to explain, as I didn't even understand it.

"Papa sent him to see how I was faring." The carriage disappeared onto the main road, and still I kept my eyes on the road. I would find a time to explain the truth to Augustus. I simply needed to figure out *how* to tell him first. A confession of that magnitude required ample thought as to how to best approach it, and, though I typically disapproved of outright lying, my situation hardly seemed conducive to honesty.

"And what did you say?"

I finally met Augustus's gaze. "That besides the matter of a somewhat irksome host, I am getting on rather well."

He laughed, pushing himself off the wall so that he towered over me. "Did you mention that you have been spending your days teaching young, impressionable minds how to flirt?"

"You are hardly that young anymore, Augustus."

He laughed. "I deserved that."

I lifted my chin. "You most certainly did."

Augustus's gaze moved to the hand at my side. "Did he bring you those?"

I glanced down, realizing he spoke of the missives from Mother I still clung to. "Oh, yes," I said, angling my body to keep him from having a closer look. "Letters from Mrs. Leavitt."

"Why did he not just have them posted?"

I gave a little shrug. "Since he could not frank it, as Papa is able, I assume he did not want the cost of it to fall to another ... not when he intended to visit."

"It is a very *lofty* sum." There were questions in his eyes.

"Is your visitor gone already?" Ruth asked, walking across the entry hall with Sarah in tow. "I had hoped to be introduced after you spoke in private."

I tilted my head to the side. "He could not stay long, but I shall gladly introduce you if he pays us another visit." I did not mention that it was not likely to occur within the fortnight.

"And he is your uncle?" Ruth bit at her lip. "No. Your cousin?"

"My father's cousin."

Ruth nodded absently. "I knew it was something like that." She hesitated. "I'm grateful you were able to see him, but he did interrupt our lesson. And I'm certain you were just arriving at the best part. You will continue?"

I laughed, gripping the letters and pinning them tight against me. "Perhaps tomorrow. I believe Augustus will quite agree we have covered enough for the time being."

"Very well." Ruth gave a small pout before something caught her eyes out the open door behind me. "Oh look, Aunt Marina has returned." Both ladies squeezed between me and Augustus, hurrying out the door to meet her.

I took a step toward the staircase. "I believe I will go and rest a while in my room."

Augustus gave a small nod before taking a step to follow Ruth and Sarah outside. He paused, glancing over his shoulder. "Do enjoy reading your letters."

All I could manage was a thin-lipped smile before he stepped through the doorway.

I TOSSED Mother's letters on the bed and stared at them. My stomach tightened at the evidence of my betrayal laid out before me. But what could I have done? The lie had been forced upon me by Papa. Yet, undoubtedly, I was the one who made the request to be free of Sandson Hall, and I had willingly complied when Papa offered me the choice. I was nearly as guilty as Papa was, and Mother would be livid to discover our deceit. For that purpose, I could not give Mother reason to suspect anything was amiss and risk leaving Fairhaven. With new resolve, I broke the seal on the first letter.

Arabella,

I hope this letter finds you well, and that the Leavitts are tolerable enough company that you have no regrets having complied with your father's arrangement. Your Aunt Priscilla has mentioned your absence repeatedly and, in truth, our entire party is keenly aware of it. I do long to know how you are faring, so please write. And do not forget your promise.

My regards,
Mother

I broke the seal on the next, unfolding it, and skimming the contents. It was, not surprisingly, similar in both sentiments and instructions, the only addition being news that my cousin, Angelica, and her husband had joined them at Sandson. The knowledge of the possible massacre I had avoided at the hands of my scornful relatives made me more grateful for Papa's intervention, despite his secrets and means for accomplishing it.

Before refolding the letter, the line before Mother's signature captured my notice.

I do expect to have a letter awaiting me when I return to London early next week. Do not disappoint me.

All too aware that there was no way forward but to continue in the deceit, I sat at the writing desk and penned a letter to Mother describing my *tolerable* time at Mr. Leavitt's. When I finished, I grabbed another sheet of paper to write Papa and demand a more thorough account of my being at Fairhaven. But it would not do to risk provoking him, nor did I trust Mother wouldn't get her hands on it first, and without a drop of ink on it, I returned the paper to the stack.

A light tap sounded at the door just as I finished. "Who is there?"

"Leah, miss."

I finished folding the letter. "Come in."

Leah stuck her head in the door, looking rather pleased with herself.

"What is it?"

"I have finished altering a few of Miss Seton's dresses. I thought you'd wish to approve them before they are returned to her wardrobe."

I stood, quelling my excitement. "Bring them in."

The door opened further, revealing several dresses already slung over Leah's arm.

I gestured her to the bed. "You may set them there."

She did so, laying each one out with care.

I leaned in to appraise the added trimmings and embellishments, as well as the more fashionable cuts she had managed to adjust on two of them. "You have quite a talent."

Leah lowered her gaze. "Thank you, miss. Would you prefer I leave them here for Ruth to have a look, or should I return them to her wardrobe?"

I looked back at the dresses, still in awe of their subtle, yet noticeable, transformation. "Here is suitable. And, Leah ..." I paused, uncertain why I suddenly wished to traverse the necessary gap between servant and mistress. "Perhaps you'd care to be present when Ruth is shown the dresses? Being that you are the one who should receive her gratitude."

Leah's eyes lifted, a tentative smile on her face. "Only if you are certain, miss?"

"I am."

CHAPTER FOURTEEN

"Oh—look at them! They are so lovely!" Ruth's gaze moved across the dresses, taking in every detail Leah had painstakingly added to improve them. "Look here, at the lace." Ruth pointed at the newly added trimming on a violet day dress. "Did you ever think such an addition could so alter the entire appearance?"

I stepped forward, appraising the bodice and the sleeves. "It is stunning. And the handiwork is meticulously done."

Ruth's arms twitched at her side, as though they longed to reach out and take hold of me. "Thank you, Bella. A thousand times over. Thank you."

"Leah is the one you should thank, not me."

Ruth spun toward Leah, moving to her side so quickly Leah had no time to prepare for the force of her embrace. "I know I'm not supposed to hug people, with me becoming a distinguished lady and all, but I cannot help myself. I am so full of gratitude."

"You are welcome." Leah was most unsuccessful at hiding her delight, and I too found myself mirroring her expression. "But they were Miss Godwin's trimmings I used."

As Ruth faced me, I waved a dismissive hand. "It is nothing."

"For you." Ruth clasped her hands in front of her chest. "But for me it means the world."

"Then I'm glad for it."

Ruth walked back over to the bed. "I wonder which I shall wear tonight to the Whitmores'."

"The Whitmores'?"

"Oh, yes. I forgot to tell you in my excitement at seeing the dresses." Ruth picked up a pink one with a newly added lace overlay on the bodice, holding it to her body and swaying back and forth. "Mother saw the Whitmores at the haberdashers today. Apparently, they requested we dine with them this evening at Safford Park."

"How delightful your families are so close that the Whitmores needn't offer adequate notice." I offered a heavy smile, hoping I had a few more in me for the night ahead. I was already exhausted after my visit with Mr. Leavitt.

Ruth returned the pink dress and reached for another, holding it up to her again and resuming her sway. "Which is your favorite? I honestly can't decide. I look at one, and I am certain that is it, then another catches my eye. I suppose it is kind of like the roses."

"Yes. Do not declare yourself prematurely." I scanned the dresses again. "Though I am partial to the—"

"The white one," Ruth said with a laugh, following my line of sight. "Refined but still breathtaking."

I shot her a disapproving look, though I could not hide my amusement. "You were eaves-dropping on my conversation with Augustus?"

She beamed back at me, returning the dress to the bed.

"It was hardly eavesdropping when you were aware I was standing the next path over."

I shook my head in disbelief.

Ruth paused, her face still alight. "May I not relish in the two of you being together again? Especially after Augustus spent years insisting it would never be so, that you were gone from our lives forever?" She clasped my hands in hers. "I never lost hope though. Well, in seeing you again, that is." She paused. "I suppose not everything can be just as I imagined it."

"Whatever do you mean?"

Ruth bit at her lip. "Do not be vexed at me for saying such a thing, but my only disappointment came in hearing you were nearly engaged to Lord Thorton. You see, I had maintained a silly hope that after all those years apart, you and Augi would find one another again and fall in love. Though he's never said as much, it is obvious he has always fancied you, and I had thought ..." Her lips jutted out into a perfect pout. "Well, it does not matter what I thought, such a hopeless romantic that I am."

"We are at least all together again." I forced my gaze from her, allowing it to drift over the dresses again. "As lovely as these dresses are, I believe you are in need of a gown for full-dress. Perhaps we could commission one in an ivory silk? I daresay that would suit you well."

"That sounds lovely!" I was relieved to see how willingly Ruth had moved on from her irksome comment, until her smile faltered. "But I hate to ask Augustus to see to such an expense." Ruth paused. "Are you aware of my situation? That I have no money of my own?"

I sent Leah a knowing glance, and she quickly excused herself.

"Augustus told me," I said, moving to Ruth's side and placing my arm around her. "And I'm so very sorry for all the loss you've had. But you must realize that you are not a burden, Ruth. I have seen it in Augustus's eyes. You are as dear to him as a sister, and surely you would not believe he would deny Sarah such a request."

"I suppose not."

"But he cannot know what you require if you do not tell him." When Ruth's countenance did not alter, I leaned in closer. "I will talk to him, if you wish."

The smile returned to her lips.

"Considering you never had a proper coming out, I might even convince him to hold a gathering in your honor—after you've completed your training, of course."

Ruth squealed in delight, twirling toward me and wrapping me in an embrace. For once, I fully welcomed it.

RUTH GAVE a pout as we made our way back to the drawing room of Safford Park. "I do wish Sarah would have been allowed to join us. Chicken and mushroom vol-au-vents is one of her favorite dishes."

I released a small sigh, in no mood to revisit Ruth's disappointment at not having Sarah here yet again. "She is not out in Society, Ruth. It is the proper thing for her to remain home."

"But she always comes to Safford Park with us."

"Not when a gentleman is visiting."

We stepped into the drawing room and meandered to the far side together. It was quite a bit grander than Fairhaven, and I could not help but admire the elegant furnishings and rich colors that were evidence of the Whitmores' wealth. "Does this room not remind you of Fellerton?"

Ruth mirrored my appraisal. "It is most similar, isn't

it?" She tipped her head to the side, as though the change in perspective would better help her identify the similarities. "How odd I should not have recognized it before now. The tapestry on the side opposite the hearth … and the maroon wall color. Even the gold framing around the paintings seem to be the very same." She righted the angle of her head and smiled at me. "Perhaps that is why I have always adored Safford Park. Well that, and the Whitmores being here, of course."

"Of course."

She paused, appraising the room a second time. "I wonder if I will now find that some of the other rooms have a likeness to Fellerton as well. Though I must admit, my memories of it are growing dim considering how long it has been since I've seen it."

"Where is Fellerton?" Mr. Treynor asked, stepping to join us. "If you don't mind my intrusion, of course."

I gave him a polite smile. "Near Bath. It is my family's estate."

"Candace mentioned the two of you were childhood friends long separated?"

Ruth bobbed her head up and down. "The best of friends, just as we are again."

"But how did—"

"Are the gentlemen not taking port?" I asked before Mr. Treynor could continue his interrogation. I was in no mood to turn tales as to the reasoning behind our separation, especially with the risk of Ruth contradicting them.

He shook his head. "I was not opposed, but Mr. Brundage preferred to defer and rejoin the group."

"Shall we begin our game of Lanterloo, then?" I glanced around to see where the others had gone, when my gaze fell on Augustus and Miss Whitmore standing together a ways off. Despite my best attempt, I could not look away as he slipped her what appeared to be a missive. Miss Whitmore glanced toward her inattentive mother before she offered Augustus a timid smile. He leaned in and whispered something to her, causing my stomach to clench at the sight. I forced my consideration back to Mr. Treynor. "I hear you enjoy horses, sir?"

Mr. Treynor illuminated. "I do. In truth, I hope to breed them one day."

"Though I have never cared much for the creatures, Ruth here adores them."

She nodded. "Oh, I do. My uncle bought me one of the finest horses in all of England before he died. Her name is Guinevere, and she is as fast as she is beautiful."

Mr. Treynor's eyes moved across Ruth's features with interest. "Do you know her parentage?"

Ruth's mouth opened then closed again. "No. I haven't much considered pedigrees before."

He gave a small nod, and silence reigned.

"Mr. Treynor, I fear I'm quite parched," I said, offering an apologetic look. "Would you retrieve me a refreshment?"

"Of course." He took two steps back before pausing. "And you, Miss Seton? Are you thirsty also?"

She shook her head.

He gave a nod and started toward the refreshments on the other side of the room.

I glanced toward Ruth. "Do you remember what I taught you earlier today?"

Her nose scrunched in confusion. "It's all a blur."

"When he returns with my drink, you must flatter him."

Ruth shook her head, a terrified expression on her face. "No. Surely I will make a mess of it."

"You shall not. Simply act interested in what he enjoys."

"And what is that?"

I repressed a moan. "Pedigrees and breeding."

Her eyes flew to Mr. Treynor as he finished filling the glass for me. "But I know nothing about any of it," she said, her voice a forced whisper.

"You needn't know a thing. All you must do is encourage and compliment him along the way."

Panic filled her features. "Why don't you do it? You said you'd show me how it's done."

"Because I know you can." I paused. "And because I'm quite certain I glimpsed a spark of intrigue when he looked at you just now."

"Here you are, Miss Godwin," Mr. Treynor said, approaching with my drink.

I took hold of it. "Thank you." My gaze flickered back to Ruth, who stood motionless with her mouth agape. "In your absence, Ruth mentioned that the reason she does not care for pedigrees is because she knows so little about them. But, if perhaps someone could assist her ..."

A small grin appeared on Mr. Treynor's lips.

"I do long to know more," she said, her blush absolutely perfect. "That is if you don't mind sharing some of what you know."

A smile filled Mr. Treynor's features. "I would be most pleased to oblige you. What is it you desire to understand?"

Her eyes moved to me, but all I offered was an encouraging nod. "Well," she said, giving him her full attention. "I suppose one must start at the beginning."

He took a breath. "Well, a pedigree is an ancestral history of the horse. Not simply its sire and dam, nor a step up in generations from there, but the tracing of its lineage to specific and notable bloodlines. You see, a winning thoroughbred will likely have a healthy mix of English and Arabian ancestry."

"And why is that?" Ruth asked, now completely focused on him.

"Well, Arabian horses are lighter and faster with more stamina. English breeds are of larger size, so when they were first bred the offspring were—"

"Larger than the Arabians, but still fast with stamina."

Mr. Treynor's delight mirrored Ruth's. "Precisely."

"It is all quite brilliant, I suppose. I can understand why you find it so fascinating." Ruth faltered ever so briefly before she found her next question. "But how do you know which bloodlines are superior?"

Not wanting to distract Ruth from her purpose, I repressed an excited smile by taking a sip of my drink. She continued on marvelously as Mr. Treynor explained how to ensure the best outcome for siring a quality racing horse. Though I cared little for such information, watching the two of them get along was preferable to watching Augustus and Miss Whitmore doing so.

Augustus stepped to my side, the warmth of him absurdly gratifying. When I saw that Miss Whitmore was no longer with him, I set my drink down and took hold of his arm. "I was hoping to have a word with you." Mr. Treynor's gaze flicked toward us, and I hurried to pull Augustus away before the interruption could disrupt Ruth's success.

We took several steps away, and he leaned in close. "What is it you wish to discuss?"

"I merely did not wish for you to disturb Ruth and Mr. Treynor when they are getting on so well." Augustus hardly looked thrilled with my reasoning, but I tightened my grip on him so he would be obliged to stay. "But now that you mention it. You have reminded me of something I wish to speak to you about. You see, I asked my maid to update a few of Ruth's dresses, and we noticed that she is in need of a gown for full-dress."

"And you wished to see about having one commissioned?"

I gave a small shrug. "If that is agreeable. One should be perfectly sufficient, or perhaps two. For she will require a ball gown also."

Augustus gave an amused shake of his head. "Two it is, but I trust you will be economical in your selections."

"I shall be as careful as if it were being made at my own expense."

His gaze moved over my gown in a way that brought a blush to my cheeks, before a teasing smile lifted onto his lips. "On second thought, you should consider inviting my mother along."

"So little trust." I nudged my shoulder into him, feeling no need to confirm I had already planned on speaking with Mrs. Brundage about the matter.

Our regard moved back to Mr. Treynor and Ruth. "And I suppose that is your doing?"

I lifted my chin. "It is."

He studied their interaction for a moment. "He does seem susceptible to such flattery, doesn't he?"

With Augustus's acknowledgment, I could not refuse a smile.

He shook his head and looked back to me. "Weren't you supposed to be the one with that focused look of fascination Ruth is now donning?"

"Sometimes one learns by watching, other times by doing."

"Well, the whole thing will end soon if he takes one

more step toward her. They are more than close enough to carry on a conversation."

I laughed, craning my neck up to look at him. "Hypocrite."

The warmth of his nearness penetrated into my skin, causing it to prickle. "I suppose you do have a point. But again, I would argue that we are an exception to the rule ... being the old friends that we are."

I lifted a brow. "And yet it seems I am not the only exception to the rule." My gaze flickered to Miss Whitmore who spoke with Mrs. Brundage and her mother on the settee. "There are apparently others privileged enough to be treated as an *old friend*."

He tilted his head to the side, his lips curving upward.

Before he could offer a retort on my jealous nature a second time, I gave a small pout. "You are absolutely tiresome. Do you know that?"

"You make it sound as though that is a bad thing."

My lips parted in exasperation. "It is fortunate for you that I am no longer an impressionable young lady."

"And why is that?"

I ignored the trembling within me. "For it is no easy thing for such a woman to discover a man's attentions are not exclusive to her alone."

His eyes searched mine, his smile fading. "I suppose it is like a man discovering that a woman's affections are promised elsewhere entirely."

The air around me grew thick, but I did not look away. I could not appear weak. I could not be that young lady I had just claimed I was not. "Then let us be glad we are friends and nothing more."

His countenance fell. "Shall we see if the others are ready for that game of cards?"

I followed him back to where Ruth and Mr. Treynor were still happily chatting.

"Forgive me," Mr. Treynor said as we approached, shooting Ruth an apologetic smile. "I fear I have rattled on far too long."

"There is no need to ask forgiveness, Mr. Treynor." Ruth fluttered her lashes at him, causing Augustus to avert his eyes in exasperation. "It was I who desired your rattling."

He smiled, his gaze resting on Ruth a moment longer.

"Yet I am suddenly most eager to begin our game of Lanterloo." Augustus took hold of Ruth's arm and placed it in the crook of his elbow.

Mr. Treynor swallowed, eagerly shifting away from Augustus. "Cousin," he called to Miss Whitmore. "Do you care to join us for cards?"

"Absolutely." Miss Whitmore whispered something to her mother and Mrs. Brundage, causing them to laugh, and started toward us. Her dark hair glistened in the firelight, and I couldn't help but notice her graceful beauty, despite my attempts to overlook it.

She flashed me a kind smile that somehow only made me feel defeated. "Are we playing three card Loo or five?"

I glanced toward the fire. "Perhaps a game of whist would be preferred?"

Ruth scrunched her nose. "But whist is only for four players, and there are five of us."

I gave her a small smile, refusing to look at Augustus. "I fear I have a headache coming on and should sit this hand out." And all the subsequent hands.

Ruth's face filled with concern. "Should we return to Fairhaven so you can rest?"

I had no intention of thwarting Ruth's continued success with Mr. Treynor. "No. It is only a minor one. I shall go sit near your aunt and Mrs. Whitmore for a time but will join you later if I feel up to it." Ruth gave a small pout, and I placed a reassuring hand on her arm. "Do not make a fuss, my dear friend. I shall be right over there, watching."

Without another word, I walked toward the settee where the two women spoke in hushed voices. Not wishing to interrupt them, I continued on and took a seat near the fire. Several minutes later, Ruth's giggle tempted my notice to the foursome seated about the card table. As my gaze skirted about their delighted expressions, it landed on Augustus, whose worried eyes met mine. I offered a quick nod and leaned into the wing-back chair, allowing the side of it to conceal me from his questioning stare.

CHAPTER FIFTEEN

*R*uth dropped her needle-work to her lap. "I still cannot believe how easy it was to encourage Mr. Treynor along in conversation." She shifted her smile to Sarah. "If only you had been there to witness it."

Sarah poked the needle through her sampler. "I would have liked to have seen your success."

The disappointment in her voice was evident, and I hated to hear it. "Perhaps we should go on a *family* outing with the Whitmores. That way you could join us."

Sarah met my gaze. "To the seaside?"

"I don't see why not, as long as your mother and Augustus are amenable."

The ladies shared a smile.

Ruth leaned back, stretching out her legs. "I do hope it can be arranged before Mr. Treynor departs."

I shimmied my needle up through the linen. "And when is that, exactly?"

Ruth pouted. "Sometime next week. He has already extended his stay a few days, but he must soon return home to help his father with some business." She released an audible breath. "At least he promised to return for my coming out event, whenever that shall be."

I lifted my eyes from my sampler. "When did he make such a promise?"

Ruth's expression grew thoughtful. "I suppose it was not an actual promise, but the terms of a wager."

"You were making bets with Mr. Treynor?" I could not keep the concern from my voice.

"I'm trying to remember exactly how it came to be." She scrunched her nose. "For some reason, he mentioned that Mrs. Whitmore believes that Augustus intends to offer for Candace soon." Ruth looked to both Sarah and me, apparently ensuring we found the notion as amusing as she did. "Apparently there is supposed to be a wedding by the end of summer."

I looked down at my sampler again, attempting to convey disinterest. "And you do not believe such an event will take place?"

"No. Augustus and Candace are dear friends, nothing more."

"And yet Mrs. Whitmore believes it a possibility?"

"Mr. Treynor said so. Then he insisted that the best of marriages are built on friendship. And though I agreed with him, I said they must also be built on love." Ruth giggled. "You should have seen the shade of red his face turned when I mentioned the word."

"And what is he to get if he wins?"

"Mr. Treynor only asked to ride Guinevere." Ruth paused, her expression full of contrition. "In truth, I am attempting not to feel too guilty about the arrangement, considering I would have allowed him to ride Guinevere if he had just asked. But my solace is that I am not wrong, so it shan't matter."

I did not glance up. "You do sound quite confident in your opinion."

"Because I am."

I tied a knot in the thread before it grew too short to work with and grabbed the sewing shears. "And why is that?"

"Because he loves you, of course."

My gaze moved to her so quickly that I clipped the tip of my forefinger with the shears. The pain was immediate. "Drat!" I cried, dropping my sampler.

I examined the damage, a trickle of blood trailing down my finger.

Ruth jumped to her feet, only to stand there motionless, the color draining from her face. "You are bleeding, Bella."

"Do sit down, Ruth." I stood. "It is only a small cut. If I can find something to wrap it with, I shall be right in no time." I glanced around for anything that could work as a bandage, but there was nothing suitable. If only I'd had the foresight to bring down my entire sewing box and not just my sampler and one color of thread.

I appraised Ruth, who stood unmoved, her focus locked on the crimson liquid. She lifted a hand to her paling cheek. "I think I may faint ... or perhaps be sick."

Shifting my hand out of view, I gestured for Sarah's aid. "Will you please help Ruth to sit while I go to my room for a piece of linen?"

Sarah nodded, and though her face was nearly as ashen as her cousin's, she assisted Ruth back to the settee.

I glanced down at the ground to make certain I had managed to contain the blood thus far. Though it was not Axminster carpet beneath my feet, even a Wilton should not have its repeated pattern soiled by red droplets, especially one of this lighter blue shade. When my eyes lifted, their terrified expressions were still on me. I offered one last smile of appeasement. "I shall dress this and be back shortly."

Hurrying into the entry hall, I began up the stairs when heavy footsteps echoed behind me.

"Bella."

I paused, concealing my hand behind my skirts. I had no desire for Augustus to catch sight of my folly. "Yes?"

"I was wondering if I might have a word?"

I glanced down at my finger, the pain increasing a touch more with each beat of my heart. "Can it wait? I was just headed to my room. I should not be long."

Augustus started up the stairs, a grin on his face. "What are you hiding?"

I angled my body away from him as he neared. "Nothing."

"Shall I guess?"

Well aware he would not soon relent, I brandished my hand.

His eyes moved from the small amount of blood now accumulating in my cupped hand to my face. "What the deuce happened?"

I started up the stairs again. "Just a slight clip with some sewing shears. I didn't have anything to wrap about it, so it looks worse than it is."

He caught up with me and reached for my hand. "Let me see it."

"I'm quite capable of dressing something as minor as this."

He laughed and shook his head, bounding ahead of me before turning to barricade my way up. "It is not you I'm concerned for, but the preservation of our carpets along the corridor." He winked and reached out his hand. "Now, let me see the damage."

I gave an audible huff to make certain he knew of my vexation, then held out my injured finger. He descended a step and took hold of my hand, cradling it in his. The tenderness of his touch and the warmth of his skin on mine sent my heart racing, my finger throbbing with each pulsation. "See, it is nothing."

"Though I believe there won't be a need to call upon the surgeon, this is hardly nothing." He tilted my hand from one side to the other to get a closer look. "You must be a very aggressive seamstress."

I lifted an unimpressed brow. "Do let me know when you are finished insulting me so I can take care of the problem at hand."

Augustus laughed, pulling a handkerchief from his pocket. "Problem at hand," he repeated, shaking his head and pressing the linen into my palm to absorb the blood. "How do you manage to be witty even in distress?"

"Because I am not in distress."

He lifted the now red-stained handkerchief and began wiping at the remaining blood along my finger with the clean portion. "Then why do you breathe like you are?"

It was only then that I noticed how quickly my chest was rising and falling, and the realization of my foolish reaction sent my cheeks ablaze. I closed my hand around the handkerchief and freed my hand from his. "Thank you. I believe I can manage from here."

A side of Augustus's mouth lifted. "But you have grown flush." He descended a stair, so that we now stood next to one another, and placed a hand on my back, gesturing me forward. His closeness did nothing to calm me. "I had best see you to your room to make certain you don't faint along the way. I know how ladies cannot abide the sight of blood."

The sight of my blood had nothing to do with my

current state, and I thought to say as much, but I was certain that was precisely what he wished me to do—thereby acknowledging that it was, in reality, he who affected me so. Well, I would not. With new determination, I lifted my chin and began up the stairs again. "What was it you wished to speak to me about?" I asked, glancing over my shoulder in an attempt to appear unruffled.

He started up after me. "I believe I may possibly owe you an apology."

I sent him a skeptical glance as he came to my side at the top. "You sound so certain of it."

"Well, the truth is, I'm not entirely sure how I offended you. That is why I need you to clarify, so that I might beg your forgiveness."

I scoffed. "I shall need more specifics than that, or you may find yourself apologizing for a myriad of things you had no intention of seeking my forgiveness for." I shot him a playful smile, but he was not looking at me.

"Last night. What did I do to upset you? You hardly spoke to me after our conversation."

I pursed my lips, pretending ignorance. "I can't think of anything."

"Was it my comment about your affections being placed elsewhere?"

My heart skipped a beat, and I rebuked it for its nonsensical reaction. It did not matter that he acknowledged his comment had been about me, nor that he cared where I should place my affections, for it would not change my course. Augustus could not offer me what Lord Thorton could—not a title, nor great wealth, nor status. And even if I could convince myself that those things did not matter, they certainly mattered to my parents. Mother would not tolerate my passing on Lord Thorton for the son of an obscure gentleman, let alone when she discovered that gentleman was Augustus. A chill ran down my spine.

"I cannot think that was it, as I did not suspect you were speaking of me in particular." I smiled through my lie, relieved to have arrived at my door. In haste, I grabbed the knob. "I thank you for your assistance and your haphazard apology. But as you can see, I am quite well and am capable of carrying on myself."

I opened the door and stepped through, but Augustus did not leave. Instead he paused at the threshold and leaned against the frame.

"What are you doing?"

He only smiled. "You were truly unaware I spoke of you?"

I turned my back on him, thankful I had the excuse of retrieving my sewing basket. "Perhaps I questioned it for the briefest of moments." I opened the top of the basket and rummaged through the contents for a spare piece of linen. There were too many ribbons and strings to sift through with one hand and, in my agitation, I overturned the contents onto the desk. "But then I also wondered if you spoke of Miss Whitmore, or perhaps another lady."

"I spoke of you, Bella, and you alone."

I froze, my mind completely going blank. The throbbing in my finger forced me to my senses, and I snatched up a partially completed sampler and awkwardly took my extra pair of shears to cut a strip off the end. Relinquishing the bloody handkerchief on top of the contents of my sewing box, I lifted the linen to begin wrapping.

"You must wash it first." Augustus gestured toward the water basin placed on a small table near the door where he stood.

I drew in a steadying breath and moved toward him, dipping my hand in the clear water and scrubbing at the dried blood until the water was tinted pink. When I finally submerged the tip of my finger, I winced at the stinging sensation, and a pitiful whimper escaped.

Augustus took a small step toward me, a look of concern in his features. "May I assist you?"

I shook my head, well aware that his touch could be my undoing. I already felt weak. I had no intention of compromising my resolve further. After drying my hands, I wrapped the linen around my finger, pulling it taut with each rotation. I could feel Augustus watching me, and after a few failed attempts to secure the end with only one hand, I held out my finger to him in surrender. "Perhaps you could tie it off for me?"

With an all-too-amused expression, he took hold of my hand a second time.

I looked toward the window, refusing to take notice of anything besides the afternoon light filtering through the panes of glass.

"There you go." His hands lingered on mine.

I swiftly lifted the bulky dressing to show off our success, hoping to keep the mood light. "Hardly noticeable, I think."

He smiled but didn't respond as he studied me.

"Well, shall we go down?" I asked a touch too cheerily, so that it sounded false even to my own ears. "I believe I left Ruth and Sarah in quite the state of distress. They shall be eager to know how I fared."

Augustus crossed his arms and leaned against the doorframe again.

I gave another small huff and tilted my head to the side. "What is it now?"

"You seem eager to avoid my declaration."

I gave a small shrug, as though my entire body was not trembling on the inside. "In all honesty, I am not avoiding it, I simply believed it to be hardly worth mentioning, considering we are *friends*, and friends should clearly be concerned with the other's welfare."

His gaze lowered momentarily before lifting again to mine. "As enjoyable as these games we play are, Bella, I am growing weary of concealing my true feelings."

The familiar look in his eyes made my heart start into a frenzy. It was a look I knew well, and I could not bear to see Augustus hurt in the same way I had hurt so many gentlemen before him. Nor could I bear the risk of seeing that same look fade over time. It would be detrimental to us both for him to declare himself. "Really, Augustus, we should go back down."

"Not until I tell you that—"

"Please stop." My voice caught, and I released a shaky exhale. "You must not say it."

He took a step closer, and the movement nearly toppled the poorly-constructed wall around my heart. "I cannot bear to know I did not take hold of the opportunity when it was given me—before it was too late."

I shook my head, frantically searching the ground at my side as though it held the inconceivable answer of how to proceed. "It could never work between us. My parents would not allow for it, and I ... well, I have plans, Augustus. You cannot simply stroll back into my life and disrupt everything I have worked for."

With one final step, he closed the space between us, and my whole being went into turmoil—my heart and my head both battling for control. His fingertips brushed down my arms, and I shut my eyes in an attempt to close myself off from the pleasurable sensation, but instead it was only magnified. Then one of his hands moved to my neck. His thumb stroked my cheek, and I opened my eyes to find his face only a breath from mine. Instinctively I tilted my chin upward. I needed to pull away, and yet I longed to draw closer, to again feel his lips on mine. I leaned in.

"Oh, heavens! Forgive me." Mrs. Brundage's quiet exclamation pierced through the silence around us, and I shoved myself out of Augustus's embrace. The shocked expression of Mrs. Brundage gaped at us from the doorway—her arm lifted as though preventing someone at her side from seeing what she had.

"What is it?" Ruth asked, peeking around her aunt's outstretched arm. Her eyes fell on Augustus then moved to me and my horrifyingly red face. "What were the two of you doing in Bella's bedroom alone? Was this another one of your assessments?"

Mrs. Brundage's confused expression lingered on Ruth then moved back to us.

"No," Augustus said, appearing utterly unaffected. "I was simply aiding Bella with her injured finger, and she wished to thank me."

I looked at Augustus in disbelief, giving a swift shake of my head. "That is not true. I would not kiss him for such a trivial thing as that."

Ruth's mouth gaped open, and she tugged Sarah into view, apparently feeling it necessary for all parties present to witness the mortifying scene. "The two of you were kissing just now?" Ruth asked, delighted.

"No." I directed my imploring gaze to Augustus, but the smirk that dominated his lips made it apparent he would be of no help to me. "We had not actually kissed … yet. Nor would we have … most likely." I cringed at my own blabbering explanation, realizing it was doing little to improve upon the situation.

Mrs. Brundage held a hand over her mouth, and my stomach clenched, waiting to see if she would break down in tears or scold us for our scandalous act. But, instead, laughter sounded through her fingers. "It seems I must keep a better watch on the two of you. If I had known I was supposed to be playing chaperone, I would have done a more thorough job of it from the start."

Augustus smiled. "Oh, do not be hard on yourself, Mother. We did not mind your negligence in the least." He looked toward me. "Did we, Bella?"

All eyes settled on me, and a second wave of heat moved through my face. "I believe the answer is quite obvious at this moment."

Mrs. Brundage pursed her lips, making Ruth and Sarah giggle.

"Well"—Augustus gave a loud clap of his hands and rubbed them together—"was your impeccable timing no more than cruel fate or was there a particular reason for it?"

Mrs. Brundage glanced toward my hand. "The girls told me of Miss Godwin's embroidery incident. We were simply coming to check that all was well."

I lifted my bandaged finger. The only evidence of any bleeding was a small spot of red that had seeped through the linen. "Good as new."

Ruth slipped through the doorway to take a place at my side. "I am so relieved. I could not believe how much blood there was. I'm not certain I shall ever be able to embroider again, knowing what the consequence could be."

I dipped my chin. "I assure you, in all my years of needlework, I have never done such a careless thing before."

Ruth nodded, hardly looking reassured.

"Oh, that is the other thing," Mrs. Brundage said,

holding out a missive for Augustus. "Owen has written to you."

Augustus took hold of the letter and broke the seal. As he unfolded it, a smaller missive dropped to the floor, and he quickly retrieved it, tucking it into his waistcoat pocket. He scanned the contents of the letter, his brow furrowing as he continued.

"What is it?" Mrs. Brundage asked, equally aware of the change in Augustus's countenance.

His eyes were full of disappointment when they met mine. "It seems I must leave without delay."

CHAPTER SIXTEEN

"*L*eave?" Mrs. Brundage asked. "For what purpose?" I watched intently as Augustus released a heavy breath, his gaze returning to the letter in hand. "Owen has uncovered evidence that could potentially affect the Setons' case."

"What evidence?" Ruth's voice was subdued.

Augustus tilted his head to one side, hesitation evident in his features. "If I discover there is something to tell you, I will."

Ruth bit at her lip. "But only if it is good news."

"Of course."

She gave a small nod, appearing relieved by Augustus's agreement.

"When do you leave?" I asked, attempting to conceal the disappointment in my voice.

"I'm afraid I cannot delay. Owen expects the hearing will take place within the next fortnight, and all evidence must be compiled before it begins."

Now it was my turn to offer a timid nod in lieu of a response, trying to convince myself it was for the good of both of us that he was leaving. I needed to fortify my defenses in his absence.

Augustus glanced around at our solemn expressions. "Come now, it should only take a matter of days."

I forced out a smile for his sake. "We ladies have much to occupy our time, don't we?" Ruth and Sarah nodded in unison, and I looked back to Augustus. "Though I may need Mr. Treynor to assist me with a lesson or two in your absence."

Augustus's lips lifted into a glorious smile, just as I'd hoped. "I must insist you hold off on those lessons requiring the aid of a gentleman until my return."

Ruth and Sarah laughed, but I gave a small lift of my chin. "Then you'd best be on your way so that you may return before I am forced to press on without you."

"You wouldn't."

I lifted a brow.

"Very well." Augustus stepped in front of me and took hold of my unbandaged hand. He paused. "Do wait for me, Bella." I was certain he spoke of more than the lessons.

My heart pattered about recklessly, and though I tried to keep myself from agreeing, my attempt was halfhearted at best. "I will."

He lifted my hand and placed his lips to my knuckles. So tender was the gesture, I dropped my gaze for fear he, or one of our onlookers, would glimpse the undeniable pleasure that coursed through me because of it. When he released my hand, I clasped it in my other, waiting for my self-control to return. When I finally looked up, he had just kissed his mother's cheek.

He offered me one last adoring smile. "Take care, all of you."

"You also," I said, and he disappeared through the open door. The room fell silent, and we listened to his muffled footsteps retreat down the carpeted corridor. A strange desire to go after him flooded over me, but I disregarded it. What good would it do either of us?

"I still cannot believe you and Augustus nearly kissed," Ruth chirped, acknowledging the very topic I most wished to avoid in his absence.

Mrs. Brundage pressed her lips together. I wondered if she meant to say something, but then she took a step backward. "I will go see about Cook packing a little something for Augustus to take with him. Do excuse me."

Relief flooded over me. The moment she left, I pulled Sarah inside with me and Ruth and closed the door.

"Ruth, you must not speak of it." I released a breath. "It was a moment of weakness, that is all."

"So you do not love him?" Ruth asked, sincere disappointment in her features.

I walked to the writing desk, righted the sewing basket, and began filling it with the spilled contents. "It would not matter if I did. A union between us is impossible."

"But why?" Ruth moved to my side to aid me in my cleanup.

Uncertain how I could even explain the situation without revealing too much, I shrugged. "It's complicated, Ruth."

"But if you love each other—"

"No," I said, a tad too forcefully out of frustration. "Forgive me. It's just that love is not an option I can consider. I am expected to marry someone of equal rank, if not higher. Someone with connections and a fortune—a gentleman like Lord Thorton." I paused, wishing I could explain that love was not enduring. That I'd witnessed its brittleness too many times. But Ruth would only assure me that Augustus would always love me. I knew better. Love always faded. Besides, Augustus had once chosen Ruth's happiness over mine, and though I could not blame him for it, it would be naïve to think it could not happen again with someone else. No, it was safer to marry for convenience. "I am told a mutual fondness often grows in such arrangements. And that is enough for me." It had to be.

"My parents never grew to love one another."

I took Ruth's hand in mine. Though I could not say as much, nor that Augustus had been my informant, I understood her plight more than she knew.

Sarah stepped to my other side, handing me the last of the ribbons she had gathered. "So there is no hope of you becoming my sister?"

My heart nearly broke. "If not sisters, then we shall always be dear friends."

She gave a small smile. "Do all ladies have to sacrifice love for a suitable match?"

Unwilling to be the bearer of the news I had discovered—that even when love was present in the beginning it soon faded—I hesitated. "I suppose there are some who fall in love with their equal, though that seems to be more the exception. But there are nearly always tradeoffs if someone chooses love."

Ruth swayed back and forth, shifting her weight from one foot to the other. "Uncle Richard and Aunt Marina married for love."

"And how did her parents react?"

"They cut her off," Sarah said in a near whisper. "They never spoke to her again. And until they both died, Aunt Susan was forced to do likewise."

The room fell silent as the realization settled in. Life was not so romantic as the novels depicted, and I hated that it had to be me who told them so. At least I could take comfort in knowing I had not completely annihilated their hope in love. That realization would come in time and from their own experiences.

Ruth released a quick breath. "I often wonder what would have happened if my mother would have disobeyed my grandparents and refused my father. Or if the gentleman she had loved had not jilted her."

I attempted to not appear startled by her declaration. "Do you know who it was—that jilted her, I mean?"

"No. I only know that Father used to say"—Ruth's gaze turned distant, as though she were trying to recall the words with exactness—"that he would not have married my mother had he known he was getting another man's unwanted scraps."

My hand shot to my mouth, covering it. "That is a horrible thing to say."

Ruth gave a nod, her eyes blinking vacantly. "If only that were the worst of it."

"He treated her that way often, then?"

Ruth scrunched up her nose. "I'm not sure I have the most accurate perception, being as I was not yet eleven when they died. But I remember when Father got in one of his moods, Mother would send me out of doors or to the nursery, and I knew I was not to return until she or my nursemaid fetched me."

My heart broke as I thought of young Ruth being my near shadow all those years. Had that been part of the reason? "Why did you never speak of it to me?"

Ruth shrugged, the corner of her lips turned downward. "I suppose I didn't know it was something worth mentioning. And it wasn't as though he was always there, nor was he always like that. Sometimes my father was very kind. Especially when we had guests, or when Augi would come to stay. Father always had a high regard for Augi." Ruth smiled, as though her words had conjured some pleasant memory. "It was quite fortunate that Aunt Marina and Uncle Henry thought to send Augi to go to school in Bath so that he could stay with us during his time off."

It seemed Augustus had been Mrs. Seton's saving grace. At least until the end. "Was your father in one of his moods ... that day?" I scanned her face to determine if I had taken my inquiry too far.

"The day they died, you mean?" Ruth thought a moment. "No. Not that I recall. He had just returned to Blacksley the day before, and Augi was there for the week's end. Father and Augi had gone shooting that morning, and when they returned, we all ate luncheon together." Ruth squinted, as though recalling the memory took effort. "Mother then asked Augi to take me out fishing so we could have fresh trout for supper—Father's favorite. And Father was in a generous enough mood that he lent Augi his new pole."

That certainly didn't sound like the actions of a man planning to commit such an unspeakable crime. But I held my tongue.

Ruth reached forward to take a short piece of ribbon from my basket and began running it through her fingers mindlessly. "By the time we returned with our catch, my parents were already dead. The whole house in commotion as they tried to figure out what had happened and what to do." Ruth fixed her gaze on the ribbon. "And that was when Augustus brought me to Fellerton to be with you." She lifted her eyes to mine, tears glinting in them.

I put an arm around her, leaning my forehead against her temple. "I am so sorry for it all, Ruth," I whispered.

She gave a weak smile. "It was so long ago that I often feel as though I'm relaying someone else's story and not my own." She paused, drawing in a shaky breath. "Sometimes I wish I knew what had happened, though I'm not certain I could bear it. It is probably for the best I shall never know."

Sarah moved to Ruth's side, and Ruth reached out to grasp her hand. The three of us stood together for some time, the combination of the silence and my churning thoughts crushing down upon me. I needed to break free from the sorrow, and I wanted to bring Ruth and Sarah up with me. "I shared a kiss with Augustus ... a long time ago."

They both turned to face me, their brows lifting to frame their widened eyes. My diversion was working, for them as well as for me, and I hoped I would not later regret my admission. "It was not long before you left Bath, Ruth," I said, sending her an apologetic smile. "And I didn't tell you because I wasn't certain what to make of it myself."

Ruth pinned me with an expectant stare. "Well you know what to make of it now, so you must not leave out even a detail."

I laughed, and the simple act lifted me further out of the darkness. "Do you recall the time you were abed for those two weeks?"

Ruth's cheery expression faltered ever so slightly, and I paused. "Go on," she said, nodding her encouragement.

"Well, despite the impropriety of it, Augustus and I met in the woods as often as occasion would permit, which so happened to be very often, him being on a school holiday and my mother away visiting her sister until near the end of it. One afternoon he was teasing me mercilessly regarding my fondness for William Morris."

Ruth's face cheered again, and she laughed.

"Who is William Morris?" Sarah asked me.

"The son of one of our tenant farmers. Augustus had been writing me love letters and allowing me to believe they came from him."

Sarah giggled. "That does sound like something Augustus would do."

"Yes, well, it worked—at least somewhat. I did not fancy myself in love with William, but I admit the thought of being in love intrigued me greatly at the time. And William was quite handsome, was he not, Ruth?"

Ruth bobbed her head up and down in agreement.

"So, what happened?" Sarah asked.

"Well, during this particular afternoon together, he would not stop bombarding me about my feelings for William. Asking me what I thought of his letters, and if I would ever consider marrying a pig man's son." A smile crept onto my lips at the memory. "His persistence drove me to near madness, and I finally marched right up to him and told him that the only reason he cared was because he was jealous of William. That he was obviously besotted with me but was too much of a coward to tell me so."

Ruth covered her mouth. "That was exceptionally bold of you."

"I don't know what it is about Augustus, but he is the only one who can provoke me in such a way—get me to behave so out of character." I paused, recalling the scene in my memory as I had done so many times. "But once it was said, he did not deny it. We just stood there staring at one another, uncertain what to do next." I shook my head, amused at our clumsy attempt at first love. "Then, without warning, he pulled me in and kissed me." Warmth settled in my cheeks. "It was perfect. Full of light and hope."

Ruth evaluated me with a creased brow. "And that was the only time?"

"Yes." I lowered my gaze. "The next time Augustus came to Blacksley …" The words caught in my throat. "Well, that was the day your parents died."

"Well, perhaps it may not be your last."

I dropped my shoulders, looking between Ruth and Sarah's hopeful glances. "I fear with him it must be. But I shall always think fondly of our time in the woods. And his kiss."

Both ladies released an audible sigh, and I couldn't be certain that I did not join them without meaning to.

THE DAYS CRAWLED by as we awaited Augustus's return, and though I refused to admit to myself how desperately I missed him, my lessons were growing lackluster and laborious as a consequence of his continued absence. The most promising part of our week was visiting the modiste and having two gowns commissioned for Ruth—one in ivory silk and the other of gold colored tulle over white satin.

In a desperate attempt to keep my thoughts from dwelling on Augustus, I encouraged Mrs. Brundage to extend an invitation for the Whitmores to join us for the evening despite the improperly late notice. Yet dinner, with its false smiles and polite chatter, was hardly the relief I had hoped for, and when we entered the drawing room, I was exhausted.

Mr. Treynor stepped in behind me, and I smiled at him. "I do hope you are not put out by being the only gentleman among us this evening. I fear I had not thought of the consequence of our offer when I encouraged Mrs. Brundage to extend the invitation."

"I consider myself fortunate to represent my sex amongst such a charming group of women."

"Speaking of charming women," I said, lifting my chin in Ruth's direction. "Does Ruth not look stunning in that color? Lilac is most becoming on her."

Mr. Treynor followed my line of sight. "I daresay you are right. Lilac suits her perfectly."

"She mentioned that she was eager to speak with you. Something about Arabian horses."

His face colored to its familiar shade of red. "Is that so?"

"It seems you have inspired her. She has spent countless hours reading about thoroughbreds these past few days, and I'm certain she has many questions." I refrained from mentioning it was at my recommendation that she did so.

His regard moved to Ruth again, a look of determination on his face. "If you would excuse me then, Miss Godwin."

"Of course." I watched Ruth's face brighten as Mr. Treynor approached her.

"They would make a lovely match." Miss Whitmore stepped to my side, her consideration on the delighted couple.

I nodded in agreement. "But whatever the outcome, it is good to see Ruth gain confidence in her abilities. She has so very much to offer, but unlike most ladies I'm acquainted with, she does not realize it." I kept my gaze on Ruth. "I believe it's part of her charm. What say you?"

Miss Whitmore paused and tilted her head to the side.

"I find her modesty most endearing, and it is quite apparent my cousin believes it to be as well."

We both laughed, and, in that moment, I wondered if Miss Whitmore and I could be friends—real, authentic friends—unlike the friends I kept in Town.

"I heard what you are doing for Ruth and Sarah," Miss Whitmore said with a kind smile. "It is good of you."

Not trusting myself to ask how she had known of it, I simply gave a nod of acceptance.

"Has Augustus sent word about when he is likely to return from Bath?"

I whipped my head to her. "Bath? Did he not go to London to aid his brother?"

There was uncertainty evident in her features. "Forgive me. I thought he would have ..." Her words halted. "Perhaps it was I who was too bold for inquiring after his destination."

I stared, unable to conceal my shock. "You spoke with him before he left?"

She nodded ever so slowly. "He stopped at Safford Park on his way out."

My heart sank at her confirmation. Augustus had gone to see her before leaving? I was tempted to ask her what his purpose had been, but I knew that was not my place. And in truth, I wasn't certain I wished to know. "I suppose he did not want to mention the details of his trip with Ruth present," I said, more for myself than Miss Whitmore.

"He is very cautious when it comes to her. And rightfully so." Her eyes settled on Ruth, and she released a quick breath. "I cannot fathom the suffering the dear girl must have endured to lose both parents, especially in the manner in which she lost them."

I gave a vacant nod of agreement. It did not come as a surprise that Miss Whitmore should know of Ruth's past; they were all dear friends, after all. Yet understanding why Augustus would take her into his confidence did little to ease my vexation at the image it conjured—the two of them alone together, speaking of such private matters. Had she cried as I had? Had he comforted her as he did me?

I looked again to Miss Whitmore, and it was then that I realized that despite any hopes of a friendship between us, we could never truly be close. Not when we desired the very same thing. I, too, desired Augustus. My heart hammered inside at the realization, and I glanced about, desperate for a diversion. "I believe Mrs. Brundage had hoped we both would agree to perform on the pianoforte this evening. Perhaps we should go see if that is still her wish?"

Miss Whitmore's brow creased together, but she gave a slow nod. "Very well."

"That does sound most pleasant," Mrs. Brundage said when I reminded her of the notion, and our group made for the music room. The small rectangular shape of the space made for a cozy atmosphere, and, at Mrs. Brundage's direction, I performed first at the pianoforte.

Miss Whitmore followed with a lovely piece she played to near perfection and, because Ruth insisted she played very ill and Sarah was not among us, I performed yet again, this time singing as well. The group offered their polite applause when I finished, and I moved back to my seat.

"That was absolutely lovely, Miss Godwin." Mrs. Brundage stood, her hands cupped before her. She looked to Miss Whitmore. "Would you care to delight us a second time, Candace, or shall we reconvene in the drawing room?"

"I have no intention of playing again, unless Ruth wishes for me to accompany her." Miss Whitmore smiled and looked to Mr. Treynor. "She has the voice of an angel."

Ruth's blush was apparent even in the dim light. Could she truly sing as well as Miss Whitmore proclaimed? And if so, how had I not known of it?

Ruth shook her head. "Oh, no. I couldn't. I don't really know many songs."

"Then why don't you sing the song your mother used to sing to you?" Mrs. Brundage said. "It doesn't require the pianoforte, and you know it well enough."

Ruth bit at her lip.

"I would love to hear it," Mr. Treynor said, offering her the most influential form of encouragement a girl could receive.

She looked to me, and I nodded.

"Very well." Ruth stood, crossing her wrists in front of her and intertwining her fingers. "Mother sang this song to me each night before bed. And though I will attempt to do it justice, my own voice is not equal to hers." Ruth closed her eyes and drew in a quivering breath. Then, ever so quietly, a pure note sounded, stilling me. More followed, and her voice flowed through the melody with little effort, creating a sad tune.

> Love is a rose bud, my dear one
> Love is a rose bud when it's found
> Lost in the frost or burnt in the sun
> Hold it tight while it's around

Her expression grew distant as she sang, and I wondered what image she conjured in her mind as her rich alto voice enveloped us. Was it her mother she visualized?

Love is a rose branch, my dear girl
  Love is a rose branch when it's yours
  But ever growin' thorn and burl
  When held too tightly, blood and sores

Love is a rose heart, little love
  Love is a rose heart buried deep
  Though all barren from above
  Still alive it e'er will keep

Even when the last notes of her song had faded, I could not remove my eyes from her. She had presented us a piece of her soul, and in some way, I felt it revealed a piece of my own. I had already learned love could be lost, and when it was, the pain was excruciating. Yet the warmth that engulfed me affirmed that real love did not die; it was simply waiting to grow anew. But was I willing to risk the loss and the pain all over again?

Applause echoed through the small space, and I pulled myself from my thoughts in time to see Ruth curtsy.

Mr. Treynor clapped most exuberantly. "An angel, indeed."

"Thank you." Ruth smiled at him, then glanced at me.

I tipped my head to the side, my heart swelling so much I nearly wept right there in front of everyone. "You are exceptional."

There was complete contentment on her face when her eyes darted behind me. "Augustus! You're home!"

It was as if a weight lifted from me so suddenly, when I spun in my seat to see him, I nearly tossed myself from the chair.

Augustus gave me a quick smile, before looking back at Ruth. "I am. And that was the perfect welcome."

Ruth hurried toward him and wrapped her arms around his waist, a gesture he eagerly greeted. "What took you so long? We expected you sooner."

He pulled out of her embrace enough to look her in the eyes. "We shall talk later. Yes?" Ruth nodded, and he looked out at the rest of us. "Are there to be more performances, or have I just made the last?"

Mrs. Brundage stood, walking toward Augustus. "The last, I'm afraid. Unless you prefer to offer us a song, dear?"

His mother's teasing smirk made Augustus laugh, and he promptly shook his head. "No, I shall spare the lot of you."

"Thank heavens." Mrs. Brundage's face beamed as she placed a welcoming kiss upon his cheek.

As if permission had then been granted, we all stood to return to the drawing room.

"Was your trip a success?" I asked when Augustus stepped next to me upon my exiting the room.

"I believe so. Though I can't yet be certain."

"And how did you find *Bath*?"

He didn't look the least bit surprised that I should have discovered his whereabouts. "I never thought I'd return to Blacksley."

"You were able to get inside despite it being shuttered up these past eight years?"

"There remains an estate manager, and he thankfully remembered my aunt fondly. When I explained the situation, he didn't hesitate to let me in."

I nodded, remembering the few times I had found the courage to go and sit outside that large, empty house over the years. I had never seen anyone about.

"Visiting Blacksley with the knowledge of what my

aunt had endured all those years was more difficult than I thought it would be." He released a breath. "But each time I felt sunken in darkness, I would go out of doors and walk the woods toward Fellerton." He looked down at me. "The memories of us would flood through me and buoy me up."

I took hold of his arm and leaned into him. "Though I am sorry for your hardship, I'm glad you were still able to find some joy there."

We neared the back of the settee in the drawing room, and I glanced to the doorway in time to see Miss Whitmore and her mother walk through it. Miss Whitmore offered a timid smile, though her mother looked rightly cross by Augustus's notice having gone to me first. A familiar pang of guilt settled inside me. But I reminded myself it was not my fault Augustus had sought me out. And besides, I scarcely could control where my rogue heart was leading me lately. Countless times since Augustus and I had nearly shared that kiss, I had found my thoughts on him, pondering what a life with him would be like. Wondering if our love could endure.

Augustus took a step closer, drawing my attention. "I missed you, Bella."

My breath hitched at his unashamed admission, but I could not hide my delight. "I am loath to admit it, but I may have missed you also." His lips curved upwards, and to make it more pronounced, I placed a hand on his arm. When I removed it again, my fingers lingered on his for an extra moment, and, as I expected, his smile grew. "Though you must not allow such an admission to give you airs."

"And yet I plan to do exactly that."

Ruth bounced to our side, nearly bumping into me in her excitement.

"What is it, Ruth?" I asked, too contented to hide my amusement.

"Mr. Treynor is leaving us in two days' time."

"That hardly seems a reason for such a state of delight," I said.

Ruth giggled. "Oh, but that is not why I am delighted. I was thinking we should go on our outing tomorrow so that Mr. Treynor could join us." She looked at Augustus. "You did promise to take Bella to the sea."

I gave Augustus a pointed glance. "That is the truth of it."

He dropped his shoulders in mock defeat, and his gaze moved to the others. "What say you all to a trip to the coast tomorrow? If the weather is anything like it was today, it should prove to be ideal, indeed."

Miss Whitmore looked to her mother, giving a small nod of encouragement.

Mrs. Whitmore's consideration stayed on me an uncomfortable moment. "I fear I have obligations tomorrow. But, if you are going, Mrs. Brundage, I don't see why Candace cannot accompany you. As to Mr. Treynor, he is under no obligation to me, and is therefore able to make his own choice on the matter."

"Count me in." Mr. Treynor's exuberant confirmation sent Ruth giggling in excitement, and Mrs. Whitmore's eyes flicking toward the ceiling.

Augustus's regard shifted. "Mother?"

Mrs. Brundage's cheeks rounded with a smile. "Of course we should go. It has been far too long since our last outing to the seaside."

Ruth squealed, and I touched her hand as a gentle correction, though she hardly appeared repentant. "Forgive me. I fear I am a touch too excited."

"But only a touch." I said, realizing my own eagerness

was nearly comparable to hers, despite my ability to conceal it better.

"What time were we hoping to depart?" Miss Whitmore asked, joining me and Augustus as Ruth made her way back to an awaiting Mr. Treynor.

Augustus's gaze shifted between us. "Do either of you hold a preference?"

I gave a small shake of my head in near unison to Miss Whitmore.

Augustus glanced toward his mother, who was once again in conversation with Mrs. Whitmore. "What if we were to leave late morning? Say around ten? That way we will arrive before the warmest part of the day. We can bring a picnic for sustenance and depart from the shore with plenty of light left to avoid travelling home in the dark."

"Mr. Treynor and I will be here at quarter to ten," Miss Whitmore said, taking a hesitant step away, her expression full of indecision.

Augustus stepped toward Miss Whitmore. "Are you leaving?"

She halted her retreat. "I thought to make a request of Mother to be on our way." Her head tipped slightly to one side, her eyes on Augustus. "I know you wish to talk to your family about what you discovered in Bath, and I fear our presence is delaying that from happening."

"If it were only you ..." Augustus's voice trailed off.

"But it is not, so I can wait until tomorrow for you to enlighten me."

"Of course. And, Candace"—Augustus gave an appreciative smile—"thank you."

My gaze followed Miss Whitmore as she rejoined her mother. "She is most considerate."

Augustus's notice had already returned to me. "Yes, she is."

I tried not to feel disappointment at his confirmation, but the need for comparison was too deeply embedded in me, and I doubted if I would have done the same. Miss Whitmore seemed to be everything Augustus should love, and a part of me was astonished that he had not yet discovered it. Would he once I was married to Lord Thorton? My heart sank at the thought, and I secretly wished he would never see her as anything but a friend.

"Farewell," Miss Whitmore called from the doorway, her mother looking anything but pleased as she bid us a parting nod as well.

Mr. Treynor stepped from Ruth's side and waved as exuberantly as Ruth often did. "Tomorrow then."

"Tomorrow," Ruth said, looking beyond thrilled as he exited the door behind them. She hurried to my side and took hold of my arm. "You are a genius, Bella. I once again did everything precisely as you taught me, and I'm quite certain Mr. Treynor's affection for me is beginning to reflect my own for him. Men are quite simple to please, aren't they?"

I covered a rogue smile with my hand.

"I believe there wasn't one thing in that comment I found agreeable," Augustus said, with a pointed glance.

Ruth jutted out her lower lip. "You simply don't like the idea of me falling in love."

"That is not true." Augustus placed a hand on her shoulder. "I simply do not want you to give your heart prematurely. You should know the person you are to marry long enough that you can be certain they are genuine—that they are the person they proclaim to be."

I knew he spoke of Ruth's father, but for some reason I felt a small prick at his declaration.

"And how long does it take to discover if someone has a sincere character?" Ruth asked.

Augustus rubbed his chin, his expression distant. "How long have I known Bella?"

Ruth's mouth parted. "I would be firmly on the shelf if I were to wait as long as that."

Augustus shrugged, making Ruth gasp, but I reached out and took hold of her hand. "Augustus is only teasing you." I sent him a pointed glance to make certain he would leave it there. "Though there is wisdom in what he says, he will be thrilled when you make a suitable match. Won't you, Augustus?"

He looked hesitant. "Just do not give your whole heart until I have judged the suitability of your suitor. Agreed?"

Ruth beamed up at him. "Agreed."

"There, now. What a lovely compromise." I paused, questioning whether Augustus was in an amiable enough mood to discuss Ruth's coming out.

He smiled at me.

"Augustus," I said, offering my most saccharine smile, "seeing as Ruth was never given a coming out dinner or ball, I thought it appropriate for you to consider holding an event in her honor. It isn't as though she has been out in Society very long, and it seems the perfect reward for all of her hard work in becoming a lady."

Ruth leaned forward in anticipation, though not a sound escaped her lips.

I pretended to remove some imaginary lint from his jacket with a few brief swipes, allowing my hand to linger. "You need not give an answer yet, as you will need to speak to your mother about it, and in such a way that does not make her feel neglectful, for many parents do not make a fuss about a lady's coming out, let alone an aunt."

Augustus considered Ruth a moment. "Mother and I had actually discussed it previously, but I regret such matters have fallen by the wayside between our mourning period for Father and the hearing on the Seton estate. But perhaps it is time we consider it again."

Ruth bounded toward him, her arms wrapping around his waist. "Thank you! I can hardly believe I shall be having a ball in my honor!"

I offered Augustus an apologetic smile. "It seems as though it shall be a ball."

He chuckled and shook his head. "Why am I not surprised?"

Ruth moved to me, clasping my hand in hers. "Do say you will return for it, Bella."

"I should like that very much, if I am able."

Ruth squealed, apparently taking my response as confirmation.

"What is all this joyous ruckus about?" Mrs. Brundage asked, stepping through the doorway with Sarah just behind her. "I wait for Branson to fetch Sarah, and you are already sharing news without me?"

Augustus returned her playful grin. "No, Mother. But I may have just agreed to hold a ball in Ruth's honor, if you are not opposed, of course."

Mrs. Brundage clasped her hands in delight. "And when is this ball to take place?"

"Perhaps after the probate hearing in the instance we may have more than one reason to celebrate?"

Mrs. Brundage drew closer, the amusement in her features replaced by curiosity. "What do you mean, dear?"

Augustus exhaled, glancing at Ruth. "There is evidence that the coroner's court was wrong in their initial ruling. Uncle Thomas's death may not have been self-murder after all."

Ruth stiffened at my side, and I grasped her hand in mine.

"The purpose for my trip to Bath was to search for evidence that could support the claim."

Mrs. Brundage's eyes flitted to Ruth. "And did you find any proof of it?"

Augustus nodded. "I believe so. I sent Owen everything I had, and I suppose he'll decide what it is worth."

Ruth gripped my hand tighter. "What evidence did you find?"

"Besides obtaining testimonies from your father's man of business, servants—including his valet—and a few individuals who knew him well, I found your father's appointment book that contained engagements scheduled well beyond his death. His financial accounts showed nothing out of the ordinary, and there was a partially finished letter I discovered written to that very same man of business. He made mention of his desire to learn more regarding a speculation he thought would perform well in the coming years. Then he requested the man report back within one week. It was dated the day of his death."

Ruth's face scrunched up for an instant before a small smile emerged. "It does seem odd for a man to continue planning his future if he is set on ending it."

"Precisely," Augustus said with a nod, and he looked at me. "A sane man intent on such a horrific crime would have altered his behavior, at least in part."

I stilled, realizing it was me that he was quoting.

He looked around at the others. "It was Bella's idea. I wrote to Owen about it, and he set out immediately to see what he could find. It seems there were a few people who already held similar beliefs, and we now have a good deal of evidence to support it."

"Then who killed Aunt Susan and her husband?"

Sarah's voice was tainted with worry, and I did not blame her. I had grown up with thinking the Setons' perpetrator had not been caught, and it had affected me for years. I stopped venturing out in the woods entirely, and despite Mother's constant badgering, I always hurried down darkened hallways with far too much haste.

Augustus reached toward Sarah, and she placed her hand in his. "We don't know who killed them. And we may never know. But whoever did this has likely fled long ago."

Despite his assurances, a chill ran down my back.

"Augustus is right," Mrs. Brundage said, clasping her hands tightly before her. "We shall consider the findings to be good news. But can the initial ruling be overturned?"

Augustus tilted his head from side to side. "In theory, the Court of Chancery holds all jurisdiction over matters of equity—the Keeper of the King's Conscience, they are called. I suppose we shall see how just and understanding that conscience turns out to be."

My thoughts were racing. "And if they do overturn the initial ruling, then everything would be returned to Ruth?"

Augustus nodded. "My uncle's estate was not entailed. Therefore Ruth, his only surviving child, was left the whole of it in his will."

Without a moment's thought I wrapped my arms around Ruth, causing her laugh to trill through the drawing room. "I thought a lady was not supposed to hug," she said as I held her tight.

"But friends are, and I am first and foremost your friend."

CHAPTER SEVENTEEN

*R*uth glanced out the carriage window. "It is a most pleasant day, is it not?"

"It is a touch warm to be honest." I ran my hand up the back of my neck, swiping at the perspiration beginning to accumulate, though I wasn't certain if it was from the heat or my growing trepidation concerning Augustus. At least Miss Whitmore and I had been spared from being crammed onto one bench as Sarah, Ruth, and Mrs. Brundage now were.

Ruth glanced over at me. "Oh, but that is what will make the day so perfect. The warmer it is, the better it will be for drying off our skirts. I can attest that the hour-long ride home is hardly ideal if you are both drenched and sandy."

I looked at Miss Whitmore who sat beside me. "And do you plan to go wading in the sea also?"

She withheld a smile, but her lips twitched at the corners. "I'm not yet certain. But I typically do enjoy at least getting my feet wet."

I nodded, glancing out the window and wondering if I

would be the only one, besides Mrs. Brundage, to forego the experience.

"Bella has never been to the sea," Ruth said to Miss Whitmore, my odd behavior apparently requiring some sort of explanation.

As though she spoke it into existence, the carriage veered, and a silver glimmer in the distance caught my eye. "There it is." I took in the great vastness of the water that stretched to the horizon and beyond.

Sarah leaned forward in her seat, attempting to catch a glimpse of it out Ruth's window.

Ruth sighed dramatically. "Is it not the most wonderful sight in the whole world?"

I glimpsed Augustus atop his steed a way off. "Nearly," I said aloud, before I could stop myself.

Ruth followed where my line of sight had just been. "Are you referring to Augustus being more wonderful to look at?"

My face pinked, and I cursed my careless tongue. Surely I knew better. "Of course not," I said, feigning innocence. "I only meant that it is difficult for anything to rival London in my eyes." But when my gaze returned to the silver line on the horizon, I knew there were two places I now preferred over London—the sea and Fairhaven.

Ruth filled the silence with her own comparison of London and the seaside until the carriage rolled to a stop.

The door swung open to reveal Augustus with his beaver hat beneath one arm, his windblown hair making him appear even more handsome than I cared to notice. Instead, I focused on the slight breeze that made its way through the open door, carrying in a waft of salt air. I drew it in, certain I could never grow tired of such an invigorating scent.

Augustus extended his hand to aid his mother from the carriage before offering it to Miss Whitmore. The way she smiled at him as she exited sent a rush of absurd jealousy through me, and I reminded myself, yet again, that Miss Whitmore's affection was of no consequence to me. After Sarah and Ruth descended, Augustus held his hand out to me.

I gripped it in mine, taking in the brilliant view as I stepped down next to him. A stretch of golden beach led right out into the sea. The others were already on their way to where the gentle waves crashed against the shore. "Look at that," I said, still in awe. "To think I might have lived my whole life with only a vague notion of what I was missing."

Augustus's eyes remained fixed on me. "I know precisely how you feel."

I laughed, refusing to take him in earnest. "Do you know what I think?" I took hold of his arm, pulling him forward.

"What is that?"

"It is most unfortunate that London Society is not agreeable to you, for I daresay you'd be quite a hit among the ladies with your constant flattery."

He squinted, looking out at the horizon. "Well, considering I only have a meager fortune and no title, I doubt I would find much success in Town."

The reminder of his situation made my stomach knot, but I waved it away as though such things didn't truly matter. "You must not underestimate how enticing you are. You could readily persuade an heiress to fall in love with you."

His eyes settled back on me. "And yet it's proving harder than I'd care to admit."

My heart leapt in betrayal, but I laughed to cover it.

"I'm taking that as an admission that any further advance on your part is solely based on your desire for my fortune."

"Don't forget your ample connections."

I dropped his arm and started forward, sending him one more playful smile before lifting my skirts to make haste towards the others. I did not trust myself to be alone with him for a moment longer.

Ruth saw me approaching and left Mr. Treynor and Sarah to greet me. "Come, Bella," she said, gripping my arm and pulling me forward. "You must come feel the water."

I planted my feet as well as I could in the sand. "Just with my hand, you mean?"

"If that is what you wish." Ruth gave my arm a tug to keep me moving forward.

I released a breath and followed, unable to find the harm in such a trivial thing.

When we reached the shoreline, I bent low to touch a wave on its retreat. Despite the heat of the day, the cold water sent a shiver through me, and I could not keep a smile from my lips.

Ruth watched me with an excited expression. "Delightful, isn't it?"

"Yes."

"Then you must go wading with us. There is nothing so grand as the pull of the water on your feet and ankles."

I stood, shaking the water from my hand. "I believe my fingers will be the only thing to venture in today."

Ruth's bottom lip jutted out in a most overdone manner.

"You must not look at me like that, or I shall be forced to inform you that it is unacceptable for a lady to remove her shoes and stockings in the company of gentlemen."

Ruth pursed her lips. "Very well. I shall not press you further to spare myself the lecture on how a proper lady must conduct herself at the seashore. I would not miss going in the water on such a fine day for anything."

I had no intention of correcting her silly logic and instead glanced around to find Augustus standing next to Miss Whitmore, watching me with a satisfied smile.

My face pinkened under his consideration. "Do you plan to wade in the sea, Augustus?"

He took a few steps toward us. "If you do."

I tipped my head to the side. "You are fully aware I will not."

"Then neither will I."

"Well, I will." Ruth sat herself in the sand and began removing her shoes and stockings. "Who will join me?"

Sarah eagerly plopped herself in the sand to begin removing her shoes also, as did Mr. Treynor with his boots and jacket. Miss Whitmore smiled at us and gave a small lift of her shoulders before doing likewise.

"It seems we are the only ones abstaining," Augustus said, looking behind us.

I glanced over my shoulder, and to my great shock, Mrs. Brundage was pulling the stockings from her feet as well. I couldn't help but laugh, and the sudden desire to join them overwhelmed me. When I tried to force it away, it refused to go.

Augustus drew closer. "You are contemplating getting in."

"No, I am not."

A smile pulled at one side of his mouth. "You are. I know that look."

The others were now entering the water, their invigorating laughs drifting on the breeze. "It would be completely improper."

"And completely enjoyable."

I bit at my lip and gave a resolute shake of my head. "I cannot."

His hand lifted, grazing my arm ever so gently with his finger. "Think of how refreshing the water would feel on your skin."

Despite the way my skin prickled from his touch, I sent him a pointed glare. "Do you have no limits to your persuasion, sir?"

He laughed. "Not when, on our last outing, you so generously admitted I need only press you a little harder and you will comply."

"You will not relent, will you?"

"I will. Once you get in."

I looked back to the sea, my heart racing as I allowed my foolish desires to overcome reason. "Very well." He was assessing me with wary eyes when I met his gaze, and I was certain he did not believe me. I hardly believed it myself. "But you must not watch as I take off my stockings."

With a hint of a smile on his lips, he turned from me.

I sat, making quick work of removing my half-boots and discreetly untying my stockings before rolling them up and shoving them inside my shoes. I pulled off my gloves, and after a brief quandary, also removed my bonnet.

My stomach was aflutter as I stood and faced him. "I am ready."

His gaze skirted over my bare feet. "You are in earnest, then? You truly intend to get in?"

I lifted an accusatory brow and set my hands on my hips. "You always were a bad influence on me."

"Someone has to be," he said, shrugging off his jacket and removing his waistcoat. It wasn't until he started untying his cravat that my gaze lifted enough to notice his amused expression.

I diverted my eyes, feeling vulnerable without the shade of my bonnet to hide my blush. "I think I shall wet my toes." As I neared the water, an incoming wave stretched up toward me, and I hitched my skirts higher than was proper, stepping into the cool water just as it retreated. The pleasure that ran through me was familiar, similar to that of wading in streams. Another wave drew close, and I took a few more cautious steps, allowing the water to wrap around my ankles.

"Bella, you got in." Ruth hurried toward me, her skirts gathered and draped in one arm, the other arm swinging at her side.

The cold water from her movement splashed on the bare skin of my arms, causing me to draw back. "But I shall not get in as deep as you," I said, noticing how the hem of her dress was already soaked through.

Ruth's gaze followed mine to her collected skirts. "It will dry." She paused before pulling back her foot and kicking water in my direction. "As will yours."

I gasped as the water made contact with my skin a second time, and my body went rigid. "You should not have done that." Ruth's hands lifted in apology, but my smile betrayed me. "I may be out of practice, but you know I could once paddle with the best of them." Gathering my skirts in one arm, I leaned down and splashed the retreating water in her direction.

A delighted squeal reached me in near unison to the water she paddled back at me.

"Where are my reinforcements?" I called, glancing at the others.

Miss Whitmore and Sarah gladly joined in, and the

sound of shrieks and giggles echoed around us, my own interspersed with theirs.

Men's laughter from the shore caught my attention, and I glanced over to find Augustus and Mr. Treynor watching us with amused expressions. "Surely you are not going to just stand there and watch me be defeated?" I called.

Augustus started in our direction, but when he came close enough, I concentrated my attack on him.

"Traitor," he said, lifting his hands to shield himself from my meager attempts.

As he neared, I moved deeper to keep him from apprehending me, the bottom of my skirts now hanging limply in the water.

"Bella," Augustus called, pointing behind me, and I thought he meant to cause a distraction when a cold wall of water hit against me with such force, it set me off balance. The momentum thrust me toward him, and Augustus reached out in time to grasp my hand as I tumbled forward onto my knees. My breath caught as the cold water moved over my lower back and legs, but Augustus pulled me upward just in time to prevent a full submersion.

Remorse was evident in his face as he took hold of my arms and lifted me to my feet. "I ..." His words trailed off as we both glanced down at my soaked day dress clinging to my body and the white muslin fabric embedded with sand. "I'm so sorry."

His apology conjured a whirlpool of memories from our youth—him always asking forgiveness for something he had convinced me to do against my better judgment. Without warning, a laugh burst from me.

"Bella?" Augustus asked, sounding more concerned by my laughter than consoled.

A confirmation of my joyous state shot through me. "I am well. More than well, actually."

A grin pulled up on one side of his mouth. "And you realize you are soaked through from the waist down?"

I nodded, burrowing my toes into the coarse grains of sand beneath my feet as another wave pressed against me. "And I have not felt so alive in years."

He looked back at the others standing in the shallower water, their expressions equally concerned. "All is well," he called. "Bella decided she would like to try sea bathing."

Without another thought, I put my arm beneath the water and pulled up a handful of wet sand, tossing it toward him. It spattered across his buckskin breeches and shirtsleeves.

He looked down at the mess I'd made, and when his eyes lifted to mine, they were full of familiar mischief.

As he started toward me, my heart leapt, and I lifted a hand in concession. "I now realize I should not have done that." My laugh betrayed me.

He shook his head as he drew closer, determination in his features. "That is twice now you have attacked me with no provocation."

Seeing as he had no intention of being pacified by my empty attempts, I turned to flee, but he bounded forward, wrapping his arms around my waist and lifting me into the air. By the time he set me down in front of the others, I was laughing so hard I could hardly draw a breath. "As you were all witness to her treason, I bring her before you to ask what punishment should be imparted." His arms remained around my waist, holding me close against him to prevent my escape. "Opinions? Verdicts?"

"Grant her mercy," Sarah said.

"I concur." Ruth smiled, taking in my drenched skirts. "She seems to have received sufficient justice already."

"Hear! Hear!" Mr. Treynor called.

Miss Whitmore also wore a smile on her face, though I was certain it could not be real, and the thought chastised me. How would I feel if the man I loved had his arms wrapped around another woman? A woman who had declared to me that she was set on obtaining someone else's suit? But was I still set on that match? With Augustus so near, I wasn't certain I was.

"See, there?" I said, attempting to twist enough in his arms to look up at him. "I believe it is unanimous."

"No." Augustus said, pulling me tighter and making my heart pound against my chest. "As I am also voting."

"The wronged do not get to sit on the jury."

"So you admit that I have been wronged?" He glanced between the others. "Does anyone wish to recant their pardon now that she has so willingly admitted her guilt?" Augustus turned us toward Mrs. Brundage. "Mother? What say you?"

"As though I would let you enact a punishment on poor Miss Godwin." Mrs. Brundage's blue eyes sparkled. "Her nature is such that she would not act without first being provoked."

Augustus's laugh vibrated through me. "Now I am to be blamed for Bella's offense? Where is the loyalty?"

"It is here," Ruth said, batting water toward us.

Following her example, everyone joined in, tossing water in our direction. Only Mrs. Brundage made her way to shore, laughing from the safety of the beach.

Augustus released me, moving between me and the others as he struck the water with such force it flew about wildly.

Laughter again danced through the air, and I remained close to Augustus, allowing his large frame to block most of the water being flung in our direction.

By the time we were too exhausted to carry on, and more sodden than any of us could have foreseen, we made our way toward the blanket laid upon the sand. The ladies sat, spreading our skirts and tucking in our feet, while the gentlemen stood nearby.

I lifted my hand to my hair, not surprised to find my coiffure askew and several pieces dislodged completely. I set about removing the pins until my dampened curls hung loose around me.

I felt Augustus's gaze upon me, and despite my better judgment, I met it. His eyes were as warm as the sun, and my skin tingled under the heat of them. I took in his sandy-colored hair, also a mess from the water and the breeze, before allowing myself the briefest glance at his dampened shirtsleeves clinging to his skin. A most pleasing physique displayed beneath the thin layer.

When I returned my consideration to his handsome face, he lifted a brow. This time, I simply smiled and shrugged off my wayward appraisal, making him chuckle.

"What is past that bend?" Miss Whitmore asked, stealing our attention.

She looked further down the beach, where the shoreline seemed to curve inward and disappear.

"Likely more beach," Augustus said, squinting in the bright light.

Miss Whitmore stood. "I think I should like to find out." She looked about our party. "Would anyone care to join me?"

"I'm too exhausted." Ruth gave an apologetic pout, leaning on her elbows in a most unladylike position.

"How about you, Augustus?"

My eyes darted to Augustus's profile, my chest constricting at the thought of them wandering off together.

He sent her a knowing smile that only served to heighten my vexation. "I would very much appreciate that."

To my shock, Miss Whitmore looked to me. "Miss Godwin, would you care to join us also?"

Though I longed to jump to my feet and make certain the two of them did not venture off alone together, what right did I have to claim him? Particularly when he seemed eager to go along. "I believe I'm too wet to venture anywhere at the moment."

Miss Whitmore's eyes flickered to Augustus, before she moved in front of me and offered an insistent hand. "There is nothing better for drying off one's skirts than walking."

I lowered my brow, completely astonished by her determination. Did she not want to get Augustus alone?

"Do come along, Bella." Augustus's voice was imploring, as was his inviting smile.

Looking back to Miss Whitmore's hand still outstretched toward me, I took hold of it, and she aided me to my feet.

"Sarah," she said, glancing to our side, "why don't you join us also?"

Sarah rose to her feet without hesitation.

"We shall not be gone long," Miss Whitmore said to Mrs. Brundage. "And I shall help you set out the picnic upon our return."

Mrs. Brundage glanced between the four of us. "Very well. But do not venture too far."

"Don't forget your bonnet," Ruth said, leaning forward to retrieve it from the spot on the blanket where I'd set it.

I glanced up at the blue sky above us, the slight breeze moving through my dampened locks. "It's too fine a day for a bonnet."

Her lips parted, but I turned to join the others before she could correct me.

We nodded our agreement and set off for the bend in the coastline.

It didn't take long before we arrived where the shore jutted inward, and we found a small cove where a rising slope eventually became a cliff face at the far end.

"How lovely." Miss Whitmore latched her arm with Sarah. "And look, a small footpath. Should we explore a little further on?" Sarah nodded her agreement, and the two made haste toward an unidentifiable path without so much as a glance behind them.

Reluctant to follow them through the unwieldy terrain, I glanced back at Augustus, who appeared unconcerned in keeping up. "Are you coming?"

He shook his head, the mischievous glint in his eyes stilling me. "They won't be away long. Come, let us talk."

The two of them disappeared from view on the other side of an incline, both moving much too swiftly. My lips parted, and I looked back to Augustus. "You planned this?"

He lifted his hands, his palms facing me, as though to demonstrate his innocence. "Candace was the instigator. And when she sets her mind on something, she's a difficult one to refuse, especially when it entails a moment alone with you."

My heart raced in my chest so swiftly I could not keep my thoughts focused on why Miss Whitmore would organize such a ruse.

Augustus extended a hand, and I glanced down at it but did not move. "I don't trust myself," I said, surprised by my own admission.

He did not lower his hand. "Perhaps you should."

I drew in a steadying breath. "No. Everything my heart is telling me contradicts what I know to be true—the very thing I have sought to obtain these last many years." And the very thing I had sought to avoid. Love.

"Could it not be possible that your heart is aware of something your mind is not?"

With every quickened beat, hope pulsed through me. Was he right? I hardly knew. But before I could stop myself, I took hold of his hand.

He pulled me closer, the heat of his body causing a shiver to move through me. I did not move away.

"Are you cold?" he asked, placing his warm hands on my arms, the gentle caress of his fingers moving along my skin.

I shook my head, unable to voice that it was his nearness that caused the trembling. I knew precisely what he meant to say to me, what I would say in return if I could not convince myself to be stronger. The thought was terrifying and yet exhilarating.

His hands settled on my waist, making my breath catch. "Bella." His voice was soft and near. "I cannot allow you to leave Fairhaven without declaring my feelings." He paused, releasing a shaky breath. "I love you, Bella. I always have."

Always.

His words stirred something deep within me, and I was reminded of Ruth's song. *Love is a rose heart buried deep. Though all barren from above, still alive it e'er will keep.* My love for Augustus had never died, just as his love for me had not, but it had simply lain dormant those eight years, weathered and broken from no fault of our own. Yet now the roots were stronger and eager to grow into something beautiful. And I yearned for it to grow again. I would give anything for it to flourish.

The realization made me want to laugh and cry all at once, but no sound came. Instead, I lifted my hands to rest upon his chest. His shirt was still damp, and the pace of his racing heart was in rhythm with my own. I could scarcely draw a breath knowing what would follow, but then I tipped my chin upward, closing the space between our lips until they were only a moment apart from touching.

His eyes shifted between mine, the air heavy between us. He lifted one of his hands and brought it to my neck, his thumb caressing my jaw. The uncertainty that had filled me only minutes before melted from the warmth of his body pressed against mine. I leaned in closer still, until we shared our very breath. "You never stopped loving me?" I whispered.

His forehead came to mine. "Never."

My chest was now lifting and falling in quick bursts, my breath attempting to keep up with my racing heart. "I never stopped loving you either." How strange the words felt to speak, as though the desire of my entire life had finally been spoken aloud.

The strength of his hand on my waist intensified, the pressure pulling me forward and upward, where the softness of his lips engulfed mine. His kiss was precisely as I had remembered it, as I had recalled it time and time again throughout the years, yet somehow it was also superior, bursting with new emotion. Hurt. Longing. And a tender, abiding love. In that moment I realized how much I had needed him. Every fiber of my soul confirmed it as my hands lifted, wrapping around his neck. Despite our closeness, I managed to pull him closer still, no longer able to resist my yearning.

Our kiss deepened and slowed before Augustus reluctantly pulled his lips just out of reach. "Will you marry me?"

My heart swelled until it nearly burst within me, and I

realized that this is what a proposal was supposed to feel like—an unwavering eagerness mixed with love and desire. All my reservations and the countless uncertainties seemed to dissolve with the realization that I could not live without Augustus. There wasn't anything I wouldn't give up to be with him. "Yes. I will marry you."

He took a step back, quirking his head to the side. "Are you in earnest?"

"Must I say it again?"

A smile touched his stunned expression. "If you would."

I took a step toward him, closing the space between us. "I will marry you, Augustus Brundage."

He yelped in excitement and lifted me off the ground, spinning me as we both laughed.

"I take it that went well," Miss Whitmore called, cautiously making her way over the incline with Sarah still at her side.

Augustus lowered me to the ground, a triumphant smile on his face. "To my great relief, it has. Bella has agreed to marry me."

Sarah's eyes widened. "Truly?"

"Yes," I said, leaning in and wrapping my arms around Augustus's waist. "Despite my better judgment, he has persuaded me to accept him."

Augustus laughed again and pulled me close to place a kiss atop my head. "Whatever it takes."

Sarah released Miss Whitmore's arm and hurried the remainder of the way to where we stood, engulfing me in an embrace. "I cannot believe I shall truly have you for a sister."

"And I, you." I squeezed her tightly as Miss Whitmore approached. She smiled with a warmth that astonished me. I was all too aware of how much practice it took to so fully conceal one's emotions, yet she managed to appear sincerely happy for us.

"Such wonderful news." She leaned in to place a kiss upon my cheek as Sarah moved to hug her brother. "Augustus has loved you since I first knew him. I am glad to know he has found such happiness."

I ached for Miss Whitmore. "Thank you. I hope you shall also find happiness."

"Yes." She took hold of my hands. "Perhaps this is just the thing to aid me in my own pursuit."

I thought to agree with her, to tell her how closure was often the thing most needed to guide us to another more promising path, but it felt too trivial to say. Instead I just smiled back at her and offered a silent hope that she would find someone who could love her as Augustus loved me, for no one was so deserving of it as she was.

"Congratulations, Augustus." Miss Whitmore moved in front of him. "It seems you finally have achieved your heart's desire."

"And, in part, I have you to thank for it." Augustus took hold of her hand, and they shared a knowing look. "Thank you."

Miss Whitmore offered him a slight smile, giving his hand a gentle squeeze and releasing it. "I believe we should go tell the others. They shall be most eager to hear the news."

THE CARRIAGE SWAYED, and I glanced out the window at Augustus, who rode his horse with such dignity I could not draw my eyes from him.

"I cannot believe you are to be married," Ruth said, for the tenth time since we had returned Miss Whitmore to

Safford Park and bid farewell to Mr. Treynor. "And I cannot believe I was not there when he asked you."

"It is not as though Candace and I were actually there to witness it," Sarah said.

Ruth huffed. "But you were there right after. Besides, you said you could see them from where you and Candace were waiting."

I looked down at my hands, mortified to think what Sarah and Miss Whitmore had likely seen if that were the truth of it. No wonder their return had come immediately after Augustus's proposal.

"It is not as though we watched them," Sarah said. "At least not once ... well, once we were certain things were going well."

I could feel the heat settling in my neck and face.

"Have you thought about when the wedding will take place?" Mrs. Brundage asked, most generously changing the subject.

She sat on the bench next to me now, and I met her gaze. "No. Augustus desires to speak to my father before we announce our engagement, and ..." My voice trailed off as I thought of all the other insurmountable hardships that were to be faced—like how I still needed to inform Augustus that my mother was not even aware of my presence at Fairhaven. I sighed. "Well, there is much to consider."

Mrs. Brundage nodded her understanding. "I know your parents allowed you to Fairhaven"—her eyes flickered to Ruth—"but with all that has passed between our families, do you believe they will bestow their blessing on the match?"

My stomach clenched. I needed to tell Mrs. Brundage the truth also. Just not yet. "I hope they will. In time." I could not keep the doubt from my voice.

Mrs. Brundage placed a hand on mine. "Well, we shall support you, however you need us to."

I smiled at her kindness. And for some reason, perhaps suddenly aware how much she had given up to marry Mr. Brundage, I felt a greater respect for her. Would I have to do the same to be with Augustus? Give up my family? My inheritance? Society? I had hardly even given a thought to the potential consequences of accepting Augustus, so set had I been in my plan to obtain Lord Thorton's proposal. I forced my worries down, committing to deal with them when the need arose, and instead clung to the happiness I had felt before now. Augustus and I would be married. A small smile touched my lips. Yes. That was enough.

The carriage shifted, rolling up the drive to Fairhaven. Mrs. Brundage looked out the window. "Who is here?"

I leaned forward, glimpsing a lovely, but thankfully unfamiliar, traveling coach. "I've not seen the likes of it."

Mrs. Brundage's face lit. "I wonder if it is my cousin, Lady Leroy. She did write to say that she would be traveling to this part of the country soon and wished to call upon me. And it is as grand a carriage as I would think her to possess." Mrs. Brundage's hands lifted to her disheveled hair. "But what a day to choose for an unannounced visit."

I leaned in close to adjust a few pins in her hair, the carriage rolling to a stop. "Thankfully you did not venture in as far as the rest of us. There." I pulled back to ensure I'd done an adequate job. "You look beautiful." And she did. Despite her wind-tossed hair and her sun-kissed cheeks, she looked lovely enough to welcome even the highest-bred relation.

She squeezed my hand in gratitude.

"And as for the three of us," I said, looking between Ruth and Sarah, "we shall make straight for our rooms."

They nodded in agreement as the carriage door swung open.

"Whose carriage is that?" Augustus asked, his voice brusque.

"I believe it is Lady Leroy's." Mrs. Brundage took hold of her son's hand, allowing for his assistance as she made her way out.

Augustus fixed his attention on me as he aided both Sarah and Ruth in their descent.

"You needn't look so worried." I sent him a playful smile, accepting his hand. "It is not my family's coach. Besides, I am not to be at Branbury for another week yet."

His gaze flickered back to the carriage, though the concern on his brow lessened.

"Oh heavens, I really do wish Lady Leroy would have written beforehand." Mrs. Brundage ran her hands down the skirts of her dress. "I suppose it shouldn't matter, being that she is family, but I should have preferred a little time to prepare." She looked to Ruth and Sarah. "Girls, follow Miss Godwin's lead, and join me when you are readied."

I watched Mrs. Brundage make her way up the stairs then turned to Augustus. "We'd best be on our way as well. It will be no easy feat to make ourselves presentable in a suitable amount of time."

Augustus surveyed my golden strands hanging wildly about me. Gently he took hold of a curl, his fingers grazing my neck and arm as he let it move through his grasp. "I think you look beautiful exactly like this."

I lifted onto my toes to place a quick kiss upon his cheek. "And that is one of the reasons I love you."

Ruth and Sarah giggled at my side, and I quickly took hold of both of their hands, leading them forward. The front door sat ajar, and I pushed it open ever so slowly, ushering them in before me and waving them upstairs. I had just clicked the door shut behind me when a voice from the drawing room reached my ears.

My blood curdled.

Mother.

CHAPTER EIGHTEEN

"*W*as she not with you?" Mother's voice echoed through the entry hall, and I tried to convince my feet forward, but they would not move.

"Well, yes. But she desired to change first." The desperation in Mrs. Brundage's voice was apparent as both women stepped into the entry hall, their gazes settling on me.

The fury on Mother's face nearly consumed me to ashes as she took in my disheveled appearance and loosely hanging hair.

"Mother." My voice was weak, and my whole body instinctively went rigid, preparing myself for her wrath. It did not come.

Instead she released a heavy breath and forced her lips into a severe smile. "Arabella, dear." Her voice was overly sweet, and I wondered that she cared to make a good impression on Mrs. Brundage. "We have come to retrieve you."

Retrieve me? With whom—Papa? Before I could inquire after her meaning, Lord Thorton and his mother stepped out of the drawing room. The Countess's curious expression transitioned to alarm when her eyes fell on me, but Lord Thorton appeared outright amused by my appearance.

My legs swayed beneath me, and I reached out a hand to take hold of the banister, ensuring I would not collapse to the ground and intensify my state of mortification. "Lady Thorton. Lord Thorton, what an unexpected surprise."

"We apologize for that," Lord Thorton said, "but when you did not arrive yesterday as expected, we arranged to come fetch you, to make certain nothing was wrong." He hesitated, his gaze sliding to Mrs. Brundage. "Though we did not realize how far such a venture would take us at the time, having only intended to go as far as the Leavitt's estate."

I stood there dumbly, unable to form one coherent thought.

Certain this moment could not grow any more unbearable, the front door swung open and Augustus stepped through. The smile on his face faded when he caught sight of me. In an instant he was at my side, his hand on my waist. "Bella? What is it?"

"Augustus." The firmness in Mrs. Brundage's voice forced his attention from me, and when his gaze settled on my mother's hateful scowl, his body went rigid. "You recall Lady Godwin?" Mrs. Brundage said, her voice entreating him to collect himself.

He blinked. "Yes, of course." He lowered his arms to offer a tight bow.

"How much you've grown," Mother said, and I wondered if everyone could perceive the hint of abhorrence in her tone as well as I could. "May I present The Countess of Thorton, and her son, The Earl of Thorton."

She gestured with a rigid arm toward Augustus. "This is Mr. Brundage. An *old* friend of our family."

Lady Thorton and her son offered a partial nod, and Augustus gave another taut bow in return. "Pleasure. I hope you were not waiting on us long."

"Nearly an hour," Lady Thorton said, evidently unamused, unlike her son.

"Oh, Mother." Lord Thorton offered one of his contagious grins. "You act as though keeping my company is an intolerable affair, indeed." He looked at me. "I have not been home three days, and she has already grown weary of my company."

I forced my lips into some sort of smile, but Lady Thorton seemed to find little humor in his words. "It is not you I have grown weary of, dear, but this hunt we have endured to locate Miss Godwin." As Lady Thorton released an agitated breath, I felt Augustus's gaze upon me, but I could not meet it. "With guests set to arrive in the next few days, I hardly had time for such an undertaking."

My lips parted to offer some sort of an explanation, but I could not coax out a sound.

"Well, we shall not delay our removal a moment longer than is necessary." Mother started toward me with purpose. She stepped between Augustus and me, her hand coming to my back, pushing me toward the stairs. "Let us go see if your trunks are readied, Arabella."

With no other choice, I climbed the stairs at her side.

Mother's glare burned into my profile, and I knew she was waiting until we were out of earshot to attack. "You foolish girl," she whispered when we started our way down the corridor. "You very well may have ruined any hope of a match between you and Lord Thorton. I don't know how we shall ever right this wrong."

"Then let us not attempt it." I did not have the courage to look at her. "I want to remain here at Fairhaven ... with Augustus."

Mother's sharp fingers clasped my arm, spinning me toward her. "You fancy yourself in love with *Augustus*, do you?"

I met her stare, attempting not to cower under the force of it. "I do not fancy myself in love. I *am* in love, and he loves me, also."

Mother's eyes moved between mine before her grip on my arm suddenly lessened. "Oh, Arabella." She shook her head. "Which *you* is he in love with?"

I swallowed, knowing too well her meaning.

Mother's gaze flitted to my unruly hair. "You have allowed Mr. Brundage to think you are still the girl he once knew so long ago, haven't you?"

Despite the quivering, I lifted my chin.

"No. You are even more foolish than that. You have come to believe your own deceit." Mother leaned in close, the sweet scent of rose water overpowering my senses. "Have you forgotten what it has taken to become a diamond of society? What aspects of your prior self you were forced to sacrifice?" Her head shifted to one side as she appraised me. "I wonder what Mr. Brundage would think of you after witnessing your talent for bringing a lady to tears with one well-placed comment. Or the tactics you have implemented to get men to fall madly in love with you, to offer you everything—including their hearts—before you decide you don't want them?"

I stilled, imagining Augustus's expression when he discovered who I really was. The admiration he thought he had for me would turn to disappointment ... to embitterment. It was as if he was standing next to me, so real it felt, and I watched as the love faded from his eyes. My head spun, and I felt I might be sick. He could not love me once he knew the truth. He had only continued loving me because he was unaware of the woman I'd become. The woman who had manipulated him with each interaction. With each smile. And with each touch. I nearly crumpled under the weight of the guilt.

"Ah." A knowing smirk grew on Mother's lips. "Mr. Brundage has been a recipient of those perfected techniques, it appears. No wonder he has been led to believe he feels more for you than he truly does."

A tear escaped down my cheek, and I swiped at it.

Mother lowered her hand until it settled over mine. "Someone like Augustus Brundage deserves a woman who is genuine and sincere, who is capable of loving him without deception. One who is capable of obtaining his love without counterfeit."

A woman who would willingly give anything to see him happy.

My thoughts went to Miss Whitmore and her goodness. Augustus did deserve a lady like her. One who was selfless, and kind, and authentic. One who did not lie to him because the truth was too difficult to speak. My heart broke when I finally embraced the truth I'd been ignoring all along. Augustus should not love someone like me. More tears rolled down my cheeks.

Mother lifted both hands to my face, her thumbs dispersing the evidence of my wrongdoing. "And you, Arabella, deserve a man who can give you the life you are accustomed to. A life of privilege and respect. You are set to be a lady of distinction, not a lady forced from Society because of an ill-suited marriage." She paused. "Do not throw away everything you have worked so hard to achieve for someone who is ignorant to who you truly are. Someone who would be heartbroken to discover the truth. For there is no undoing what you have done."

She was right. After too long allowing my heart to lead me amiss, I compelled my mind to resume its rightful place. A shaky breath escaped me. "I was a fool, Mother. But I will right this."

"Of course you will." Mother's posture relaxed a touch, but then she lifted a finger to point at me. "And do not think you have freed yourself from explaining how this whole debacle occurred. If we had more time and my nerves were not already spent, I'd pull it from you now. As it stands, I will first write to your father for his account. I'm certain he had something to do with this. Cursed man."

"It was—"

"And do not take the blame for him. You are crafty, but not so much so that you could accomplish this without your father's knowledge." Mother placed an arm behind me, pushing me forward again.

Without a word, I led her to my room where Leah was hurrying to gather the last few items to place in my trunks.

"You have not finished yet?" Mother asked Leah, glancing around the small room with distaste.

"I just have, my lady." Leah kept her eyes on the floor.

"Then I shall inform the servants to retrieve the trunks straightaway." She paused, appraising my dress with disgust. "And do help Arabella change into something suitable. She looks dreadfully ridiculous in such a state."

Leah curtsied her acknowledgment.

When Mother had walked from the room, I glanced around at the friendly room, wishing it was not time to leave it.

"Miss?" Leah knelt beside my trunk.

"Forgive me. I did not hear your question."

"Which dress would you prefer? A traveling or a day dress?"

"My blue travelling dress if it's accessible."

Leah rummaged through the trunk, pulling out the chosen dress, as well as some necessary underthings, before rising and moving toward me. Though she kept her gaze down, the redness of one of her cheeks caught my eye.

"Whatever has happened, Leah?"

She lifted a hand to cover the red mark. "It is nothing, miss."

My stomach knotted. "Did my mother do that?"

Leah's silence confirmed it.

My throat went dry, knowing the fault was mine. "I am so sorry," I whispered.

Leah drew in a shuddered breath. "Let me help you change."

As she moved to lay the garments on the bed, I caught sight of my *dreadfully ridiculous* state in the vanity mirror. Augustus had just assured me that I looked beautiful just as I was, but my tangled, wind-blown hair and sun-bitten face were testament to what Mother had said. Augustus was not in love with me, but with the lady he thought me to be—a lady I scarcely recognized in my reflection.

WITH A FRESH GOWN and a bonnet to cover my hastily arranged coiffure, I made my way downstairs to join the others. My heart nearly faltered as I stood outside the threshold of the drawing room, but with one last fortifying breath, I found the courage to step through on trembling legs.

The room fell silent as I walked in, but I did not let my gaze waver from Mother's. "I am ready."

"Are you truly leaving then?" Ruth asked, rising to her feet.

"Yes." It was no easy feat concealing my utter disappointment as I took in her sorrow-filled face. "But I shall write to you very soon."

Ruth gave a pout, and her gaze flickered behind me. "But what of Augustus and—" Mrs. Brundage placed a cautioning hand on Ruth's shoulder, and to my great relief, Ruth held her tongue.

"Yes," I said, sending a forced smile to where Augustus stood watching me with narrowed eyes, his arms crossed over his chest. "I should like to bid ... *Mr. Brundage* farewell also." Sensing Lord Thorton watching us, I dipped into a small curtsy. "Thank you for everything, sir."

Augustus gave a subtle shake of his head as his only response, and I quickly turned from him, unable to bear the disenchantment in his eyes. Had I only kept my distance, I could have prevented his pain and my own. Such a fool I was. At least now Augustus would not become trapped in a marriage where he would soon grow to despise me.

"Well, then." Lady Thorton rose to her feet. "Let us be on our way." She paused briefly before Mrs. Brundage, her face void of emotion. "Thank you for your hospitality."

Mrs. Brundage gave a nod of acknowledgment. "It was our pleasure."

Filling the spot Lady Thorton had just left, Mother looked to Mrs. Brundage. "And thank you for taking care of Arabella when the Leavitts were no longer able to host her."

Mrs. Brundage's brow wrinkled, and she looked to Lady Thorton who waited impatiently by the drawing room door. "Of course." Her words came hesitantly. "We were pleased to have her here."

Mother reached out her arm to me, commanding me forward. "Come, Arabella."

Unable to glance at the faces watching me for fear my heart would burst with shame, I moved to Mother's side and followed her out the door behind Lady Thorton. Lord Thorton stepped in behind us.

The sunlight was now nauseatingly bright and the heat most unwelcome as we made our way to the carriage. Relieved to find Leah already positioned upon the coach box, I lowered my head, allowing my bonnet to block the world from view.

"Farewell!" Ruth called from the doorway.

Unable to resist, I glanced over my shoulder to find Ruth and Mrs. Brundage on the front steps. Ruth's waving hand dropped to wipe her eyes, and my heart constricted.

Lord Thorton offered me his hand. "May I assist you?"

I glanced from his hand to our mothers already situated in the carriage and back to Ruth. "Forgive me. I only need a moment."

He gave a nod, positioning himself to await my return.

Hurrying up the stairs, I didn't hesitate to wrap my arms around Ruth's neck with all the fervor of love I could muster. "Oh, my friend, how I shall miss you."

She welcomed the embrace, sniffling into my ear. "And I, you."

Mrs. Brundage wore a sad smile on her face. "Take care of yourself, my dear girl."

"Thank you for everything. I hope you know ..." My words trailed off, unable to find any acceptable reason to pardon my behavior and now the consequence of it.

"I do know." Mrs. Brundage squeezed my hand in hers. My gaze fell to the empty entry hall behind them, and my heart sank. "Tell Sarah I shall miss her also." I swallowed. "And tell Augustus ..." A tear escaped down my cheek, and I quickly brushed it away. "Just tell him that I hope he finds a woman deserving of him. And how very sorry I am."

Mrs. Brundage's lips turned downward at the corners, but she nodded her agreement.

"Arabella, dear." Mother's voice splintered through my hesitation. "Do make haste."

With one last glance at the place where my treacherous heart was certain Augustus would be, I swallowed my disappointment and made my way back to Lord Thorton. "Forgive my delay. I ..." I attempted to think of an excuse that would not make me appear foolishly sentimental and weak.

"You needed a proper goodbye," he said, an expression of understanding on his face. He grinned at me, extending his hand. "I can understand that."

Lady Thorton, on the other hand, appeared rightly cross as I settled into the rear-facing seat of the carriage next to Mother. "I still do not understand where the miscommunication took place." Her consideration moved from Mother to me, as her son moved on to the bench next to her. The carriage started forward.

Mother's eyes darted in my direction, letting me know that she intended to answer. "As I've thought about it, I believe there were simply too many last-minute changes occurring all at once." She gave a small lift of her shoulders as the carriage rolled forward. "I had only just returned to London when I received your missive inquiring if Arabella and I could join you at Branbury Court early. Though I sent letters to both Arabella and

Mr. Leavitt detailing our newly arranged plans, those letters obviously did not arrive in time. Nor did Mr. Leavitt's letter relaying Arabella's removal to Fairhaven, which I'm certain he wrote, reach me before my departure." Mother shook her head. "The timing is all quite bizarre."

The carriage swayed as we turned onto the main road, and I glanced out the window at Fairhaven. I hadn't realized how fond I'd grown of the place until it disappeared from sight, and I knew I would likely never see it again. I lifted a hand to cover the ache in my heart that was threatening to consume me.

"And why did you not simply accompany the Leavitts to the coast?" Lady Thorton's question was directed at me, forcing me from my anguish. "It seems most unusual for a relative to situate you elsewhere without first obtaining your parents' consent."

I sensed Mother grow rigid at my side, and I knew exactly what lie was expected of me. I straightened my slumping shoulders and met Lady Thorton's gaze. "With Mrs. Leavitt's quickly declining health, Mr. Leavitt thought it best to spare my sensitive nature. Returning me to London hardly seemed ideal, knowing I would simply arrive in time to make the journey right back to Branbury."

Lady Thorton's head tipped to the side. "But why the Brundages?"

Mother leaned forward. "Well the—"

Lady Thorton lifted a hand to silence Mother, keeping her sharp focus fixed on me.

I suppressed my shock at Lady Thorton's display of power over Mother. "Their location was ideal, being so near the Leavitts' estate, but mostly because the Brundages' niece, Ruth, was my dearest friend growing up in Bath." My gaze flickered to Mother. I would not allow her to take Ruth from me. Not again. "Mother has always been so very fond of her, so I suppose it seemed a natural solution to Mr. Leavitt."

Mother's lips pulled tight into a sort of grimaced smile. "Ruth was always a delightful girl." The glint in her eyes informed me she was up to something. "Though her past is a most unfortunate one."

I gave a small shake of my head, willing her to stop.

She released an exaggerated sigh, her defiant gaze returning to Lady Thorton. "You may recall the Seton case that occurred eight years past?"

Lady Thorton looked to her son, who shook his head. "I don't believe so."

"It was all quite tragic, really. The Setons, Ruth's parents, died in Mr. Seton's bedchamber. The Coroner's Court ruled it a murder and self-murder at the hand of Ruth's father."

"Oh, heavens," Lady Thorton whispered, lifting a hand to cover her mouth. "Poor dear."

I looked to Lady Thorton, hoping I had correctly discerned her feelings on the matter. "It was dreadful what happened. And I'm certain you can imagine what it could do to their daughter's reputation. But my parents realized it was no fault of Ruth's, so they have allowed us to maintain our relationship all these years." I glanced back at Mother, reaching out to take hold of her hand in a false display of sincerity. "I feel so blessed to have a mother like her."

Mother straightened, her hand clenching into a fist beneath mine. "It is I who is grateful for such an obedient daughter."

Lady Thorton gave a thoughtful nod. "Why did you not tell us as much earlier, Lady Godwin?"

I placed my hand back in my lap. "Oh, she is far too modest to tout her own praises."

Lady Thorton lifted her chin decisively. "Well, I think it is very noble of you, Lady Godwin." Her gaze met mine. "And I do hope absconding with you like that has in no way jeopardized your relationship. We would have been more cautious had we known the particulars."

Well aware I had accomplished my goal, I forced a smile to my unwilling lips. "I thank you for your sentiment, and I shall write to Ruth and ensure all is well. But she is the kindest person I know and will likely not think twice about it." I glanced at Lord Thorton, but he watched me with such unwavering consideration that I looked to his mother again. "I do hope you know how sorry I am for this debacle. Especially when you have so much to do to prepare for your other guests."

Lady Thorton hesitated only a moment before her posture relaxed slightly. "Well, it is done, so let us not speak of it further."

Mother and I nodded our understanding.

"Oh, I have also received word that your friend, Lady Beatrice Hancock and her companion will be joining us after all."

"Miss Marianne Browning?"

Lady Thorton gave a small lift of her shoulders. "I believe that was her name."

"I shall be glad to see them." And in part, it was the truth. The haunting look of disenchantment in Augustus's eyes pierced me each time my thoughts returned to him, and I longed for something to distract me from the pain, to help me forget what anguish I had caused him. Perhaps Lady Beatrice and Miss Browning would help me rebuild some semblance of what my life had been before going to Fairhaven.

CHAPTER NINETEEN

I pulled at the needle on my embroidery, my thoughts miles away at Fairhaven.

"Miss Godwin."

When I lifted my gaze, Lady Beatrice was wearing an exasperated expression. "What is it?"

Lady Beatrice shook her head. "Did you not hear a thing I said?"

I dropped my needlework to my lap. "Forgive me. I was lost in thought."

Lady Beatrice and Miss Browning shared a knowing glance before Lady Beatrice placed a stiff hand atop mine. "You have not been yourself since our arrival. What is the matter?"

"Nothing at all."

Lady Beatrice scanned my masked expression and removed her hand. "I had asked you if you had noticed that Miss Hutchison wore that same day dress not two days past?"

I glanced over at Miss Hutchison who sat contentedly reading on her own, her light pink day dress hardly familiar to me. "She appears content with her appearance and likely does not care much for our opinion."

Lady Beatrice nodded, as though my declaration had somehow proven her point. She lowered her voice even more. "I heard her mother speaking to some of the other ladies. Apparently, Miss Hutchison's incessant reading has become quite the problem as she will speak about nothing but books."

I released a slow breath. "And yet I can't help but think such conversation is likely more stimulating than most."

Lady Beatrice's eyes flickered toward her, not at all affected by my declaration. "Well, she shall never find a husband with such untoward behavior. No man wants a wife that reads."

I glanced down at my embroidery, attempting to conceal my irritation. "That is quite the generalization."

"Name a man you know who would prefer it."

I searched my thoughts. "Perhaps Mr. Morland."

Lady Beatrice pursed her lips. "I suppose he may, but Mr. Morland is a ninny so he does not count. What are your thoughts, Marianne?" Lady Beatrice glanced back toward her friend, apparently needing a more accommodating opinion.

Miss Browning lifted her gaze readily. "My father nearly refused to teach us to read on the off chance we would become overly fond of it."

Lady Beatrice nodded as though the admission had somehow proved her point. "It is lucky for me she holds no title, for I shall not find her seated near me at dinner. I cannot tolerate a bore."

I could not sit by a moment longer and allow them to carry on so. Placing my sampler on the settee next to me, I glanced over at Miss Hutchison. "Pardon me." Several ladies looked up from their stitching. "Miss Hutchison, is it?"

The young lady looked up from the pages of her book, an uncertain expression on her face. "It is."

I smiled sweetly at her. "I was wondering if you would care to join us for a bit. We were just discussing how captivating your book appeared to be, and we hoped you would be willing to tell us about it."

She looked slightly wary of the invitation. "I would be delighted to join you." She stood and started toward us.

Lady Beatrice scowled at me, gesturing for Miss Browning to scoot so that Miss Hutchison could take the seat farthest from her on the settee.

I held out my hand for her book as she approached. "Evelina," I read, examining the front cover before handing it back. "And you say it is good?"

She took the book from me, clasping it to her chest. "It is better than good."

I gestured for her to take a seat. "Will you not tell us about it? I fear we are in desperate need of amusement."

With only one hesitant glance toward Lady Beatrice, she began. Miss Hutchison spoke of a young heroine's entrance into Society, Evelina's innocent nature leading to constant ridicule as well as hilarious blunders. My thoughts returned to Ruth time and time again as she spoke, and I could not help but laugh and worry along with Miss Hutchison's explanation.

"But what of Lord Orville?" Lady Beatrice asked, apparently forgetting her disinterest.

Miss Hutchison lifted her shoulders. "I haven't read far enough to know."

Miss Browning sighed dreamily. "You will tell us when you have finished, won't you?"

"Of course I shall." Miss Hutchison stood, looking

down at me. "Thank you for inviting me to join you, Miss Godwin."

The sincerity in her words warmed my heart, and I realized I felt more myself in this moment than I had felt in days. Though Mother would be vexed with my social blunder of associating with an outsider, I thought of Augustus. Perhaps he would have been proud of me for using my influence to lift another. Not that such a small act would budge the scale of wrongdoings. "Thank you for sharing the story with us, Miss Hutchison."

Lady Beatrice released a thoughtful hum. "I suppose if all books were so entertaining as that one, I would not oppose reading so much."

I could not hide my delight at my small success. "I'm certain Miss Hutchison could provide you with recommendations of equal caliber."

Lady Beatrice lifted her chin. "Do you know when the gentlemen are set to return? I thought there was to be a picnic."

"I believe the picnic is set for Thursday."

Lady Beatrice released an overdone sigh. "May we at least go outside for a turn about the grounds? I feel so cooped up."

Without a moment's hesitation, I stood. "That sounds ideal. Shall we?"

The fresh air engulfed me as we wandered out of doors. I closed my eyes, lifting my face to the sun.

"You don't wish to freckle, do you?" Lady Beatrice watched me with an odd expression.

"If it means my skin can feel the warmth of a summer's afternoon, I shouldn't mind at all."

Lady Beatrice secured her bonnet more tightly under her chin, as though my very suggestion might freckle her.

Lord Thorton's booming laugh sent us turning. A

group of more than a dozen gentlemen were walking toward us from the stables.

"Out for a stroll?" Lord Thorton deviated from the other gentlemen toward us.

I gave a small curtsy as he approached. "Yes. It is too fine a day to stay indoors."

He glanced around. "May I join you?"

Lady Beatrice and Miss Browning both nodded their agreement, and I offered a hesitant smile. "Please do." He extended an arm toward me, and I accepted it. "Did you enjoy your morning ride?"

"Yes. Some of the men wished to see Branbury's property lines, so it took a bit longer than I had originally planned."

"I did not think I'd see you until dinner, so this is a pleasant surprise."

He appraised my profile. "Is it?"

"Of course," I said, feeling that all-too-familiar prick of guilt.

"Well, I'm glad to hear it."

We followed Lady Beatrice and Miss Browning in relative silence to the large gardens situated behind the house.

"Miss Godwin, I can't help but wonder if there is something amiss."

"Not in the least."

He paused his steps, causing me to stop also. "And yet I am perplexed by you."

My chest tightened. "I'm not certain what you mean."

A smirk came to his lips. "I'm trying to make sense of it myself, though I'm having a difficult time of it." He heaved a heavy breath. "When we came to retrieve you from Fairhaven, I wasn't expecting to find you so ..."

"Disheveled?"

His laugh boomed, causing Lady Beatrice and Miss Browning to glance over their shoulders at us. "I suppose that is part of it, and yet I'm pleased I glimpsed you in such a state. You stirred something inside of me that day, and I long to witness it again."

It was then that I noticed the unusual glint in his eyes. It could not be. I wanted no false expectations in a marriage partner. "And here I thought you sought an impeccably-trained lady, my lord."

"I do. An impeccably trained lady with a spark about her."

I glanced away, allowing my bonnet to conceal my pained expression. The spark Lord Thorton spoke of had been ignited by a man now gone from my life forever. A spark I was certain he would never be the cause of.

"Miss Godwin, could I speak candidly?"

"Is that not what you have been doing?" I asked, a laugh behind my words to soften them.

"Yes, I suppose I have."

I drew in a calming breath, setting my gaze on Lady Beatrice and Miss Browning several paces in front of us. "But, by all means, please continue."

"It is apparent our mothers are quite set on seeing us married."

My stomach knotted. "Yes. I believe they are."

"And from what I know of you and your collection of refused offers, yours is not so different a past from my own. The only variation seems to be how we go about rebelling. I refuse to offer for the women my mother attempts to throw at me, while you refuse to accept the men your mother thrusts at you."

Lord Thorton's reasoning was as good as any I could offer and far preferable to the truth that I'd come to understand at the beach—that my love for Augustus was the actual reason behind every refusal. But Augustus could not be my reason any longer. "And yet it seems you have the upper hand." I forced a playful smile. "No one knows of how often you disobey your mother's wishes, while all of the Beau Monde whispers of mine."

"And that is precisely why I have never judged you for your reputation. I always assumed we were similar in that regard."

"Yes." Why did the admission feel so painful? Lord Thorton and I were a suitable match, and I had known it all along.

He hesitated. "And that is also why I believe we should both agree to lower our guards and actually get to know one another. We may soon discover we are as compatible as our mothers believe us to be."

I met Lord Thorton's gaze, refusing to let my thoughts drift to Augustus. Lord Thorton was not only my last viable option, but a man comparable to myself. I could no longer hope for more. And though I wished to reason with him, to tell him that we would both be happier if we did not allow emotion to guide us in our union, I would not extinguish the inkling of hope I glimpsed in him. If an empty hope is what it took to obtain his offer, so be it. Better his eventual dissatisfaction than Augustus's. For, from what I had heard of Lord Thorton's reputation, he would not hesitate to find delight elsewhere once he tired of me, where Augustus would remain loyal in his misery. "I believe I could agree to that."

I GLANCED AROUND THE ELABORATE, mahogany furnishings of the Rose Room. The bed was nearly double the size of the one at Fairhaven, with large posts on the corners that seemed to reach up to the ceiling. The walls were a deep shade of burgundy, and the golden framed portraits commanded the eye. Even the chaise lounge by the fireplace was exquisite, with its scarlet, striped fabric and golden piping. It was all so elegant, yet it felt somehow ... inhospitable.

Leah moved to my side. "Do you need anything else, miss?"

"No." I glanced at my readied reflection, attempting to muster some sort of pleasure at how handsome I had been made to look. Yet the image I saw was Augustus's expression when he'd looked at me that first night at Fairhaven when I'd worn this very gown. I shook the thought from my mind. Augustus was far better off without me.

A sharp knock echoed through the room, and Leah sent me an uneasy glance.

"Perhaps it is Lady Beatrice." My false hope was evident in my tone.

Leah nodded and moved to the door, opening it just enough to see out.

Mother stepped through so swiftly that Leah was forced to take a step back to prevent the door from hitting her.

"Arabella, I must speak with you."

My eyes flickered to Leah. Though I dreaded being left alone with Mother, I could not allow Leah to be caught in the crossfire again. "Leah, will you go see Lady Beatrice's maid about the recipe we were just discussing? The rose lip salve?"

Leah bobbed her head at my hastily created excuse, curtsied, and left.

I focused on the full-length mirror, attempting to convey a sense of composure despite my racing heart and damp palms beneath my gloves. "What is it you wish to speak to me about?"

"Much." She paused. "I have finally received a letter from your father."

My chest constricted, and though I tried to remain unaffected, I could not stop myself from glancing at her reflection.

"Ah. Did you think I had forgiven you your deceit?" Mother stepped behind me, focusing on our reflection. She placed her hands on both of my shoulders, leaning in close to one ear. "I have not."

I swallowed, searching for the courage to tell her I had my own inquiry to make as to her threatening Ruth. But the courage did not come.

"And though I do enjoy watching you squirm under the weight of your own conscience, I fear there is no time before dinner for your confession." Mother dropped her hands. "Instead I have come to ask why you have not yet received Lord Thorton's offer?"

I lifted my chin, unwilling to tell her of my half-hearted attempts to let down my guard so Lord Thorton could come to know me. "We have only been at Branbury a week."

"And yet you have known him longer than most men who have offered for you."

"Lord Thorton does not seem as eager as other men to enter matrimony, but I assure you I am doing everything you taught me to do in order to secure him."

"Then why is there talk below stairs that leaves me questioning how thorough a job you're doing? For as dense as gentlemen are, even they can recognize when a lady's thoughts and affections are otherwise engaged."

The air felt thick as I drew in a breath. "There is talk of such things amongst the servants?"

"Besides you and me, there were only three other people who witnessed your folly: Lady Thorton, Lord Thorton, and your maid."

"Leah would not spread such a tale."

Mother narrowed her eyes, as though she could sense my lapse in not keeping a necessary detachment toward my servant. "I do not believe it was your maid, as I made it quite clear what the consequence would be if she betrayed me again. And Lady Thorton, thank heavens, has seemingly decided to overlook your recklessness and continues to hope for a forthcoming engagement. Which leaves us …?" Her voice trailed off expectantly.

"Lord Thorton," I whispered.

"Precisely. His concerns were likely shared with his valet who proceeded to share it with the rest of the servants. Vile creatures with their need for gossip."

"One mention of a concern does not mean he has lost interest, Mother."

Mother clasped my upper arms, the tips of her fingers digging into the delicate skin beneath. "Interest gets us nowhere, Arabella. You must convince him of your devotion, for I am not certain how well I will bear another of your disappointments."

I pulled in a shaky breath, distinguishing the threat in her tone and the distress it caused. And suddenly I became aware that I would do anything to be free of Mother and her vicious control of my life. "I will, Mother," I said with new conviction. "I will convince Lord Thorton."

She tossed my arms from her grip and faced the mirror, smoothing her hands over the emerald silk of her gown and readjusting her matching necklace. "Now go." She flicked her wrist toward the door. "Dinner will be announced in twenty minutes and you have much to accomplish."

Without a word of protest, I glided from the room, rubbing at the tender spots on my arms as I made my way downstairs. *I will soon be free of Mother* was my rallying cry as I glanced around the drawing room. Lord Thorton's awaiting gaze met mine. There was no more delaying. I would demonstrate that my affections were his and his alone. It didn't matter that my heart constricted at my resolve, for the sooner I could achieve his offer, the better. I moved toward Lord Thorton with determination.

"Miss Godwin." He stepped away from the group of gentlemen he'd been speaking to and bowed, sending me the smile that had once made my whole being alight with pride. "You look absolutely ravishing this evening."

I dropped into a brief curtsy, locking my eyes with him as I lifted. "Thank you, my lord. I could easily say the same of you."

He gave a hearty laugh, and I felt several gazes shift to us. "I believe I should like to hear it from your lips. Please go on."

My cheeks warmed at his affront, but I stepped closer, revealing to him that I appreciated his encouragement. Or, at least, appeared to. "Perhaps we could find a moment later ... when there are not so many listening ears about to overhear my praise?"

A mischievous smirk touched his lips. "I have been longing to steal a private moment with you, so that sounds delightful." He glanced behind me. "And speaking of delightful, the last of our party arrived a little over an hour ago."

I tilted my head, attempting to recall which of the guests were missing. I could think of no one. "Remind me who it is we were waiting on."

He flicked his head, and I followed his line of sight just over my shoulder. My heart thudded to a halt. "Augustus?"

Augustus's severe expression appraised me momentarily before he offered a stiff bow. "Miss Godwin."

No matter how much I willed it, I could not pull my gaze from his look of betrayal.

Lord Thorton took a step closer to me, leaning in until I could feel his breath on my ear. "I hope you don't mind my being so bold, but I thought to surprise you by the gesture." I blinked several times, as though I might be imagining the whole thing. But Augustus did not disappear.

I glanced back toward Lord Thorton, expecting to find malice or spite in his expression. Yet I found nothing but curiosity. "How unexpected, my lord." My voice came out hoarse, and I cleared my throat.

"Miss Seton is here also."

"Ruth is here?" I glanced around in a panic, hoping none of the ladies had gotten to her first. She would be eaten alive in this pack of venomous creatures.

"She is taking dinner in her room." Lord Thorton placed a light hand on my back, directing me toward where Augustus stood. "Is that not correct, Mr. Brundage?"

Augustus gave a brisk nod. "Yes, she did not believe she could be readied in time to join us, but she will be down to socialize after dinner."

I swallowed, sensing both men watching me. "I am most eager to see her. I have hardly felt myself since our hasty goodbye."

Lord Thorton gave a satisfied smile. "I'm glad you are pleased, Miss Godwin." He glanced toward the entrance where his mother stood glaring at him. "If you will both excuse me one moment. I believe I am needed."

My lips parted, longing to protest being left alone with Augustus, but Lord Thorton walked away before I could offer an excuse. I glanced around at the familiar faces, none of which seemed to be taking particular interest in Augustus and me. "What are you doing?" I hissed.

His jaw slackened. "As though I am the one that owes you an explanation?"

"You wish for an explanation?" I lifted my chin, willing it not to quiver. "I made a mistake in accepting your offer. It could never work between us. It is better for us both if we find a more suitable situation." The words were half-truths, but I would not give more.

"I can see you've wasted no time."

I took a calming breath, not wishing to draw unnecessary attention. "You knew of my intentions, so don't make me out to be some kind of conniving temptress that lured you along without your consent."

His ire reflected back at me. "Pardon me if I'm making you out to be something you aren't."

Tears pricked my eyes. "Think what you like. It cannot matter."

"Let me tell you what I think, and you can decide if it matters or not." The force of his gaze bore into me. "You are scared, Bella."

I glanced toward Lord Thorton to make certain his notice was still elsewhere. "And what is it I am scared of?"

"Besides your mother? You fear marrying beneath the expectations placed upon you. You fear a lowering in your social standing." He lifted a knowing brow. "But more than all of that, I'd say you're most terrified of being loved."

"That is ridiculous."

"Is it? Then why have you rejected every man who has offered for you?"

I swallowed. "That is not your concern."

"Considering I am now one of those men, I believe it is."

I skimmed the room, deciding what I could say to appease him without revealing the truth—none of the others were him. And yet, I did not deserve him. I lifted a casual shoulder. "When the time came to accept, it simply never felt right."

A muscle in his jaw flexed. "Not even with me?"

My heart ached, and I could not force the lie from my lips. "This is not the time to discuss such a thing."

"It seems with you there is never a good time to discuss the difficult topics."

I knew he was referring to Mother and concealing my stay at Fairhaven from her, but what good would it do to acknowledge it or explain to him my reasonings? The sooner he realized the kind of person I was, the sooner he'd let me go.

"And who is this handsome gentleman?" Lady Beatrice stepped to my side with Miss Browning in her wake. "I am certain we have not been introduced."

With every last bit of will power, I forced a smile to my lips. "Mr. Brundage is an old friend of mine."

"He seems very much worth mentioning, yet I don't recall you telling me of him." Lady Beatrice assessed him with far too much pleasure. "Will you not provide an introduction, Miss Godwin?"

My body trembled from suppressing too many emotions, but I glanced back toward Augustus. "Mr. Brundage, this is Lady Beatrice and Miss Browning."

Augustus bowed. "It is a pleasure."

Lady Beatrice gave a generous crack of her fan to open

it before moving it in an amorous flutter. "I assure you, the pleasure is mine."

My stomach clenched at her brazen display, though I was thankful Augustus had missed my discussion with Ruth and Sarah on what the swift movement of her fan indicated.

"So, how is it you know one another?" Lady Beatrice took a step nearer Augustus.

"As Miss Godwin stated, we are just *old* friends. Nothing more."

I swallowed. "His cousin was my neighbor in Bath. She will be down after dinner, though I have already introduced you both to her at Lord and Lady Brimhall's ball three weeks past."

Lady Beatrice and Miss Browning shared a questioning glance.

"A Miss Ruth Seton?"

Lady Beatrice's eyes lit with recognition. "Oh, yes. Your *neighbor.*"

I gave a nod, hoping they would consider the connection and therefore decide to leave Augustus alone.

"She was a delightful girl." Lady Beatrice smiled sweetly at Augustus with not even a hint of the repulsion she'd displayed that night. "With lovely brown eyes and hair to match, if I recall correctly."

Augustus nodded. "Yes."

Lady Beatrice closed her fan and tapped Augustus on the arm with it. "So tell us. What was Miss Godwin like when she was younger? Did she collect as many unwanted hearts in Bath as she has managed to collect in London?"

His forlorn gaze slid to me. "Not that I'm aware of. But then I don't believe she was set upon collecting hearts when I knew her."

Despite the touch of benevolence in his voice, Lady

Beatrice giggled, her lips parting as though he had dealt me a great blow.

"Oh, look." In an attempt to prevent Lady Beatrice from offering any more of her opinions on the matter, I directed the others' notice to Lady Thorton. "I believe it is time to walk in to dinner." And to my great relief, the women truly were beginning to arrange themselves discreetly in order of highest rank. Lady Beatrice sent Augustus a small pout. "I suppose we shall have to continue our conversation after dinner."

"Yes, you shall." I smiled, never so grateful that Augustus did not hold a title, for he would not be seated anywhere near Lady Beatrice.

CHAPTER TWENTY

"*B*ella!" I cringed inwardly and glanced toward the drawing room door as Ruth's high-pitched tone drew the collective attention of the ladies. I had spent the first while after dinner keeping an attentive eye on the entrance in hopes of preventing this precise welcome, but when Ruth had not come, I had let down my guard, thinking she had likely opted to stay in her room for the night.

Ruth gave a foolish wave and hurried toward me, making me curse myself for not being more vigilant. "Oh, Bella. How I have missed you this past week."

I reached out my hands to grasp hers, ensuring she would not wrap me in an embrace. "I can hardly believe you are here. I did not know the room in which you were staying, or I would have come to you earlier."

"Oh, I wish you had. I've been ready for quite some time, but I wasn't certain I would find the courage to come down on my own. Thankfully Leah had heard of my arrival and came to greet me. With a little persuasion, here I am."

A smile touched my lips at hearing of Leah's kindness. "And look how lovely your gown turned out." I took a step back to appraise Ruth.

Ruth lifted her skirts with one hand, swishing her new gown from side to side. "I didn't think it would be ready in time, but Augustus paid an additional sum to have them both finished before our departure. And I cannot wait for you to see how well the ball gown turned out. "

I glanced around at the curious faces observing Ruth's display, before noticing Mother's glare. She flicked her head toward Lady Thorton, and I realized our oversight. "And have you greeted Lady Thorton yet?"

"No." Ruth's eyes widened. "I have erred already, haven't I?"

I stepped to her side, and latched my arm through hers. "You were just excited to see me. Lady Thorton will understand that."

Ruth's body was rigid as I led her forward. "Oh, but I'm so nervous."

Though my stomach clenched at our upcoming inter-action, I could not let Ruth sense my hesitation. "There is no need to be nervous. Just remember what I taught you."

Ruth's elbow tightened around my arm. "I can't remember a thing right now, let alone what you taught me." She shook her head. "I'm destined to make a fool of myself. I just know it."

As we approached the group where Lady Thorton and Mother stood, I lowered my voice. "Just don't speak until spoken to, and try to curb your excitement."

Ruth gave a quick bob of her head just as we stopped before Lady Thorton.

Lady Thorton gave a regal nod of acknowledgment. "Miss Seton. How delighted we are to have you at Bran-bury Court." I pressed my hand against Ruth's arm, reminding her not to speak until I was certain Lady Thorton was finished. "Did your aunt not join you?" she asked, glancing behind us.

Ruth shook her head. "No, my aunt does not care for house parties in the least, not even one in so grand a place as Branbury Court."

I stifled a wince, wondering how Lady Thorton would take Ruth's unintended slight.

Lady Thorton gave a hesitant nod. "And who has accompanied you as your chaperone? My son did not say."

Ruth quirked her head and scrunched her nose. "Chaperone? I did not even think about such a thing, being as I've never had need of one before. I suppose Mrs. Whitmore might have been a chaperone of sorts while I was in London, but I never referred to her as that."

Mother cleared her throat. "If you are without, I shall gladly accept the role."

I studied Mother, trying to determine if her offer was given out of false charity or with a more calculated purpose in mind.

"Oh, that would be delightful. Thank you, Lady Godwin." Ruth directed her wide smile at me. "How alike the two of you are."

Mother's gaze met mine, and her stone smile was evidence that she was as insulted by the compliment as I had been.

"It is the least I can do." Mother reached a hand out toward Ruth, which Ruth eagerly accepted. "Arabella, go introduce Miss Seton to some of the other ladies, and I shall find you both for proper introductions when the gentlemen return."

I nodded, inducing Ruth along with a gentle tug.

Ruth paused, dipping into a haphazard curtsy. "Thank

you again for allowing me to Branbury, Lady Thorton. I am utterly thrilled to be here with Bella."

Mother sent me a pointed look, and I pulled a touch harder, leading Ruth away from the amused whispers.

Ruth leaned in close as we made our way across the drawing room. "Are you vexed?"

I had spent the last fortnight advising Ruth against almost everything she had just done, but when I met her worried expression I could not say as much. "No. You did very well." I paused. "Perhaps a touch exuberant, but do not fret, I believe it was just nerves."

Ruth released a small huff. "I hope I don't prove an embarrassment to you."

I stopped to face her. "You could never be an embarrassment to me."

She gave a contented smile.

"There is something I must ask you." I drew in a breath, and glanced around to ensure no one was near enough to overhear. "Does Augustus despise me now?"

Ruth's shoulders dropped, and she leaned her head to one side. "No. He is hurt and perplexed, but I'm certain he could never despise you."

My heart nearly broke at her declaration. It somehow seemed worse that he wouldn't hate me for what I had done. And though a part of me longed to explain myself to both of them, I knew it wouldn't help. I was set on my decision. Augustus deserved someone worthy of his love.

"And don't worry, Augustus already told me I must not speak of what happened between the two of you."

I breathed a sigh of relief at Augustus's foresight. "He is right. It must not be spoken—"

"Miss Seton, is it?" Lady Beatrice sent Miss Browning a knowing glance, stepping to join us.

"It is." Ruth wrinkled her nose before a touch of recognition lit her eyes. "We met at the ball given by Lord and Lady Brimhall, did we not?"

Lady Beatrice lifted her chin, as though insulted by the very idea that Ruth wasn't certain of their introduction. "Yes, though we did not have the opportunity to speak for long."

"And remind me of your names?"

I squeezed Ruth's arm. "This is Lady Beatrice Hancock," I said, in a tone that urged her to remember. "And Miss Browning."

"Oh, of course." There was uncertainty in Ruth's expression. "Lady Beatrice Hancock and Miss Browning." She spoke the names slowly, as though committing them to memory. "It is such a pleasure to see you again."

"Yes." Lady Beatrice looked to Miss Browning. "Were we not just saying how we long to know Miss Seton better?"

Miss Browning nodded in eager agreement.

I tightened the fist at my side, too aware of Lady Beatrice's reason for befriending Ruth.

"That would be wonderful." The sincerity in Ruth's voice irked me as much as the genuine smile on her lips. Why could she not be wiser to the ways of the world? "And to think I was nervous about meeting Bella's friends. How silly of me."

Lady Beatrice pressed her lips together, clearly suppressing her amusement. "We already had the privilege of meeting your cousin, Mr. Brundage. He seems a most agreeable gentleman."

Ruth bobbed her head. "Oh, he is the best of men. I don't know what I would do without him."

"How endearing." Lady Beatrice sent Miss Browning another knowing glance. "And, if I might be so bold, is your cousin spoken for?"

Ruth's gaze shot to me. "Well ... I ..."

"He is." I squeezed Ruth's arm tightly, hoping she would not contradict me with the perceptive eyes of Lady Beatrice upon us. "An engagement is expected to take place between Mr. Brundage and a Miss Whitmore." I could feel Ruth's gaze searching my profile, but to my great relief she said nothing.

Lady Beatrice gave a pout. "How unfortunate."

I lifted a hand toward Lady Beatrice. "You never finished telling me of your visit to the Meads and how you came to shorten your stay."

Lady Beatrice flicked her nose at Miss Browning, as though she could not be bothered to relay such a tale yet again.

Miss Browning gave a small nod, realizing her role. "The vixen, Miss Gilbert, conveniently had relatives not three miles from the Meads and arranged to stay with them for the summer. Though Mr. Mead swore to his parents that he did not know of it, he was all too eager to accommodate Miss Gilbert's outwardly innocent excuses to meet while she was nearby. Within a fortnight, he had offered for her."

I tilted my head, returning my regard to Lady Beatrice. "I am so sorry to hear of how it all came to be."

Lady Beatrice flung her wrist upward. "You well know that men like Mr. Mead are amusing distractions and nothing more. As with you, I could never settle on a man without a title, despite his fortune."

Ruth's mouth gaped open, obviously taking it as a personal insult. "Amusing distractions?"

I gave a subtle shake of my head, willing her to hold her tongue. "She speaks of my previous offers, that is all."

Ruth glanced between us. "I simply don't believe a

person should be refused because they lack a title or a fortune."

Lady Beatrice smirked, but Miss Browning sent her an understanding look. "And yet it is the way of things."

"Miss Seton." Mother stepped to my side. "The gentlemen have finished taking their port. Come with me, and I shall make introductions."

"Very well."

I gave a farewell nod to Lady Beatrice and Miss Browning and stepped to join them.

Mother held out a hand to stop me. "You may stay here."

"But I'm certain Ruth will be more at ease if I join you."

"And I'm certain you have a task of your own to see to."

I did not move, unsure if I wished to defy Mother for such a trivial thing as introductions.

Mother's pointed look softened when it shifted to Ruth. "Come, dear. I shall return you to Arabella the moment we are through."

Ruth obediently released my arm, sending me an apologetic glance as Mother led her forward without me. Instead of dwelling on my dismissal, I searched the men flowing into the drawing room, looking for Augustus's sandy-brown hair and handsome smile.

But no. He could not matter. Instead I set my focus on Lord Thorton who had stopped to speak with his mother. I felt nothing when I looked at him, yet that is exactly what I required. And I was more certain of that now than ever. The disenchantment I'd seen in Augustus's eyes during our last two interactions was enough to haunt me for a lifetime, but to contemplate facing it every day for the rest of my life was too much to bear. No. A marriage of convenience to Lord Thorton was my only option.

"How is it Miss Seton and her cousin came to be here at Branbury?" Lady Beatrice asked, following Ruth with her eyes.

I looked toward Ruth to find Augustus at her side, and Mother looking less than pleased with his intrusion on the introductions. He didn't seem to care. I turned away before my amusement could show. "Lord Thorton invited them."

"But for what purpose?"

I shrugged, unwilling to speak my conjecture.

Lady Beatrice scanned her friend's thoughtful expression. "What is it, Marianne?"

Miss Browning hesitated. "I feel as though I know the name Seton, but I can't seem to place it. You said she was your neighbor in Bath, Miss Godwin?"

I nodded slowly, contemplating whether I should confess Ruth's past before Miss Browning recalled it on her own. "Her parents died about eight years ago. It was quite a tragic situation."

Miss Browning's eyes widened with horror at the realization. "Those were Miss Seton's parents?"

Lady Beatrice looked from Miss Browning's shocked expression to me. "What happened?"

I made certain Ruth and Augustus were still across the room from us. "The court determined that Mr. Seton killed his wife and then killed himself." Lady Beatrice lifted a hand to her mouth as I hastened on. "But there is recent evidence to suggest it was not so."

The two ladies shared a look of misgiving.

"The case will soon be heard at the Court of the Chancery, and it is very likely the initial decision will be overturned."

"What is it that has you ladies so enthralled?" Lord

Thorton asked, stepping to my side with Mr. Green and Mr. Oliver in his wake.

Lady Beatrice pulled out her fan, giving it a soft flick of her wrist. "We were discussing Miss Seton."

"And what of Miss Seton?" Lord Thorton stepped closer to me, giving space for his friends.

"I was explaining a bit of her past and the hardships she has endured."

Lord Thorton's consideration landed on Ruth who was offering Lord Hancock an awkward curtsy under Mother's vigilant eye. "For such a tragic past, she sure has a lot of spirit."

The five of them laughed, and though my chest heated with indignation, I forced out a smile. "Yet who could blame her?" Their mocking snickers halted, awaiting my revelation. "One set to inherit such a large fortune can afford to have less care for others' opinions."

"She is an heiress?" Lady Beatrice asked, appearing quite startled by the news.

I paused, deciding how much stretching of the truth was acceptable in shielding a friend—and in some part myself—from mockery. "It is not yet official, but shall likely be soon. Her father, after all, was a man of immense wealth."

The shared looks of astonishment told me I'd perhaps gone a touch too far.

Mr. Green's gaze lingered on Ruth a long moment. "Even without a fortune, Miss Seton seems a lady worth knowing."

My heart lifted at his acknowledgment, and I censured myself for ever having thought Mr. Green beneath my notice. "I assure you, she is."

❧

Notwithstanding the lateness of the hour, Mother insisted on accompanying me to my room before bed. When the door was secured behind us, she turned on me. "Did you know of their arrival?"

There was no way to feign ignorance as to what she was speaking of. "No. Lord Thorton relayed that he wished it to be a surprise."

"Why in heaven's name would he bring the one man ..." Her words trailed off, before her piercing glare returned to me. "It is a test."

I swallowed, her words confirming my own fears.

"It seems Lord Thorton is not as big of a fool as the rest of his sex." She released a puff of air. "You must prove to him where your devotion lies."

Despite the constriction in my chest, I straightened my shoulders. "But what if it does not lie with him?"

Mother's palpable abhorrence nearly silenced me, but now that I had begun, I refused to cower.

"Does Lord Thorton not also deserve a wife that prefers him above all other men?"

Mother scoffed. "No. Nor should you be foolish enough to expect the same from him. Marriage is a business union, little more. So long as you do what is expected of you as a wife, and use discretion in everything else, you will make Lord Thorton an equitable match."

My stomach twisted at her insinuation, and I shook my head. "Marriage can be more than that."

Mother's laugh mocked me. "You still fancy yourself in love with that pitiable, untitled man, Mr. Brundage?"

Resentment coursed through my veins, but I knew my defiance would not only serve to worsen my own consequence, but that of Ruth and Augustus as well. "No. I was mistaken in my feelings for Mr. Brundage. Just as I was mistaken with the other gentlemen I encouraged before him."

"Do not lie to me, Arabella. I was the one who taught you the art of deception."

My teeth clenched at the reminder of her part in all of this—in her making me into someone unworthy of Augustus's love. "If you expect the truth from me, then I will hold you to that same standard."

"Arabella—"

"Explain why you allowed me to believe for years that I had been forgotten by Ruth and Augustus."

Mother lifted her chin. "It was necessary."

"As was your threat to Ruth, I suppose?"

"You know nothing. And yet you stand on your moral high ground, unaware that it has crumbled beneath you long ago."

"You threatened to ruin an innocent child." My voice quivered, and I cursed my weakness.

Mother did not respond for some time, her eyes fixed on me. "A threat that apparently needs reinstating."

Though my legs trembled beneath me, I grasped at my waning courage. "You no longer hold any power over her. I have told the others of her past."

"What have you told them? That Ruth's father took her mother's life, then his own?"

The boredom in her voice sent a shiver through me. "What do you know?"

"What if I told you that the Setons' deaths were not committed at the hand of Ruth's father?"

I lifted my chin. "Evidence in support of that very conclusion has already been gathered. It is likely already being reviewed at the Court of Chancery."

Mother's brow lowered. "And what conclusion is being sought?"

My throat grew tight, and I wondered if I should tell her. "Only that it could not have been Mr. Seton who committed the crime." Mother's sigh of relief filled the space between us, and I leaned a hand on the wall to support my unsteady legs. "Do you know who committed the murders?" I whispered.

"Regrettably, I do."

I shook my head and took a step away from her. "Why did you not tell the authorities?"

"Life is not that simple."

My head throbbed, attempting to understand what she was alluding to. Had Mother something to do with their deaths? Had Papa?

"And let's just say, it would do no one any good to have the truth revealed now, especially not Ruth."

"You have lied to me before in order to get me to comply. Why would you not do so now?" My voice was weak and full of doubt.

"Perhaps you should ask your father when he arrives at the week's end. He was made to see the wisdom of concealment. And though he did err greatly by allowing you to Fairhaven, I'm certain he is once again steadfast in his resolve."

My courage waned, but I pressed one last time. "Tell me who killed them."

"No." Mother released a heavy breath. "Despite what you believe, I do care to protect you."

A light knock sounded at the door, and we both stilled.

Mother's eyes narrowed. "Are you not going to answer it?" Though her voice was soft, her tone was foreboding. "I am most curious to see who would be visiting at this late hour, as you've not yet rung for your maid."

I offered a silent prayer that Augustus would not be so

foolish as to visit my bedchamber and opened the door, just enough to see out.

The sight of Ruth standing there, her candlelight dancing in the darkness, could not have been more welcome. "Ruth. What is it?"

"Oh, Bella, I fear I cannot sleep."

I held out my own candle to more fully illuminate her, noting that she still wore her gown. "Have you tried?"

She shook her head. "No. But I'm just so certain I won't be able to. My room is so big and dark, and I was shaking just standing alone searching for the bell pull to call for my maid. The mere thought of trying to sleep in such a state …" She bit at her lip. "May I come in with you?"

I glanced over my shoulder at Mother. The absence of the candlelight shadowed her, leaving me uncertain what I should say. I could not risk Ruth becoming a target of Mother's vexation.

Mother took hold of the door and pulled it from my reluctant grip, revealing herself to Ruth.

"Oh, forgive me." Ruth lifted a hand to her mouth and glanced between us. "I hadn't realized you were here, Lady Godwin. I can come back later … or perhaps just wait out here until you are through speaking."

Mother forced a tight smile to her lips. "I believe we have discussed quite enough for one night." She took hold of my candle and stepped out the door, pausing next to Ruth. "What a delight it is to have you here." The false sincerity in Mother's voice nearly fooled me.

"And I'm so grateful to be here." Ruth returned her smile without reservation. "And thank you again for your kindness today. I hope acting as my chaperone will not be too much of a burden on you."

"Not in the least. I'm certain the arrangement will

actually prove most advantageous." Mother glanced back at me. "Do you not agree, Arabella?"

I did not answer.

Mother turned from us. "Sleep well," she said over her shoulder as the darkness dispersed from her retreating figure.

I drew in a shaky breath and gestured Ruth inside. "Do come in. Leah can help you ready for bed also." I stopped to pull the ornamental bell lever to inform Leah she was needed.

"Is that what that is?" Ruth held her candle up to the bronze circle, a small handle protruding from one side. "Silly me. I was looking for a bell pull in my room, not a lever."

Retrieving another candle, I brought it to hers and waited for the wick to take light. My hand still shook, but the flickering light thankfully concealed it. "Did you enjoy your evening?" I asked, desperate to take my mind off my encounter with Mother.

"I suppose so. At least once my nerves settled a bit."

"And what did you think of Mr. Green? He seemed to pay you a particular interest after your introduction."

"Do you think?"

"Absolutely."

Ruth gave a hesitant smile. "He is very handsome."

"And he is the son of a baron. A second son, mind you, but he likely has many advantageous connections."

"You would consider him a suitable match, then?"

I smiled, too aware of what a marriage to Mr. Green could do for Ruth's reputation. The shelter it could provide her. Besides, Mr. Green was Lord Thorton's oldest friend, so if an arrangement could be made between Ruth and him, she would surely remain a constant in my life. "It would do you no harm to determine for yourself if he was."

Ruth tilted her head thoughtfully, her nose wrinkling. "But what of Mr. Treynor?"

"He is a good man. But he has not spoken for you, nor mentioned his intentions of doing so. Or am I mistaken?"

Ruth shook her head.

"Then why not allow Mr. Green a chance to win your approval? And by doing so, if you determine Mr. Treynor the superior choice, then you will be more certain in where to place your encouragements."

Ruth bit at her lip absently. "I suppose you are right. I'm not even certain what Mr. Treynor's feelings are toward me, though I had hoped they were similar to my own."

I moved to the vanity and began removing my jewelry, withholding my assurance that a few more interactions with Mr. Treynor, and Ruth would very likely have an offer from him. Even still, if she could secure it, Mr. Green was the better match. For both of us. Then Ruth and I could always be together. "It is easier to discover if a man is left wanting when you compare him to another of high standing."

Ruth followed me, her eyes on my darkened reflection. "Is that why you decided against Augustus when Lord Thorton arrived? Was Augi left wanting?"

"Of course not." I faced her. "In truth, I've never met a man Augustus was inferior to."

"But then why—"

"I am the daughter of a viscount." I stated the fact as though it was the definitive reason. I couldn't tell Ruth that I would have given it all up if I had not been shown my own inferiority. It was Augustus who was superior in every way. "I have a responsibility to my family."

Ruth gave a small huff. "I know. It's just you don't look at Lord Thorton the way you look at Augustus."

Another light knock sounded, and Leah stepped in, her eyes moving to Ruth.

"Ruth is going to sleep with me tonight."

"Very well, miss." Leah skimmed Ruth's dress. "Should I fetch her nightclothes?"

I gave a vacant nod. "Yes."

"Here. I shall go with you." Ruth stepped to Leah's side. "I know right where everything is, so I'll make quick work of it. I simply did not wish to go alone." Ruth stopped, and turned toward me, a folded missive in her outstretched hand. "Oh, and Augustus wished for me to give you this once we were alone. It arrived for you not long after you left for Branbury."

It was not from Augustus, then. My brief excitement had faded before I had been able to reprimand myself for it. I took hold of the letter. "Thank you, Ruth."

She smiled happily and linked her arm through Leah's in an endearing, though utterly inappropriate, manner. The two figures disappeared through the threshold, Ruth's hushed voice drifting through the open door. I drew near the candle, holding the sealed letter to the light. It only took me a moment to recognize the familiar seal, and I broke it open.

Arabella,

Change of plans. Remove to Branbury without delay.

Papa

How strange that those two lines could have prevented so much heartache had they been read in time. But they hadn't. And now all that was left for me was an inescapable sorrow. Crumpling up the letter, I threw it into the darkness then wrapped my arms tightly about myself, refusing to let my thoughts focus on anything but the emptiness around me.

CHAPTER TWENTY-ONE

"*H*ave I been keeping you awake at nights?"

I glanced at Ruth, her pleased expression taking in the garden around us. "Not at all." In truth, Ruth's even breaths and the warmth of her next to me had proven just the thing to lull me to sleep the past several nights, somehow staving off the nightmares I'd had since leaving Fairhaven.

"I'm glad to hear it. But you must tell me if it gets burdensome, and I'll …" She paused. "I was going to say I'll sleep in my own room, but I believe I would prefer the chaise lounge near your hearth to being alone."

I smiled at her ridiculousness, the thought of having her with me bringing me more comfort than I cared to admit. "There will be no need for that. You are always welcome with me."

Ruth tilted her head, appraising me. "I've hardly seen you smile since we arrived. At least not a real authentic smile like that." She flicked her chin toward me. "What has been on your mind?"

"Why did Augustus agree to come to Branbury?" I

blurted the question before I had time to consider the possible implications.

Ruth shrugged. "We received Lord Thorton's invitation a few days after you left. Augustus was set on declining at first, but with a little persuasion from Aunt Marina, Sarah, and me, he changed his mind."

"But why?"

Ruth studied me without answering, then she dropped her gaze to her hands. "Are you unhappy we came?"

"No. Of course not." I touched her arm, and she lifted her head. "I could not be more thrilled that you are here." I paused, dropping my hand to my side. "It just seems odd that Augustus would come. Especially considering he has avoided me since our first conversation days ago. I know we hardly see the gentlemen during the days, but when we come together in the evenings, after dinner, he makes no point to seek me out."

"Do you wish him to?"

"No, of course not. In truth, I don't know what I wish." A sigh slipped from my lips. "Forgive me. I should not have mentioned it."

"Bella, I hope I do not upset you by asking, but why did you tell Lady Beatrice the evening of my arrival that Augustus would soon offer for Miss Whitmore? I have thought of it countless times these past few days, but I cannot figure out why you ..."

"Why I lied?"

Ruth bit at her lip, offering a timid nod.

"It's complicated." The moment the excuse slipped from me, I realized I had given Ruth the very excuse Mother always gave me. It would not do. "I lied because I was trying to protect Augustus from the cunning designs of Lady Beatrice. An upcoming engagement was the first thing that came to my mind, and I said it."

"But Lady Beatrice does not seem cunning. Erroneous at times, but not full of guile."

"She allows you to see what she wants you to see. She is a spiteful creature, and I will not have her play with your cousin's emotions, even if I must lie to keep her from doing so."

Ruth gave a small huff. "I suppose I can see why you felt inclined to say such a thing."

We continued on, the buzzing of insects and the calls of birds filling the silence.

"There is to be a ball next Friday," I said, desperate to counter the melancholy I'd caused.

Ruth cheered. "Truly?"

I pulled a vibrant green leaf off a bush we were passing, twirling the stem between my thumb and index finger. "Yes."

Suddenly Ruth stopped, a look of panic on her face. "But you never taught me to dance."

I paused, facing her. "You said you knew some dances."

"Simple country dances. Surely those are not what will be performed at this ball."

I took in the worry tainting her lovely face, then lifted on to my toes, scanning the top of the hedges to ensure no one else sought refuge in the garden. "Come." I took hold of her hand and led her to a decent-sized alcove off the garden path.

"What are we doing?" Ruth asked.

I untied my bonnet and tossed it to the side. "I am teaching you the waltz."

Ruth's eyes widened. "But how shall that work? We are both ladies."

"How difficult can the gentleman's part be?"

Ruth gave a shrug and removed her own bonnet.

"Stand here next to me on my right and face the same

direction as me." Without a word of complaint, Ruth stepped to my side, and I placed my right hand on her waist. "Put your hand over mine, and now extend your left hand so that I may take hold of it." I inspected the stance. "Very good. This is the starting position. Now we will walk forward, both of us stepping with our outside foot first. But step slowly." We stepped. "Now the other foot. Slow step. Good. And two more times."

"That isn't so hard."

I smiled. "Now face me, lifting your left hand while it is still in mine, bringing it to the center just above us. Good. Your right hand will move to my waist, and my right will remain on yours."

Ruth giggled. "I can see why some people believe the waltz to be improper. We are so very close. I'm certain when it is a gentleman I'm partnered with, I shall have a constant blush the entire set."

"The dimly lit ballroom will allay the effect." I thought through the next movements, attempting to recall the stepping order of the gentleman. "This is where it gets a touch more difficult. We are going to circle one another, you starting with your right, and me, I believe, with my left." The gravel shifted beneath us, making the movement a touch clumsy. "Now step with your left and rotate on it."

Ruth leaned too far to the side at the same moment that I mis-stepped. The laughter that erupted from us both did little to help us to right our error, and we nearly toppled. Ruth caught hold of my arm, balancing me. How good it felt to laugh again.

"What are the two of you up to?" I stilled at finding Augustus standing in the alcove's opening, the corners of his mouth twitching as though refusing us his smile.

I straightened my posture. "I was just teaching Ruth the waltz."

He quirked a brow. "And how was that going?"

Ruth covered her mouth, and I gave a small shrug. "Well enough." I paused, waiting for him to fill the silence, but he didn't. "Aren't you supposed to be out fishing with the gentlemen?"

"I've had my fill and decided to return early."

I glanced toward Branbury. "Did you come to the gardens by way of the house?"

Augustus shook his head. "I walked from the pond, so I came the back way into the gardens."

My relief was instantaneous, knowing Mother could not be aware of his being here. I took in his solemn expression, and I longed to say something to bring a smile to his lips, but instead I looked at Ruth. "Now that your cousin is here, he can assist you."

Ruth's eyes lit with excitement, the dark chocolate color radiant in the daylight. "In truth, I believe it would be most helpful to see the two of you waltz."

I shook my head. "That is hardly neces—"

Ruth placed her hands on her hips, sending me a pointed look. "You always say lessons are easier to recall if you can visualize them."

Augustus's expression was as hesitant as my own.

"Come you two." Ruth urged me forward. "I simply must see it done."

After a moment, Augustus gave a slow nod, acknowledging his willingness.

I drew in a breath, attempting to calm my racing heart that was plotting an uprising within me. "Very well." I stepped to Augustus's side, keeping my gaze forward. It was only a dance. Nothing more.

His hand moved to my waist, and though his touch was gentle, the penetrating warmth stirred memories within me, stealing my breath. *Only a dance.* I inhaled, placing my hand over his, before extending my other out. He took hold of it and effortlessly led me forward. When we had taken four steps, we rotated into one another, our hands lifted high between us. The warmth of his breath touched my cheek, making my heart stutter. I placed my hand on his waist and we began turning, each movement bringing our bodies closer together.

His intent gaze held traces of sadness that I could hardly endure, yet I could not look away. We transitioned into the stepping movement again, his touch lightening so it was hardly perceivable on my waist and hand. It made him feel disconnected from me, and I longed for things to be the way they had been when I had first arrived at Fairhaven. But there was too much unsaid between us, too many things to seek his forgiveness for, and I could neither find the words nor the courage.

"Bella." His voice was quiet as we faced one another a second time. He drew in close. "I must know if this is what you truly want."

My heart beat wildly, uncertain what he was referring to.

"All of this," he said, his eyes flicking to Branbury.

"Oh." I swallowed my disappointment, too aware of the lie that must be said. "It is what I want."

As we turned, his grip suddenly tightened on my waist in a way that made my body tremble with desire. "Then I am happy for you."

I nearly missed a step. "You are happy for me?"

"Well, I am determined to be." He released me to resume the forward position again. "I thought I was coming to Branbury to convince you to change your mind, to show you that I could provide you the greatest happiness." We stepped forward, my legs threatening to give out under me with each movement. "But if you believe it is Lord Thorton that can provide it, then I will accept that. I only want your happiness. It is all I have ever wanted."

My thoughts whirled as we faced one another again. I scanned his expression, so full of heartbreak. I could not take it. "I must go."

We stopped, dropping our arms, but neither of us stepped away.

Augustus's hand lifted to my face, and it was only then I realized that a tear had escaped onto my cheek.

He gave a small smile, his hand lingering on my neck. "Tell me what you want of me. Tell me, and I'll do it." His eyes moved between mine with such intensity I thought he might discover the answer on his own.

Attempting to find any bit of strength I could hold onto, my focus landed on Ruth just behind him. Her hopeful expression was precisely what I needed. If I could not lie for my own sake, I would lie for hers. I lifted my hand to cover his. "I want you to find happiness also." I drew in a steadying breath. "But you deserve someone worthy of your love. Someone like Miss Whitmore." His brow pulled low, but I stepped away, holding on to his hand until the last possible moment. "Forgive me."

Without a glance behind, I lifted my skirts and hastened toward the house, tears now streaming down my face.

MR. GREEN and Ruth stood observing a hand of cards being played at a nearby card table. He leaned in and whispered something to Ruth, and she lifted a hand to her mouth, laughing.

Lord Thorton leaned in close. "I believe my friend finds your friend very intriguing."

I forced a smile to my lips. "I believe you are right. And I do not oppose it in the least."

"But what do you say of her cousin? He looks far from thrilled by the notion."

I followed Lord Thorton's gaze to Augustus, whose unwavering focus on Mr. Green was thick with distrust.

"I believe his misgiving is not particularly Mr. Green himself, but his dislike of any man showing interest in Ruth."

Lord Thorton laughed, causing Augustus's glare to slide to us. "I shall not complain, not when he has proven himself impartial to my regard for you."

I looked away, not wishing for Lord Thorton to perceive how distressing his comment had been. "Had you thought it would be otherwise?"

"I admit, I had. I saw so much life in you during those brief moments at Fairhaven, but when we returned to Branbury the light seemed to dim."

My gaze remained forward.

"That is why I invited Miss Seton and Mr. Brundage here. I needed to see the light again." He paused. "And I needed to see which of them ignited it in you."

I drew in a slow breath and looked at him. "And did you find what you hoped?"

"I believe so." He studied me. "Unless you wish to inform me otherwise?"

I shook my head, not trusting myself to speak.

He smiled, that all-too-familiar glint in his eyes. "When does your father arrive again?"

My chest constricted. "Friday morning."

"Very good. I am eager to speak with him." Lord Thorton paused. "Do you care to play a hand with me?"

"I fear I will be a very ill partner tonight. I'm far too tired to think clearly."

Lord Thorton scanned the large room where six tables had been set up, most of the chairs already filled with guests playing cards. "As your friend has commandeered my typical partner, I shall convince Mother to play a hand with me. She always claims I neglect her when I'm selecting a partner despite knowing she is superior." He chuckled. "If only that were the truth. But now seems as good a time as any to lose some money for the sake of appeasement."

"Is it not amazing the things we will do to content our parents?"

Though I'd not meant the comment as a jest, Lord Thorton's laughter trailed behind him as he crossed the large room.

He easily persuaded Lady Thorton to join him before aiming his smile at Mother. Mother gave an imploring nod to me, indicating she wished for me to join also. With no other option, I started toward them when, to my surprise, Lord Hancock neared the small group. I halted, waiting to see if I had been offered a windfall from Lady Beatrice's father. To my great relief, she stepped in next to Lord Hancock and meandered to the table with the others where Lord Hancock pulled a chair out for her. With one last warning glare in my direction, Mother sat, her back to me.

"What do you know of Mr. Green?" Augustus asked, stepping near me.

My heart raced foolishly at his proximity, and I took a small step away to settle it. "He is a gentleman." Augustus's attention remained fixed on Ruth and Mr. Green as I continued. "As well as the second son of a baron."

"And that's it? You are encouraging Ruth toward Mr. Green based on those two facts alone?"

"Does it not say something about his character that Lord Thorton holds him as a close friend and has since childhood?"

"No. It does not. The only comfort I take in any of it is that Ruth has no fortune to tempt *a second son of a baron.*"

I swallowed and clasped my hands tightly in front of me, fixing my gaze back on Ruth and Mr. Green.

"Bella? What have you done?"

I could not look at him. "I mentioned that Ruth could inherit a small sum if the court case is overturned."

"A small sum? How small did you say?"

I bit at the inside of my lip. "Perhaps I did exaggerate a bit, but I did it for Ruth."

Augustus took a step toward me. "Please tell me you are jesting?"

I lifted my chin. "I don't see the harm in it."

"Do you not?" Augustus ran a hand through his hair. "Look at me, Bella."

Tears welled in my eyes, and I shook my head.

"Unless you desire a scene, please look at me."

Ever so slowly, I met his gaze, blinking back my tears.

"You had no right to do that—to tell them of the court case and Ruth's lost inheritance. She may never get that back."

"I simply wanted her to be accepted." I glanced around the room to make certain we had not drawn anyone's attention. "It was only a matter of time before everyone here discovered her past, and I thought it would be most beneficial—"

"For whom, Bella? Was it most beneficial for Ruth or for you?"

Anger surged through me. "I would not have been

forced to say such a thing had you declined Lord Thorton's invitation like any reasonable man would have done. Surely you are just as much at fault as I am."

"Do you hear yourself?" Augustus shook his head. "I feel I hardly know you."

"This is me, Augustus." A tear slipped down my cheek, and I swiped it away. "Do you now see why I could not marry you? You were made to believe I'm still the girl I once was, but I'm not." My voice faltered. "I fooled you, and I fooled myself. It is better that you realized the truth before you were stuck in a marriage with someone you would certainly grow to despise."

"Is that why you left Fairhaven?" Augustus's expression softened, but I did not answer. "It's not true you know. Not a word of it."

"It is." I lifted my shoulders and shook my head in defeat. "And I have no power to change it."

"We always have the power to change."

"No, we do not. I do not."

Augustus released a heavy exhale, staring vacantly at the others. The mindless chatter buzzed in my head, and all I wanted was to be rid of it. My hands were trembling, and I drew in a slow breath, suppressing my rising emotions. Better numb than mad.

"I never thought you unchanged." Augustus's voice was gentle and close. "I love you, Bella. Not solely the girl you were, nor the woman you've become, but the whole of you. Everything that brought you to this moment and everything that will follow after. Forever." My soul quivered at his declaration, but I would not look at him lest he discovered it. "Despite what you believe, you deserve to be loved that fully. Not in spite of your imperfections, but in addition to them."

How I longed to believe him, but the imperfections he

spoke of were only a small portion of the ones I possessed. Perhaps he could love a woman who had lied, who had showed she cared too much for status and fortune and reputation. But to love a woman who had formed a reputation for hurting others intentionally, who was continually selfish and false and manipulative? That was impossible.

"If you knew ..." My voice trailed off. He would not understand. I did not wish him to understand. For I would turn out no different than Mother, just as she had not deviated from her mother. I already was more like her than I cared to admit.

"There you are, Mr. Brundage." Lady Beatrice walked toward us, a sultry smile on her face. "I need a partner for whist. What say you?"

His eyes flitted to me. "I had not intended to play this evening," he said, barely able to conceal his irritation at her arrival.

Lady Beatrice glanced between us with interest. "Have I interrupted something?"

"No," I said, trying to appear unaffected. "Not at all."

Apparently appeased by my assurances, Lady Beatrice's beseeching eyes settled back on Augustus. "I truly cannot convince you?"

"I fear I'm in no mood for games."

Augustus glanced at Ruth, and Lady Beatrice followed his gaze. "I see you are once again playing the role of the vigilant protector." She fluttered her lashes at him, but his eyes did not return to her. She stepped to his side and placed a hand on his arm. "In that case, it might be relevant to know that it was Mr. Green and Miss Seton who I had hoped to oppose. Surely that would be a more beneficial location for you than standing all the way over here with only Miss Godwin for company."

It was my turn to conceal my irritation.

Augustus glanced down at Lady Beatrice's hand before meeting her gaze. "I prefer to watch their interactions from a distance. But I thank you for the offer."

I stepped toward her. "If Mr. Brundage is certain of his intentions, I would gladly partner with you, Lady Beatrice." If I could not right my many wrongs, I could at least ensure Mr. Green's intentions toward Ruth were sincere. Besides, I could not trust myself to stand here a moment longer with Augustus and his heart-wrenching declarations.

Lady Beatrice gave a small pout. "Very well then, Miss Godwin. I believe the game they are observing is nearly finished."

Not willing to glimpse Augustus's disappointment, I lowered my head and stepped in next to her.

～

RUTH PULLED down the coverlet and sprang into bed.

Leah pressed back a smile. "Do you require anything else, Miss Godwin?"

"No. Thank you."

Leah dipped into a brief curtsy and left.

I glanced at Ruth sprawled on the bed, smiling up at the ceiling foolishly. "You seem content."

She lifted onto her elbows. "Mr. Green has told me that he prefers my company over that of any other woman. Can you even believe it? Someone prefers me. Not to just one, but all other women."

"You should not be the least bit surprised." And yet, even as I spoke the words, I could not push the thought of Mr. Green as a fortune seeker from my mind. I had watched Ruth and him closely all evening, and he seemed genuine in his interactions, yet did people not often think *me* genuine? "Though, despite his declarations, you must be cautious."

I climbed in the bed next to her, and she rolled to her side, propping her head up with her arm. "But you have been singing his praises since I arrived."

"I believe the prospect of us marrying such close friends may have influenced my regard for him."

Ruth's eyes gleamed in the candlelight. "I did not even think of that. How wonderful would that be? Dearest friends marrying likewise."

I rebuked myself for having put such an influential thought in her mind. "Yes, but that is not a reason to marry someone. Remember what Augustus said about truly knowing a man before you fall in love with him? Though I believe Mr. Green to be a good man, it is sometimes difficult to truly know a person's intentions."

"Yet what reason could he have for falsehood? I have no fortune, at least none as of yet. And there seems to be nothing else he would gain from pursuing me."

I bit back my admission, as well as my comment regarding what some men hoped to achieve through such endeavors. She need not worry herself, for I would keep a vigilant watch on them both. "Regardless, do promise you'll be careful."

Ruth leaned back and pulled a pillow over her chest, squeezing it with a ridiculous smile on her face. "Very well."

CHAPTER TWENTY-TWO

*T*he servants buzzed around us, attempting to keep our plates brimming and our cups full as we reclined on the blankets that had been laid out for us.

Lady Thorton shooed away a young servant attempting to place another sandwich on her plate. "Would anyone care for a game of bouts-rimés or perhaps charades?" She glanced around at the idle members of our group, who were now too full and too hot for any sort of exertion. "There is also rowing on the lake. And there are wild blackberry hedges nearby if anyone cares to see if they are ripe."

Ruth tapped my arm. "Blackberries sound delightful. Would you care to go with me?"

Before I had a chance to convince her against the idea of venturing out in this heat, Mr. Green stood up and reached out a hand for her. "I will accompany you, Miss Seton."

I suppressed a groan, watching her stand. "As will I."

"Well, I cannot let you eat all the berries without me."

Lord Thorton rose and extended a hand to aid me in standing. "Does anyone else care to join us?"

A few others nodded their agreement and stood.

Ruth faced Augustus. "Do you wish to join us, Augi?"

I followed her gaze to find Augustus leaning back on his elbows watching us. Every interaction with him tore at my heart, so when he shifted forward, I knew I could not allow for him to come along. "Ruth," I said, my voice loud enough to carry, "your cousin looks the picture of leisure. Perhaps if I assure him that I will be most vigilant in my care of you, he need not be troubled to move from where he is."

Augustus's eyes narrowed.

"Unless you do not trust me, Mr. Brundage?"

The collective regard of the group shifted to Augustus. "I've seldom had reason not to."

His declaration stung, but I offered him a tight smile.

"Let's be off then." Lord Thorton extended his elbow to me, and I took hold of it.

We walked along the shore of the lake for a while before coming to the end of a grove of trees. A large area opened up that was overgrown with countless blackberry bushes as tall as Lord Thorton.

"What a sight," Ruth exclaimed from Mr. Green's arm. "There are so many bushes, it would take all of us days to pick the berries from them. Too bad I did not think to bring a basket for collecting."

Mr. Green looked down at her. "And yet, the delight of eating blackberries straight off the bush is one of those pleasures best seized in the moment."

Ruth smiled up at him innocently. "I believe you must be right. We have blackberries at Fairhaven, and also bilberries, though they usually aren't ripe until the end of July." Ruth examined the blackberry bush they had just stopped in front of, her shoulders falling. "Oh, these are not yet ripe either."

"There are some," Mr. Green said, plucking one and holding it out to Ruth. "We simply must search a little harder for them."

Ruth bit into the berry, her face alight. "Oh, that is delicious!"

Lord Thorton searched the bush, located one, and popped it in his mouth. "It seems the most logical plan is to all spread out and search," he said, glancing at the others. "And, just so everyone is aware, there are wild strawberries that should be ripe, if you look for them."

The small party dispersed, and I led Lord Thorton to the bush where Ruth and Mr. Green were now searching.

"Here's a patch." Lord Thorton stopped to grab a couple from the top of the bush. "It seems the ones with the most sun ripen first."

I pulled off my gloves, and he placed three berries in my palm. The warmth of them tantalized me, but I resisted the urge to eat them all at once. The sweet juice of the first teased my tongue, and I ate another. "These are delightful."

Lord Thorton continued searching the higher areas of the bush, alternating between eating them and handing them to me to partake. I glanced over at Ruth a few bushes away, laughing as she tossed a berry at Mr. Green. Though Ruth was a tad excessive in her flirtations, she also managed an air of innocence that seemed to balance it. She tossed another berry and started into a fit of giggles.

Lord Thorton followed my gaze. "Would it not be a pleasing arrangement if friends were to marry friends?"

"It would have its benefits. Though we must not be too hasty in our hope as Mr. Green and Ruth have only just met." I summoned all my courage, knowing I was running out of time to secure Lord Thorton. "And I have not yet received an offer myself."

Lord Thorton took hold of my hand and led me through a gap in the hedge. My heart pounded in my chest, but not in a way that made me feel alight and giddy. "You have not yet received an offer because I have not spoken to your father. But I intend to do so first thing when he arrives tomorrow."

I forced a smile to my lips. "You do me a great honor."

Lord Thorton laughed. "You needn't sound so formal about it. I'm asking him for your hand because I wish to marry you. We will make a good match, and heaven knows it's high time I settled down."

Despite Lord Thorton's reasonings being identical to my own, my stomach dropped.

He closed the space between us, placing a hand on my waist. "Are you pleased?"

My head spun, and I placed my hands on his arms to steady myself. "Exceptionally," I lied, my chest rising and falling, but not from longing.

He glanced down at my hands grasping his waistcoat sleeves. "I feel the same." Before I had time to prepare myself, he pulled me forward, pressing his lips roughly against mine. My breath hitched, and I stiffened, causing him to pull back briefly, a look of utter amusement on his face. "It seems not all the rumors are true."

I knew his meaning, but I could not bring myself to tell him that despite all my offers and my reputation, I'd only ever been kissed by one man. A man whose kiss felt nothing like his.

He stepped close again. "Do not worry. I will be gentler now that I'm aware of your innocence."

My lip quivered, but what choice did I have? I could

not leave now and risk everything. I closed my eyes as he drew close, attempting to soften my lips as his met mine. His mouth moved in some sort of rhythm, and I attempted to follow his movements, counting the seconds until he released me again.

He looked down at me, a wicked smile on his lips. "I believe you will suit me just fine."

I stilled. "I should go check on Ruth."

"Don't be too hasty in your pursuit; they could be finding their own enjoyment."

Bile rose in my throat. Without a backward glance, I left Lord Thorton. "Ruth?" I searched where she had been only minutes before. "Ruth?" I attempted to keep my voice calm, though my pulse was accelerating. Why had I ever left her?

"Has Miss Seton come this way?" I asked a few members of our group that were still working their way down the bushes. They all shook their heads.

I scanned the area again, wondering which direction to continue my search when I caught sight of Augustus walking toward us with Lady Beatrice on his arm.

"See there, everyone is still picking berries just as I said they would be." Lady Beatrice gave a pleased smile. "I do hope you left some for us, Miss Godwin," she called, when she caught sight of me.

Panic rose within me. I had assured Augustus I'd keep her safe, and yet I had no idea where she was.

"Where is Ruth?" he called, dropping his arm from Lady Beatrice's grasp and hastening toward me.

The accusation in his voice was nearly too much to endure in my current state, and I blinked away the tears that blurred my eyes. "I'm sure she is not far. She was right here only a moment ago."

Augustus's posture went rigid, and his eyes swept the hedges. "Ruth!" he called, stepping around me.

Lord Thorton approached us. "They have likely just gone in search of strawberries. There is no need to overreact."

"Ruth!" Augustus moved forward with increased determination, attracting the gawking stares of some of the other berry pickers.

Hesitantly, I lifted my skirts and followed.

He pressed through a narrow divide in the hedge. "Ruth!" he called, from the other side.

Taking hold of my bonnet and lowering my chin, I pushed through after him, the thorns taking hold of my day dress. Despite the snags it would cause, I forced my way through. "She could not have gotten far. We only left her for a moment."

He spun toward me. "You said you'd keep an eye on her. You said I could trust you, and yet you left her. Why?" My face flushed red, his expression shifting from bewilderment to anger. His jaw tightened and his teeth clenched. "Do not tell me it was for a rendezvous in the bushes to further along your suit?"

I drew in a shuddered breath. "It was only a moment."

He shook his head. "What kind of friend are you?" A tear escaped onto my cheek, but Augustus turned from me, jogging forward. "Ruth!"

Lady Beatrice muttered under her breath, pressing through the same bush Augustus and I had gone through. "Wretched plants," she hissed, smoothing out her skirts. "I have just snagged one of my best dresses."

I started forward again.

"Have you located them?" Lord Thorton stepped through a much wider opening in the hedge a few yards in front of us, and Lady Beatrice blew out an exasperated breath.

"Not yet."

"Why did you not tell me there was a larger opening?" Lady Beatrice demanded, scowling at Lord Thorton.

Not a touch of remorse was evident in his features. "Why did you not wait behind like I instructed?"

Lady Beatrice huffed indignantly. "Why I never—"

The sound of a faint cry compelled me forward to a small copse of trees. "Ruth!" I took hold of my skirts and ran, the sound of men arguing growing louder.

A small clearing opened, and I caught sight of Augustus pinning Mr. Green to the trunk of a large tree. Ruth watched in terror, tears streaming down her face.

"Ruth!" I called, gesturing her to me.

Her widened eyes met mine, and she made haste to where I stood, collapsing into my embrace with a sob.

"How you call yourself a gentleman—" Augustus growled through gritted teeth.

Mr. Green glared back at him, his face growing red with anger in his futile attempts to free himself from Augustus's unrelenting hold.

I heard Lady Beatrice gasp and the hurried footsteps of Lord Thorton from behind.

"Release him, Mr. Brundage." Lord Thorton pressed past me.

Augustus's gaze landed on Lord Thorton, a look in his eyes I had never seen in him before—absolute loathing. He did not relent.

Lord Thorton lifted his hands in a gesture of peace. "Let him go, and we will discuss this."

Augustus's chest heaved as he pressed harder into Mr. Green, but then he gave one final push on Mr. Green's chest and stepped back. Mr. Green hurried to right himself, tugging at the bottom of his jacket to straighten out the creases left by Augustus's grip.

Augustus pointed at Mr. Green. "Don't you ever come near Ruth again."

Mr. Green looked up at Augustus, his face still red with fury. "I only acted in accordance to Miss Seton's inducements."

Augustus's eyes flashed to me, and I dropped my gaze, unable to bear the accusation in them. "Had she known of your intentions, she never would have encouraged a degenerate like you."

"And yet here we stand." Mr. Green's eyes flicked toward us, a slight smirk on his lips. "Witnesses to attest to what has transpired between us."

My lips parted, and I held a hand over Ruth's ear, pressing the other against me, as though that would somehow keep Mr. Green's accusations from sinking in.

"You scoundrel." Augustus started forward again, and Lord Thorton stepped between them, his large arms outstretched to prevent another altercation.

"Come now, gentlemen. Let us be reasonable."

"Reasonable?" Augustus threw up a hand toward Mr. Green. "How is one to be reasonable when it is evident what his purpose is?"

"I love her," Mr. Green said, causing Ruth to lift her head. "I love you, Ruth. I did not mean to frighten you, but I could not restrain my desire for you."

"Liar." Augustus stepped in an attempt to block Mr. Green's view of Ruth. "Your only desire is for her supposed fortune."

Ruth went rigid in my embrace.

Augustus shook his head, the muscles in his jaw flexing. "Well, I've never been happier to inform someone that she has no fortune. I received a letter two days past informing me that the Court of Chancery ruled against our appeal. The Crown is officially the sole inheritor of the Setons' estate."

As we all stood in stunned silence, the hurt began to set in. My dearest Ruth had nothing, and Augustus had not confided in me about it.

Augustus drew in a breath and directed his vehement glare back on Mr. Green. "Will you still profess your love for her when she is as poor as you?"

Ruth's breath halted as though in anticipation of the answer, or perhaps in response to the hurt Augustus's words had caused. I held her tighter, compensating for my own unsteadiness.

Mr. Green's eyes lingered on Ruth a moment before he lowered his gaze, his silence louder than anything.

Augustus moved toward us, his focus locked on Ruth. "Let's go home," he whispered, holding his hand out for her.

With one uncertain glance at me, she left me and sunk into his embrace.

I looked to where Lady Beatrice had been, only to find her retreating figure nearly at the hedges. She was likely eager to tell the others of the encounter before I could swear her to silence. Wretched gossip.

Lord Thorton had a hand on Mr. Green's shoulder. "Miss Godwin, go now, and I will be along shortly."

Attempting to not show my relief at his command, I started toward the hedge. When I had made it to the other side and out of view of Lord Thorton, I hurried to rejoin Augustus and Ruth. "Wait, please," I called when I was only a few paces behind.

Augustus paused but did not look back at me.

My breathing was heavy as I drew up next to them,

Ruth's tear-stained face wrenching at my gut. "I am so sorry. I never meant for any of this to happen."

Augustus started forward again, and I took hold of his arm, stopping him. "Please. Let me try to make amends."

"How could you possibly undo this damage, Bella?" All the warmth was gone from his eyes.

Ruth released a quivering breath. "This is not Bella's fault."

"No. The blame is mine." Augustus met my gaze. "Bella attempted to warn me against the type of woman she truly was, and I refused to believe her."

My heart shattered, the pain of it surging through my entire being.

"What do you mean?" Ruth's voice hitched.

A tear rolled down my cheek. "I was the one who told Mr. Green that you were an heiress."

Ruth's brown eyes grew wide with understanding.

I wanted to shrink away, but in desperation, I took hold of her hand. "My reasonings were misguided, but I assure you they were not ill-intentioned."

The hurt in Ruth's features did not lessen, and she pulled her hand from me. "Augi, I want to go home," she whispered.

Augustus nodded, leading her forward again, but I did not have the strength to follow this time. I watched, motionless, until they disappeared. My legs trembled beneath me, and I looked around for somewhere to take cover. A large tree near the bank of the lake caught my attention. With its massive trunk and the overgrown bushes surrounding it, it seemed an adequate spot for privacy. I staggered my way to it, arriving just as my strength gave out, and crumpled to the ground, sobbing.

CHAPTER TWENTY-THREE

"*W*here in the heavens have you been, child?" Mother scanned my dirtied dress and red, blotchy face. She drew closer, so as not to be overheard. "And why do you look so unkempt?"

I glanced around to find the picnic area emptied and the guests loading into carriages. Had Lady Beatrice not shared the scandal with everyone as I'd expected, or had the rumors simply not yet met Mother's ears? "Ruth and Augustus are leaving," I said, flatly.

"They already have. I saw them load into their carriage well over an hour ago."

I nodded, my heart sinking at the confirmation.

Mother's eyes narrowed. "Do you mean they are removing from Branbury?"

I gave a second nod, this one even slower.

Mother took hold of my arm, pulling me a tad farther from the curious gazes directed at us from the carriage windows. "What happened?"

"Mr. Green attempted to get Ruth in a compromising

situation. Apparently he believed ..." My voice quivered, unable to confess my folly to Mother.

"That she was an heiress?"

"Yes." My voice was quiet and distant.

"Yes, I heard rumors of your foolish tale." Mother shook her head. "Though I suppose it's all for the best."

I flinched. "All for the best? Ruth's reputation will likely be marred because of me." Emotion touched my voice, but I swallowed it down.

"Yes. Quite ironic, really." Mother gave an amused smirk and glanced behind us. "Now dust yourself off before Lord Thorton returns. We cannot have him believing you've been hiding away moping."

My energy expired, I simply stood there staring at her.

"Arabella," Mother hissed, motioning to my dress.

I looked down, shaking the loose debris free and plucking off a few stubborn bits with my fingers. The hem was soiled but there was nothing to be done.

"Miss Godwin." Lord Thorton approached from behind, his eyes skirting over my dress in agitation. "Where have you been? I have been out searching for you for nigh on thirty minutes."

Mother gave a subtle lift of her brow, making it clear what she expected.

"Forgive me. I got turned around on my way back to the picnic." I looked down at my ruined dress. "And I took a tumble during my attempts to find my way back."

Concern touched Lord Thorton's features, the hard set of his jaw softening. "I forget that a woman is not equal to a man when it comes to navigating out of doors. Forgive me. I should have seen you back safely."

All I could do was nod.

He released a heavy exhale. "Let us be glad you found

your way back. I was returning to organize a search party."

Several gentlemen waited just outside of the carriages. Had it been me they were waiting on? I suppose I hadn't thought of the consequence of my absence, but I also hadn't realized how soon the group had intended to leave or I would have returned sooner. Perhaps we would make it back before Augustus and Ruth could depart Branbury. I brightened a little at the thought, until I realized they would likely not speak to me even if they were still there.

"Are you not glad, Arabella, that a search party was not required?" Mother's voice sounded distant in my ears.

"Yes." Mother nodded, pressing me on. "And I am sorry if I caused any of you a scare, my lord."

"No harm done." Lord Thorton's gaze snaked down my figure in a way that made me want to wrap my arms around myself. "Except to your lovely dress, perhaps."

"Yes. Such a shame." Mother put a hand behind my back, guiding me forward. "Let us be on our way. I'd hate to keep Lady Thorton waiting on us any longer."

Lord Thorton stepped into our path. "I was hoping I could have a brief word with your daughter in private, Lady Godwin?"

Mother's false smile for Lord Thorton faded as her eyes moved to me, relaying her expectations without needing to say a word. "Certainly, my lord," she said, leaving us to talk.

Lord Thorton faced me, his large frame blocking out the watchful gazes from the carriages lined up behind us. "Miss Godwin, I am sorry for how things turned out with your friends. I did not bring them here to be thus treated. But I must assure you that Mr. Green is the best of men and meant no ill will toward Miss Seton."

I stared up at him, unblinking. "Best of men? The

supposed gentleman who just attempted to take advantage of my dearest friend? *That* Mr. Green?"

Lord Thorton's eyes shot to the side. "I can understand that you're angry," he whispered. "But Mr. Green swore he meant no harm by his actions. He said he only intended to have a little fun with the girl, seeing how encouraging she had been toward him."

Rage pumped through me with each racing beat of my heart, and I fisted my hands at my side. "Your friend is a cad."

Lord Thorton appraised me, then one side of his mouth lifted in a partial smile.

"What about this could you possibly find humorous, my lord?"

He rubbed a hand over his mouth to cover his growing amusement. "Nothing. I assure you I take the accusation of cad very seriously."

My whole body shook. "If you will excuse me. I cannot tolerate being mocked in my current state." I moved to step around him, but he took hold of my upper arm.

"Miss Godwin, please." He looked down at me, pinning me with an obnoxious frown. "I do not mean to make light of the situation. It is just that I'm overjoyed to see the spark in you again."

I did not respond.

"If it will vindicate you, I will admit Mr. Green can be a cad at times."

"It is not I who requires vindication," I spat.

Despite his best efforts, his lips curved upward again, and I forced my arm from his grip. Countless wide-eyed faces followed me to the carriage, yet I found I didn't care at all. Perhaps this would give them something to gossip about besides Ruth.

When I climbed into the carriage, Lady Thorton

pulled her skirts against the bench so they would not be sullied by mine. "Heavens, child. You look as though you have been out wallowing in the mud."

I had nothing to offer but a wearied expression. "I was."

Lord Thorton lumbered in behind me, the carriage dipping beneath his weight, when he caught sight of his mother's shocked expression. "Miss Godwin got lost on her way back from picking blackberries." His tone was matter-of-fact, free of any discernable emotion.

Lady Thorton arched a brow. "It is quite a feat to get lost at such a location as this."

"Arabella gets lost wherever she goes." Mother's dishonesty grated more than usual. "I don't know how many times we had to send the servants out to find her at Fellerton Hall."

The suspicion in Lady Thorton's expression lessened, ever eager to believe Mother, lest she was forced to confront the truth so plainly before her. I was no more than a compilation of lies Mother had fed her.

The carriage started forward, the rumbling of the wheels a welcome respite from the buzzing inside me.

"And what are the gentlemen's plans for tomorrow, Lord Thorton?" I could hear the victorious tone in Mother's voice, having successfully righted yet another of my follies. "I am hopeful my husband will arrive before the group sets out."

Uninterested in his reply, I shifted my attention out the window, allowing the voices to fade and the void within to consume me.

~

Lord Thorton's booming laugh reverberated through the carriage, pulling my thoughts from the emptiness.

Mother glanced past me, out the window. "Are we nearly to Branbury already?"

Lady Thorton nodded. "It will come into view just ahead."

I took in the large hedge. Blurred from the movement, it appeared to be one giant plant. The scene conjured a memory I longed to repress. Yet as Branbury came into view, I was transported back to my first time viewing the large house on my way to Fairhaven—Augustus's warm breath on my neck and his hands firmly on my waist. My breath hitched, and instead of pushing it away, I closed my eyes to keep hold of the sensations for as long as I could.

"It is quite a sight, is it not?" Lord Thorton was watching me when my eyes fluttered open.

I gave a slow nod.

He smiled, and leaned back into his seat. "Should you like to be mistress of such a place?"

Mother and Lady Thorton shared a meaningful glance in my periphery, and I looked back out the window toward the grand house and its imposing grounds. I did not answer.

"Arabella," Mother said, a warning in her tone. "Lord Thorton has asked you a question."

The lie nearly choked me as I forced it out. "I should like it very much." I kept my eyes fixed on Branbury, and my thoughts turned to Ruth. Then Augustus. Were they still here or had they managed to pack their things and set off already? Despite having no notion what I would say to either of them, I could not help but hope I had not missed them.

"Arabella, dear?" Mother's overly-sweet tone sent a shiver through me.

Slowly, I turned to face her.

Her taut expression informed me I had earned myself a scolding. "Are you well, darling? Or have your adventures today exhausted you?" She pulled a glove from her hand and touched my cheek with the inside of her wrist, the unfamiliar image of a caring Mother. "Perhaps you should take a rest before dinner."

When the carriage came to a stop, Lord Thorton opened the door but did not yet move, awaiting my response.

I lifted a hand to the spot on my cheek Mother had felt, suddenly desperate to accept her bait in the slight chance that Ruth and Augustus were still here. "I do feel rather out of sorts. Too much sun, perhaps."

With my confirmation, Lord Thorton climbed out of the carriage to assist me. "I shall look forward to seeing you at dinner, Miss Godwin."

I swallowed down my resentment. "Yes."

Lady Beatrice and Miss Browning alighted from the carriage behind ours, but I did not even glance at them, hurrying up the exterior staircase and into the house.

"What is the matter, miss?" Leah asked after I shut the door of my room behind me.

My breaths were coming fast from the exertion of running up the stairs. "Have they gone?"

Her expression filled with understanding, and she dipped her chin. "Yes. A quarter hour ago. They seemed to be in a great hurry. I helped ready Ruth's trunks myself."

I rested my head against the door and closed my eyes. I had hoped in vain. All truly was lost.

"Come sit." Leah came to my side. Taking hold of my

arm, she led me to the chaise lounge. "I shall bring up some tea."

I shut my eyes again and leaned into the angled back, unable to so much as utter my thanks.

After several minutes, a sharp knock echoed through the room. I did not move.

The door creaked open and shut again. "What in heaven's name are you doing?" Mother's voice infiltrated the silence.

I did not move. "Resting."

"You know precisely what I mean. Do you know what Lady Thorton just asked me?" Mother's voice was near.

"No."

"She inquired if your melancholy has to do with the departure of a *certain friend*. And she did not mean Miss Seton."

I heaved a sigh. "I am tired, Mother."

"You are tired?" Her voice drew closer still. "Think of what I'm constantly made to endure because of your flippant behavior. You exhaust me, Arabella. But you will not disappoint me again."

I finally opened my eyes, meeting her glare with a wearied expression. "No matter what I do, I will be a disappointment to you. I have sought for years to obtain your acceptance, yet nothing I do is ever enough. Even Lord Thorton will not be enough. I am through trying to please you. I am through trying to be loved and falling short." I drew in a breath, drained of all care. "And I will not marry Lord Thorton."

Mother took hold of my wrist and yanked me to my feet. "You *will* marry Lord Thorton."

Tears blurred my vision. "Ruth's reputation is already tainted, and neither she nor Augustus will likely ever see me again. What can you possibly hold over me now?"

"Besides your inheritance, your very position in our family?"

"You would disown me for going against your wishes?" I gave an unamused laugh. "Go ahead. I don't want any of it."

Mother's lips parted. "You would give everything up now that you are so close? You shall be the wife of an earl, Arabella. Do you realize there will be few women with a higher status than you? You shall want for nothing."

"I shall want for so much."

Mother clenched her jaw, her eyes moving between mine. "You selfish girl. Thankfully, there is one bartering chip I still possess."

"Then use it, for I no longer care."

"If you insist." Mother forcefully released my arm and took a step away from me. "I shall write to Ruth directly and inform her that it was her *mother* who killed her father before taking her own life."

Her words knocked the breath from me.

Mother took in my rigid posture. "I will gladly inform her that it was you who encouraged me to share the life-altering news with her."

"You lie."

Mother's hand reeled back so swiftly, I had no time to prepare for the impact. Her palm slapped my cheek. My ears rang with pain, and my skin stung, but I righted myself, lifting my chin defiantly. "Hit me all you like. I shall never believe such a thing. Ruth's mother was kind, and she loved Ruth with all her heart."

"Which is precisely why she did it."

I stilled, uncertain why the notion penetrated my core. My resolve faltered.

Mother lifted a triumphant brow. "Ah. Willing to listen now?"

I swallowed but did not answer.

Mother released an aggravated breath. "Your father maintained a … fondness for Mrs. Seton up until the time of her death. I had warned him that her husband would not abide their continued friendship. Mr. Seton was a violent man who did not spare his wife when his temper flared. But your father would not see reason.

"Apparently, Mr. Seton began taking his anger out on Ruth as well. Despite his wife's best efforts, a particular occurrence ended with Ruth abed for a week or two. The bruising was apparently quite extensive, and the servants were told that she fell down the stairs, unwitnessed by any of them."

My legs felt weak beneath me as I thought of those weeks Ruth had been made to stay abed—the weeks Augustus and I had carelessly traipsed about the woods together without an inkling of Ruth's suffering. "How do you know this?"

"Partly from servants' gossiping lips and partly from a letter that came for your father the morning of the Setons' deaths. He was not at home at the time, and my curiosity got the better of me, for Mrs. Seton had never been so brazen before in her antics. In the letter she explained her fears for Ruth and the threats Mr. Seton had laid against them. She said that she could not bear the idea of harm coming to her daughter again, but nor could she bear the shame and the consequence of having taken a life, even one so awful as her husband."

I felt I might be sick. "You did nothing when you read of her intentions?"

Mother let out a shaky exhale, and the slightest flicker of remorse was visible in her expression. "I had thought it was an attempt for attention, a vain hope of hers that your father would come to her rescue." She paused, her gaze now distant. "It was not. By the time he returned home, we had already received word of their deaths."

"And you did not turn the letter over to the authorities?"

"We couldn't. We could not risk becoming involved. Our family's good name would have been tarnished, and your father's political career undermined from a scandal. Who knows what people would have thought about his involvement? No. It was not an option."

We stood a moment in strained silence before she lifted her chin. "So, now that you know the truth, can you imagine how such knowledge would affect Ruth? How heartbroken she would be to know it was her mother, a woman she loved more than anything, that she likely venerates to a fault, who had done something so unspeakable? What would others think of it? A woman, after all, does often follow in her mother's footsteps."

My head spun, and I dropped back onto the chaise lounge, no longer able to stand under the weight of it all.

"So you see, Arabella, I do still hold something over you. Something that I hope will allow you to see reason."

I swallowed, giving only the briefest of nods.

Mother released a pitiable sigh, as though burdened by my forcing her coercion. "I expect you to be yourself again by dinner. Lord Thorton must know he is not mistaken in offering for you."

Even after Mother had gone, I had no tears to cry. I sat and stared at the sooty hearth, my thoughts as empty as my heart.

"Miss Godwin?" Leah placed a tea tray on a nearby table and moved to my side, crouching down in front of me with a cup and saucer in hand. "I have brought you tea with lemon, just how you like it."

I blinked, my eyes flickering to her offering before settling back on the fire.

"Miss Godwin, you are pale." I could hear the concern in her voice, and she lifted the cup again. "You must drink something."

I took hold of the cup and lowered it to my lap.

Leah did not move, nor did she speak.

My whole life was a lie. I was a lie. When Ruth and Augustus left Bath, I had no one. Even Papa withdrew from me after that. Mother's abrupt interest in righting my upbringing became all I had. I thought if I could become what she wished me to be ... if others thought me to be that also ... then I would find the love I sought. But it would never be enough.

I took in Leah's sympathetic expression. "I will never be enough. Not for Society and not for Mother." My throat tightened. "And now I have lost the only people who still loved me because they realized what I have become—a mere shell of the girl they once knew. A hollow, empty shell and nothing more."

"If I might be so bold, miss, you have too often been told of your faults. I have seen your goodness. Your kindness." Leah's hand came to rest upon my wrist. "Perhaps all is not lost."

I thought of Mother's threat against Ruth. Even if I could right my relationship with Ruth and Augustus, a task in itself that seemed impossible after all I had done, I would not risk causing Ruth such pain. Her mother was everything to her. The truth would leave her broken. "I fear it is."

∾

LADY BEATRICE'S fan sliced the air between us, so rapid were its movements. "Miss Godwin, what was it you and Lord Thorton were discussing with such feeling before we left the picnic?"

I glanced at Mother standing nearby. Her vigilant gaze had hardly deviated from me all evening, nor did she lessen her watch now that the gentlemen were taking port. It was at her insistence that I'd even come to speak with Lady Beatrice. To make it appear as though I was not upset by her venomous gossip that had spread like a fire among the guests.

"Miss Godwin?" Lady Beatrice's brows were lifted, her irritation obvious at being made to wait.

"We were also speaking of the occurrence with Mr. Green."

Lady Beatrice and Miss Browning shared a meaningful look. "It was quite unfortunate. To think poor Mr. Green nearly embroiled himself with a girl of impoverished means. I wouldn't be at all surprised to discover a proposal had been Miss Seton's purpose from the beginning with how shamelessly she flirted with him. But I suppose you would not think that, being her friend."

Though I wanted to scream, to tell her what a vile, unfeeling gossip I found her to be, with Mother's penetrating eyes burning into my profile, I bit my tongue.

Lady Beatrice closed her fan and rested it on her collar bone. "I do hope the encounter has not caused any discord between you and Lord Thorton?"

The lie felt bitter on my tongue. "Not at all."

Lady Beatrice sneered. "Well I'm relieved to hear it. Especially considering how there are whispers of your supposed regard for Mr. Brundage."

I did not respond.

"Are you not shocked at hearing that?" Lady Beatrice

appraised me, disappointment pulling her mouth into a frown.

My false smile was meant for Mother, not Lady Beatrice. "With you encouraging the rumors along, I confess I am not surprised in the least."

Lady Beatrice gawked at me. "Come, Marianne." She turned her back on me. "I believe we shall find more tolerable companionship elsewhere."

Miss Browning paused just before passing me. "I am sorry for what happened with your friends, Miss Godwin. I hope you know that."

Before I had time to acknowledge the unexpected kindness, she was gone.

I did not move, listening to the ladies' excited murmurs. The chorus of their voices created a sort of hum like the wind through the trees. It made me feel distant. Alone. Had I not just been one of them weeks ago? Had I not yearned to be here at Branbury, with the victory of having attained Lord Thorton's offer as I soon would? How swiftly things could change.

The men's loud laughter echoed through the drawing room, but instead of moving toward them, I took a seat on a nearby settee.

Lord Thorton came to stand before me. "What are you doing sitting so far off from the others? Are you still upset about the occurrence with Miss Seton?"

I lifted my gaze. "I'm simply exhausted."

"You should retire."

"I do not believe sleep can cure the exhaustion I suffer, my lord."

He appraised me briefly. "What sort of exhaustion is that?"

Mother's eyes were fixed upon me from the other side

of the room, and the small surge of courage vanished. "It is nothing."

Lord Thorton let out an exhale and took a seat next to me on the settee. "I am not a fool, you know."

I stared at my hands clasped in my lap. "I did not think you one."

"Perhaps not, but you have certainly not been forthright with me as you agreed to be."

I stilled.

"I am well aware of your regard for Mr. Brundage. As I already shared, when I first brought him here, I had hoped to discover that it was not so. I even gathered evidence to the contrary for a time. But you have made it far too obvious for me to pretend otherwise any longer."

He glanced over at me, but I could not make myself meet his gaze. Not when all I saw in my mind's eye was how furious Mother was going to be with me when Lord Thorton did not make his offer, and how she would take it out on Ruth. I couldn't let that happen. I shifted to face him, panic rising in me as I attempted to rally myself for the greater cause. "Forgive my failings and the boldness with which I am about to speak. I admit I have been blinded by my infatuation with Mr. Brundage, but I am well aware that a union could never work between us. I'm confident my disappointment shall soon pass, and I will move on. As you have already stated, we are a good match and equal in many important things." I paused, knowing it was time to seal my fate—if I'd not already lost the chance. "Though I can understand if you no longer wish to make me an offer, I believe we could make a good life together."

Lord Thorton considered me. "Do you know what amazes me about all of this?"

I shook my head.

"When I finally came to terms with your regard for Mr. Brundage, and after being assured by your mother that a match to him would not be permitted, I found that I still desired to offer for you."

"You did?" My emotions were all muddled, and I simultaneously felt great relief and overwhelming displeasure at his declaration.

Lord Thorton straightened in his seat, his broad shoulders pulling back. "The only way I can seem to make sense of it is to compare it to something I actually understand. You see, I am a hunter. And when hunting, every so often there is an animal that is capable of evading the best of us; the more it does, the more fiercely we hunt it. You, Miss Godwin, are a rare vixen, and I mean that in the best sort of way. Your beauty and your poise alone make you a catch worth having, but you are also cunning and caring. Each suitor who attempts to entrap you has ended up empty-handed, and yet it only adds to your allure. That is why I must have you."

As the truth set in, so did the ache inside me. To Lord Thorton I was nothing more than a trophy to be had. And the worst of it was that I had lived the last eight years of my life for that purpose, without realizing the consequence. And now I was trapped. "Tell me, my lord, as I'm not a huntress, is there a scenario where the vixen comes to a favorable end?"

CHAPTER TWENTY-FOUR

*S*tubborn pieces of hair stuck out of my coiffure at odd angles, the ringlet curls near my face askew. Leah stepped back, chewing on her lip as she likely assessed what could be done.

"I fear I did not sleep well." It was an understatement, but the dark circles contrasting my splotchy, swollen face were evidence enough of the night I'd had. Nightmares had awoken me more times than I cared to remember. But I had been too exhausted to keep myself from sleep, so I would close my eyes and allow them to haunt me again. Endlessly staring out the window waiting for Augustus. Mrs. Seton poisoning her husband before putting a vial to her lips and drinking it herself. Papa standing trial for murder. And, the nightmare that had left me drenched in sweat and trembling—me poisoning Lord Thorton on our wedding night. I shook the vivid recollection from my mind.

Leah froze, a pin halfway pushed into my unkempt hair. "Did I hurt you?"

"No. Not at all."

The door creaked open and Mother strode inside, pulling on her gloves. "Are you ready, Arabella? The ladies are beginning to gather for our shopping expedition." Mother's eyes landed on my reflection, and her eyes narrowed. Swiftly she moved to my side, taking hold of my chin and forcing me to look at her. "You look dreadful. You cannot accompany us to town in such a state. Your hair ... and your face." Mother shook her head in disbelief, turning on Leah. "Have you tried any facial powder?"

Leah's arms were rigid at her side, her gaze set on the floor. "We tried that, my lady. I fear it made her look chalky, so she had me remove it."

"Will you be able to make her presentable by dinner?"

"I believe all that is required is a bath."

Mother gave an irritated huff. "Very well. I shall inform the servants to bring up a bath at once. We must have you looking fit enough to play the part of an Earl's future wife." Mother gave a tight smile. "Lord Thorton has spoken to your father, and despite all my fears, I am assured that he intends to offer for you this evening."

"Papa is here?"

Mother's eyes flicked upward in aggravation. "Did you not hear me?"

"I heard you." I lowered my gaze to my lap. "And I shall be put to rights by dinner."

"You should aim to be readied before that, in the event Lord Thorton desires a private audience with you beforehand."

"Yes, Mother."

Mother placed a hand on my shoulder, but there was no warmth in her touch. "I know it does not seem so now, but you shall one day be grateful for what I have done."

I stared vacantly at my own pitiful reflection.

"Speaking of what has been done ..." She paused. "If

your father returns with the gentlemen before we do, I have forbidden him to speak with you until I am present. We have many things to discuss, the three of us together."

"Yes, Mother." My voice was empty, hollow. Just as I was.

Mother released my shoulder and walked to the door, stopping when her hand grasped the doorknob. "Do not thwart me again or there shall be severe consequences." The door closed behind her.

Leah's gaze continuously returned to my reflection as she removed the ineffective pins from my hair, but I had no strength to meet it and witness her pity.

When the servants had towed in the bath, filled it, and departed, Leah helped me to undress. As I soaked in the warm water, I felt no pleasure and no cleaner. Perhaps it was because I was sullied on the inside, and no amount of water could wash that away.

When I was all dried and dressed, Leah began combing through my hair, her hands gentle as she worked through the knots. She continued combing long after the knots were all removed. She hadn't spoken a word since Mother left, but I felt her care in her silent tenderness.

"I am grateful for you, Leah."

She gave a small smile.

"I hope you will choose to stay on with me when I marry."

Her comb stopped midway through my hair, and I glanced at her reflection, nervous to discover regret on her face. Losing Leah would be unbearable in this moment. To my great relief, she nodded. "I will be happy to stay on with you *wherever* you go, miss."

I reached up for her hand, and she placed it in mine. "Thank you."

A soft knock sounded.

Leah moved to the door and slowly opened it.

"Is Arabella readied enough to see me?"

"Papa." I was already on my feet as Leah let him in and slid out the door, closing it behind her. "Mother told me you were out with the gentlemen."

He shook his head. "I informed them I was too exhausted from my travels these past few days to join them." He lifted a finger. "And it was not a mistruth as it was a very trying trip. Just this morning, on the last leg of our journey, the axle broke on the carriage."

"Oh, Papa." Worry pulled at my brow. "How fortunate you did not get injured."

"Yes." He stepped near enough to place a welcome kiss on my cheek. "And thankfully we were not far from the posthouse where we'd changed horses. The postmaster recommended a very capable coach-maker who is already working on the repair. He said he could have the carriage delivered as soon as Tuesday."

I attempted a smile, but my lips would not accommodate me.

"You have had a rough go, haven't you?" There was discernment in Papa's eyes.

"Yes." I hesitated. "And you should know that Mother told me not to speak with you until her return."

"Yes. She told me likewise. But her presence will hinder my explanation—the explanation you deserve after everything you were made to endure because of my folly. Both past and present."

"I've learned much of it on my own already. And Mother told me of the Setons." I paused. "And who was accountable for their deaths."

He nodded, not a hint of surprise in his expression. "Did she tell you why I complied with her demands? Why we kept Ruth from you?"

My throat went dry. "No."

He moved to the wing-backed chair, gesturing for me to take a seat across from him on the chaise lounge.

There was hesitation in his features as he leaned forward in the chair, his feet wide and his elbows resting on his knees. "Susan—Ruth's mother—and I had grown up with the understanding we would one day marry. I had loved her since I was a young boy, though I didn't recognize it as love until too late. You see, your grandfather had gotten into a bit of a financial scrape, so much so that when your mother came along with her tempting fortune, he asked me to consider her instead of Susan. Fellerton was near ruin and we needed the funds." Papa leaned back, his expression stern. "I was enchanted by your mother's beauty, the way she mesmerized me with her flattery. I was too young and too foolish to realize the consequences of my choice, not only for me, but for Susan as well. I broke Susan's heart and married your mother.

"After Susan married Mr. Seton, he moved her away to one of his estates just south of London, and for years we did not see one another. Nor did our neighboring families speak. When Susan's parents died, she inherited everything and convinced her husband to remove their family to Blacksley. Mr. Seton was often away, and, with your mother finding little delight in my company and motherhood, she too would be gone for weeks at a time visiting one of her sisters."

I nodded, all too aware of Mother's neglect those first dozen years or so of my life.

Papa set his gaze on his folded hands. "It was during this time that Susan and I became reacquainted. It might have been wrong, but we were lonely … and you and Ruth took to each other instantly. We used to picnic—"

"Out by the stream." I offered Papa a sad smile. "I remember."

"Yes, I suppose you would." He glanced toward the vacant hearth. "For years we managed to maintain our ... friendship. But then one day, her husband happened upon us locked in an embrace on his way home to Blacksley. We didn't see each other often after that, and it broke us both, but especially her." Papa's jaw clenched, and his hands tightened into fists. "The fiend treated her terribly ill, and year by year the life slowly faded from her. I wanted to intervene, but I never did." Papa lowered his head, lifting his hand to cover his eyes.

I stood and walked to his side, kneeling at his feet.

His shoulders heaved forward with a sob. "I should have done something." His words were hardly understandable. "I could have saved her."

I took his hand in mine, my desire to comfort him stronger than all my uncertainty. "You cannot allow yourself to carry the blame for others' choices."

"Then let me at least carry the blame for going back on my word, for keeping Ruth from you."

I swallowed, my fingers tightening around his hand. "What was your reasoning for doing so?"

"Susan wrote to me the day she died, having discovered I would not be at home so I could not stop her. In the letter she explained her intentions. Her reasons. And then ..." He blew out a shaky exhale. "She asked me to care for Ruth once she was gone."

I stiffened. "Mrs. Seton asked you to be Ruth's guardian?"

"I'm not exactly certain what she meant by her request." He sniffed and lifted his reddened eyes to mine. "But no, not even I took it as that. Another guardian had been named for Ruth in Mr. Seton's will, a relative of his, I believe. And when they declined, Mr. and Mrs. Brundage gladly claimed their right, being next of kin.

"But I intended to play my part and ensure Ruth was given everything her mother wanted, including maintaining the friendship between the two of you. Your mother was wholly set against it. She believed any continued interaction with Ruth would make people question my reasoning, make them wonder if Ruth was my illegitimate child or if I'd had a role in the Setons' deaths. She also mentioned your attachment to Augustus and how, if we allowed it to continue, it would ruin your future prospects. It was all preposterous really, and I told her so. I stated she had always loathed Susan, and therefore loathed Ruth and Augustus also. She did not deny it."

Papa glanced at the window. "Her chance came to undermine my intentions when the Coroner's Court ruled the killings a murder and self-murder at Mr. Seton's hand. They had found no evidence of an outside perpetrator and, because of his past dealings with his wife, it was assumed he had killed her himself. Your mother and I were the only ones who knew the truth."

"And you did not want the authorities to know it?"

Papa's countenance grew severe. "Do you know what they do to a person who has committed self-destruction? What they did to Mr. Seton thinking he had carried out the act?"

I gave a timid shake of my head, not certain I wished to know.

"Such people are not given a proper burial. Instead they are taken at midnight to a crossroads, where the evil spirit will be diffused in four directions." He winced. "And before they are buried, a stake is driven through their heart to prevent their ghost from walking."

A small gasp escaped me, and I released his hand to

cover my mouth.

"Your mother said that if I did not agree to her demands, she would give the authorities the letter which she had managed to seize without my knowledge. That my beloved Susan would be defiled even in death." Tears welled in Papa's eyes, but they did not fall this time. "I could not bear it, Arabella. Such a cruel fate was befitting of a man like Mr. Seton, but not his gentle, kindhearted wife."

I rested my head on Papa's knees, and his hand moved to my back. We did not move for some time, nor did we speak. In the silence, my mind churned over what I had been told, my heart softening. Though I could not completely pardon the choices he'd made, I could now understand them. Everything Papa had done was because of his love for Ruth's mother.

Papa cleared his throat, and I lifted my gaze to his. "That is the wrong I meant to right. When I saw Ruth that evening at the ball, it was as though I saw Susan. And when you mentioned how different she would have been if her mother had been alive, I knew I had failed them both. And I had failed you.

"I admit that my plan to get you to Fairhaven was not very well thought through, especially the bit about falsifying an invitation from the Leavitts. But I could not tell you the truth and risk your mother finding out, nor was I certain you would agree to the arrangement if it was not forced upon you." Papa pressed his lips together. "I was all too aware of the hurt you endured thinking Ruth and Augustus had forgotten you all those years ago—a hurt you needed to understand had not come from them."

"You could have explained it in the letter you sent with Leah."

"I tried to pen an explanation several times. But in the

end, I took the coward's way out and trusted you would discover the necessary truths on your own." His expression softened, and he cupped my face in his hand. "If I could have foreseen the complications that arose, I would not have sent you to Fairhaven."

"No, Papa. I would not have missed Fairhaven for anything. My time there was the happiest I've been since Ruth and Augustus left."

Papa tilted his head to the side, studying my face. "You love him, don't you?"

Ever so slowly, I nodded. "I do love him. But it cannot matter. Mother has threatened to tell Ruth of her mother's role in the deaths if I do not marry Lord Thorton." I glanced down. "Besides, Augustus would not have me."

"Did he tell you that?"

I rose to my feet, moving to the window. "I saw it in his eyes, Papa. He finally realized what kind of woman I have become."

"And what kind of woman is that?"

My chin trembled. "One just like Mother."

Papa moved up behind me and lightly rested his hands on my shoulders, following my gaze to the garden below. "You are nothing like your mother, despite her attempts to make you so. You are thoughtful, and kind, and good."

Tears blurred the bright colors of the summer afternoon. "No. I have fooled you as I have fooled everyone."

"How have you fooled us?"

"I have been catty and judgmental. I have fed my vanity and my pride, and I have treated others abominably. I have lied, Papa. Too many times to count. And worst of all, I have hurt Ruth and I have hurt Augustus."

"So, you *have done* these things."

I nodded.

"*Have done* is different than *are doing*, Arabella. And

realizing our mistakes is the only way forward. If you don't want to be the person you are, choose to be the person you wish to become."

A tear slipped down my cheek. "I have done too much, hurt too many."

"People are not the sum of all their wrongs. They must also be willing to take into account all their rights. And if the sides are not equitably proportioned, make them so. At least that is what I am trying to do." Papa's hands moved down my arms before dropping to his side. "And if I had to wager a guess, I would say Mr. Brundage would be likely to see it the same way."

A warm sensation buzzed in my chest as the image of who I yearned to be clarified in my mind. I wanted to be carefree, like the girl I once was. I wanted to be a lady who laughed readily and smiled easily. A lady who trusted and hoped and was kind. And mostly I wanted to be someone who loved and was loved in return. My heart nearly burst at the simple freedom Papa had handed me. I had a choice, and I would choose to be— I froze. "I can't choose who to be, Papa." I turned to him, despair supplanting all hope. "Mother will tell Ruth about Mrs. Seton's death. She could not bear it, and I will not ruin her happiness for mine."

Papa's eyes twinkled. "That is the other reason why I came to speak with you. When Mother wrote to me of my unpardonable meddling and the consequences of it—your *troublesome* affections being placed on someone other than Lord Thorton—I made a decision that I will not let you suffer as I have because of her demands." He reached into the pocket of his waistcoat and pulled out a letter, handing it to me. "You must keep this."

I looked down at it. "What is it?"

"The letter from Susan."

My gaze shot to Papa's. "You want me to take it?"

"I did not go through such a painstaking endeavor of retrieving it simply to read it myself." His jest was null on me, and his weak grin fell. "It should be in the possession of Ruth's rightful guardians, the Brundages, and they must decide how to move forward with the knowledge."

My eyes settled on the missive, again amazed that such a small thing could so fully alter so many lives. I took hold of it, handling it with care. "But Mother can still tell Ruth what she knows."

"Yes. She can. But she no longer holds the strongest cards, for I am calling her bluff and quitting her game."

I quirked a brow.

"Do you know the highest punishment for withholding evidence here in England?"

My entire body went weak from the realization. "Death ... by hanging."

"Precisely. And my guess is that Mother will be as eager to avoid the noose as I am."

My face blanched.

"Do not worry, Bella." Papa patted my arm, his hand tarrying a moment. "It is not likely we would be prosecuted, seeing as it would require the Crown to reinstate the majority of Ruth's inheritance. And even if we were charged, the consequence would likely not be severe. For what incentive have they to condemn a loyal peer, or his wife, harshly?" He paused, a slight lift at the corners of his mouth. "But your mother does not know that. Nor will she tempt fate by threatening the people who hold such a powerful card in their hand. Ruth should be safe."

"I understand what you are suggesting, but there were too many *likelys* in your explanation. Any possibility for prosecution is too much." I held out the letter to him. "You must keep this."

Papa's expression grew solemn. "Just like you, I'm ready to change. I'm ready to amend the wrongs I have committed." He paused, his gaze dropping to the missive. "The Brundages deserve to know what is contained on that paper. They deserve the protection it could provide Ruth. And if, after thinking on it, Mr. Brundage decides to bring the matter to court, I will testify to the letter's authenticity, no matter the outcome."

It seemed a foolhardy decision, yet I understood it. I would do anything to right the wrongs I had caused Ruth. The Brundages. Augustus. I pulled the letter to my chest protectively. "Thank you, Papa."

He released an exhale and took a step back. "Now, I told Lord Thorton just this morning that I will consent for you to marry *any* man you love."

I did not move, teetering between shock and joy.

"Let me rephrase that. Unless you truly desire to marry Lord Thorton, you'd best be off."

Needing no further prompting, I lifted onto my toes to place a kiss upon Papa's cheek. "Thank you," I squealed, glancing around the room and considering how best to proceed. I wasn't certain how long I had before Mother's return, and I wondered if we could get my trunks packed and on the carriage before— My shoulders dropped under the weight of the realization, and I looked at Papa. "We have no coach."

Papa smiled. "We have horses and Mother's side saddle. She likely will not miss it until tomorrow morning."

My hands and legs tingled at the very thought of climbing atop such a large creature after years of refusing to ride. "Very well. But I shall need to go now before I change my mind."

Papa laughed. "Tell our groomsman to accompany

you. I should join you myself, but I must be here to deal with your mother and the social mayhem your sudden absence will surely cause."

"Thank you, Papa." I placed the letter in my reticule and opened the door, sending him one last smile.

"Where in heaven's name are you going in such a state?" My head whipped around to find Mother stepping into the doorway, her look of disgust lingering on my dampened, loose-hanging hair.

I opened my mouth but no words came out.

"What are you hiding?" She pushed past me and her eyes landed on Papa. "What is this? Did I not specifically tell you both to wait to speak until I returned?"

I took several steps backward.

"I believe you did," Papa said, his voice emotionless. "But I wished to see Arabella before her departure."

Mother's gaze narrowed. "Departure?"

Papa moved to my side, placing himself between Mother and me in an undeniable display of protection. "She is leaving Branbury without delay."

Mother's glower did not veer from Papa. "She is going nowhere."

Papa looked at me. "What say you to that, Arabella?"

"I am leaving." My voice was weak at first, but Papa gave an encouraging nod, and I gathered my courage. "I will not marry Lord Thorton."

Disbelief touched Mother's features. "You certainly will. I will not allow you to ruin this family's reputation, not after all the work I've done to right your wrongs. Besides," she said, one corner of her mouth lifting ever so slightly, "have you already forgotten what I have in my possession?"

"*Had* in your possession," Papa said coolly.

Mother's gaze flew to him.

"Sit," he said, gesturing her to the chaise lounge, "and I will enlighten you on how things are to be from now on."

"I absolutely will not."

Papa did not move, his arm still extended invitingly toward the sitting area.

"Perhaps you should do as Papa says." Though my legs shook beneath me, it was not from fear but from the release of a great weight being lifted off me. "I believe it would be the wisest choice for all involved."

Mother crossed her arms defiantly.

"Sit!" Papa commanded, his volume rising just enough to make Mother startle. With lifted chin, she moved past Papa, lowering herself onto the lounge without a word.

Papa gave a small shake of his head at her obstinance before turning to me. "Be safe, my darling."

"Thank you, Papa." I looked to Mother, whose eyes were fixed on the hearth. "Farewell, Mother."

She did not turn around, nor did she speak.

Yet, for the first time in years, I did not care what she thought. With a lightened step, I moved to the door. "Oh, and Papa?"

He had just settled in the chair across from Mother. "What is it, Arabella?"

"Will you have Leah sent to me as soon as it can be arranged?"

"Of course."

Mother did not move. "And where is it your maid should be sent?" she asked me, unable to conceal the curiosity in her voice.

"Fairhaven, of course."

Mother spun in her seat, her look of utter shock sending a satisfied smile to my lips, and I hurried from the room.

CHAPTER TWENTY-FIVE

"This is it." My words seemed to blow past me as I slowed my horse to a trot, taking in the familiar sight of Fairhaven. My back ached from the hours atop the horse, though I was relieved it hadn't taken quite as long as I had thought it might. Not even three hours with one break in between to have the horses tended to.

"We arrived just in time, miss." Brown glanced upward at the sky. "An hour later and it'd be gettin' dark."

I smiled. "Yes. Now help me down from this cursed creature."

The wrinkles around Brown's aged eyes deepened with his chuckle, and he dismounted, moving to assist me.

When my feet were again on solid ground, I placed a hand on the horse's sweat-soaked neck. "I do believe I may grow to like you yet."

He whinnied, and I handed the reins to Brown. "You can walk them back to the stables. I'm certain the Brundages won't mind."

He nodded and led the horses in the direction I'd gestured.

My heart was thudding in my chest, and I stopped on the top step to draw in a calming breath. I looked down at my dusty, wrinkled day dress and wished I'd had the patience to have changed into my traveling dress. After shaking my skirts and running my hands through my curls—which had been dried by the wind into a mess of tangles—I lifted a hand and rested it on the knocker. "I can do this," I repeated under my breath, clenching the heavy, circular handle.

But could I? What if Augustus couldn't forgive me? Or Ruth? Was it worth the risk if they would simply tell me to leave? I dropped my hand, and the metal knocker gave a muted clank.

The door creaked open, and the butler's gaze locked on me, his eyes widening. "Miss Godwin?"

My apprehension grew. If he was this shocked to see me, I wondered what welcome I would receive from the others. "Hello, Branson. Is Mr. Brundage at home?" I needed to tell him of Mrs. Seton's letter to Papa. Then I would know how to proceed with Ruth.

He stepped back and opened the door to let me in. "He is. If you'll wait here."

I was listening to his fading footsteps when Ruth's excited voice floated out the open drawing room door. "And to think I hadn't realized they'd grown to love one another."

Unable to resist my curiosity, I tiptoed closer, peeking inside.

Ruth and Sarah giggled, their backs to me and their attention out the drawing room window. Mrs. Brundage stood a few steps behind them, facing the same direction.

"Girls, we really should give them privacy." Mrs.

Brundage peered over their shoulders, with no apparent determination to heed her own advice.

I thought to announce myself, but my interest to discover who *they* were urged me forward.

Ruth shook her head. "I can hardly believe it. Mr. Treynor will tease me mercilessly when he discovers he has won our wager. I was so adamant that there would not be a marriage this summer."

My feet grew heavy beneath me, and it was then I caught sight of who they were observing. Not twenty paces from the window Miss Whitmore and Augustus were locked in an embrace. I blinked, but they were still there. I could not convince my eyes to look away, my heart breaking with every lingering moment they spent in one another's arms. Suddenly, it felt as though I was living my nightmare; though Augustus stood right there outside the window, he would never come. Not for me. I would wait forever.

My legs swayed beneath me, and I reached out a hand to steady myself on a nearby chair. But why should I be surprised? I had done this. I had told Augustus to offer for Miss Whitmore. Was I cursed to ruin everything?

"Bella?" I lifted my gaze to find Ruth watching me with an awestruck expression. "What are you doing here?"

Sarah and Mrs. Brundage spun toward me.

I tried to force the rehearsed words from my mouth. Any words. "I … I came to beg your forgiveness."

Ruth's head tilted to one side, and she raised an eyebrow. "You came all the way here from Branbury for that? Could you not have written with an apology?"

I drew in a breath, reminding myself that Augustus was not the only reason I had come. Ruth was my dearest friend, and I could not lose her. "I needed to tell you, in person, how sorry I am. I should never have shared the untruth about your inheritance. And I certainly should not have encouraged you toward a match whose only observable merits were a handsome face and good connections. You deserve someone infinitely better than that wretched man who does not even warrant having his name uttered."

The corner of Ruth's lips twitched, giving me hope.

"I have been so foolish. Could you ever forgive me?"

Ruth pursed her lips before a smile lit her face. "Of course I shall. I cannot stay angry at you. And I do not blame you for what happened. You offered me sound advice countless times, and I did not heed you. I only hope I've learned from my errors, for I know Augustus cannot always be there to stop every"—Ruth quirked her head—"what did he call Mr. Green again?"

"Scoundrel?"

"Not that one."

"Liar?"

Ruth shook her head again.

"Degenerate?"

"That's it." Ruth smiled. "Degenerate. Augustus cannot be there to stop every degenerate I encounter. Though I'm glad he managed to stop this one before anything scandalous happened."

Relief flooded over me at her light-hearted confirmation that nothing too detrimental had occurred. "As am I."

Mrs. Brundage and Sarah both nodded in agreement, and I turned to them. "I also need to apologize to you both. I gave you false hope, placed you in an uncomfortable situation, and left after breaking my agreement to Augustus. But I need you to know that I should have very much adored being a part of this family."

Sarah offered a timid smile. "I should have liked that also."

Mrs. Brundage nodded. "We all would have."

"Miss Whitmore will be an exceptional addition. Far better than I ever could have been." I glanced out the window, but the happy couple was no longer in sight. My heart began racing, and I quickly moved forward, giving Mrs. Brundage and Sarah a hug before stopping in front of Ruth. "How dear you are to me. I hope you know that."

She wrapped her arms around me so tightly, I never wanted to leave. But I needed to before I would be forced to face Augustus in my disappointment. My strength was spent. I could not bear it. I would write to him and tell him of Papa's revelation. I pulled back from Ruth, tears threatening to fall. "I shall be in touch."

Ruth gave a pout. "You are leaving already? But you have just arrived."

"I know. But I cannot stay longer." I swallowed, taking a few steps away. "I only came to apologize to all of you, and now I must be on my way."

"That is the only reason you came all this way?" Augustus's voice came from behind.

I did not turn around. I could not bear to look at him and remember the embrace he had just shared with Miss Whitmore, nor the whispers of their engagement I had heard. Instead, I glanced to the side, my gaze fixed on the ground. "I did wish to speak to you, but it seems I have come at an inconvenient time. I can pen you a letter instead."

"I'd prefer to hear what you have to say in person."

Mrs. Brundage shooed Ruth and Sarah out the door. "We will let the two of you speak in private."

Realizing it would be ridiculous to continue facing an empty room, I slowly turned toward him. Augustus leaned against the doorframe, his wary eyes on me. "What is it you wish to discuss?"

I glanced behind him, wondering if Miss Whitmore had returned home to announce their betrothal to her soon-to-be delighted mother. Had their embrace been one of farewell or would she be joining him here momentarily? "Are you certain I am not imposing on you?"

He hesitated, then pushed himself off the doorframe and started toward me. "I'm not certain. But I'll let you know if that changes."

I gestured behind him with my chin. "You may want to shut the door."

He paused, glancing behind him. "And why is that?"

I lowered my voice. "Ruth should not overhear us."

After a moment's hesitation, he moved to the door and closed it. "Better?"

I nodded.

"Now what is it that has you acting so mysteriously?"

"I know what happened to Ruth's parents."

His eyes narrowed. "What do you mean, *you know*?"

I retrieved the letter from the reticule I clutched and held it out to him. "Read that."

His gaze darted from the letter to me and back again before he carefully took hold of it, avoiding contact with my hand. He unfolded it, and I watched as his eyes moved over the words, his brow drawn low. When he finished, he looked at me. "Where did you get this?"

"It was sent to my father the day your aunt died, only my mother got hold of it first. She used it to coerce him into abiding by her demands, threatening to reveal the truth if he did not comply. One of the things she demanded was keeping Ruth and you from me. In return, Mother would not hand over the letter to the authorities, ensuring your aunt was not disinterred and subjected to the standard self-murder burial. The very idea of someone Papa loved so dearly enduring such an awful fate was too much. He could not oppose Mother."

Augustus skimmed the letter again.

"I only ask that if you decide to use it to substantiate Ruth's case, then you say it was found at Blacksley when you were going through papers. Papa said withholding evidence can be punishable by hanging, and though you may think my mother or even my father deserves such a fate, I beseech you to refrain from retribution. Though I understand ultimately it is up to you what you do with it, as well as whether or not you will tell Ruth."

Augustus drew in a long breath, releasing it in a quick puff. "There was a part of me that always wondered if this was the truth of it." He lifted the letter and gave it a slow shake. "The day of their deaths, I noticed Aunt Susan's lingering gaze on Ruth time and time again. There was so much love in her eyes ... and there was sorrow." He dropped his head, his thumb and forefinger settling on the bridge of his nose.

Not certain how to comfort him in his grief, or if it was my place to do so at all, I wrapped my arms around my midsection and waited patiently.

"Forgive me." Augustus's head lifted a touch, though his focus remained on the letter. "And what would you do with this evidence?"

"I thought about it some on my journey from Branbury, and I simply do not know. On one hand, it could right the injustice of Ruth losing her inheritance."

"But?"

"On the other hand, I cannot help but think of the damage it would cause Ruth. It would break her heart and force her to grieve a second time. And the grief would be a crushing thing to bear, especially if it came to be known publicly." I paused, the fast pace of my heart reverberating through me. "I'm now certain all the money and esteem in the world cannot compensate for a broken heart." A truth I had learned too late.

Augustus's discerning eyes moved across my face, and he dropped the letter to his side. "I cannot abide the thought of telling her, of having her discover such a thing after so long. Perhaps someday, when she is ready, but not yet. Besides, the case has already been ruled on, and I'm not certain if we could attempt another appeal." He hesitated. "Ruth did not, in actuality, lose everything. The Court rewarded Ruth with her mother's dowry as well as the money that had been set aside for her own dowry. She is also allowed her parents' and her own personal items that have remained at Blacksley all these years."

The shock I felt at hearing the news was quickly replaced with relief for Ruth. "I am so very glad to hear that."

He rubbed at his jaw. "I am sorry I did not tell you. I simply did not want Mr. Green to discover that Ruth's fortune could very well have paid off his debts."

The mention of Mr. Green and Augustus's underlying message—I was not someone he could confide in—pricked me. "I am sorry that I behaved in a way that betrayed your trust."

He did not refute my claim.

I looked back to the letter at his side, and I was suddenly eager to be on my way. "If you could keep that somewhere safe, I would greatly appreciate it. It is one of the protections to keep my mother from telling Ruth."

Augustus quirked a brow.

"As I was leaving, Papa was informing Mother that if she attempts to threaten me or Ruth again, he shall tell the authorities of your aunt's letter and their role in withholding it. It is only a ploy, of course, Papa would not really do so and certainly not without your agreement."

Augustus's brows lifted, and he looked as though he was attempting to make sense of it all. After a moment, he slipped the letter into his waistcoat pocket and gave a resolute nod. "I shall keep it safe."

"Thank you." We stood in awkward silence. "I'd best be on my way."

Augustus straightened. "Yes. I suppose you should."

Though I felt like weeping, I managed a strained smile. "And congratulations on the upcoming wedding." Unable to endure his confirmation, I ducked my head and stepped past him toward the door.

"Bella?"

I glanced over my shoulder to find a small lift on one side of his lips. "Yes?"

"Branson mentioned you arrived on horseback."

"I did."

Augustus took a step toward me, making my heart patter recklessly. "I thought you no longer rode horses."

"I don't … well, I did, but I …" My words trailed off as he took another step closer, making my heart lift in empty anticipation. What was he playing at?

"So, *you* rode a horse all the way *here* from Branbury?"

I knew I should take a step away from him, but I couldn't. "Yes."

"What I can't understand is why a lady—one who declares she has not ridden in over eight years and does not care for riding—suddenly feels it a necessity to get on a horse and ride for over two hours."

"Our carriage was being repaired. It was the only way to get here."

Augustus nodded, his gaze moving to the window.

"And where do you expect to stay tonight? Certainly you will not ride to Branbury in the darkness."

I lifted my chin. "I am not returning to Branbury. I will likely stay at a nearby inn or go to my father's cousins' house. Mr. Leavitt told me I'd always be welcome."

Disbelief touched his expression. "You are truly not returning to Branbury?"

I shook my head, wondering whether he felt remorse for so quickly asking for Miss Whitmore's hand. No. I would not allow such thoughts. I was determined to change.

"And why would you not stay here, then? With us?"

"I do not wish to impose, nor do I wish to ruin anything between you and Miss Whitmore."

His brow quirked upward.

"When I first arrived, I saw you out the window, embracing. And I overheard Ruth mention the wedding."

Augustus nodded, denying nothing.

"So that is why I cannot stay. It seems the only thing I'm really good for is causing damage in my wake."

"You do excel at it." A smile warmed his face, and my heart sank further. It would not be for much longer that he could offer me such smiles. "May I show you something before you go?"

I glanced out at the late afternoon light, certain I should be on my way now that I would be required to seek lodging. But I did not wish to disappoint him again. A brief observation of whatever it was he wished to show me was the least I could do. "I suppose, if we are quick about it."

He extended his arm to me and, with a shaky hand, I took hold of it.

"Are you two finished?" Ruth asked, as we stepped into the entry hall.

"Not quite." Augustus led me forward, opening the front door. "We will be back shortly."

All three women were smiling, and Augustus closed the door behind us.

We made our way to the back of the house and started toward the rose garden. Augustus walked so swiftly, I was barely managing to keep up with his long strides. "Forgive my haste. Are you managing well?" He led us through the back of the garden onto the small walking path we'd taken to the holloway.

"Yes. But could I ask where we are going?"

"Only a little further, I'm nearly certain of it."

I tightened my grip on his arm. "You don't know where we are going?"

"Not precisely." He stopped at a crossing footpath and glanced side to side, then stilled.

"What—"

He placed a finger to his lips and listened, a smile lighting his handsome features that nearly drove me to madness. "This way." He led me forward again, until the sound of voices could be heard somewhere in front of us.

"Candace," Augustus called, and the voices stopped.

"Augustus?" Miss Whitmore's voice sent a wave of shock through me, and I planted my feet, releasing Augustus's arm.

Augustus reached a hand toward me. "Come, Bella."

I recognized that mischievous glint in Augustus's eyes instantly, the one that had always come before we got into trouble, and I shook my head.

"Augustus? What are you doing?" Miss Whitmore rounded the path and stopped mid-step when her gaze fell on me. Her lips parted. "Miss Godwin?"

I forced out a smile. "Miss Whitmore. I hope you are well?"

Her eyes flicked back to Augustus and his tiresome grin. "Very well. And you?"

I lifted my shoulders, powerless to explain how utterly out of sorts I was.

"Candace, what is it?" Another man's voice immobilized me, and when he stepped into view, my jaw dropped. I glanced between Augustus and this man who looked bafflingly similar—the same sandy-colored hair, the build, even an equivalent amused smile on his lips.

He glanced from Miss Whitmore to Augustus before he took notice of me standing there gaping at him.

Augustus gestured toward me. "Owen, you remember Bella?"

Owen's face lit with recognition. "Of course. How could I forget her with the way you babbled on about her for years?"

"Owen?" I whispered, still attempting to make sense of all this in my head. I looked back at Augustus. "This is your brother, Owen?"

Augustus took a step closer to me. "Yes. And Miss Whitmore's fiancé."

I reached out toward Augustus, feeling unstable on my feet, and he moved to offer his support.

"Very recent fiancé," Owen said, sending his brother a pointed glare. "So recent that we had sought a moment together. Alone. Without so many watchful gazes upon us. And yet here you are."

Augustus chuckled. "As though you don't owe me for being your postal boy this past year while you've been in Town."

I furrowed my brow. "Those were the letters you were passing to Miss Whitmore?" The question slipped from me before I considered how meddlesome I appeared, but I didn't care.

Augustus's expression softened. "Yes."

Owen quirked a playful eyebrow at Augustus. "You said no one ever saw you."

"I meant Mrs. Whitmore never saw me."

Owen nodded, the smile growing on his lips. "I see how those two statements could be conflated. Not that it matters now anyway, considering Candace's mother has given us her *most reluctant* blessing."

Augustus offered an obligatory smile without ever removing his gaze from me.

"Well, seeing that it looks as though the two of you have as much need for privacy as we do,"—Owen offered his arm to Miss Whitmore, who gladly accepted it—"we shall excuse ourselves." Miss Whitmore's cheeks pinkened beautifully, just as I felt my own cheeks grow warm. "Bella, I hope there will be much time for talking later."

I glanced at Augustus. "I hope so also."

Miss Whitmore directed a smile at me. "And thank you, Miss Godwin."

Before I could ask what her gratitude was for, Owen led her away.

"It wasn't until you showed up that Mrs. Whitmore finally accepted there was no future for Candace and me. You well know how stubborn mothers can be when it comes to marrying off their daughters."

Despite all the hurt I'd felt regarding Mother, I laughed. "Entirely too well."

Augustus lifted an arm to me. "Shall we find somewhere we will not be interrupted?"

I smiled up at him. "Yes, please."

We started back in the direction we had come, now at an unhurried pace.

I looked up at the tall trees surrounding the path. "I do believe Ruth was right. Fairhaven is the most glorious place I've ever been. I shouldn't mind staying here all my life."

"Are you certain of that? Will you not come to regret your choice and all that you will be required to give up?" Augustus searched my profile. "I cannot give you the life you are accustomed to. No grand balls. No expensive furnishings. Far fewer fancy dresses."

I pursed my lips in exaggeration and put a finger to them. "How many fewer dresses are you talking?"

He laughed.

I leaned into him, tightening my hold on his arm. "Someone wise once told me that regrets come with any choice that is made. We simply need to sort out which of those choices offer the regrets we can live with." I lifted my gaze to his. "I've already sorted it out, and I can't live without you. Whatever is lost to me because of my decision, it is because I have chosen something greater."

His other hand came to rest upon mine. "I believe you have just made me the happiest man in all of England."

"Only England?"

He laughed. "The territory will no doubt expand once I forgive you for thinking me engaged to Miss Whitmore. One full day, Bella. That is how long I was home. Perhaps had you given me a week I might have offered for her, but a day?"

I scoffed and nudged him with my shoulder.

His eyes were a warm brown in the golden light, and his smile was even warmer. "I have loved you my whole life, Bella. And that will never change."

My whole being was aflutter as we stepped onto the familiar path that led to the holloway. The ground grew up high above us, and the dimming light made everything appear magical. Augustus stopped and faced me. "I'm sorry I did not tell you of my brother and Miss Whitmore.

I assure you, I would have if I had not been sworn to secrecy."

"You know that is not true. You clearly enjoyed using the situation to your advantage, provoking my jealous nature."

Augustus grinned. "A man must do what he can to win a woman's heart. Especially when that woman is the only one he has ever loved. The only one he ever will love."

"But can such a man overlook all her flaws? Her failings? As numerous as they are and have been?"

He stepped closer and lifted a hand to my face, his fingers softly caressing my cheek and causing my breath to catch. "If she can trust him when he declares that he values every aspect of her. Each flaw. Each failing. All of it. And when she forgets it, he will tell her again."

I lifted my hands to rest on his chest. Despite his calm demeanor, his heart pounded as readily as mine. "I suppose I shall allow for such declarations as long as it is not done to excess. You would not want your praise to become disingenuous."

He laughed. "I shall try my best, but I make no promises." His hand slid to the nape of my neck, and he leaned forward, placing a kiss upon my forehead. The warmth of his lips sent shocks through me. "You are kind." His mouth grazed my skin until he placed a kiss upon my temple. "And intelligent." My cheek. "Beautiful."

His lips grazed my other cheek, and I closed my eyes. An energy surged through me, congregating wherever his lips touched. "Witty." My other temple. "Strong." The warmth of him waned, and I opened my eyes to find his gaze upon my mouth. "A remarkable kisser?"

I smiled. "Was that one a question?"

A side of his mouth quirked upward. "Discerning."

Without a moment's hesitation, I pulled him toward

me. His lips melted against mine, and it was as if, in that moment, we became one. The movements of our kiss, our hands, our very bodies were in sync with one another. His hands on my waist tightened and eased in rhythm to everything else. And though I had never experienced anything like the longing that coursed through me in this private moment of healing and passion, I yearned for more. I wrapped my arms around his neck, my back arching to draw us together until we could not be any closer, the whole of my body now flowing with energy from his warmth against me.

Our kiss slowed, and I moved my hand to his jaw to feel the deep, unhurried movements beneath it. My head spun from exhilaration, my hands and legs trembling from desire, when he finally pulled away. He rested his head on my forehead, our heavy breaths mingling between us.

"I am happy to report you are undeniably a remarkable kisser."

I lifted my chin, placing a light kiss on his lips. "I will try not to be offended that it took you three separate occasions to make the determination." I tsked my tongue. "It only took me one kiss to come to the realization myself."

He laughed, his eyes full of so much love I thought I might weep from the sight of it. "On second thought, I recant my declaration altogether and will continue to gather evidence until I'm unequivocally certain of my opinion."

I lifted an unimpressed brow.

"It will easily take a lifetime to make a sound judgment on the matter, and I intend to gather thorough evidence at every encounter."

I released an overdone sigh. "I suppose if you must."

His hand wrapped around my waist, pulling me toward him but stopping just before his lips touched mine. "Oh, I must."

I closed my eyes, allowing his warmth to consume me again.

EPILOGUE

*R*uth swished the lavender skirt of her ball gown. "I still cannot believe your parents took on the expense of my upcoming Season, Bella. It was so generous of them."

"Considering the Court of Chancery is taking so long to return your inheritance, my parents were happy to oblige you." Or at least Papa was, as he continued in what ways he could to amend his wrongs.

Ruth shook her hands at her sides before clasping them in front of her. "Oh, heavens. I am so nervous. What if I make a fool of myself in front of everyone?"

I stepped up behind her, placing my pearl necklace around her neck and fastening it in place. "You will do no such thing. You are a well-trained lady now."

"Am I? I feel very much the same but with more things to fret about."

I suppressed my amusement and glanced at Leah who stood watching us. "What say you, Leah? Is Ruth ready for her coming out?"

Leah smiled her assurance. "I've hardly met a finer lady."

"Thank you, to the both of you." Ruth appraised her lovely reflection in my full-length mirror. "I suppose it is hard to see the transformation in ourselves sometimes." She smoothed her gown. "Do you think Mr. Treynor will notice the change in me? It has been four months now since his visit."

"From what I know of Mr. Treynor, he will be eager to appreciate your every quality—both old and new."

Ruth giggled. "I still cannot believe he came for my ball, especially considering I lost our bet two times over."

"If I had to venture a guess, Mr. Treynor's coming has little to do with the bet."

The bedchamber door creaked open, and heavy footsteps sounded behind us.

A smile came to my lips, but I did not glance behind me. "But don't tell Augustus I said as much, for he will rightly be cross at my encouraging you."

"What encouragements are you giving her?" Augustus asked, stepping to my side and placing a kiss upon my cheek.

I turned to face him, the perfect picture of innocence. "Nothing you need worry about, husband."

He couldn't refuse me a smile. "If this has anything to do with a certain person who will be in attendance this evening, I shan't hear a word of it. I'm already regretting approving any gentlemen being invited at all, let alone one as eager as Mr. Treynor."

Ruth's eyes brightened. "Eager? How amusing you should choose the very same word as Bella to describe him."

Augustus hardly looked pleased with our like-minded comment.

"What are you hiding, Augi?" Ruth asked, and it was only then I noticed his hands situated behind his back. "Is it for me?" Ruth stepped to his side to try to catch a glimpse.

He shifted away from her. "Patience."

I stretched my neck to do likewise, but he noticed my attempt and took a step back, pinning us with a most ineffective glower. "You two are absolutely tiresome. Might I at least give my speech before I present what I have?"

Ruth and I shared a glance, and I folded my arms across my chest. "How long is this speech to be?"

He lifted his brow. "Would it matter?"

"It most certainly would. If it is to be one of your monologues, I should like to take a seat before you begin. Make myself comfortable."

He laughed. "I shall be brief."

"Go on, then," Ruth said, excitement lighting her expression.

Augustus straightened. "Ruth, these past few months, despite my attempt to overlook the truth before me, I've noticed the exceptional woman you have become." Ruth's gaze flicked toward me at his confirmation. "A woman more capable than I had permitted myself to believe."

The utter delight on her face displayed her gratitude perfectly.

"As such, I believe you are more than ready to discover something I've kept from you all these years."

My stomach clenched. Surely he would not tell her of her past now, right before she was to go down and begin welcoming the guests to her coming out ball.

Augustus's eyes lingered on me a moment. "And Bella's frantic look tells me I should assure you, and her, that my revelation won't ruin your night in the least." He paused, the corners of his mouth twitching. "Or I hope it doesn't."

I flicked my eyes upward and gave a subtle shake of my head at how amusing he found himself.

He moved closer to us again before turning his attention back to Ruth. "As you are well aware, Bella's mother was not able to make it to our wedding, nor is she accompanying Lord Godwin on his current visit to Fairhaven." He paused. "And though I won't go into the particulars of why until you feel you are ready to know of them, you should be made aware that it was at Lady Godwin's insistence that you and I were not able to maintain a friendship with Bella once you came to Fairhaven. A task, I fear, I was forced to help execute."

Ruth's gaze shot to me, and I nodded, hoping Augustus had a point to all of this.

"I only tell you that, so this"—he brought his hand in front of him, a stack of missives tied together with a string in his grip—"is given context."

Ruth stepped closer to him. "What are those?"

"All the letters Bella wrote to you after you came to live at Fairhaven."

Carefully Ruth reached out her hand and took hold of them, clasping the letters to her chest. "And what of all the letters I wrote to her? Were they never sent?"

"They were not." Augustus revealed his other hand that held an even larger stack than the first. "These, Bella, are all the letters Ruth and I wrote to you throughout the years."

I stared at his offering. "You kept them?" My gaze lifted from the bundle with amazement. "All that time apart and you kept them?"

He shook his head, smiling. "Why do you always act astonished by my devotion to you?"

I blinked, unable to take my eyes off the letters. "Why did you not tell me?"

"I had planned to give them to you earlier, but I thought it would be more meaningful if I presented them to you both at the same time. That way, when you wish it, you could share the experience."

Tears blurred my vision as I reached out and took hold of the priceless treasure. "Thank you." I lifted my gaze. "You don't know how much this means to me."

"Or me," Ruth said, having successfully freed a missive from the bundle and unfolded it.

Augustus leaned in, and I welcomed a lingering kiss from him.

"Listen to this." Ruth stepped to our side, unaware of our affectionate exchange. "My dearest Ruth. I cannot understand why I have not heard from you yet, and I'm loathe to admit that I miss you desperately. My life has become monotonous without you and Augustus to keep me company. Mother has taken control of my training, and I absolutely abhor every moment of it. I don't know why she feels it so necessary to make me into a well-trained lady. I had to wear a backboard the whole day until it was time to dress for bed, and I'm now certain there was never a worse invention in all of history." Ruth flashed me an amused smile and dropped the letter to her side. "It shall be so delightful to read through these."

It was strange hearing my own words so long forgotten, and I longed to open a letter and see what Augustus had written to me. I sighed and walked to my desk, placing the stack carefully in the corner. I rubbed my fingers over the top letter. "As much as I wish we had the time to read them now, I do not want to rush the experience. I have waited this long; I suppose a few hours more will do me no real harm." It took every bit of self-restraint to leave them there and return to Augustus's side.

A knock sounded at the door and Leah moved to answer it.

"I came to see if Arabella and Ruth are ready." Mrs. Brundage's cheery voice sounded through the room.

Leah opened the door wider, allowing Mrs. Brundage a clear view inside.

"Oh, Ruth, how stunning you look. The very likeness of your mother." Mrs. Brundage hurried toward us, her eyes glistening as she wrapped Ruth in an embrace. Her hand found mine, and she looked over at me. "And you, Arabella, ever the vision of feminine beauty."

Augustus crossed his arms over his chest and cleared his throat. "And good evening to you, Mother."

Mrs. Brundage's cheeks rounded in a teasing smile. "Oh, do not be sour, dear," she said dismissively. "You look well enough."

"Well enough?" Augustus scoffed. "Surely you might have offered something like—the epitome of masculine charm."

Mrs. Brundage tilted her head, appraising him. "If you say so, Augustus."

He threw up his hands and laughed. The sound reverberated around us, and we could not help but join him.

"I think you look dashing," I said, smoothing the lapels of his double-breasted tailcoat.

"That is an improvement to looking *well enough*, I suppose."

Ruth leaned forward and whispered to Mrs. Brundage, and Mrs. Brundage nodded. Her eyes were dancing as she sent me a meaningful glance. It was time.

"Now I have a surprise for you," Ruth said, looking at Augustus.

He appeared completely perplexed by the notion. "And what is that?"

"Sarah," Ruth called. "Come in!"

Sarah took a hesitant step into the room wearing a beautiful white ball gown, her hair set in a lovely coiffure with loose curls positioned around her face.

"What is this about?" Augustus asked, his brows set low.

"She is also having her coming out tonight," Ruth said matter-of-factly. "We decided not to tell you until the last minute—which is now."

Augustus stared at his sister for a time, then lowered his gaze to me. "Did you know of this?"

I attempted an air of innocence. "As though I would go behind your back and help plan such a thing."

"You did, and you didn't tell me." He shook his head, his jaw slackening in offense, though a slight upward curve at the corners of his mouth betrayed him.

I pinned him with an overdone pout. "Would you have allowed it if I had?"

His eyes widened. "No. Absolutely not. She cannot come out into Society yet, she's still far too young."

"She absolutely can," Mrs. Brundage said, beckoning Sarah to her. "She underwent the same training as Ruth, she is old enough, and Ruth wishes with all her heart to have the two of them share their coming out."

Ruth linked her arm with Sarah. "It will bring me so much comfort to know she is there with me."

Augustus was still gawking at his sister, who did not shy away from the attention as she once would have done. "This is absolute madness. She is but a chi—"

I put a hand on his arm, giving a subtle shake of my head to silence him.

His shoulders lowered in defeat, and he released a heavy breath.

"You look exquisite, Sarah," I said, smiling at her. "And I believe you are ready to take on the world." I glanced at Ruth. "You both are."

Augustus pointed a finger at them, attempting to appear stern. "If a gentleman so much as looks at either of you wrong, I shall revoke his invitation immediately and physically see him from our home—just so you are both aware."

Taking that as apparent permission, Ruth and Sarah embraced, giggling in utter delight.

"What is all the fuss?" Our small group turned to find Owen and Candace walking into the room through the open door when Owen's gaze landed on Sarah. "Why is Sarah dressed for the ball?"

"They all decided she would have her come out with Ruth tonight," Augustus said. "Without telling me. And apparently you either."

Owen's gaze turned to his mother. "You cannot be serious. She is but a child."

"She is seventeen," Candace said with a smile. "The same age I was when I entered Society. Besides, she has been trained, and it is Ruth's dearest wish that they could come out together."

Augustus's lips parted, and he pointed his finger again. "Those are the exact same reasons Mother gave, Candace. Did all five of you conspire against us?"

Owen glanced at Candace, dumbfounded. "You knew of this?"

She lifted her chin. "Of course I did." Candace fixed him with a pointed stare. "And I don't think you need even ask why I didn't mention it to you. You have made it quite obvious."

Augustus and Owen shared a sympathetic glance. "Owen, you can help me keep an eye on the gentlemen."

Owen took in Sarah and Ruth. "This is going to be a long night."

Victory was ours!

After greeting Ruth, Sarah, and Mrs. Brundage, Candace came to my side and linked arms with me. "That went better than expected."

"Thank heavens, considering we included both Ruth's and Sarah's names on our invitations."

Candace smiled, glancing over at Owen. "I have news."

"What is that?"

"It seems Mother is not nearly as dissatisfied with my choice to marry Owen as she is at living in that large house all alone. We shall be moving into Safford Park with her at the end of the month. She also said that she has already left it to us in her will."

I took hold of Candace's hand that rested in the crease of my elbow. "Oh, how wonderful. Now I shall have to think of my next wish, for they all seem to be coming true as of late."

She pulled me a few steps away from the others. "Perhaps you might consider giving our child a playmate as your next wish."

My eyes widened, and I glanced down at her stomach before I could stop myself. "You're with child?"

She drew closer. "Yes. But I wish all the attention to be on Ruth and Sarah tonight, so we will not announce it yet."

My heart warmed. "I am so happy for you both. You will make wonderful parents."

"What are the two of you whispering about this time?" Augustus asked, pausing his conversation with Owen.

I smiled at him. "You shall come to know in time."

"Time? Oh, look at the time," Mrs. Brundage interjected suddenly, scooting Ruth and Sarah to the door. "Our guests will begin arriving any minute. Come on, everyone downstairs." We all moved to the door, but Mrs. Brundage stopped in the doorway. "Oh, Bella, dear. I forgot to mention that your father arrived and said he would be down as soon as he was cleaned up."

"Wonderful, thank you for telling me."

"Come on," she said again, guiding the others out ahead of her. As my bedchamber emptied, I took hold of Augustus's hand, halting him.

He looked down at me. "What is it?"

"I believe I know my next wish."

"Your next wish?" Augustus lowered his brow. "Whatever do you mean?"

I smiled, lifting on my toes to place a light kiss on his lips. "We must go down now. But do remind me to tell you later."

THE END

NEXT IN SERIES: "The Cottage by Coniston"

by Deborah Hathaway

DID YOU ENJOY "A WELL-TRAINED LADY"?

As an author, reviews are *critical* to my success. It would mean so much to me if you would take a moment and submit a review on Amazon, Goodreads, Bookbub, or wherever you buy books. There are so many stories I'd love to write, and your assistance is a vital part of bringing those books to fruition. Thank you so much for your support!

Also, if you'd like to receive updates regarding: future projects, release dates, giveaways, and other important information, I would love for you to join my newsletter! Subscribe at JessHeileman.com.

Other places to find me:
Instagram: @AuthorJessHeileman
Facebook: AuthorJessHeileman
Facebook Group Admin: Sweet Regency Romance Fans

ACKNOWLEDGMENTS

Where would I be without the countless people who helped and encouraged me along the way? I certainly wouldn't be here—that's for sure. This book was so much harder for me to write than my first, and it truly took a team of people to get me through it. So here's my meager attempt to thank those who made publishing "A Well-Trained Lady" a reality.

First, I need to thank my husband. He is my sanity, my biggest support, and my best friend. He is always thrilled to read my work, edit what I need him to, and handle all that goes by the wayside while I'm writing. I love him more each and every day.

My wonderful children are incredible. They not only are understanding of me as I pursue my dream of writing, but they support me, cheer for me, and love me through all the ups and downs. Despite not having read either of my books yet, they are very adamant about being my top fans.

My amazing parents, my wonderful in-laws, and my brothers and sisters—thank you. Thank you for supporting me in my dream and helping me wherever you are able. Thank you for taking the time to care about what I care about, and putting up with all my silliness and the demands on my time. Thank you to my extended family, which has been so supportive. My family—grandparents, aunts, uncles, and cousins—is honestly the best group of cheerleaders, and I love them all!

My amazing friends, you are so often my strength and my joy. You are always there for me when I need you most, and I cherish each and every one of you. Thank you for always lifting and inspiring me.

The group of writer friends I have found in the community of authors is incredible. I don't know how I published my first book without them. They are there to help and encourage me whenever I'm in need. There are so many of them, I wish I could name them all, but there are a few who have been vital in my success.

To my local writer friends: Celeste Cox, Kaleena Shreeve, and Amy Standage, I treasure the friendships we've made and our girls' nights out. To my Hidden Springs friends—I love you all! It is an amazing thing to find more of "my people" in this vast world, and I'm thrilled I have.

My fellow admins of Sweet Regency Romance Fans: Sarah Adams, Sally Britton, Jennie Goutet, Deborah Hathaway, Martha Keyes, Ashtyn Newbold, Kasey Stockton, and Mindy Strunk I adore each of you! Thank you for allowing me into this group, and then keeping me once you got to know me. It is amazing to have friends whom you can rely on without fail.

Thank you to my critique partners: Emily Beeson, Martha Keyes, and Kasey Stockton. Every week I looked forward to our meeting, not just for your great feedback but to chat and laugh with you. You have been a constant support throughout this entire process and have taught me so much.

And a huge thank you to my beta readers that took something rough and made it resemble a book. Jennie Goutet, Deborah Hathaway, and Clarissa Kae your input was beyond helpful and insightful. I'm in awe at the knowledge you each have regarding what makes a good story and good writing, as well as your unique abilities that added so much depth to my story. Thank you.

Ashtyn Newbold, thank you for helping me design my cover. You have so many talents that I should really stop being surprised each time I learn of yet another thing you are capable of.

A huge thank you to Jenny Proctor, my editor, for the feedback and fixes you sent me. I was amazed at your ability to pinpoint the weak spots of my manuscript and for your knowledge of story and grammar. This book is so much better because of you!

I am so grateful for all the ARC readers who were willing to read my book and review it (also thank you to those who sent me errors along the way). I treasured each email I got from you. Huge hugs from me to each of you for your time and effort on my behalf!

Susan Kuechenberg, Angie McCain, Julie Carpenter, Priscila Perales Borda, and Whitney Wright, thank you for your extreme care in catching so many of those pesky errors that have eluded me and countless others. You amaze me with your knowledge and your willingness to assist me.

And a special thanks to Elise Griffin for proofreading my book. I feel so much better sending "A Well-Trained Lady" into the world knowing your well-trained eyes were on it. It always amazes me how many things you catch in a manuscript I had thought to be fairly clean. Thank you!

Lastly, and above all, I want to thank God for the talents He has given me, His steadfast love, and His blessings when I need them most.

ABOUT THE AUTHOR

In kindergarten, Jess won a first prize ribbon for her original creation *Pigs in Wigs*. The storyline was solid: there was this pig that wore a wig—and it rhymed. Not impressed? Neither were her children when shown the very masterpiece that influenced her to become an author. "You won a ribbon for that?" Yes. Yes, she did.

Thankfully, life has since exposed her to a thorough education with its share of awards and accolades—and, more importantly, to the trials and human experiences that form the heart of a storyteller and the substance of great stories.

Besides her love of writing, Jess is an avid reader, shameless people observer, international café loiterer, and partially retired photographer. She loves being a mother to five amazing humans and a wife to the greatest man she knows.

Made in the USA
Las Vegas, NV
01 May 2023

71393914R00225